CW00958450

Losing Sam

Nicole Maser

Copyright © 2023 by Nicole Maser.

All rights reserved.

No portion of this book may be reproduced in any form without written permission from the publisher or author, except as permitted by U.S. copyright law.

Contents

Chapter 1

"Cut! Cut!" Jess yelled at one of the younger girls on the team. What was her name? Marin? Morgan? Something with an "M" in it, for sure. All the freshmen looked the same, or at least acted the same. All giggly and happy, even at the last early morning practice of the season.

They always started like that. But she'd been around long enough to know it didn't last. By sophomore year, the novelty of it all will have worn off, and the six AM practice giggles with have turned into grunts, groans, and complaints.

"Cut!" Jess yelled one more time to Marin Morgan as she cradled the ball at the top-center of the arc.

She watched M decidedly *not* cut, and instead drift further to the left half of the arc.

A whistle blew.

"Alright, time's up!" Coach Lowe called behind them. "We'll finish running through these plays next practice. Clean up the cones, and move the goals back near the shed. Congratulations on making it through your last two-a-day practice of the year!"

Jess lowered the head of her stick, letting the ball roll out onto the ground.

"What was that?" she demanded, making a beeline toward freshman M. "I told you to cut like three times and you just stood there."

The girl froze like a deer in headlights.

"Uh—" Her cheeks grew red, glancing around them. "I—I didn't know you were talking to me."

Jess gritted her teeth. Sure, she hadn't said her name, but she'd looked directly at her. That was more than good enough. Besides, M was actually a pretty good player. Jess had noticed her skills right away when Coach Lowe pulled her up to Varsity that summer, along with a small handful of other freshman that he thought showed promise. She'd been with them long enough now that she should be catching on to these things.

"If someone looks directly at you and says something, is it not obvious they're talking to you?"

The girl's cheeks somehow darkened another shade, and her eyes dropped to her feet.

"Um—yeah. Yeah, you're right. I'm sorry, Jess. It won't happen again."

A throat cleared beside them. Jess glanced over, temporarily distracted from her angry tirade. Scarlett stood there, giving her a pointed look. Then she turned to M.

"It's okay, Mia," Scarlett said with an apologetic smile. "It happens to the best of us sometimes."

Mia. That's right.

The girl smiled back at her appreciatively, her shoulders relaxing like it was the first time she'd taken an actual breath in the last thirty seconds. Another freshman called to her from the other side of the field, and she carefully avoided Jess' glare as she turned to leave.

When she was a few paces away, Jess turned to Scarlett and crossed her arms.

"I wasn't wrong. She was completely clueless out there."

"Yeah," Scarlett replied, bending over to pick up one of the cones near them. "But you yelling at her won't help."

"I didn't yell," Jess muttered. "She's one of the best younger players out there. She could be really good in a couple of years if she pays attention and does what I'm telling her."

"Yeah, but to her, and probably the rest of the freshman, you just look like an ass."

Jess pursed her lips. "I'm just trying to help her."

Scarlett picked up another cone, then stopped, turning it over in her hands as she looked at her. "Look, I know you care. But they'll never know that if you don't say it or show it. No one can read your mind."

Jess rolled her eyes. They should all be better at taking negative feedback. Obviously, it's for their own benefit. They should know that.

She walked past Scarlett, picking up the rest of the cones before heading to the locker room. That was the worst part of morning practices. The rush to shower and get ready for school with only a few quick minutes to spare. And sharing three showers between twenty-two girls on a chilly morning was less than ideal.

After she'd finished drying her hair and changing into her clothes for school, she pulled her phone out. There was one new notification. An email from the guidance counselor asking her to come by her office that day.

3

Great, another thing to add to the list.

She tucked the phone back into her pocket, then spotted Mia putting on makeup near the sink. Jess stood up from the bench and walked toward her.

"Hey, Mia," she said, working to make her voice sound more gentle than it usually did.

The girl turned to her, a momentary glimpse of fear passing over her face. Jess stopped herself from rolling her eyes.

She folded her arms and cleared her throat awkwardly. "I wasn't trying to be harsh earlier."

The girl looked at her, as if waiting for her to continue. When she didn't, she nodded, accepting the non-apology. "Okay."

Jess pursed her lips. "You're good. Really good." The girl instantly brightened, a surprised look filling her face. "Some of your passing and cuts could use some work, though. If you want, I could help you with them at the next practice. There are some tricks I could show you to make it easier."

Now the girl was absolutely beaming. "Yes, for sure," she grinned. "That would be amazing! Thank you!"

Jess nodded. "Sure."

She turned and walked back to her locker to grab her backpack. Scarlett stood there, waiting for her with an amused smile.

"Don't." Jess growled, shooting her a glare.

Scarlett chuckled, pulling her own backpack onto her shoulders. "Come on, we're gonna be late."

***

"What do you mean, they've already filled the first spot?" Jess asked, in disbelief.

Miss Williams sighed, pushing a few college brochures to the side of her desk. "They did, but there's still one more student they'll accept from our school this year and you definitely have a great shot at getting it."

Jess glared at the cheesy motivational posters on the wall. She'd worked her whole life for this. Every decision she'd made, everything she'd sacrificed had been to get into Trinity University. And receive early acceptance, no less.

She had to get in. No matter what.

"Did you apply to your second choice like I told you?" Miss Williams asked, picking up a new brochure and flipping through the pages. "Bucknell has a great lacrosse program, too. It's really not a bad backup to have."

Jess leaned back in the plastic blue chair and crossed her arms over her chest. "Backup plans are for people who don't think they can win."

Miss Williams shot her a pointed look, dropping the brochure back onto her desk. "I'm surprised you want to go to Trinity at all. They have such strict—*lifestyle rules* and expectations for their students. It's a perfect fit for our students who are very church-oriented and religious, but you've never struck me as that type."

Jess' eyes flicked to the window on the wall beside them. Groups of students made their way across the quad, finding their friends for lunch.

5

The woman paused, carefully treading through the next few words. "Jess, do you mainly want to go to Trinity because that's where your mother went?"

Jess' hands clenched involuntarily as an uncomfortable feeling spread through her stomach. She shot the guidance counselor a dangerous look and stood up, pushing the chair back with more force than was really necessary. Then she grabbed her backpack off the floor and turned toward the door.

"Okay, wait!" Miss Williams called out. "I'm sorry. Please, sit down," she asked, motioning toward the chair.

Jess glared at the closed door of the office, refusing to turn around.

"I have something you can do to help your chances of getting into Trinity." She paused. "If that's really what you want."

Jess turned her head and eyed the woman suspiciously, waiting for her to continue.

"Your academics are already one of the highest in the class and obviously your extracurriculars are great with lacrosse and those clubs you were in last year." She pulled a piece of paper out from the top drawer of her desk. "The only area where I think you could improve is your community service."

Jess immediately shook her head. "I already volunteer every summer through the church and I included that with my applications."

"Yes, but this would be different." She held out the paper for Jess to take. "The college admittance boards are giving seniors a chance to do one last project that will be factored in with their application. It's a volunteer program, but you create a video project of the experience. Think of it as a last chance for extra credit. Each student gets to pick one option on the list and volunteer there for the rest of the semester.

You have to create a video essay of your experience and submit it right before winter break when they make final decisions on early admissions."

Jess' eyes scanned the paper carefully, reading over each program. She already had so much on her plate between school, college prep courses, and lacrosse, adding anything else would definitely be a stretch. But if it meant giving her a better chance at getting in, it was worth it.

"You really think this will help?" she finally asked, her words laced with a precise balance of both hope and suspicion.

"I do," Miss Williams answered. "I've already informed most of the other seniors who are waiting on acceptances and so far, everyone has agreed to do it. Gabby Earnheart, who I know is also competing for the last spot at Trinity, told me yesterday that she's going to participate."

Jess rolled her eyes. *Of course she is.*

Gabby always competed with her for everything, ever since they were children. When Jess started playing lacrosse, Gabby had to join too. When Jess won the spelling bee in fourth grade, Gabby had to beat her in the talent show that year. If Jess received an award for something at church, Gabby made sure she won two awards. So when Jess told the girls on her lacrosse team about applying to Trinity, she wasn't surprised when Gabby announced soon after that she was as well.

Miss Williams pulled another paper out of her desk that had names scrawled in one long column. She began counting off each name, whispering the numbers to herself.

"Perfect." She smiled and looked up from the paper. "We have room for one more person. They're only allowing one student per program, so there's a limited number of spots open."

Jess scanned the program options again. She saw the hospital near the top of the list and knew that it would be her best choice. Luke's mom was a nurse there, so she figured she could help get her some good footage to use in the video.

"Okay," she finally agreed. "I want to sign up for the hospital program."

Miss Williams shook her head. "Not yet. Each person will get an equal chance to sign up for the program they want. The sheet will be posted in the library today after lunch. It's first come, first serve, and you can sign up right when the last lunch bell rings."

Jess nodded, making a mental note as she tucked the paper into her backpack. Another to-do added to the never-ending list.

"Make sure you get there early, though. I've already heard a few students say they want to do the hospital program. That'll definitely be one of the first to go."

"Okay." Jess pulled her backpack over her shoulders and walked toward the door. Then she paused, turning her head back halfway. "Thank you."

Miss Williams gave her a small, satisfied smile, as if she'd been waiting for that. "Of course."

Jess pulled the door open and stepped into the busy hallway. The scent of microwaved pizza and lukewarm hamburgers wafted by as students rushed past her on their way to the cafeteria and courtyard for lunch. She glanced each way down the hall, searching for her friends. After a minute of waiting, she pushed through the crowd and sat down on the bench on the other side of the hallway.

Jess pulled the program paper out of her backpack and scanned through the instructions again, her lips pursed in frustration. She had enough on her plate without adding a useless video project into the mix. And there was nothing she hated more than last minute changes to her workload.

"Jess!"

She looked up and saw Scarlett waving at her from the other end of the hall.

She stood and slipped the paper back into her bag. "What took so long?"

"The boys had to grab a snack on the way because they couldn't wait five more minutes to eat," Scarlett answered with an eye roll.

Jess looked further down the hall and saw Luke and Malik following close behind, hands full of chip bags and cookies.

"Hey babe." Luke smiled as he approached and leaned down to kiss her cheek.

"You guys are such children." Jess shook her head, wiping crumbs off of his face.

Her relationship with Luke had been an accident. Something that sort of just happened because neither of them did anything to actively stop it. If she really thought about it, there wasn't even a time when they'd actually become an official couple. There wasn't any defining moment where he'd asked her to be his girlfriend, or she asked him to be her boyfriend. They'd each just been friends with Scarlett and Malik, so when those two started dating, they all four spent a lot of time together. Then slowly the group hangouts began to feel more like double dates. The goodbye hugs lasted a few seconds too long. The drunken nights together produced sloppy, drunken kisses. And eventually it was just understood by everyone that they were off limits to anyone else. Jess hadn't even really thought about it. She just accepted it like everyone else did.

Malik laughed, offering one of his cookies to Scarlett. "Hey, we're trying to bulk! We need our calories."

"I'm good," Scarlett grimaced, looking over at Jess. "Wanna go get coffee?"

Jess looked down at the time on her phone again. "Yeah, but it needs to be quick. I have to be back at the library right when lunch ends."

Luke grunted, a few crumbs falling out of his mouth and onto the chest of his black shirt. "Why? Aren't you done for the day?"

Jess pursed her lips. "Not anymore. Apparently, Trinity already chose the first student from our school—"

"Seriously?!" Scarlett cut in. "Wow, not that I'm super wild about you wanting to go there, but I really thought you'd be the first one chosen."

"Yeah, I thought so too," Jess replied, frustration evident in her voice. "So now there's only one spot left. I guess they're giving some seniors a chance to do a volunteer program for the rest of the semester as a last way to impress the colleges." She pulled out the list, handing it to Scarlett.

"Damn, that sucks," Luke said, washing his food down with a loud gulp of his soda. "Is it like an everyday thing you have to go to?"

Jess nodded, glancing at the crumbs still littered across his chest. "Yeah, the paper says a minimum of six volunteer days a week until winter break."

Malik took the paper from Scarlett, scanning over the list. "Hey, the hospital is on here. You should try to get that one."

"Oh, nice!" Luke yelled, wrapping his arm around her shoulder. "If you do that, my mom could probably get you out of having to go on all the days."

Jess took the paper back from them. "If everyone else is doing the full schedule, then I will, too. I'm not going to cheat."

Luke frowned. "Okay, well then, at least pick that one so I could come and hang out with you while you're working."

Jess gave him a small smile. "I'll try. I can sign up after lunch, but its first come first serve."

"Oh, shit yeah, we need to hurry then," Scarlett said, grabbing her bag off the floor and giving Malik a quick kiss. "We can go through the drive-thru."

Luke squeezed Jess' hand and flashed her a big, boyish grin. "Text me when you guys get back."

Luckily, most of the seniors had already left for lunch, so the parking lot was almost empty. They wasted no time crossing the lot and getting into her car. As she slid into the driver's seat, Jess glanced at the tiny, circular gold pin attached to the visor above her. It was her mother's college pin that she'd received when she graduated from Trinity. Jess performed her daily ritual, kissing her fingers and pressing them against the pin before buckling her seat belt.

Glancing at the clock on the dashboard, she checked the time and turned the key in the ignition. They'd need to be quick, but should make it back in time.

They drove the short few minutes in comfortable silence, listening to whatever songs came on the radio.

As they veered off the main street, she could see the coffee stand drive-thru line wrapping around the side of the building and snaking its way through the rows of the parking lot.

"Great," Jess muttered, glancing at the clock again.

"Looks like it's moving fast. We should be fine," Scarlett said before looking down to scroll through her phone.

Jess pulled the car up to the back of the line, behind a motorcycle. The seat of the bike caught her attention for a split second. It was bright lime green on an otherwise fully black bike.

"I can't believe they didn't pick you first," Scarlett muttered absentmindedly, still scrolling through her phone.

Jess shrugged, looking off to the side through the window. She was sick of thinking about it. She'd had her time to sulk. Now it was time to move on and do something about it.

"I mean really, if you don't qualify as a top choice, then what the fuck does that mean the rest of us normal people are?" Scarlett muttered.

Jess snorted, shaking her head. The line moved up, and she released her foot from the brake to inch the car forward, following the motorcycle in front of them.

"This volunteer thing is gonna be tough with the longer practices we have now leading up to the finals," Scarlett said, finally looking up from her phone. "Are you sure not trying to do too much at once?"

Jess shot her a pointed look, cocking one eyebrow.

"I'm not saying you can't handle the workload," Scarlett continued. "We both know you can. I'm just trying to make sure you don't burn yourself out or something."

"It's fine," Jess muttered, glancing at the clock again. "It's only like six weeks and then I'll be done for the rest of the year. Besides, if Gabby can do it, I definitely can too."

Scarlett gave her a disgusted look. "Of course she's doing this, too. If she did anything original without copying it from you, I'm pretty sure the fucking world would end."

The line moved up again, finally leaving just one person in front of them. Jess glanced down at the clock again, feeling a twinge of anxiety at how quick the time had gone by. She tapped her fingers against the steering wheel, hoping they'd order quickly.

The barista leaned out of the window to greet them. Jess watched the rider flip the front of their helmet up, replying in some way that made the girl laugh and lean in a little closer.

Jess drummed her fingers the slightest bit harder.

The barista stayed partially hung out of the drive-through window, giving the rider a sultry smile as she tapped their order into the iPad resting in her palm. They talked for a few more seconds before the girl reluctantly pulled herself back into the coffee stand.

"Come on," Jess muttered. "Hurry it up."

Scarlett laughed. "Hey let the poor girl shoot her shot at hot motorcycle guy,"

"Not if it makes me late. And how do you know he's hot? He's literally fully covered. You can't see a single part of him."

Scarlett shrugged. "Anyone on a motorcycle is hot."

Jess chuckled, shaking her head.

The barista returned to the window with a small bag in her hand. She handed it to the rider, flashing a big smile. The rider said something that made her laugh again, looking a little flustered.

"Oh my god, seriously!" Jess snapped, her frustration hitting a boiling point. "I don't have time for this."

She watched the girl scribble something on a napkin, then she handed it over with another coy smile.

Scarlett laughed. "Oh my god, she really is shooting her shot!"

The rider nodded, tucking the napkin into their pocket. Then they flipped the visor on the helmet down and accelerated forward, out of the drive-thru line.

"Finally," Jess hissed, pulling the car up to the window.

They hurried through their orders, and the coffees came out within a minute.

Jess sped back toward the campus, going at least ten miles over the speed limit. When they reached the parking lot, she checked the time again. One minute past the time of the last lunch bell.

"Shit," she hissed, slamming the car door closed behind her and running toward the library building.

"Good luck!" Scarlett yell from behind her.

A group of students opened the doors and made their way outside as she approached the building. She ran up and squeezed between them, pushing her way into the library. Her eyes scanned the far wall until they spotted Miss Williams standing near the back corner between some round wood tables. A small group of students lined up in front of her single file, each one signing their name on the clipboard she was holding. Jess jogged up and stopped at the back of the line, panting heavily.

The few kids in front of her took a minute to sign their names and then finally it was her turn.

Miss Williams looked at her with a frown. "I told you to be here early."

"I know, I'm sorry. We got stuck in traffic. Is the hospital program still open?" she asked, eyes wide with hope.

The woman shook her head. "It was one of the first to go." She looked down at the clipboard. "Actually, you're lucky to be getting any program at all. It looks like there's only one left."

Jess grimaced. Great. The one no one else wanted.

"Which one is it?" she asked, mentally running through the other programs she'd seen on the list.

Miss Williams glanced down again, double checking the entry. "The addiction recovery clinic at the community center."

*Awe*some. Something she knew absolutely nothing about.

"Are you sure that's the only one left?"

"Yes."

Jess pursed her lips, thinking it over one last time. It would be extremely tough to fit another thing in on top of her schedule. The hospital would've been a little easier since she knew someone there that could've helped her. But this one would be a completely different story. She thought about all the late nights she'd already spent the last few years to get into Trinity. She was so close. She'd just have to find a way to make it all work.

"And you're *sure* this is my *last* option for impressing the board of admissions at Trinity?" she asked.

"This will impress both Trinity *and* Bucknell," the woman responded.

Jess considered it for a moment. Then she leaned over and signed her name on the line next to the addiction program. Her jaw tightened when she saw the name "Gabby Earnheart" scrawled next to the hospital. Of course she'd been the one to get it.

"Perfect," Miss Williams smiled at her and turned around to grab something off the table, "And now you can take one of these." She handed her a small black padded camera bag. "We're loaning each student a camera to film their project."

Jess took the bag from her.

"You're free this period, right? No classes?" the woman asked.

"Yeah."

"Good. Each student needs to go meet their program director today to finalize their volunteer schedule for the remaining weeks of the semester."

"Right now?" she asked, exasperated as she placed the camera strap over her shoulder. It somehow felt even heavier than her loaded backpack.

Miss Williams nodded. "They expect you to start immediately."

Jess frowned. She made a mental note to remember to text Luke, letting him know she wouldn't be able to meet up with him after all. Dealing with him being butthurt about her bailing on him again would be the cherry on top of an already crappy day.

"You know, you're lucky to even have this opportunity, Jess. You should be a little more grateful," Miss Williams said with a disappointed look.

Jess looked down, a tiny twinge of guilt emerging beneath the irritation. Or maybe it was just the coffee she'd gulped down in a rush, deciding to upset her stomach. "Sorry. I am grateful. It's just that right now it feels like one more thing being thrown on the pile for this semester."

Miss Williams nodded like she understood, although she probably didn't.

"Thank you for your help. I really do appreciate it," Jess said. The small feeling of guilt pushed out an even smaller, but genuine, smile to accompany the apology.

Miss Williams smiled back. "You're welcome."

Jess turned and made her way out the library doors. She pulled out her phone, clicking on the maps app. Then she typed in the name of the community center as she crossed the grass between the library and the parking lot. The phone's mechanical voice rang out before showing her the fastest route.

Ten minutes. Not bad. At least she wouldn't be stuck driving all over the place every day.

When she got in the car, she decided to call her dad on the way to let him know she'd be home a little later than usual. He wouldn't care, but it would at least save her having to explain later that night when she was exhausted from the long day.

She clicked on his contact and heard the phone ring as she put it on speaker and dropped it onto her thigh.

It cut off halfway through the third ring. "Hey Jess, it's Matt."

"Hey," she glanced down at her phone to make sure she'd dialed the right number, "Is my dad there?"

"Yeah, he's a little busy, though. We got a DV call across town, and he's talking to the suspect right now. Want me to get him for you?"

"Oh," she answered, glancing over her shoulder as she pulled out of the parking space. "No, that's fine. Can you just let him know I'll be home a little later today? I have a school thing at the community center that I have to go to."

"Yeah, no problem. I'll tell him," he answered. "Be careful, though. We get calls near there all the time. That area usually attracts the kind of people you want to avoid."

She put the car back in drive and sped through the now mostly empty lot. "Thanks," she muttered, already mentally checked out of the conversation. "I'll keep that in mind."

She heard some commotion in the background, then Matt mumbled a quick goodbye and hung up before she could answer.

She rolled down the windows and continued the drive in silence, listening to the swish of the icy wind whip by. The air smelled crisp and wet, a reminder that fall was nearing its end, which meant that the school semester was too.

Before she knew it, her phone declared her arrival, and she pulled up near the front of an outdated red brick building. She put her car in park and scanned the area.

The building had a few small windows that she could see, all of which were lined with green frames, although, the paint had clearly faded over the years and was now more like the ombre of half dead grass. The main double doors had the same distasteful green trim with the paint peeling off in all the corners. There were some words printed in white on one door, but they were too worn down to be legible.

Two large men stood a few feet from the main doors, smoking. Another man sat on the ground, leaned against the wall on the opposite side of the doors. She hated to admit it, but the thought flashed through her mind that maybe Matt was right and this wasn't a good place for her to be spending time every day.

She opened her glove box and pulled out the small key chain of pepper spray that her dad had given her years ago. He'd chosen the hot pink version even though she'd never once in her life had anything pink. When he gave it to her, he'd said something about how it would match her outfits.

She turned it in her hand, wiping some weird gunk off the handle. He'd given it to her so long ago, she wondered if it would even still work. Maybe not, but she attached it to her keys anyway, thinking that it couldn't hurt to have it just in case.

Jess scanned the building once more and stepped out of the car. As she took a few steps forward, she was relieved to see a friendly looking, middle-aged woman walk out of the doors. The woman smiled and said something to the men, who responded by dropping their cigarettes on the ground and stomping them out before walking into the building. The woman reached down and picked up the smashed cigarettes, throwing them into the trash near the door.

Jess approached her before she could follow the men back inside. "Excuse me! Do you, by any chance, work in the center?"

"I do," the woman responded with a warm smile. "Can I help you with something?"

"Yes, actually. I'm here for the student volunteer program."

"Oh my goodness, that's great!" the woman exclaimed. "Wow, to be honest, I halfway didn't even expect anyone to pick our program."

Jess' eyes bounced away to the peeling paint on the doors. "Yeah. Well, I'm here to help now in any way you need me to," she said, finishing with a tight smile.

"That's wonderful. We're so grateful to have you here! I'm Laura," the woman said, holding her hand out toward Jess.

"Jess," she responded, shaking the woman's hand firmly.

"Jess," Laura repeated with a smile. "Great to meet you. I don't really have time to give you a tour right now, but—"

The sound of a loud motorcycle drowned out her voice as it pulled into a parking space near the front of the building. Jess turned toward the sound and froze. Right there, bright as day, was the lime green seat on the motorcycle.

"Oh, what perfect timing!" Laura exclaimed. "Sam can give you a tour and show you around." She waved her hand, motioning for them to come over.

Jess clenched her jaw. Of course, this would be her luck. Not only is he the reason she's stuck in this program, now she also has to work with him.

Asshole, she thought to herself as she watched the rider kick down the stand and cut off the engine.

Then, they took off their helmet and Jess' mouth fell partially open.

The *girl*, still straddling the bike, smiled back at them.

"Hey Sam, come here! I need to introduce you to somebody!" Laura yelled to her.

She swung her leg over the bike and flipped her long, wavy brown hair behind her. She removed her jacket and walked toward them.

Jess tried her best to mask the look of both shock and disdain that was surely painted over her face at that moment.

"Sam, we have a new volunteer. This is Jess," Laura said, motioning toward her.

The girl gave her a wide, genuine smile and extended her hand. "Nice to meet you."

Jess reluctantly reached her hand forward, shaking it lightly with a curt nod.

"I was just saying that this was perfect timing," Laura began. "I don't have time to do a tour right now, but you would probably do a better job than me anyway," she finished, smiling at Sam.

"Oh yeah. No worries. I can do it," Sam replied, adjusting the helmet under her arm.

"Great!" she turned back to Jess. "The schedule is Monday through Saturday, after school, and after any extracurriculars you may be in. Does that work?"

Jess nodded reluctantly. "Sure."

"Perfect," she answered with a smile, turning to walk back inside. "You can just do the tour today and make your first full day tomorrow."

Jess gave another small nod.

After a few seconds of silence, Sam smiled warmly at her. "So what made you want to volunteer here?"

Jess' anger surged again, and she couldn't help the glare that filled her eyes. "It wasn't my first choice."

The girl laughed in a way that sounded completely unbothered and carefree. The lightness of it struck a new match of irritation.

"Ah, okay. That makes a little more sense. So you got stuck with us?"

"Mhm," Jess grumbled, glancing over at the motorcycle.

"Well," Sam continued, "I guess the faster we get this tour done then, the faster you can go home."

That was the last straw. "Surprised you care about other people's time now."

Sam jerked her head back, her eyes widening slightly. "Uh—what?"

Jess crossed her arms over her chest and glared at her. "Today. The coffee stand."

Sam raised her eyebrows and tilted her head to the side. "Did I accidentally take your order or something?"

Jess rolled her eyes. "You were so busy flirting with the girl at the window that you made me late getting back to school. Since I was late, I was the last one to pick a volunteer program." She waved her hand toward the building. "This was the only one left."

It took a moment, then Sam's confused expression changed to one of amusement. She bit her lip, as if she was desperately trying to hold back a smile.

"It's not funny," Jess seethed. "You screwed up the plan I had."

Sam couldn't keep it in any longer and broke out into laughter. "You're mad because I cost you, like what, an extra *minute* in the drive-thru line?" she asked, cocking her head.

"It wasn't just a minute," Jess growled.

Sam smiled even bigger. "Why were you even getting coffee in the first place if you were on *such* a tight schedule?"

Jess huffed. "Well, I didn't think I needed to factor in extra time waiting behind someone who was just there to get a date."

Sam laughed again, shaking her head. "Look, I'm sorry I—"

"I think I'll pass on the tour today," Jess said, cutting her off.

"Uh—are you sure?" Sam asked. "We could—"

"Yeah. I'm sure." And with that, Jess spun on her heel, charging back toward the parking lot.

She reached the car and wrenched the door open, throwing the camera bag onto the tan, worn leather of the passenger seat. How could the day have gone so wrong? Senior year wasn't supposed to be like this. It was supposed to be the perfect ending to a long four years of hard work. When everything came together and she finally got everything she'd always wanted.

Now instead, it felt like everything was falling apart.

Chapter 2

S hit. Two minutes behind the target time.

Jess glanced back up from her watch, feet pounding against the hard pavement. Her foggy, jagged breath came out in forced puffs, partially blocking her view in the gray morning light.

Pumping her arms harder, she made the last turn on the road.

Through the short blasts of cloudy air rushing from her mouth, she could just barely make out her house at the end of the block. She sped up her pace, kicking her legs as hard as she could. Her lungs burned with every new breath of the icy morning air. Her legs vibrated and tingled under the pressure of each thud as her foot hit the ground.

She glanced down at her watch again when her left arm swung up toward her chest. The seconds ticked by, and she realized there was no other option but to sprint the last thirty yards to the front door.

Her legs kicked as hard as they possibly could. The steady burn in her lungs immediately turned into a white hot, searing pain that filled her entire chest and abdomen. Her arms swung harder as she hit the bottom of the driveway and accelerated up the red brick steps to the door.

She shoved the door wide open and burst into the entryway of the house, immediately doubling over to catch her breath.

She tilted her wrist. The corners of her mouth bent up into a small smile. Four seconds to spare.

"Hmph." She heard her dad grunt from the kitchen. "Cutting it a little close. What happened?"

Jess' smile dropped as she straightened up and ambled through the small living room and into the kitchen where her dad stood in front of the stove, cooking breakfast.

"Little off, I guess," she answered, dropping into one of the wooden chairs at the table.

He glanced at her for a moment before looking back down at the pan full of eggs. Every morning was the same. Eggs. No bacon, or sausage, or potatoes. Just eggs. She'd gotten sick of them years before, but kept it to herself. It seemed to be the only thing he really knew how to make that didn't somehow involve a grill or microwave. He'd never explicitly said so, and she'd never asked, but the lack of breakfast variety over the previous twelve years since her mother passed told her enough. So there she was. Another morning choking down the over-salted, under-peppered yellow globs.

He stirred them a few more times and then grabbed two white ceramic plates from the cabinet. He scooped a few spoonfuls of eggs onto each plate, grabbed two forks from the drawer, then walked toward the table.

"When's your first semi-final game?" he asked, scooping half his plate into one massive bite.

"Couple weeks."

"Think you're ready for it?"

She nodded, stabbing her fork through a chunk of egg that had more pepper than the rest. He watched her for a moment and then stood up, walking back to the stove.

"So," he continued, picking up the pan and moving it into the sink, "why'd they assign you to the recovery center for this project?"

Jess stopped chewing. She'd filled him in on the project the night before, but chose to leave out a few details.

"I was trying to get the hospital, but someone else got it before me."

"Did you ask Luke if his mom could help? I'm sure she could call in a few favors and get you in."

She shook her head. "It's fine. I agreed to do this, so I'm sticking with it. It's only for a few weeks, anyway."

He looked at her with a pointed expression. "I don't really want you hanging around there. It's not safe for young girls. We get calls in that area all the time."

Jess stood up from the table with her still mostly full plate. "It's not a big deal." She put it in the sink in front of him. "Besides, it's not like I'll be alone. Other volunteers and workers will be there with me."

He continued silently scrubbing the pan in the sink.

Jess watched him, waiting a few seconds for a response before realizing the conversation was over. It wasn't surprising. This was how things usually went between them. Jess had never been a huge talker, but he was on a whole other level.

She walked out of the kitchen and trudged up the wood stairs, her tired legs burning in protest with every step. She went into her room first and grabbed a shirt and jeans out of the top drawer of her dresser. Sunlight streamed through her window, reminding her of the time.

She rushed through a hot shower and tied her wet hair up into a messy bun.

The thud of the front door closing echoed through the house as her dad left for work.

Shit. That meant she was definitely running late.

She slipped on a pair of sneakers and threw a hoodie over an old lacrosse t-shirt. Then she grabbed the video camera bag sitting by her bedroom door before jogging out and down the stairs.

She made a beeline for the kitchen and opened the fridge, spotting the row of canned lattes exiled to the back of the shelf. Usually she refused to drink these monstrosities that her dad insisted on buying, but even canned coffee would be better than nothing.

She grabbed one off the shelf and headed for the front door to grab her keys. Her pace slowed as she walked by one of their family pictures hanging on the wall. It must have been taken when she was two or three. Her mom and dad stood smiling widely at the camera, with her as a toddler standing between them. She looked at it for a second before kissing her fingers and pressing them against her mother's beaming face. The glass there was smudged with fingerprints from this daily ritual, and Jess made a mental note to clean it at some point that week.

The drive that morning was a little longer since her house was farther from the center, and she put on an audiobook for her AP literature class to pass the time. Only half listening, she thought about how the day might go. If she was being honest, she didn't have a clue how addiction centers operated or what type of volunteer work they needed. The most she knew was from what she'd seen in TV shows, and even that was minimal at best and grossly inaccurate at worst.

She was still pondering this as she entered the parking lot and pulled her car into a spot close to the front doors, frowning when she saw the lime green seat on the motorcycle in the space next to her. For one brief second, she considered pulling the car back out of the lot, going home, and calling in sick for the day.

That thought lingered for a moment, then she took a deep breath and gathered her coffee can and camera bag from the passenger side seat before making her way into the old building.

The worn brass door knob screeched as it turned, and she had to shove her hip against it to jolt the door open.

The inside of the building was about as outdated as the outside. It smelled like a mixture of dust and a sink drain that desperately needed cleaning. Faded light blue walls lined with cork boards and paper announcements encompassed the hallway she'd stepped into. One paper on the upcoming events board caught her eye. A concert in the park that had happened three years before.

Maybe the volunteer work would consist of trashing old bulletins. They clearly needed it.

The floor comprised alternating red and white scuffed tiles. Although the white had turned more into the yellow tint of stained teeth. It reminded her of the old checkerboard in the chemo room of the hospital where they treated her mother. One of the friendlier nurses on staff would play with her while her mother slept in the pink recliner, an IV feeding supposedly life-saving poison into her arm. That checkerboard was just about as worn as these floors.

Maybe mopping would be another part of her volunteer work.

"Hey Jess!" Laura's voice floated toward her. The woman stood in front of a large curved reception desk further down the hallway.

"Hey," Jess replied, smiling politely. As she approached, she could see Sam sitting on the other side of the desk, typing furiously on a laptop resting on her thighs.

"I heard you weren't feeling well yesterday. Some bad coffee or something?"

Jess shot a glare over the desk at Sam and could swear she saw the ghost of a smirk on the girl's lips.

"I'm feeling much better today," she replied, looking back at Laura. "Definitely ready to get to work."

"Oh, good!" Laura said, smiling as she walked to the other side of the desk. "I'll be busy running meetings all day today, so I'll mostly need your help with filing."

Wonderful. Because it definitely wouldn't be more beneficial for her to be spending her afternoons studying and working on her college prep courses. No, filing useless papers trumped all of that.

Laura grabbed a stack of folders and papers from the floor and put them on the desk before running through the instructions.

"Okay," Laura said once she finished. "I think that's it! If you have questions or need anything, I'll be in the main room. Oh, and feel free to film anything you like besides the meeting attendees. Obviously, they need to remain anonymous."

"Sounds good, thanks," Jess replied, setting her camera bag and coffee can down on the desk as Laura walked away.

"Did I fully ruin coffee stands for you?"

Jess glanced up and saw Sam looking at her coffee can with a small, amused smirk.

"I was running late and didn't want to risk getting stuck behind someone again," Jess said, sitting down at the desk. She saw a wide smile break out across Sam's face as she turned back to her computer to continue typing.

Jess opened the black case and pulled out the camera. She pressed the power button and the device immediately blinked to life. She waited a few moments for the screen to illuminate with the view in front of her, but it remained black. Turning the camera around, she verified the lens cap was off and that nothing was blocking it. She pressed one of the many buttons on the back of the camera and some type of error message popped up that she didn't understand.

She exhaled a puff of air, her frustration growing while she tried to figure out which combination of buttons to try next. She clicked a few at random and the camera beeped before showing a new error message.

Great, I'm going to fail and not get into college because I can't figure out how to use a stupid camera, she thought, jabbing a new combination of buttons. Another error message popped up, and this time stayed blinking on the screen.

"Do you need help?" Sam finally asked, shooting her an irritated look.

Jess glared back at her. "I got it."

Sam reached forward, snatching the camera out of her hands.

"Hey! I said I had it," Jess exclaimed, reaching for the camera.

Sam moved it out of her grasp. She glanced at the screen for a split second before rolling her eyes and reaching into the camera bag. She searched through a few of the pockets before pulling out a small, thin, black square. Then she pushed it into a slot on the side of the camera, pressed the power button, and handed it back to Jess all in one fluid movement.

Jess looked down at the camera screen, watching as it filled with a clear view of the desk in front of her.

"Mm, thanks," she muttered reluctantly.

Sam looked back at her laptop with an even expression and continued typing, once again fully engrossed in whatever she was doing.

If Jess didn't despise the girl so much, she might actually be impressed with her level of focus. That was something she admired about people.

She set the video camera on the desk and filmed a few clips of the filing she'd been instructed to complete.

The work was simple, and she quickly made it through the first stack of papers, then moved to grab the next stack from the floor. As she bent over, reaching for them, she caught a glance of a notebook peeking out of Sam's backpack on the floor.

"You go to Kenton?" she asked in surprise.

Sam glanced at her, one eyebrow raised.

"The high school," Jess explained, nodding toward the notebook.

Sam looked back at the screen. "Uh, yeah," she muttered.

"I thought they said only one of us could be assigned to each project," Jess said, irritation finding its place in her once again. "I signed up for this one. It's mine."

"Okay?" Sam answered, not bothering to look up from her screen.

Jess huffed. "So *you* have to do a different one. I won't risk getting in trouble because we hand in a video essay on the same program."

Sam finally looked up from her laptop, blinking a few times before her face filled with understanding. "Calm down. I'm not here for a school project."

"Then what're you here for?" Jess quipped, wondering why she was being forced to spend time with this girl every day.

The amused look dulled from the girl's face, and she turned back to her computer, leaving the question hanging in the air.

Jess gritted her teeth and reluctantly continued sorting the stack of papers in silence.

Within a few minutes, the doors to the main auditorium opened, and people began slowly drifting out. Some gave her small nods or polite smiles on their way past the desk, but almost all of them greeted Sam with genuine happiness.

After a few minutes, Laura walked through the doors, trailed by a tall, slender young man. They both walked up to the desk.

"What's up Sammy?" he asked with a wide grin.

She returned the smile, shutting her laptop.

"Ricky, this is Jess," Laura said, motioning her hand toward her. "She's a volunteer from the high school."

"Hey, nice to meet you. I'm Ricky," he said, smiling warmly at her. Then he looked back at Sam. "Convinced someone else to be a nerd like you and spend all their free time here?"

Sam laughed. "Hey, I had nothing to do with this one. She came all on her own. Well–" she paused, and Jess swore she could see a smirk on her face. "She *sort of* came on her own."

Jess glared at her, swallowing the urge to interject and explain how she really got stuck there.

"Are Megan and Sara here? I want to say hi," Sam continued.

"Yeah, yeah. They're waiting outside," Ricky replied, nodding at the entrance. "Guess I better head out, anyway. We have to rush over to Sara's dance practice," he said before smiling at her again. "Jess, it was great meeting you."

"You too," Jess replied with a small, genuine smile, before he and Sam turned to walk toward the front entrance.

Laura sat down in Sam's chair and began filling out a form on her clipboard.

"She seems to know everyone here pretty well," Jess said, continuing her filing.

"Hm? Oh, Sam? Yeah, we're very lucky to have her," Laura replied, turning on the desktop computer in front of her. "She's one of those computer whiz types. She set all of this up for us." She waved her hand at the computer on the desk. "Some people here knew her when she was little and her mom was still in the program." Laura typed into the computer, pecking the keys one at a time. "Gosh, she spent more time here as a kid than she ever did at home. I still remember helping her with her homework when we had slow days," she recalled with a laugh.

Jess nodded slowly, letting the silence hang in the air as she absorbed this new information. Hearing intimate details about someone's life without them being there felt wrong.

"So, do you mainly run AA and NA meetings here?" she asked, gently changing the topic.

Laura clicked some icons on the computer. "Mm yeah, mostly, but we also do some group events, too. The next one is the flag football game, which is everyone's favorite."

"Oh, that sounds fun," Jess replied. The prospect of doing something competitive would at least give her one thing to look forward to.

"Definitely bring your camera to that one. You should be able to get some good footage. It gets pretty serious," Laura said with a smile.

"Good to know. I'll keep that in mind."

The main door opened, and they looked up to see Sam walking back in.

Laura stood from the seat and gathered her things. "Do you have any questions for me while I'm here? Anything you need me to show you again?"

"Um—no." Jess glanced around at the paperwork in front of her. "I think I'm good for now. Thanks."

"Okie dokie," Laura replied with a smile. "Holler if you need anything." She walked back to the auditorium, where new attendees had already begun gathering for the next meeting. Sam circled the desk and sat back down in her chair, opening her laptop again.

The rest of the day flew by, with Laura bringing her new office tasks to work on in between meetings. By the time she finished for the day, she felt confident that she knew the system pretty well and could jump right in the next time she was there. Sam remained sitting next to her the whole day, headphones on, fully engrossed in her computer.

When it was finally time to leave, Jess gathered her things and stood, tossing the coffee can into the trash beside her.

She paused for a moment, contemplating, then turned to Sam. "Thank you."

Sam looked up at her questioningly, pulling her headphones off.

"Thanks," Jess repeated through pursed lips. "For helping me with the camera."

"Oh, yeah, no worries," she replied absentmindedly. "It was the SD card. You need to have that in the camera in order to film and save videos and what not."

"Right," Jess muttered, having no idea what that meant and knowing she'd forget the second the conversation was over.

She swung the bag over her shoulder and walked toward the front door.

First day down.

Chapter 3

"This means that anyone who belongs to Christ has become a new person. The old life is gone; a new life has begun! Love yourself as God has always loved you..."

Jess' eyes glazed over as she stared through the overly excited pastor on stage.

As a young girl, she'd counted the wooden planks on the walls to pass the time, and once she got older, she started running lacrosse plays in her head and quizzing herself for upcoming school tests. She figured that was at least a better use of her time than staring at the wall.

A soft snore came from her left on the wooden pew where her dad sat, slightly slumped to the side. She knocked her knee against his and watched his head jerk up in response. He glanced around in alarm before giving her a small, embarrassed smile as he straightened up in the seat.

It was times like these that made her feel pity for the man. Church had always been her mother's thing, not his. He and Jess only tagged along because her mother had always insisted. After she died, though, her dad kept up the routine and made sure they never missed a single Sunday.

Although it felt tedious at times, she really was grateful to have that one thing that made her feel close to her mother, like she still had some small part of her. She'd passed when Jess was six, but she'd been sick long before that. In her stongest memories, their relationship existed within hospital visits and appointments. And before that, it existed through hugs and bedtime stories and all the typical things that a parent does for a young child. But there was nothing special or specific about the things she remembered. There was no smell of perfume that would suddenly transport her into a fond memory. She didn't have a special pancake recipe that she made every Saturday morning or a favorite song she always played. At least, none that Jess could recall. The memories she had of her mother before she'd gotten sick were so generic she sometimes worried she'd made them up entirely from watching mothers interact with their children in shows or movies.

As a child, this had been fine. She'd remembered tight, soothing hugs, and the way her mother held her as she cried. But as she got older, those memories no longer felt like enough. She wanted to know who she was as a woman—as a person. What did she believe in? What made her happy or sad? What did she struggle with?

Once, when she was twelve, she'd worked up the courage and asked her dad what her mother was really like. She would never forget the way he recoiled. An instant uncomfortable air settled around them, and he never answered the question. She felt sick the rest of the day as they both avoided each other around the house. The old, unhealed wounds torn freshly open once again.

It did, however, produce one positive. Later that week, she'd walked into her room to see an old photograph of her mom resting on her pillow. It showed her mother standing in front of a large concrete sign that read "Trinity University". A small gold pin clung to the corner of the photograph. A circle of gold with the letter "T" in the center.

"Thank you, everyone," the pastor said, cutting Jess out of her daze. "And I look forward to seeing you all next Sunday!"

She glanced at her dad, who still looked half-asleep, but clapped nonetheless.

He cleared his throat, looking over at Jess with a sheepish grin. "Good sermon, huh?"

Jess smirked and shook her head. "It must've been. You only slept through like half of this one instead of the whole thing."

He grunted, rubbing the back of his neck as the surrounding people began to stand up and disperse. Jess watched them filing out the door.

"I think I'm gonna go to the center again today. I need to get as much footage as possible, and I didn't really get much yesterday."

He nodded. "Alright. I'll be on shift after this, but I should be home around dinnertime. I can grab something on the way if you want."

"Yeah, sounds good." Jess stood up, stretching her arms and legs.

"Babe!"

She looked to the right and saw Luke coming toward her with a wide smile.

"Hey," she replied, smiling back and picking her things up off the pew.

He spotted her dad and immediately slowed his approach. "Oh, hi Mr. Miller."

Her dad nodded. "Luke."

"Where do you want to go for lunch?" Luke asked, leaning over to kiss her cheek.

"Oh, I can't go today, sorry," she said with an apologetic look. "I'm going back to the center today."

"What?" he frowned. "I thought you said you had Sundays off?"

Jess hated when he gave her that sad puppy dog look. It was one of those things that made her irrationally annoyed. Then she felt bad for being so annoyed. And that also annoyed her.

"Yeah, but I need to get as many shots as I can for the video."

He stuck his bottom lip out dramatically. "Please, just skip it for today. I miss you."

"No. This is important." She turned back to her dad. "Are you ready to go?"

He groaned, slowly standing up and stretching his back. She took that as a yes and gave Luke a quick side hug, ignoring his overly sad demeanor. "I'll see you tomorrow."

"Kay," he muttered, as she walked toward the doors at the back of the church.

***

When she pulled up to the community center building, it surprised her to see that the parking lot was nearly full. Small clusters of people stood outside talking and smoking, while others walked in and out of the doors. She grabbed her things and weaved her way through them to the front door. A few people lingered inside the front hallway too, and she made her way past them to the desk where Sam sat, talking to a young man.

"Hey," Sam said, glancing up at her. "I thought today was your day off?"

Jess set her things down on the desk. "Yeah, but I figured I should come in and get a few extra shots for my video."

"Jess!" Laura called as she walked up to them. "So glad you're here. The community center in the next town over had to shut down for the day because of a plumbing leak. Now we have to host all of their attendees, so it'll be a busy day."

"Oh, I'm glad I came in then. What do you need help with?"

"Can you both help me get the auditorium filled with more chairs?" she asked, looking between Jess and Sam.

"Yeah, of course," Sam said, standing up. Jess followed her as she walked down the hallway. This part of the building seemed to be empty of people, mainly consisting of storage rooms and closets. The dirty sink drain smell worsened the farther they went.

"So, you had nothing better to do than come hang out with us?" Sam asked, throwing a playful smirk over her shoulder.

Jess shrugged. "We went to church this morning. I figured I should use the rest of the day to get ahead on school work."

Sam nodded as she stopped in front of one of the closed doors, opening it to reveal a large storage closet with stacked chairs and other equipment.

"We probably need at least two stacks," she muttered mostly to herself, looking at the chairs.

They each grabbed as many as they could carry and headed back down the hallway toward the auditorium. Then they dropped the chairs and began separating and dispersing them evenly throughout the room.

When they got back to the desk, the hallway had mostly cleared out, with people either leaving or heading into the next meeting. Jess waited another minute for the hall to clear, then she quickly set up her camera halfway between the desk and the front entrance to film from a different angle as she completed her next tasks.

Time flew by as she worked through one filing task after the other in a peaceful flow. It was almost enjoyable. She finished another set of tasks and went to move her camera to get a different angle. As she approached the front doors, she thought she heard shouting outside the building entrance. She waited there for a moment, watching the doors, but couldn't hear anything else. Finally, she turned back to the camera and flipped the latch to remove it from the tripod.

Suddenly, the front door burst open in a commotion.

A sharp, wiry man stood there, his eyes darting back and forth between her and the rest of the hallway. When his gaze landed on her camera for a split second, her grip subconsciously tightened. His face looked hollow, with the cheekbones protruding like knuckles in a skeletal hand. A faded gray shirt hung off of his body like a wet rag with a ring of sweat around the collar, circling his neck. The yellow tinge told her it'd been there for a while.

"What?" he demanded, staring at her with a spiteful look in his eyes.

Jess took a step back instinctively, but her brain froze, refusing to fill her mouth with words.

"You got a fuckin lighter?" he asked, taking a step toward her. The stench of cigarettes and body odor filled her nostrils.

"Uh—no, I don't think we have one here," she answered, trying to sound more sure than she felt.

He shot her an irritated look. "How 'bout you go back there and check?"

She saw his eyes flicker down to her camera once more.

"Uh—"

She jumped in surprise when suddenly, a strong hand closed around her arm from behind. She felt herself being pulled gently, but firmly, backwards. Then Sam stepped in front of her.

"Hey man," she said, voice steady and uncharacteristically commanding. "We don't have any lighters here, but there's a gas station across the street you can get one from."

He scoffed. "Nah, your girl here can go check in the back for one."

Jess' eyes flickered to Sam.

"Like I said," she began, crossing her arms loosely over her chest. "You can get one across the street."

Her tone remained calm, but there was something in it that left Jess feeling uneasy.

The muscle in the man's jaw twitched back and forth as he took a quick step closer to them.

"And like *I* said, she can go look for one."

Jess instinctively stepped back, but Sam remained firmly in place.

"You should leave. Now," Sam said in a low, but commanding tone.

"I don't needa do shit!" he snapped, stepping forward, leaving only inches between him and Sam's face.

"Leave or we'll call the police," she said.

"Fuck you," he spat.

Then, in a flash, he shoved his hands hard against Sam's chest. She fell a step backward, catching herself against the wall. He threw a hard punch toward her head, and she moved just fast enough to miss most of the contact, but it still caught the corner of her eye socket. Sam ducked slightly and then threw a punch back. It landed between his jaw and neck.

Jess watched in shock for a split second, then turned and ran toward the desk. By the time she grabbed her cell phone and looked back up at them, Sam had pinned him against the wall, knocking down some of the cork bulletin boards that hung there.

"Help!" Jess screamed toward the auditorium as she dialed 911 on her phone. She looked up and saw them struggling against the wall. Then Sam turned him just enough to slam them both down to the ground.

"Hey!" a man yelled, as he ran toward them from the auditorium. Another one quickly followed.

The 911 operator answered, and Jess quickly explained the situation as she watched the men working to pull him away. The operator told her that officers were on their way, and Jess hung up the phone, running back toward them to help. By the time she got there, the two men had pulled him away from Sam and had him pinned against the ground while he continued yelling a string of profanities at them.

She ran to Sam, who slumped on the floor, leaned against the wall. Her arms rested on her knees, and her head drooped between them, moving with each breath she took.

"Hey," Jess said, trying to keep her voice calm. "Look at me."

Sam raised her head, turning slightly toward her, but she kept her eyes glued to the man still writhing on the ground. Blood dripped from her lip and a small gash on her left temple. The eye on that side was also a little swollen, and Jess knew it'd probably turn purple and blue within a few hours.

"Oh, my god!" Laura's frantic voice rang out behind her. "Sam, what happened? Are you okay?"

"Fine," Sam muttered, still watching the man intently as he struggled against the men holding him down. "Just a strung out asshole."

"The cops are on their way," Jess said.

Laura nodded gratefully at her, then looked back to Sam. "Are you okay? Do you need an ambulance?"

Sam snorted. "Definitely not. I'm fine."

"No, you're not. You're bleeding," Laura said, frowning at her. "Jess, there's a room down the hall with a first aid kit. Can you take her there and get her cleaned up? I'll wait here until the police arrive."

Jess nodded. "Yeah, of course."

She grabbed onto Sam's arm and gently pulled her to her feet. They slowly made their way through the crowd that had gathered in the hallway.

"Where's the room Laura said to go to?" Jess asked softly, her hand still clutched firmly around Sam's arm.

"A little farther down on the left."

When they reached the room, Jess let her hand drop to push the door. It opened to a dimly lit room filled to the brim with old office chairs. Reddish orange cabinets lined every wall, with one small countertop beneath.

"Sit down," Jess said, as she began opening the cabinets in search of the first aid kit.

Sam did as she was told, sitting in a chair near the countertop.

Luckily, it only took Jess a few tries before she found the cabinet that held the first aid kit. She pulled out the bright red bag and set it on the countertop. She pulled open the zipper and fished through the contents, quickly finding gauze and anti-bacterial wipes. Pulling another chair up, she sat in front of Sam, close enough that she had to fit both her knees in between the other girl's legs. Sam leaned forward a bit, letting Jess' hand gently hold her chin.

"This might sting," Jess muttered. Sam gave her a slight nod.

She rubbed the anti-bacterial wipe across the cuts and was surprised when Sam gave almost no reaction. Jess then pushed some gauze against the wound on her head, applying pressure to stop the bleeding. Again, she expected some type of reaction to the pain, but Sam seemed oblivious to it.

"Hey," Jess said, gently lifting Sam's chin to get her attention. "How's your head feeling?"

"Fine," she said with a shrug.

Jess frowned. "I'm worried about where he hit your head. You could have a concussion."

Sam shook her head slightly. "I don't have a concussion, trust me. It wasn't that hard."

Jess watched her carefully for a minute, trying to decide whether she should insist that she go to the hospital. Finally, she gave in, deciding to drop it.

"Fine, but you need to monitor your symptoms for the rest of the day. And if you feel sick or anything like that, then you need to go to the hospital right away. Okay?"

Sam laughed lightly. "If you say so."

Jess nodded, satisfied with that answer. She finished wiping away any blood from the girl's face and placed a bandaid on the cut near her eye.

"You'll probably get a black eye," she said, standing up and looking over her work one more time.

Sam stood up with her. "All done?"

"Yeah," Jess replied, putting the supplies back into the first aid bag.

They both walked back out into the hallway, Jess following closely behind her. As they approached the front area, Jess could see that the crowd had mostly dissipated.

"Dad?" she asked in surprise, seeing her father standing near the front door talking to Laura.

"Hey," he looked up at her, his eyes showing a mix of frustration and relief. He walked towards her, pulling her into a tight side hug.

"This is Sam," Laura said to him, placing her hand lightly on Sam's shoulder.

He released his daughter and looked over at the other girl. "Hi Sam, I'm Officer Miller. Do you mind if I ask you a few questions about what happened?"

"Yeah, sure," she said, leading them to the pair of chairs behind the front desk.

Jess remained in the hallway, watching as her dad began running through his list of questions. She knew he had the tendency to intimidate people, but it looked like Sam was mostly at ease.

"How are you doing?" Laura asked from beside her. Jess realized that Laura also seemed to be closely watching the interaction between the two of them.

"I'm okay," she answered. "It was a little scary, though."

Laura looked at her sympathetically. "I'm so sorry, honey."

"It's not your fault," Jess said, giving her a small, reassuring smile. "I'm glad she's okay, though, and I'm glad I wasn't up here by myself."

Laura nodded. "Me too."

46

Jess continued watching from the hallway, waiting for them to finish up while Laura went back into the auditorium, where a few members were waiting for the next meeting to begin.

A couple more minutes passed before her dad finally stood up from the chair.

"Thank you, Sam. That should be enough, but if there's anything else you want to add to the report, just give us a call."

Jess approached the desk. "Did you arrest him?"

He nodded. "He's in the car with Matt. We'll drive him down to the station." He paused, clearing his throat, "I texted one of the nurses I know at the hospital. She said they can make an exception and let you volunteer there for your project."

Jess raised her eyebrows in surprise. "Why'd you do that?"

"After what happened here today, I think it's pretty clear that this isn't a safe place for you to be," he said through a tight jaw.

"Dad that's not—"

"I don't want to hear it, Jess. These aren't the kind of people I want my daughter hanging around every day," he said, raising his voice.

Sam stood up from the chair, grabbing her headphones off the desk. She walked around Jess and headed toward the mess of cork board and papers that had been knocked onto the ground in the hallway.

Jess gritted her teeth, lowering her voice. "I didn't want to be here either, but I made a commitment. I won't back out now and leave them hanging."

He huffed. "I don't care about your commitment. I care about your safety."

She crossed her arms defiantly. "Dad, I'm fine. Nothing even happened to me."

"Yeah, not this time, but what happens the next time some guy comes in and loses it after a bender?"

"Well then, it's a good thing I'm not alone and there are other people here with me," she replied, glancing down the hallway to Sam, who was cleaning up the mess on the floor.

He grunted, crossing his arms over his chest.

"I'm not quitting," she said, looking back at him. "Besides, this is only until the end of the semester, anyway. It'll be over before you know it."

He glared at her, shaking his head, before finally giving in. "Fine, but you need to check in with me while you're here, and you need to keep your pepper spray with you at all times."

Jess nodded. "Deal."

He sighed, dropping his arms. "Don't stay late today. I expect you to be home by the time I get off my shift."

"Okay," she replied, watching him gather his things.

She walked with him down the hall to the front door. They shared another awkward side hug and then he walked out to where Matt was waiting outside with the squad car.

She turned back and walked up beside Sam, kneeling down to help pick up the things that had fallen on the ground. Sam had her headphones covering her ears. They worked in silence for a few moments, before Jess looked up at her, motioning for her attention. The girl removed her headphones, and the low buzz of music floated out.

"Thank you," Jess said seriously.

Sam looked back down at the ground and continued picking up debris. "It's no big deal."

"It is," Jess replied. "I wouldn't have known how to handle it if I was alone." She paused, looking down at the pile of papers she was sifting through. "So—yeah, thanks."

Sam didn't reply this time, but she left her headphones resting around her neck instead of putting them back over her ears.

Jess took a deep breath, knowing what she wanted to say next, but not knowing how to say it. "Also, I'm sorry for what my dad said. About the people here." She paused for a moment. "Laura mentioned that your mom used to come here or something."

Sam stopped what she was doing. Jess thought she could see her jaw tighten, but she wasn't sure if it was just from the slight swelling that had started to appear on her cheek.

"It's cool," she muttered, standing up and taking the pile of papers to the desk.

Jess felt both relieved and a little more anxious by the conversation being over. She took her time picking up the rest of the items on the ground, then went to work hanging the cork board back in its designated spot on the wall. A little while later, Laura asked for her help cleaning up the auditorium.

By the time she finished the task and returned to the front desk, Sam was gone.

Chapter 4

"Are you guys okay to lock up?" Laura asked, peering through the door from the hallway.

That Monday had come and gone in a flash. The day had flown by in a flurry of school, lacrosse practice, and volunteering. Not even one full week on the new schedule, and it was already beginning to take its toll.

Before she knew it, nine o'clock rolled around, and they were cleaning up the auditorium to prepare for the next day. Her eyes burned from exhaustion and dust as she dragged the broom across the scuffed wood floor.

"Yeah, we got it," Sam replied from the corner where she was stacking the chairs.

Jess glanced up at her as she mopped. She'd been mildly disappointed that day when she arrived to find the awkward air between them still painfully present. Sam barely acknowledged her, keeping her headphones on and her eyes glued to the laptop, as usual. At least on the other days she'd said *hi* or given her a smile, or something. But this time, her intense focus seemed like an impenetrable force field. Honestly, Jess really didn't care if Sam ever acknowledged her again.

She loathed small talk anyway. It made her feel disingenuous. But she hated walking on eggshells even more.

"Thanks girls," Laura flashed them a bright smile before retreating down the hallway. "And make sure you walk to the parking lot together. Neither of you should be out there alone at night."

Jess nodded, her eyelids sagging, the weight of her head feeling unusually heavy on her shoulders.

Between the two of them, it only took a few more minutes to finish emptying the trash cans and setting out the pamphlets for the next day. Once they were done, they both gathered their things, shut off the lights, and headed out the front door.

As Jess stood beside Sam, waiting for her to retrieve the key from her backpack, she mentally reviewed the assignments due the following day. It would take at least a few more hours. Maybe half the night. Grabbing some type of caffeine on the way home would probably be a good idea.

"These locks can be a pain sometimes," Sam muttered beside her, jiggling the key in the lock.

Jess nodded, surprised to hear the friendly lilt in her voice. Maybe she'd misread her that night and she truly was just super focused on whatever she'd been working on. It was definitely plausible. Her observational skills probably weren't at their peak, given her extreme level of exhaustion.

The key finally scraped through, locking the door. They both turned to walk toward the parking lot.

"Night," Sam said with a quick smile as she reached her bike.

"Yeah, see you tomorrow," Jess mumbled, a yawn muffling her words.

She walked the last few feet to her car and quickly slid in, locking the door beside her. That had been another rule her dad had given her if she was going to stay late at night.

She put the key in the ignition and twisted.

The engine squealed like an injured animal before sputtering a few times and dying out.

She tried again, and the noises repeated once more before she released the key.

"Shit." She closed her eyes for a moment, leaning her head back against the headrest.

Of course. This was just her luck.

She grabbed her phone from the passenger seat and pulled open the glove box, searching for the AAA card her dad had put in there for her.

As she sifted through yellowed papers she'd never bothered to look at before, a knock on the window made her jump. Her eyes shot up to see Sam watching her with a concerned expression.

"I don't know what's wrong. It won't start," she huffed, pushing the door open.

"Yeah, I figured from the sound," Sam replied, matching her irritated tone. "Can you pop the hood?"

Jess released a frustrated sigh as she fished for the lever beneath her seat. She pulled and heard something click.

Sam walked to the front of the car and lifted the hood, propping it open with a thin metal rod. Jess stepped out of the car, following her.

With the flashlight on her phone, Sam examined parts of the car that Jess had never laid eyes on before.

That continued for a few minutes until Sam finally pulled the rod out and lowered the hood, letting it pop back into place.

"I think you're gonna have to get it towed."

Jess groaned, shaking her head. At this rate, she probably wouldn't make it home for another hour or two at the earliest.

"If you want, I could give you a ride home," Sam offered. Although the look on her face made it obvious that she hoped she'd say no.

Jess stared blankly at her. "On that?" she asked, jerking her head toward the motorcycle.

Sam scoffed. "Look, it's not my favorite solution either, but I also don't want to sit here with you all night waiting for a tow truck."

As much as Jess hated the idea, she also knew Sam was probably right, and this was her best option. Her dad was on a shift and it was too late to bug Luke or Scarlett to come pick her up.

Her eyes drooped lower by the second.

"Fine," she grumbled.

She walked back to the driver-side door and grabbed the camera bag, then sent her dad a quick text, explaining what was happening and asking if he could have her car towed at some point the next day. Once that was taken care of, she joined Sam by the motorcycle.

She watched with an apprehensive look as Sam pulled out a second, smaller helmet and handed it to her.

"I can attach the camera bag to the back so it's secure." Sam paused for a moment, thinking. "You're gonna be behind me, though, so you'll have to wear my backpack."

"Uh—okay," Jess replied, looking down at the bike, her palms beginning to sweat.

Sam handed her the backpack, and Jess slowly put it around her shoulders. It was still warm from Sam's back, giving her a bit of comfort in the frosty night air.

Sam checked the latch on Jess' helmet and then sat down on the bike. She turned the key in the ignition and it roared to life.

Sam looked up at her expectantly. "Alright, get on," she said, her voice a little louder over the rumbling of the engine.

Jess swallowed, her muscles going rigid. "I've—uh—I've never been on one before."

Sam stared at her, and Jess could see that she was making a conscious effort to not look too annoyed. She was failing miserably.

"I promise you'll be okay," Sam said. "You don't have to do anything but hold on and lean with me."

Jess swallowed thickly.

"Here," Sam said, handing her phone to Jess. "Put your address in so I know where I'm going."

Jess tapped in the string of numbers and letters, then took a timid step toward the bike. She lifted her leg clumsily over the seat, lowering her body into a sitting position. Her stiff hands hung at her sides, unsure of what they should be holding on to.

Sam spoke over the roar of the engine. "Okay, hold on and lean your body with me when we turn."

Jess nodded, unable to form any words. Her hands shook as she searched for a spot on the bike to hold on to.

Sam kicked the shifter on the bike and released the clutch, causing them to roll forward. When she shifted up, they accelerated, and Jess' body jerked backwards. She yelped in surprise and instinctively grabbed the back of Sam's jacket in front of her.

Sam's entire face was covered with the black helmet, but Jess could swear she heard a quiet chuckle.

She kept her hands on Sam's back, knuckles white as they clung to fistfuls of the jacket. They approached the end of the parking lot where it met the main street and her anxiety spiked again.

Sam turned her head. "Remember, lean with me!"

Jess gripped more of the jacket as they slowly went over the dip and started the turn onto the street. The bike tipped to the side, and her stomach dropped.

They were falling. She squeezed her eyes shut, bracing for the impact.

Then, a second later, she felt Sam lean into the turn. She remembered what Sam had said and tried her best to mimic the movement, even though her brain screamed to do the opposite.

A split second passed, then she felt the bike speed up, and the force seemed to pull them upright. Sam's body shifted beneath her hands, straightening back up on the seat.

An involuntary exhale of relief left her mouth. Her fingers ached from holding on so tight, and she released her grip by just a fraction to keep her muscles from cramping.

"See, you're a natural!" Sam yelled back to her.

Jess could hear the hint of a teasing smile in her voice. She didn't respond, instead keeping her full focus on the road and her iron grip.

Now that they were on the main street, the bike moved much faster, and to her surprise, it actually made it feel more secure. They weaved in and out of traffic, and Jess leaned each time she felt Sam move beneath her hands. If she wasn't so terrified, it might have actually been kind of fun.

They zipped down the long roads, the icy wind whipping past them, biting at the exposed flesh on her face and hands. She shivered beneath her thin long sleeve shirt. If she'd known it'd be this cold, she would have grabbed the spare hoodie she always kept in her car.

As they pulled up to the next stoplight, her hands and body were trembling in full force. The area looked familiar, and she knew they were about halfway to her house.

Sam turned to her, flipping up the visor on her helmet. Her brows furrowed, watching her for a moment. "Are you okay?"

"Y—yeah. Ju—just cold," Jess answered through the chattering of her jaw.

Sam frowned. Then she turned back and flipped the visor down once more. When the light changed to green, she drove them through the intersection and slowed down, immediately turning into a vacant parking lot on their right side.

She pulled them into a spot and kicked the bike stand down.

"Wh—what are y—you doing?"

Sam flipped her visor up again and then unzipped the front of the jacket she was wearing. It revealed a black hoodie that she had on underneath. She quickly swung the jacket off her shoulders and handed it to Jess.

"Here."

Jess shook her head. "N—no, it's okay."

Sam rolled her eyes. "Take it. I know how cold it is riding at night without one."

Jess paused for a moment, then finally gave in. "Th—thanks," she said, taking the jacket from her.

She removed Sam's backpack from her shoulders, setting it on the seat between them. Her arms slid into the jacket, and she immediately felt warmth enveloping her. Every muscle in her body relaxed.

She looked up at Sam, who watched her with a small, satisfied smile. "Better?" she asked.

Jess nodded. "Much better."

"Sorry, I don't have any extra gloves, but if you keep your hands in the jacket sleeves, they shouldn't get too cold."

Jess nodded, pulling the cuffs down to cover her white knuckles.

Sam faced forward again and flipped the visor back down. She kicked the stand up and, within a few seconds, they zipped back out onto the main road.

With the jacket keeping her warm, it became much easier to relax. She watched the buildings and houses whip by. It was pretty. Almost enjoyable, even.

She let her eyes and mind wander as they road down the winding roads, and before she knew it, they were turning down the street she'd grown up on.

The bike slowed to a roll in front of the driveway, and Sam glanced down at her phone to check the address.

"This is it," Jess said.

Sam left the bike running and flipped the visor up. Jess took the backpack off first, then the jacket, handing them both back to her.

"Thanks for taking me home," she said, unhooking her camera bag from the back of the bike. "I really didn't want to have to wait for the tow truck."

Sam chuckled. "Yeah, me either." She put the jacket back on and then swung the backpack over her shoulders, pulling on the straps to tighten it.

Jess paused for a moment. The realization hit her that she probably wouldn't have her car back by the end of school the next day. She could ask Scarlett or Luke for a ride, but she knew it'd be out of their way.

"Um, actually, is there any way I could ride with you to the center tomorrow after school?" Jess asked. "I don't have lacrosse practice, so you wouldn't have to wait around or anything."

Sam tilted her head with an amused smile. "You're not too scared? I mean, I'm pretty sure you almost ripped the back of my shirt a few times with that grip you had."

Jess rolled her eyes, but couldn't help the small smile that filled her lips.

"Okay, I admit, it definitely was not my favorite thing in the world. But I don't really have another option, so I guess I'll have to deal with it."

Sam shook her head with a smile. "Alright, if you say so."

Jess took her phone out of her pocket, handing it to Sam. "Here, put your number in and I'll text you after the last bell so we can meet up in the parking lot."

Sam quickly typed her number and handed the phone back to her.

Jess looked down at it for a moment before returning it to her pocket.

"Okay, well, goodnight," she said. "And uh—thanks. Again."

Sam smiled with that same amused look in her eyes. "Yeah, see you tomorrow."

Jess trudged up the steps and unlocked the front door, listening to the roar of the motorcycle as it went back down the street.

Chapter 5

"Jess...?"

"Jess?"

"Jess!"

She jumped, the world suddenly rushing back to her. Her eyes shot frantically around the room.

Shit.

Mr. Arnon, the economics teacher, stood above her, a concerned expression pulled across his wrinkled face. A few students watched and giggled as they walked out the door into the hallway.

"Jess, are you alright?" he asked, pushing his thick black glasses up the bridge of his nose. "It's not like you to sleep during class."

She straightened up in her chair.

"Yeah," she answered, clearing her throat. "Yes. Sorry, just a little tired this week. It won't happen again."

He studied her for a moment. "Okay. I'll give you a pass just this once, but make sure you're getting enough sleep at home."

Thank God. Detention was the absolute last thing she needed.

"Yeah. Thanks," she muttered, quickly gathering her things. She stood and scurried out the door into the hall before he could change his mind.

Weaving through students, Jess plodded down the hallway toward Miss Williams' office. Luckily, even with her impromptu nap, she hadn't forgotten about the college prep course form she needed to drop off.

"Oh, hey! I was hoping you'd stop by today," Miss Williams said, looking up at her from behind the desk as she entered.

"Yeah. I'm sorry I completely forgot yesterday." Jess pulled the form out of her backpack and handed it to the counselor.

Miss Williams glanced over it with a satisfactory smile. "Perfect, thank you."

Jess nodded and immediately turned to head back out into the hallway.

"Hey, wait!" Miss Williams called after her. "How is the volunteer project going?"

Jess paused in the doorway. "Um—it's good. It's been interesting," she answered slowly, letting out a small laugh.

The woman smiled at her. "Well, that qualifies as a win in my book. How is the video essay coming along?"

"It's okay. I'm kind of having a hard time thinking of what to film, though. So far, we've been doing the same stuff every day, and it's basically just been office work."

Miss Williams nodded thoughtfully. "Well, I'm sure you'll think of something. Remember, they're really looking to see what's below the surface of these projects. They want to see that you found meaning in it."

"Right," Jess nodded. "I'll work on it."

She turned again to leave.

"Oh, actually," the woman stopped her. "One more thing. Do you, by any chance, see Sam Hayes while you're volunteering? I know she spends a lot of time there."

Of course Miss Williams' would know her. It seemed like everyone knew Sam on some level.

Jess pushed down the urge to tell her that Sam was the reason she was stuck volunteering there in the first place.

"Yeah, I'm about to see her now, actually."

"Oh, perfect!" She pulled a folder out of her desk. "Would you mind giving this to her? She was supposed to come by last week to get it, but never showed up."

She handed the folder to Jess. It was a red college brochure with the letters "MIT" printed in the center.

"Woah," Jess muttered, her head jerking back in surprise. "She's going to MIT?"

Miss Williams nodded. "Most likely. She has a great shot at it as long as she can stop skipping so many classes. Getting her to actually show up at school since she moved here has been—well, challenging, to say the least."

Jess smirked, shaking her head. For some reason, that didn't surprise her.

She agreed to pass along the brochure and re-entered the busy hallway. Students filled the halls, rushing to leave for the day. She pulled out her phone and sent a quick text to Sam while she weaved through the crowd.

When she exited the building, she saw Scarlett standing near the edge of the parking lot.

"Scar!" she yelled.

The girl turned around, quickly locating her in the crowd.

"Hey," she answered, walking toward her. "What're you doing right now? Wanna go get lunch?"

"I wish," Jess frowned. "I'm going to the community center."

"Oh, is your car fixed already?"

"No, but hopefully it'll be done by tomorrow. Someone's giving me a ride today," Jess said, glancing toward the parking lot and quickly finding the familiar motorcycle parked near the curb. "And there's my ride now," Jess murmured, watching Sam approach the bike.

Scarlett followed her gaze. She cocked her head slightly. "Wait—why does that bike look so familiar?"

Jess watched her, waiting for the dots to connect.

"Wait! Oh my god. Is that hot motorcycle guy?!" she said, slapping Jess' arm. "You're telling me, hot motorcycle guy is actually a hot motorcycle *girl*?!"

Jess chuckled, shaking her head at her best friend's choice of words.

"And wait—that's your ride?! How do you even know her?" she asked with a disbelieving grin, clearly loving the turn this conversation had taken.

"Yeah, she sort of volunteers at the clinic, so I met her there on the first day. Trust me, I was shocked too, but she's actually not that bad. She's helped me out a few times."

"Wow, I never would've seen this coming." Scarlett watched Sam with an amused smile. "Okay, well, are you gonna introduce me to your new friend?"

Jess chuckled and walked toward Sam, with Scarlett following closely behind.

"Hey," she said as they approached.

"Hey," Sam replied with a smile as she unhooked her helmet from the back of the seat.

Jess glanced back at Scarlett, who wore a wide, childish grin behind her. "Uh—this is my friend, Scarlett."

Sam gave her a polite smile. "Hey. I'm Sam."

"Right. I kinda feel like we've already met," Scarlett answered. Jess cringed, knowing where this was headed.

Sam raised an eyebrow and tilted her head in question. "Have we?"

Scarlett laughed. "It feels like it."

Jess groaned. "She was in the car with me that day at the coffee stand."

Sam looked at her with a confused expression.

Jess rolled her eyes and muttered, "You know, when you made us late getting back to school."

Sam paused for a moment before laughing, finally realizing what Scarlett was referring to. "Oh!" she exclaimed. "Great. Apparently, that wasn't really the best first impression."

Scarlett laughed with her. "Hey, I didn't care. Jess was the only one with a stick up her ass that day."

"Hey!" Jess said, slapping Scarlett's arm but chuckling with them. "I was right to be annoyed, okay?"

Sam laughed, shaking her head.

"So, are you new here?" Scarlett asked.

"Uh—yeah, sort of," Sam replied. "I transferred in at the beginning of the year."

"In your senior year? What'd you get kicked out of your old school or something?" Scarlett asked with a teasing look.

Sam smirked, shaking her head. "No, nothing like that. My uncle came back from his tour in Iraq, so he let me move in with him."

Scarlett nodded while Jess absorbed the new information.

"Hey!" a boy called from behind them. They all looked up to see Malik and Luke walking toward them.

Luke flashed a big smile at Jess before pulling her into a hug and kissing her cheek.

"Hey," Scarlett said, giving Malik a quick kiss before turning back to Sam. "This is Sam. She volunteers with Jess."

The boys both greeted her politely, each introducing themselves.

"I thought only one person was allowed in each program?" Luke asked.

Sam nodded. "Yeah, I'm not doing the project that Jess is."

"Is this your bike?" Malik interrupted with an excited smile.

"Yeah," Sam answered, smiling back at him. "My uncle had a few lying around that he wasn't using. None of them worked, but I was able to fix this one up with a few spare parts. Unfortunately, this was the only seat I could find that fit this model."

"That's awesome," Malik said, stepping up to the bike to take a closer look. "I want one so bad. I'm definitely gonna get one once I graduate."

Luke turned to Jess while Malik continued questioning Sam about the bike. "Wanna get lunch?" he asked hopefully.

"I can't, sorry. We have to leave right now," Jess replied with an apologetic frown.

Luke gave her a puzzled look, glancing back at Sam and the bike. "You mean you're riding on that?"

"Yeah, I told you my car is still in the shop. She's giving me a ride."

"Are you sure?" he asked, frowning at her. "My mom always talks about how many motorcycle accidents come into the ER."

Jess pursed her lips. That was the last reminder she needed. "It's fine. It's not far from here."

He nodded reluctantly, letting the matter drop.

"We should probably get going," Jess said, looking at Sam, who was excitedly explaining something to Malik about the bike.

"Sam," Scarlett added, "my parents are gonna be gone all weekend, so we're having a party at my house this Saturday. You wanna come?"

"Uh—yeah, sure," Sam answered, picking up her helmet. "Sounds fun."

Scarlett flashed her a big smile. "Great. Jess can give you the address," she said, taking Malik's hand and pulling him away from the bike.

Luke leaned down and gave Jess a quick kiss before the three of them walked away.

"Sorry," Jess said, picking up the helmet she'd worn the night before. "Scar can be a little pushy sometimes. You don't have to go to the party if you don't want to."

Sam chuckled. "She was fine. It does sound fun. I haven't really been out like that since I moved back here."

Jess smiled appreciatively as Sam handed her the large jacket again. "Oh, then yeah, I think you'll have fun. Scarlett definitely knows how to throw a good party."

Jess put her arms through the jacket, zipping it up to the base of her neck. Sam took her backpack and camera bag and tied them down to the back of the bike before handing Jess her own backpack and settling in on the seat. Jess threw the backpack over her shoulders and sat down behind Sam, leaving a few inches of space between them.

Sam put her helmet on and slipped the visor down over her eyes before turning the key in the ignition and starting the bike.

Anxiety crept back up into Jess' chest.

She put the helmet over her head and buckled the strap, pulling it tight beneath her chin, before taking a deep calming breath. The air tasted like gasoline.

"Ready?" Sam asked over the rumbling of the engine.

"Yeah," Jess nodded, grabbing a fistful of the black hoodie on Sam's back.

The bike rolled backward out of the space, and they slowly navigated through the busy parking lot. Jess leaned into the turn as they went over the bump and sped out onto the main street. Again, her nerves calmed a bit once they reached a higher speed and eventually coasted along the road.

They pulled into the familiar parking lot and drove into a space near the front of the building.

"How was it?" Sam asked, sliding her helmet up over her head. "You seemed a little more comfortable today."

Jess slowly released her grip on Sam's back and stretched out her sore fingers. "Yeah. Not as bad as last night."

Sam hooked the helmets onto the bike, then they each grabbed their things and headed inside. The hallway was quiet, and as they approached the front desk, they could see Laura running a meeting in the auditorium. Sam pulled her laptop and headphones out of her bag and plopped down into her usual chair.

As Jess set her things down, she remembered the folder that Miss Williams had given her.

"So, I didn't realize I was hanging around a genius every day," Jess said with a teasing smirk, pulling the folder out of her backpack.

Sam gave her a questioning look until she saw what Jess was handing her.

"Miss Williams asked me to give it to you. She said you didn't show up to get it last week."

"Oh, yeah," Sam muttered, taking the folder and flipping through the first few pages. "Guess I forgot."

"You're going to MIT?" Jess asked with genuine interest.

Sam shrugged. "Maybe. I haven't been accepted yet."

"Well, Miss Williams seems to think you'll get in."

Sam snorted, shaking her head. "It's her job to make us believe that stuff."

"Yeah, I guess," Jess chuckled in agreement. "She also said you never show up at school, which explains why I've never seen you around there before today."

Sam shrugged again, tossing the folder onto the desk. "I don't really need to. I'm already done with all my high school credits. The only classes I'm in now are for getting ahead on college courses."

Jess raised her eyebrows. That was impressive. She spent practically every waking moment working to get ahead and get into her first choice university, but this girl was still miles ahead of her.

"How'd you do that?" she asked, hoping she sounded more impressed than jealous.

Sam flipped her laptop open. "Uh—there wasn't much to do in the last foster home I was in," she answered nonchalantly. "I had a lot of free time, so I just got really ahead on everything."

Jess nodded, mentally cataloging this new piece of information. She'd probably learned more about Sam in the last hour than she had in the last few days they'd worked together. A pang of guilt ran through her. She was probably the one to blame for that. She made a mental note to try being more friendly while she was there.

"That makes sense," Jess replied, keeping her response general enough for the conversation to either continue or finish, depending on what Sam was comfortable with.

"So what college are you trying to get into?" Sam asked, turning to her with a smile.

"Trinity University," she answered with a pause. "And I guess Bucknell too. But I just applied there as a backup."

"Trinity," Sam said, thinking for a moment. "Isn't that the Christian college that's like an hour from here?"

Jess nodded. "That's the one."

"Hm," Sam grunted, turning back to her laptop.

"What?" Jess asked.

"Nothing," Sam replied, still looking at her computer. "You just don't seem like the typical person who would go there."

"What do you mean?"

Sam shrugged. "They're pretty strict, right? I assumed the only people who went there were people who went to private religious schools their whole lives or something."

Although she said it in a matter-of-fact tone that lacked any hint of judgment, it still bothered Jess.

"I didn't choose it because it's a religious college," she said, trying to keep the irritation out of her voice. "They have a great lacrosse program and good academics."

"Yeah, but don't they like only accept people who believe the same stuff they do and follow all of their rules?"

Jess gritted her teeth. She wouldn't admit it now, but this was actually something that bothered her about Trinity. They expected all of their students to live their lives according to their moral code, and Jess didn't necessarily agree with everything they believed in. Deep down, what bothered her even more was wondering what her mother had believed in since she'd been a student there.

She chose to avoid Sam's question. "Not all people that go to Christian colleges go for the religious aspect. People go for lots of different reasons."

Sam looked up at her, probably detecting the irritation in her voice. "So what's your reason, then?" she asked.

Jess paused, an uncomfortable feeling settling in her stomach. She wasn't in denial. She knew the real reason why she was going. It was a way for her to feel close to her mother and get to know who she was when she was Jess' age. It didn't take a therapist to figure that out, only someone mildly self aware. But even though she'd admitted it to herself, that didn't mean she wanted to discuss it with anyone else.

Before she could think of an answer, the door to the auditorium swung open and people flowed out into the hall. Saved by the bell.

"Um—I have to go ask Laura something," Jess muttered, pushing up from her seat. She circled the desk to the auditorium door, purposely avoiding Sam's curious gaze.

She quickly caught up with Laura on the tasks that needed to be done, then found the perfect opening to ask her for a favor.

She'd had an idea earlier that day to switch up the video essay by doing interviews with anyone that was willing. And she figured Laura would probably be the best first candidate.

Luckily, she was right.

Laura easily agreed to the interview, and Jess spent the rest of the time hurrying through her tasks and preparing a set of questions. It was also a bonus that it meant she could basically avoid Sam the rest of the day, ensuring their previous conversation wouldn't have the chance to continue.

When they were finally done for the day, Jess began packing up her things at the front desk to head home. As she was stuffing the camera into the padded black bag, her phone rang.

"Hello?"

A man from the repair shop greeted her. Then he proceeded to explain that one of the parts they needed was on back order and wouldn't be delivered for another two to three weeks.

Just another thing to add to the list of recent inconveniences.

"Everything okay?" Sam asked, shutting her laptop and pushing it into her backpack.

Jess slid the phone back in her pocket. "That was the car place. They said they're waiting on a part and it won't be in for another few weeks."

"Oh, that sucks," Sam said, frowning at her.

"Yeah," Jess muttered, shoving the rest of her things into her bag.

"Do you need a ride after school every day, then?" Sam asked. "Until your car is fixed."

Jess looked up at her, surprised. "No, that's okay." She shook her head. "I can't ask you to do that. I have practice and games on some days, so you'd be stuck waiting around for me."

Sam shrugged. "I don't mind. I can work on my laptop pretty much anywhere. Besides, it'd only be for a couple of weeks, right?"

"I mean, yeah, but are you sure?" Jess asked seriously. She hated the thought of being an inconvenience to someone. Especially someone she barely knew. "You really don't have to. I can always Uber or something."

Sam shook her head. "Really, it's no big deal. Think of it as me paying you back for being the reason you got stuck with us in the first place," she answered with a playful smirk.

Jess chuckled. That did seem sort of fair. "Okay, fine, I'll take that."

Sam smiled widely at her, the playful look still present in her features. Jess found it hard not to smile back when she gave her that look. It felt almost contagious.

They finished packing their things in comfortable silence and said goodbye to Laura before walking outside. Jess tied her backpack and camera bag down as Sam unhooked their helmets and pulled her spare black hoodie off of where she'd tied it to the bike. Jess watched as she slid it over her head, pulling it down to cover her tight white t-shirt. Sam handed over her backpack and the jacket before she sat down, put on her helmet, and started the engine. Jess joined her, leaving an inch or two between them, and gently rested her hand against the other girl's lower back.

Once she felt the bike roll backward, she added a second carefully placed hand and tightened her grip. Then, taking a deep breath, she tried to relax her body as much as possible and remind herself of how short the ride would be.

The beauty of the lights streaking by them in the night seemed to distract her brain just enough to almost forget the anxiety still present in her chest.

At some points, she felt so relaxed watching the world rush by that she worried she might doze off.

Eventually, the bike rolled to a stop in front of her driveway and she let her hands release their tight grip on the hoodie in front of her.

She stood up, resting her hand on Sam's shoulder for balance as she swung her leg over the seat. Then she pulled the backpack off her shoulders and handed it to Sam, along with the jacket.

"Thanks. Again."

"You're welcome. Again" Sam nodded at her.

Chapter 6

The frigid air stung her nostrils and throat, like salt water on a paper cut.

Her breath came in short bursts, perfectly in sync with the gentle thud of her feet hitting the pavement. It was colder and darker outside than it usually was during her morning run, and the air reminded her of that each time it entered her lungs.

Even through the extreme exhaustion all week, she'd struggled to get a solid night of sleep, tossing and turning every hour. When she finally woke again and saw gray light illuminating her bedroom window, she decided sleeping was a futile effort. The next best option: run.

Jess took a deep, steadying breath as she jogged past the small hill outside her neighborhood. This was usually her favorite part. Dark green plants and shrubs covered the hill, and they bloomed with flowers in the spring and summer. Now, as the season changed from fall to winter, the plants hardened and died off with the harsher conditions. But even then, she could still smell the faint hints of fresh greenery, accentuated by the morning dew.

She closed her eyes for a split second, inhaling the wet, earthy scent.

Then the moment was over.

She increased her pace, relishing the way her legs stung as they worked twice as hard. Clearing her mind, she focused entirely on the last stretch, mentally calculating the changes her body needed to make. She swung her arms harder, and her eyes darted to her watch as her left arm came up towards her body.

She turned the last corner onto her street. Seeing her house at the end of the block spurred her to run even faster. She pumped her arms tight across her body, building fresh momentum.

Each house became a mental countdown.

5.. 4.. 3..

Almost there.

She hit the bottom of the driveway and sprinted, lunging up the front steps before crashing through the door.

Bending over, her chest heaved as she gasped for air. She rested her hands on her knees, catching a glimpse of her watch. A small smile made its way onto her lips.

Drawing in a few more deep breaths, she smelled eggs and coffee. She looked up and noticed the lights on in the kitchen.

She straightened up and took a few steps further into the entryway.

Her dad stood in front of the stove. He glanced at the clock on the microwave.

"Hmph," he grunted, not yet looking at her. "Who would've known getting up earlier would make you faster?"

She smirked to herself. "Yeah, too bad they don't schedule our games at six in the morning."

He continued stirring what Jess knew were scrambled eggs. She spotted the steaming coffee pot next to him and went to pour herself a cup, grabbing the largest mug she could find.

The delicious, bitter scent assaulted her nostrils as she poured until the deep brown liquid reached the brim.

She glanced out the kitchen window into the backyard. The gray morning had lightened into blue and white as the first real rays of sun found their way into the sky.

She carefully lifted the mug and grabbed her phone from the countertop before settling into her usual seat at the table.

"Why are you up so early? Big plans for the day?" her dad asked.

She shrugged, taking a sip of the coffee. The hot liquid burned against her cold lips.

"Woke up and couldn't fall back to sleep. But yeah, we have the flag football game today for the volunteer program, so I'm going over there soon."

Even though she could still feel a tired fog clouding her senses, the excitement of doing something competitive was enough to energize her for the day. Or at least a few hours.

"Need a ride? I'm off today."

"That's okay," she muttered, unlocking her phone. "Someone's picking me up."

He finished stirring the eggs and loaded up two plates, walking them over to the table. They each grabbed a fork and ate in silence, scrolling mindlessly through their phones.

Once Jess finished her breakfast and coffee, she put her dishes in the sink and headed upstairs. Showering seemed like a waste of time before the football game, so she decided to spend the rest of the morning getting ahead on her homework while she waited for Sam to pick her up.

Over the years, she'd become an expert at squeezing in quick work sessions throughout her busy schedule. Waiting for someone to pick her up was one of her best opportunities to get extra homework done.

AP Calculus was her least favorite and always took the longest. She wasn't even halfway done by the time her phone buzzed on the wooden nightstand beside her with a text from Sam.

Like always, she'd prepped her bag with all the necessities the night before.

She grabbed it off the floor by her bedroom door and trotted down the stairs. She could already hear the roar of the motorcycle from outside by the time she hit the bottom step.

"Is that your ride? The girl from the center?"

She looked up and saw her dad peering through the blinds to the driveway.

"Yeah," she answered, putting on her shoes that were sitting near the front door.

He grunted. "I think I should drive you."

She rolled her eyes. "Dad, it's just a motorcycle, and it's a short ride."

"The motorcycle is fine," he replied. "But I don't think she's the type of person you should be hanging out with."

Jess stopped tying her other shoe, looking up at him in surprise. "What? Why?"

He grunted again, turning away from the window. "Because I said so."

"Dad, that's ridiculous. She's already here to pick me up," she replied, brushing off his odd behavior.

He looked at her for a moment. Then he pursed his lips and turned to walk back toward the kitchen. "Well, next time let me know, and I'll drive you."

"Okay, well next time you have the day off, I'll ask you instead," she said, trying not to get annoyed as she watched him walk away from the window and disappear into the kitchen.

She waited a few seconds for an answer. "Okay, bye?" She finally called after him when she realized he wasn't returning.

One thing she could be proud of that day: her nerves on the bike seemed to be improving. Every day she'd ridden with Sam that week, she'd gotten better and better. With almost a full week of riding under her belt, she felt almost at ease. It did also help that she'd begun to actually trust Sam as the driver.

When they arrived at the field, Jess saw people scattered about in athletic clothing, stretching and talking. They crossed the dewy grass and said hi to Laura before dropping their things near the silver metal bleachers. Sam sat down on a dry patch of grass and began stretching her legs and back. Jess decided to join her, although her muscles still felt loose from her run that morning. It was really more of an excuse to find something to do since she didn't know anyone else there.

"Ready to get your ass handed to you?" Sam asked, throwing her a smirk as she folded her body over to touch her toes.

Jess snorted, realizing she should've expected this. "When was the last time you even played a sport?" she asked, shooting her a teasing look. "And video games on your laptop don't count."

A man burst into laughter somewhere behind them. They turned around to see Ricky walking towards them in a tank top and shorts, carrying a football in one hand.

"Glad we finally have someone that can keep up with the shit talking," he said, chuckling.

Sam shook her head with a smile as she continued her stretch. "You can have her on your team. You guys could use the help from someone who's actually athletic."

Jess smiled, loving the competitive banter. This had always been one of her favorite parts of lacrosse.

Sam stood up slowly, stretching her arms over her head. She stripped off her hoodie and pulled her sweatpants down, revealing a pair of navy blue soccer shorts underneath. This was the most Jess had actually seen of Sam's body, given that she was usually covered in pants and a hoodie. It surprised her that she actually seemed to be in good shape, with muscles toned enough to sculpt shapes through her thin clothing. She let her eyes linger for a second before looking away. Maybe Sam would be better competition than she thought.

"Jess, have you played before?" Ricky asked, taking a long drink from his water bottle.

"A couple times when I was younger, but I play lacrosse now."

"Well, that's more experience than anyone else on our team," he said with a chuckle, glancing around the field at the other patrons.

"Oh, don't make excuses. You're no better than they are," Sam said, giving him a light shove.

"Hey, go easy on us. We can't all be soccer super stars like you, Sammy."

She rolled her eyes. "Yeah, yeah, go round up your team before they get lost."

Jess smiled at their interaction. It reminded her of how she and Scarlett behaved while at practice.

"Soccer super star, huh? So you do, in fact, do more than just play video games," Jess said with a smirk.

Sam laughed, looking back at her. "Definitely not a superstar. I haven't played in years. And where did you get this whole video game thing from? I don't think I've ever once played a video game on my laptop."

"Well, you always seem so into whatever you're doing. I figured it had to be something fun."

Sam chuckled, shaking her head. "I'm working," she said. "I do freelance coding projects."

"Wow, Ricky's right. You are a nerd," Jess replied with a chuckle, although she was actually a little impressed.

"Well, this *nerd* is about to kick your ass," Sam replied with a smirk as she dropped her hoodie and sweatpants onto her backpack.

"Yeah, right."

The game moved at a quick pace once they started. It didn't take long for Jess to realize that most of the players were younger and middle-aged guys who played great in the first ten minutes, but couldn't last past that. At first, she had a tough time outrunning them, but once they tired out, she could easily beat them on both offense and defense.

By the time halftime rolled around, it seemed like it was basically her and Ricky versus Sam, with the other players just trying their best to stay upright.

When Laura eventually blew her whistle for the break, everyone trudged off the field, practically collapsing on the sideline.

Sam jogged up next to her, wearing a cocky grin and looking like she'd barely broken a sweat. "So even when it's basically just two against one, I can still kick your ass."

Jess snorted and shoved her lightly. "Ricky," she called to him as he walked a few yards away. "I'm guarding her in the second half," she said, nodding her head in Sam's direction.

He shook his head, still breathing hard. "Go for it."

Sam smiled at her, dropping onto the grass near their bags. Jess grabbed her camera from where she had it set up to film the game and started watching the footage.

"So what kind of stuff do you need to film for this thing?" Ricky asked, taking a big gulp of his water.

"Honestly, I'm kind of stuck on that. I feel like it's been boring so far with me just filming the stuff I've done. I was hoping to do some interviews of people in the program, but I doubt anyone would want to do it since everything is centered on being anonymous."

He shrugged. "You can ask me the questions if you want."

"Really?" Jess asked, shooting him a hopeful look.

"Yeah, I don't mind," he answered, taking another drink. "Ask away."

"Thank you! This is going to help a ton!" Jess said with a wide smile. She held up the camera and pressed the button to record.

"Okay, um—" she paused, trying to think of an appropriate question. "What is the hardest part of being an addict?"

He thought for a moment. "Trying to be a good husband and dad," he finally said, looking down at the grass as he gently swirled the water in his bottle. "Always wondering and worrying about how this is affecting her. Not knowing how much of it she'll remember when she grows up," he paused, clearing the emotion from his throat. "Forgiving myself for not being a better dad when she was younger."

Jess watched him intently through the camera screen. The normal thing to do would be to respond in some nice, comforting way. Her brain tried to come up with something to say to fill the silence.

"You're a great dad. She's lucky to have you." Sam said from behind her. "She could have it a lot worse."

Of course Sam would know the perfect thing to say. She seemed like that type of person. Comforting, but genuine.

Ricky looked at her with a sad but appreciative smile. Sam stood and walked over to Laura near the end of the bleachers.

Ricky continued in a lower voice. "I kinda knew her mom before she died," he said, nodding toward Sam. "She'd been in the program for a while before I started coming."

Jess' body tensed and her heart instantly ached, hearing that her mother had died. Her eyes darted to where Sam stood, talking to Laura.

She paused the camera and set it down in the grass, not wanting to record these private details.

"She had Sammy pretty young and already had some drug problems before that, I guess. Man, I felt like *I* was just a kid when I first started coming here," he continued, glancing over at Sam. "But she was *really* an actual kid."

He watched her for a few seconds before clearing his throat and turning back to Jess. "Anyway, that's part of what motivates me to be the best I possibly can be for my daughter. Sam's great even after all the shit she went through, but I *never* want to put my daughter through something like that."

Jess gave him a small nod of understanding. This time, she didn't bother trying to think of something nice to say.

81

After a few moments of silence, she asked him a couple more general questions for the video, but her thoughts kept returning to Sam and her mother. It left an unwelcome ache in her chest.

A few minutes later, Laura blew the whistle, signaling the start of the second half. Jess was grateful to have a distraction.

She stood up, walking back onto the field as everyone slowly got into position for the kick-off.

They kicked the ball to the other team, and she watched one of the younger guys easily catch it and charge toward them. After running a few yards, Ricky grabbed his flag, stopping the play.

They lined up again, with Sam standing just a few feet away. Jess stood in front of her, watching her body language carefully for clues of where she would run.

"Don't feel too bad if you can't keep up," Sam said, flashing her a wide smile.

Jess snorted and rolled her eyes, but couldn't keep the smile from breaking out across her face. Something about the other girl's smile felt contagious, and Jess couldn't help but mirror it, as the uncomfortable feeling in her chest finally felt some much needed relief.

They hiked the ball, and every player on the line charged forward. Sam ran a few steps, looking directly at her with that cocky smirk. Then, when she was a foot or two away, she suddenly jerked hard to the left. Jess had been so focused on watching her face that she missed seeing her hips twist. By the time she recovered, it was too late. Sam easily lost her, catching the pass a few yards away.

She ran a couple of yards down the field before a younger woman on Jess' team caught up with her and managed to pull her flag.

As they lined up again, Sam shot her an amused smile. "Distracted?"

Jess glared back at her, this time determined to keep her focus.

The man from the opposing team hiked the ball again, and Sam immediately sprinted forward. Jess watched her carefully this time, staying glued to her side. After a dozen or so feet, she saw Sam look up at the sky. She followed her gaze and saw the ball spiraling toward them. It looked like it might overshoot them by a few feet, so Jess kicked her legs harder and turned around to fully face the ball. She took a few steps backward and jumped, letting her momentum carry her as she raised her arms.

The ball inched closer, then suddenly, her back slammed into something hard behind her. She shot her hands back, trying to catch herself, but instead they grabbed and tangled in the shirt of whoever she'd run into.

She fell hard to the ground, shutting her eyes as the air rushed out of her lungs. It took her a second before she opened her eyes again. She shifted, putting her weight on her elbow to sit up, and felt a person move beneath her. She looked down and saw Sam, face contorted in pain.

"Oh my gosh, I'm so sorry!" Jess said, pushing herself off of her and falling onto the grass. "Are you okay?"

Sam lifted her head off the grass and started laughing. She slowly raised her arm, revealing the football clutched tightly in her hand.

Jess broke out into laughter, dropping her head between her hands.

"Told you you wouldn't be able to keep up," Sam said, rolling onto her side with a big grin.

Jess rolled her eyes and shoved her shoulder.

"Hey, take it easy," Sam groaned dramatically. "I could be hurt by that tackle you just did."

"Yeah, yeah," Jess muttered. "You look fine to me." She pushed herself up off the ground and knocked the ball out of Sam's hand.

Sam laughed again, pushing herself up off the grass and popping onto her feet.

The rest of the game went by in a similar fashion, with her and Sam evenly matched.

By the time Laura blew the last whistle, Jess felt thoroughly exhausted. She made her way off the field and collapsed next to her camera.

She hadn't expected to work so hard during the game, but once she started guarding Sam, her competitive nature took over and she couldn't stand the thought of letting her win.

Sam dropped onto the grass beside her, still breathing hard. "Well, that was more of a workout than I expected to have today."

Jess smirked. "Me too. I guess I didn't expect you to *not* suck."

Sam smiled wide with her eyes closed, head leaned back facing the sky.

***

"So, you guys seem to be getting along pretty well now," Scarlett commented as she poured two shots.

The party had started, and the house was already packed with people. Sam had arrived a few minutes before and greeted them before being dragged away by Malik and some of the other boys to talk about her motorcycle.

"Yeah, I guess we are. She's different from how I thought she was at first. I actually don't mind hanging out with her now." Jess glanced over to where Sam was standing in the living room with a group of guys.

She was clearly telling a story and everyone surrounding her was laughing, hanging on every word she spoke. This was something that kept surprising her; the way Sam seamlessly blended with any group of people. It was like she was magnetic and everyone naturally gravitated to her in any situation.

"You're not the only one that thinks that. Pretty sure Malik has found his new best friend," Scarlett said with a laugh, nodding her head towards them.

Jess laughed, shaking her head. "Cheers." She clinked her shot glass against Scarlett's.

She threw the liquor back and felt the burn drip down her throat, settling deep in her stomach. Scarlett gave her a disgusted look before taking a big gulp of soda to wash it down. Then they weaved between groups of people, making their way through the crowded living room toward their friends.

"Hey babe," Luke said, leaning down to kiss her cheek as they walked up to the circle of people.

"Hey," she said, giving him a quick glance before letting her eyes drift to Sam, who was still looking at Malik, laughing at something he'd said.

"Sorry boys, we're stealing her," Scarlett said, grabbing Sam's hand and pulling her forward. "She hasn't had a drink with us yet and we need to get a few down before beerpong."

Sam laughed, shooting Jess an amused look as she squeezed past her. Jess smiled and shrugged, following them back to the kitchen.

Scarlett pulled three plastic shot glasses out of the bag they'd bought earlier that day and set them on the granite island.

"I'm so glad you came tonight!" Scarlett said, shooting her a wide smile as she poured the new round of shots.

"Yeah, me too," Sam replied. "Thanks for inviting me."

Jess smiled at them and picked up two of the full shot glasses, handing one to Sam.

"Cheers bitches!" Scarlett yelled, knocking her plastic shot glass roughly against theirs.

They all gulped them down. Jess noted that it went down easier than the last one. She took a sip of soda to wash away the bitter taste before handing the cup to Sam so she could do the same.

"Wow, maybe you should include this in your video essay," a voice said from the other side of the kitchen.

Jess looked up and rolled her eyes when she saw Gabby walking in along with Jacie, another girl on their lacrosse team. Jacie gave her a warm, shy smile, but Jess noticed that her eyes immediately drifted to where Sam stood beside her.

"Didn't realize you were coming, Gabby," Scarlett replied in a flat tone.

"Well, Jacie wanted to come and asked me to DD for her since she knew I wouldn't be drinking. You know, don't want Trinity to think I'm not serious about getting in," she finished, throwing a judgemental look toward Jess.

"Oh, you're trying to get into Trinity too?" Sam asked, clearly unaware of the group dynamic.

Gabby looked at her for a moment, like she was trying to figure out if she was worth answering.

"Yeah," she finally drawled as she gave Jess a pointed look. "And I take their rules seriously."

Before Jess could spit out the angry retort that was bubbling up in her throat, Jacie cut them all off.

"I'm Jacie, by the way," she said, holding her hand out to Sam with a smile that stretched from ear to ear.

"Sam," she replied with a polite smile, shaking her hand. Jess noticed that Jacie's wide grin remained planted on her face well after Sam let her hand go.

"Okay, we're playing beerpong," Scarlett said, shooting Jess a look that said she couldn't handle another minute with Gabby. "Jacie, help yourself to any of the drinks," she said, giving her a warm smile as they walked back out to the living room.

"Okay, thanks!" Jacie replied, her eyes still following Sam.

As they entered the living room, Sam leaned into her, dropping her voice slightly. "Well, Gabby seems great."

Jess glanced at her and saw the small smirk on her lips. Apparently, she'd been more in tune with the situation than Jess had realized.

She shook her head and snorted. "Yeah, she's something."

"Babe!" Scarlett yelled to Malik. "Come, be on my team for BP!"

Malik and Luke both walked toward the table they were standing at.

"We'll play you guys," Luke said, motioning between himself and Jess.

"No," Scarlett said, pulling two balls out from one of the cups. "Sam's on her team this round."

Luke shot her a disappointed look, but nodded in understanding, walking off to the side of the table.

"Hey, maybe now you'll win something today," Sam said, giving her that cocky smirk that was starting to feel familiar.

"Oh shut up," Jess said, laughing and shoving her arm.

"Oh yeah, who won at football today?" Scarlett asked, positioning the cups on the table.

Sam smiled at Jess, waiting for her to answer.

She rolled her eyes with a sigh. "She won. Apparently, in addition to being a computer genius, she's also a secret star athlete."

"Oh man," Malik laughed. "That's dangerous beating Jess at something. I'm pretty sure she's the most competitive person I know."

"Oh yeah, I found that out today," Sam said with a chuckle. "She basically tackled me, trying to get an interception. I still caught the ball, though," she said, throwing Jess a side smirk.

"Shit, she tackled me once trying to get to the ball, and we were just in practice—not even a real game!" Scarlett said, laughing.

Jess rolled her eyes, laughing along with the group. "Okay, okay, we get it. I like winning," she said, turning to Sam. "Which means you better not suck at beerpong."

"Ya know, I might actually be better at beerpong than I am at football," Sam said with a smirk.

Jess smiled back, shaking her head. Playing against Sam that day had been fun, but she was already enjoying being on the same team much more.

"Alright, eye for eye." Malik said, tossing the ball towards them.

It bounced a few times on the table before Jess snatched it up. "I got it."

They started playing and, within a few turns, it was clear to Jess that this was, in fact, another thing that Sam seemed to excel at. The two teams were almost evenly matched, with Sam and Malik both making one shot after another.

Sam took her shot and easily made a cup, leaving only one left. Jess cheered as Malik pulled the ball out and lined up his shot. He extended his arm, releasing the ball from his fingertips as they all watched it seamlessly drop into the second to last cup. Jess cursed, shaking her head as Scarlett celebrated, kissing her boyfriend.

"You're up," Sam said, handing her the ball with an encouraging smile. "Make this, and I promise I'll sink mine after you."

Jess smiled, rolling her eyes, but feeling secretly fueled by her over confidence.

She lined up the shot, took a few steadying breaths, and then let the ball fly toward the other end of the table. They all watched as the ball circled the last cup once, then dropped into the water.

"Damnit!" Scarlett yelled. Malik frowned, pulling the ball out of the cup.

"Hell yeah! Good job," Sam said, nudging her shoulder with an excited smile.

"Alright, you're up, superstar. Don't break your promise," Jess said with a smirk.

Sam grinned as she picked up the other ball.

"House rules. If she makes this, then we win with no rebuttal," Jess said to her friends at the opposite end of the table.

"Yeah, yeah, just shoot," Scarlett said dismissively, watching Sam like a hawk.

She lined up the shot and smoothly threw the ball.

It landed perfectly in the center of the cup with a small splash.

"Yes!" Jess yelled, throwing her arms around Sam's neck and pulling her into a tight hug. "You're amazing. I can't believe that!"

She felt the girl shake in laughter beneath her arms.

"You're not so bad either," Sam said. Jess felt the warmth of her breath near the top of her ear.

She let her arms drop, pulling back to look at her with a wide grin. The haze of the alcohol swarmed her head and body. The area on her ear still tingled where Sam had spoken to her.

"Okay, we need a rematch," Scarlett said, barely masking the animosity in her voice.

"Dude, I'm playing for someone in the next game," Luke said from where he was standing off to the side of the table. "I'm sick of watching."

Jess laughed. "Someone else can play this one. I need a break first," she turned to Sam, grabbing her hand. "Come on, I'm not letting anyone else steal you for their team tonight. You're stuck with me."

Sam laughed as Jess pulled them away from the table, weaving through the crowd of people toward the kitchen.

"Want one?" Jess asked, motioning toward the liquor bottle on the island as they entered the kitchen.

"Yeah, sure," Sam answered, taking a sip of the soda that was sitting beside it.

"Hey guys," they both looked up, seeing Jacie walking towards them with a friendly smile. "Can I have one too?"

"Yeah, of course," Jess said, returning the smile as she pulled out a third plastic shot glass.

The clear liquid sloshed over the side as she poured. She reached out, handing one to her teammate, who stood close to Sam's side.

"Cheers," Jess said, as they all clinked their glasses together.

She threw the shot back, barely noticing the taste this time. Her mind felt foggy, and she closed her eyes for a second as she rocked on the balls of her feet. When she opened them, she immediately noticed the way Jacie's eyes were examining Sam take another sip of the soda.

"Hey," Jess said, placing her hand lightly on Sam's arm. "Can you go outside with me for a minute? I just need some air, I think."

"Yeah, of course," Sam said, quickly filling a red solo cup with soda.

When she was done, Jess took her hand again, leading her out of the kitchen toward the backyard. She pretended not to notice the disappointed look on Jacie's face as they made their way past her.

Jess weaved them through the crowd, eventually making it to the back sliding glass door. She slid it open and stepped out into the frigid night air, thick with the scent of cigarettes and weed mixed with wet grass. Clouds covered the moon, but a single well-placed porch light managed to cast a soft light over most of the backyard. Jess spotted the small wooden bench that she and Scarlett played on when they were kids.

She pulled Sam with her, and dropped her body onto it, hearing the wood creak and groan in protest beneath her.

Closing her eyes, she leaned her head back and inhaled the icy air, hoping it would help clear her mind.

The bench was barely large enough for two people, but she felt Sam squeeze in beside her and instantly appreciated the warm contact from her body.

"You okay?" Sam asked, a slight hint of concern in her voice.

"Mm—yeah, just needed a break," she said, keeping her eyes closed. "Thanks for coming with me."

"Honestly, I kinda needed one, too."

"What, you couldn't deal with everyone loving you so much?" Jess asked, pulling her head back to reveal a teasing smile.

Sam laughed, shaking her head.

"Seriously," Jess continued. "I swear everyone that meets you instantly loves you."

"Not everyone," Sam snorted. "If I remember correctly, you hated me before we even actually met for the first time."

Jess smiled, shaking her head as she thought back to that day. "Yeah, and now we're friends. It just took a little longer than usual."

"Friends?" Sam said, looking at her with that signature teasing smile. Jess stared at it for a second before responding.

"Only when you're not beating me at something," Jess answered seriously. "Today in the football game, we were definitely *not* friends."

Sam laughed, knocking her shoulder against hers.

"I have to admit, though," Jess continued with a smile. "I was impressed."

Sam shrugged, an uncharacteristically shy smile filling her features.

A beat of silence passed between them before Jess asked, "Why'd you stop playing soccer? Sounds like you were pretty good."

Sam looked up, watching two people exit the house onto the back porch. "Uh—it wasn't really working out once I was in foster care," she said, clearing her throat. "They're usually not super flexible with different schedules and getting to games and stuff like that."

Jess gave a small nod. "How old were you when you went into foster care?"

Sam paused, looking across the yard as she thought. "Uh—twelve. That's when my mom OD'd," she said, clearing her throat again. Jess felt the ache in her chest from earlier resurface. "I played for one season in high school, but then I had to transfer homes again and it just didn't work out with the next one."

Jess waited to see if she would continue, but she remained silent, eyes blankly staring off across the yard.

"You didn't have any other family to live with?" she finally asked, watching her intently.

"Not really," she answered, shifting on the bench. Jess felt the loss of contact against her right side and immediately missed the comforting warmth. "I never knew my dad. Both my mom's parents died when she was young, and I had my uncle, but he was constantly deployed."

Jess nodded slowly, absorbing everything. "I'm sorry, that must've been really difficult."

Sam finally looked at her, giving her a small, sad smile that didn't reach her eyes. She leaned back on the bench, and Jess relaxed again, feeling the warmth of her body resume its place against her side.

It felt odd, talking to someone who'd experienced a loss similar to her own. As a child, her grandmother had once taken her to a support group to help her open up about her grief and process what she'd been feeling. But even then, she didn't feel like anyone there actually understood. And hearing the other people speak made her feel even more alone when she realized that none of them were thinking or feeling the things that she was.

But sitting there, listening to Sam and hearing the thinly veiled pain in her voice, she felt almost understood in a way. She felt mesmerized by the way this girl could tell her about the painful events of her past and come out the other side unscathed. Even as the words left her lips in a soft whisper, Jess could still see the strength and power behind her eyes, like speaking about these terrible things fueled her to some degree.

"My mom passed away too," Jess whispered, barely loud enough for her own ears to hear. She cleared her throat and blinked hard, wondering for a moment if she'd even said anything aloud or if she'd imagined it.

Sam was quiet for a moment. "I'm so sorry."

Jess gave a small nod of acknowledgement, staring at the hands fidgeting in her lap. They felt entirely separate and far away from her body, like a foreign alien object.

"How old were you?"

Jess cleared her throat, looking up at the other girl. Her light green eyes distracted her from the uncomfortable feeling that had risen in her chest.

"Uh—I was six," she answered, thinking for a moment. "Almost seven." Jess swallowed hard again, keeping her eyes on Sam, like she was the gravity preventing her from breaking apart and floating away. "She was diagnosed with cancer," she continued softly, surprising herself. "It all went pretty fast, so I don't think I really fully understood what was happening."

Sam nodded. "Kids aren't supposed to have to know those things at that age."

Jess pulled the solo cup out of Sam's hand and took a long drink. "They're not supposed to have to know about drug addiction either," she replied, looking into Sam's eyes as she carefully placed the cup back in her hands.

Sam held the eye contact, slowly lifting the drink to her lips and taking a sip. Jess felt an uptick in her heart rate and opened her mouth to continue—

"Guys!" Scarlett yelled from the back door. Jess' body jumped, the sudden interruption reminding her of their surroundings. "Come on!" she said, waving them over.

"Uh—yeah," she muttered. "Yeah, we're coming!" She looked back at Sam, who gave her a small smile.

"I—" Jess started. "I'm really glad you came tonight."

Sam gave her a warm smile and Jess swore she could feel its heat radiate through the cold night.

"Me too," Sam replied, standing up from the bench and stretching her arms above her head. "Come on, let's go beat them again," she said with a smirk.

Jess drifted through the rest of the night, some details sticking in her mind more than others.

The second round of beerpong was against Scarlett and Luke, but she and Sam beat them by more than a few cups.

Afterwards, she watched as Sam and Malik shot-gunned beers together, with half of the party there to cheer them on. And then, before she knew it, the party had thinned out and there were only a handful of people left lingering, waiting for their rides home.

"Sam," Scarlett mumbled after they'd said their goodbyes to Malik and Luke. "Did you drive here?"

"Mm—yeah," she said, from where she was sitting on the couch, with Jess curled up next to her.

"Sleep here," Scarlett said. "Don't try to drive or anything."

"Kay, thanks," Sam said, fighting to keep her tired eyes open.

"Jess, are you sleeping in my bed?" Scarlett asked from the hallway.

Jess shifted, sitting up-right before dropping her head onto the cushion beside Sam's shoulder. "No, I'm fine out here," she mumbled.

Scarlett chuckled and shook her head before tossing them a blanket. "Okay, make sure you drink enough water before you fall asleep."

Jess felt the blanket being laid over her, and she curled closer into the warm body beside her. She took a deep breath, inhaling a scent that reminded her of freshly brewed mint tea and eucalyptus. It felt soothing in her chest.

"Mm—you smell good," she muttered, more to herself than anyone else.

She felt the body beside her head vibrate with soft laughter, and that was the last thing she remembered before falling asleep that night.

When she awoke the next morning, she was alone on the couch, with the blanket wrapped around her and a water bottle set beside her.

Chapter 7

Each day followed the same pattern, and after almost two weeks, Jess felt herself wearing thin.

She woke up early, did her morning run before eating breakfast with her dad, and then rushed off to school. She hurried through her classes, finishing as much of the homework as she could during the school day. Then she headed to practice or a game, if she had one that day, while Sam waited for her.

Most days, Sam waited in the library and worked on her computer, but on game days, she watched and cheered her on from the bleachers. Then they'd meet up after and ride together to the community center.

"How was it?" Sam asked from behind her as she reached the parking lot.

She shrugged, turning her head. "Cold. Pretty sure my muscles were on the verge of cramping the entire time."

"Yeah, I'm not surprised. It's freezing out here," Sam replied with a shiver.

They both automatically slid into their familiar routine, with Jess tying down her bags and Sam pulling out the helmets and untying her hoodie and the heavier jacket from where she left them every day on the bike.

They each put on their things, and Jess waited for Sam to get seated. Once she did, Jess lifted her leg over and settled in a half-inch behind her before resting her hands on the other girl's hips.

Sam started the bike and they were off.

The wind felt colder than usual, nipping at any exposed flesh. Jess pulled her hands further up into the jacket sleeves, blocking them as much as possible.

When they arrived at the center, Laura was standing outside talking to an older man. She saw Jess and instantly lit up, waving her over.

"Jess! Perfect timing!" she yelled to her.

She took off her helmet and stood up from the bike before walking over to them.

"Jess, this is Mike," she said, motioning to the man next to her. "He's been a long time attendee here. I was telling him about your volunteer video and he said he'd be willing to do an interview for you!"

"Oh," Jess said in surprise. "That would be amazing! Thank you so much."

He smiled warmly at her. "No problem. I'm happy to help. I have a daughter your age and she's doing the whole college application thing right now too, so I know how stressful it can be."

Sam walked up to them, holding Jess' camera bag and backpack.

"Thanks," Jess said with an appreciative smile as she took the bags.

"Hey Sam, good to see you again," Mike said.

"Hey, you too. It's been a little while."

"Yeah, I've been going to the center that's closer to my house. It's been a busy few weeks."

Sam nodded in understanding.

"Thanks again, though, for helping Kara with that computer project. I think she misses spending time with you. Hasn't stopped talking about you since," he said with a laugh.

Sam chuckled with a shy smile. "No problem. Glad I could help."

A big gust of wind blew by and Jess watched Sam shiver, the bare skin on her arms now exposed without her hoodie.

"Come on, it's freezing out here. You're gonna get sick or something," Jess said to her, nodding toward the door.

They all shuffled into the building and Jess walked to the desk, dropping her things onto the floor. She realized she was still wearing the heavy motorcycle jacket and stripped it off, setting it on the back of Sam's chair.

They both settled into their usual routines, and Jess began tackling the tasks that Laura had given her for the day.

The evening went by quickly once she started her interview with Mike. It ended up being the perfect addition, since he talked more about the community and resources available for addicts. She thought it would balance well with the more intimate interviews she'd already done with Laura and Ricky.

Mike left shortly after the last meeting finished, with Laura following suit. Jess had one more stack of filing before she would be ready to leave for the night. While she worked on that, Sam cleaned up the meeting room and got it ready for the next day.

"You ready?" Jess asked, leaning against the doorframe.

"Yeah," Sam answered, returning the broom to the corner of the room.

They packed their things and headed toward the front doors.

The second the door swung open, the sound of pounding rain filled the air.

"Shit!" Sam said from behind her.

Jess peered out at the motorcycle in the parking lot. Rain ricocheted off every inch of the shiny black metal.

"Will the bike be okay?" she asked with concern, looking back at Sam.

She grimaced. "Yeah, it'll be fine, but it's not really safe to drive when it's like this. I'll roll it up here so it can dry off, but we probably shouldn't leave until the rain stops."

Jess frowned, mentally calculating how late she'd need to stay up to finish her homework. That seemed to be a new pattern in her life. And it was one she wasn't particularly enjoying.

Sam stripped her backpack off her shoulders and set her things on the ground in front of her.

"Do you need help?" Jess asked, over the roar of the rain.

"It's fine, I got it." Sam said, before running out into the dimly lit parking lot.

It took her a few seconds before she rolled the bike up onto the sidewalk and made her way toward the overhang by the front doors. By the time she made it to where Jess was standing, she was completely soaked. Beads of water dripped off her hair, with some strands sticking to her face and neck.

Jess watched as she set the bike up, her white shirt fully soaked through, clinging to her arms and stomach.

"Fuck," she muttered, untying her hoodie from where it'd been attached to the bike. It fell to the ground with a plop, instantly bleeding water out onto the concrete.

Sam grimaced at the soaking mess, droplets of water running down her face and neck, dropping onto the floor beside the hoodie. She looked up, glancing around the parking lot for a few seconds.

"Want to get some food while we wait?" she asked, nodding toward the small diner that shared the parking lot with the center.

Jess followed her gaze. The building was probably only about fifty feet away.

"Sure. I'm starving anyway," she said, looking back at Sam.

The girl seemed to almost be glowing with the lights of the parking lot reflecting off the water that dripped down her body. Rain looked good on her.

They scaled the building beneath the small overhang until they reached the closest point to the diner.

"Ready?" Sam asked, looking at her with a daring smile.

Instead of answering, Jess sprinted out into the parking lot, instantly feeling the heavy water droplets beat against her shoulders and back. Sam's laugh floated faintly behind her, drowned out by the sound of rain hammering the pavement. Water splashed up against her ankles as she jumped up over the curb and ran the last few feet to the door of the diner. She bent over slightly, catching her breath and inhaling the icy air as Sam sprinted up beside her. Jess wiped the dripping water off her face that fell from her now wet hair.

Sam pushed open the door to the small diner and Jess felt her body relax as the warm air hit her skin, followed by the smell of buttery hash browns and syrup.

"Hi girls." A friendly older woman greeted them from behind the counter as she poured coffee. "Give me a minute, and I'll be right with you."

They waited at the front until she came out and led them to a booth in the far corner, handing over a set of sticky, laminated menus. Although Sam didn't seem to need them. She quickly ordered an array of sugary items off of the kids' menu without looking.

Their food came out quickly, and they began eating in comfortable silence.

"Sam?" an older man asked, approaching their table. He wore a white shirt and apron that almost matched that of their waitress.

"Oh my gosh, Jerry!" Sam answered excitedly, shooting up from the booth. She wrapped her arms around him in a tight hug.

"I can't believe it," he said, before letting go and pulling back to scan her from head to toe. "You've grown up so much. I hardly recognized you."

Sam laughed, a wide smile stretching across her face. "Yeah, I guess it's been a pretty long time."

"How are things? How's your mom doing?" he asked. "When you stopped coming around, I just assumed you guys had moved or something."

Sam glanced down, her smiling falling from her eyes.

"Yeah," she began, clearing her throat. "My mom actually passed away a few years ago."

He frowned, the wrinkles on his forehead deepening. "Oh Sam, I'm so sorry to hear that."

She nodded, her eyes dropping their gaze for a moment.

"You know, I was always rooting for her—and you. I wish I could've done more to help."

Sam gave him a small smile. "You helped us a lot."

He nodded, returning a sad smile. "So, you're back now?"

"Yeah," she said, the upbeat tone in her voice returning slightly. "At least for now to finish senior year."

"That's great, Sam. I'm proud of you," he said, squeezing her shoulder before looking down at the table. "And I can't believe you're still ordering the same sugary crap you did back then," he said with a bellowing laugh that only the lungs of an older man could produce.

Sam laughed with him, giving that rare shy smile. "Old habits, I guess."

He laughed, shaking his head at her. "Well, I'll let you get back to your food, but you let me know if you need anything at all, okay? I mean it."

"I will," Sam replied with an appreciative smile. "Thanks Jerry."

He smiled once more at both of them before leaving for one of the other nearby tables.

"Seems like you know a lot of people around here," Jess commented as Sam slid back into her side of the booth.

"Yeah, I guess I do," she replied with a fond smile, taking a bite of her waffles and whip cream before continuing. "My mom used to take me here sometimes after her meetings."

Jess watched her carefully, noting the tiny changes in her expression as she mentioned her mother.

"The waiters loved it," Sam chuckled, looking down at her food. "She'd talk to them for hours. There was something about her that just made everyone love her."

"You must've gotten that from her then," Jess answered with a small smile.

Sam smiled shyly down at her food, running her hand through her wet, messy hair. Jess felt an almost imperceptible burn in her chest,

103

and the corners of her smile curved a little higher. She wondered how a person could transition so seamlessly between confidence and endearing humility.

"I always wondered what happened to everyone after I left," Sam said, looking around the diner.

"That must've been hard to leave everyone you know. Especially being that young."

Sam shrugged, looking back down at her food and fidgeting with her fork. Jess wondered if this was how she looked when she talked about her own mom's death.

She wasn't sure if it was the rain, or the comforting feel of the diner, but this night felt different. There was something cathartic about listening to Sam talk about these things. Like hearing her speak these words somehow made her feel more at peace.

"Its weird being back now," Sam said, barely loud enough for Jess to hear. Her voice sounded the slightest bit strained, and Jess felt her chest instantly constrict at the sound. "I don't think I talked about her or even said her name out loud for years because I was never around anyone who knew her. But now that I'm back here, it's like she's just—everywhere."

She paused, using her fork to push some bits of waffle around her plate. Droplets of rain dripped from her hair down onto her neck. Jess watched the way her eyes glazed over slightly, and she knew there were memories, or ghosts, dancing behind them.

"I think I was starting to forget her," Sam whispered.

Jess felt the words pierce her heart. They'd come from Sam's lips, but without knowing it, she'd spoken for them both. That had been the fear keeping her up most nights since she was a child. The terror that gripped her, squeezing until she could no longer breathe. It was always there, waiting for the moment she tried to recall a memory of her mother that didn't exist. Or maybe it existed at one point, but had long since faded. And if she could forget some things about her, then one day maybe she could forget everything. Maybe there would come a day where there was nothing left of her besides the knowledge that she had once existed. And maybe one day there wouldn't even be that.

She'd never spoken these words aloud, not even to herself. Just the thought of it made her stomach turn. But hearing Sam say them felt like they'd come out of her own mouth. It felt like an unbearable weight had been lifted from her shoulders and replaced with an equally unbearable ache as she watched Sam endure the pain of the confession. It wasn't fair that this girl could liberate Jess' heart with eight simple words and then be forced to suffer the consequences of them alone.

Jess placed her hand on the table, only an inch away from Sam's. A second passed before she slowly lifted her thumb, setting it on Sam's hand.

Then she began stroking small circles against it.

Sam's eyes flitted up, looking first at their hands together and then meeting Jess' gaze.

She watched the life return to Sam's eyes, like she was finally being released from the haunted memories that had abducted her. Jess felt the weight ease in her own chest and throat, like her body was a mirror of every feeling that passed through the other girl.

Her thumb vibrated where it touched Sam's hand. Every nerve ending screamed at her to stop. Or maybe they were screaming at her to *never* stop.

"Hey ladies," the waitress said from beside the table.

Both girls jerked back in surprise. Jess pulled her hand back, squeezing it into a tight fist in her lap.

"Sorry, I just wanted to let you know my shift is ending in a few minutes. Would it be okay if I closed out your tab?" she asked with an apologetic smile.

"Oh—uh—yeah, of course," Sam stuttered, clearing her throat. Jess' eyes stayed glued to her lap, staring at the hand that now felt like it'd been burned.

"Thanks," the woman said, taking the card that Sam handed to her. "I'll be right back."

When she walked away, Jess remained still, avoiding the other girl's gaze that she could feel still lingering on her.

The waitress returned to the table a minute later with the card and receipt, handing it to Sam.

"Oh," Jess said, shaking her head as she returned from her daze. "Sorry, here, I have cash."

"It's fine," Sam said, shaking her head as she signed the receipt.

Jess frowned, but didn't have the energy to protest.

Sam glanced up at the window, looking out into the parking lot. "I think the rain stopped."

Jess followed her gaze.

Sam looked back at her. "Want to finish your food and then we can head out?"

Jess looked down at her mostly full plate, her stomach now filled with a feeling she wasn't familiar with. "That's okay. I'm done."

Sam watched her curiously for a moment, like she wanted to say something.

Jess hoped she wouldn't.

Finally, Sam nodded and began gathering her things.

Jess followed suit, and they silently made their way out of the diner.

Cold air, thick with the smell of wet asphalt, rushed at them when they opened the door. It was enough to briefly distract her from the feeling in her stomach.

They quickly crossed the parking lot to the front of the building, where the motorcycle waited beneath the overhang. Sam used her hand to wipe away a few small droplets of water from the bike seat, leaving it mostly dry. She then pulled the dry heavy jacket off of where it hung on the bike and handed it to Jess.

Jess placed her hand on the hoodie that Sam usually wore, checking to see if it had dried out at all. Water squeezed out, coating the palm of her hand.

She frowned, handing the dry jacket back to Sam. "Here. You need to wear it tonight."

Sam shook her head as she sat down on the bike. "It's fine. I'm more used to riding in the cold than you are."

"No." Jess crossed her arms. "You're still soaking wet. You'd be freezing."

"I'll be fine," Sam replied, shaking her head.

Jess glared at her, refusing to give in.

Sam watched her for a moment before sighing. "Okay, if I start to get too cold, then we can pull over and switch. But you start with it."

Jess rolled her eyes. "Fine," she muttered, putting her arms through the jacket.

She tied her things to the back of the bike and then sat down behind the other girl. When she set her hands on her hips, she could feel her trembling.

"You're already shaking."

Sam snorted. "Shivering won't kill me."

Jess frowned, annoyed at the girl's stubbornness.

Then she had an idea.

She unzipped the jacket she was wearing and scooted herself forward on the seat. She moved slowly, feeling her inner thighs slide against the outsides of the other girl's legs. Jess stopped suddenly when she felt Sam's back hit her core.

Chills ran up her spine, and a warm feeling settled low in her stomach. She swallowed the thick feeling in her throat before continuing, slowly inching her hands forward from Sam's hips to the area where her thighs met her stomach.

Sam suddenly went still, her hands frozen on the helmets in front of her. Jess continued gliding her hands across the girl's stomach until her arms were fully wrapped around her torso. Her hands gently grasped each of her sides, and she pulled herself closer until every inch of her chest and stomach were pressed against Sam's back, with her head naturally resting on Sam's right shoulder.

Jess swallowed, tilting her head slightly until she could almost feel the warmth of Sam's neck beneath her lips.

"Better?" she whispered.

She felt a tremor run through Sam's body, her stomach tightening beneath her arms. Sam remained frozen for a second before giving an almost imperceptible nod.

It took another second before Sam's hands began moving again, unhooking their helmets from the front of the bike.

She handed one over her shoulder to Jess and then slid the other one down over her head.

Jess put her helmet on, snapping the buckle in place, and then wrapped her arms around her again, trying to give her as much warmth as possible.

Sam started the bike without another word and took off on the familiar route to Jess' house.

It felt different riding this way. Each time they leaned into a turn, she felt the muscles in Sam's stomach and back tense and move with the bike. Every tiny change and movement in the girl's body seemed to ripple through her own.

She felt safer in this position, but there was a new anxious feeling in her stomach. It wasn't like the nerves she usually experienced on the bike. It was different. Something she couldn't quite place.

When they turned onto her street, a strange feeling filled her chest. Almost like disappointment. Or maybe relief. Or a mix of the two.

The bike rolled to a stop at the bottom of the driveway, and Jess let each of her feet down onto the wet pavement. She released her hands from Sam's sides and slid her arms out from where they'd been snaked firmly around her body.

Jess stood up, easing her leg over the bike, and slid the helmet up off of her head. Then she unzipped the jacket, stripped it off, and handed them both to Sam.

She quickly unhooked her things from the back of the bike, and when she was done, she paused, glancing up at Sam, who had her helmet visor down, covering her eyes.

Jess cleared her throat awkwardly. "Mm—thanks for dinner."

Sam nodded.

Jess swallowed, glancing down at her hands. She wasn't sure what exactly she wanted to say, if anything, but the thought of Sam leaving made her feel uneasy for some reason.

"See you tomorrow?" Sam asked, kicking the bike into gear.

Jess nodded, ignoring the disappointment that bloomed in her chest. "Yeah. Yeah, see you tomorrow."

She turned and walked to her front door, an unfamiliar feeling settling in her stomach as she listened to the bike's roar slowly disappear into the night.

Chapter 8

"Jess, here!" Scarlett screamed at her from the other side of the field.

Jess turned, carefully cradling the ball, and sprinted down the field toward her. A large defender on the other team stuck closely at her side, trying and failing to knock the ball out of her stick.

Scarlett cut across the field, losing her defender. She made a beeline toward the goal.

Jess' eyes flitted across the players surrounding her. She knew there would be a small window of opportunity to make a pass to her best friend before another defender picked her up.

Jess made a quick cut to the middle of the field, just fast enough to make her defender fall one step behind.

"Scar!" she yelled as she pulled her arm back and lobbed the ball toward her.

It sliced through the air with perfect accuracy.

Scarlett leapt forward, catching the ball seamlessly on her way to the goal. She dodged around another defender and shot at the upper left corner of the net, narrowly avoiding the other team's goalie.

"Yes!" Jess yelled, pumping her arms in the air and running toward Scarlett, along with the rest of her team.

This put them ahead by two goals with only two minutes left of the game, basically securing their win.

She gave Scarlett a tight hug before turning to look at the people in the stands. Her eyes scanned for a second, then easily located Sam sitting next to Malik and Luke in the bleachers.

Their eyes met, and Sam gave her an impressed smile. Jess couldn't help the wide grin that broke out across her face, feeling the pride swell inside her. She saw Luke clapping and cheering along with Malik and flashed him a quick thumbs up before resetting at the circle of the field.

The last two minutes of the game ticked by uneventfully, securing their win and placing them in the district semi-finals.

When the final whistle blew, Coach Lowe gave them a quick congratulations and, as a reward, canceled the practice they had scheduled that upcoming Saturday on the morning of Winter Formal. The girls on the team cheered again, thanking him before dispersing to join their families in the bleachers.

Her dad was on a shift and hadn't been able to make it, so she walked instead to where Sam and the boys stood at the base of the metal bleachers.

Luke ran up to her as she approached, picking her up and swinging her around.

"You did it!" he cheered. She laughed as he set her back down on the ground.

"Fuck yeah we did!" she heard Scarlett yell from behind her.

"Good job, babe," Malik said with a smile, wrapping her in a tight hug.

Jess then glanced at Sam, who shot her a proud smile.

"Clutch pass at the end," Sam said, nudging her shoulder.

"Thanks," she smiled, warmth flaring in her chest.

"And because of how awesome we are," Scarlett said, "coach gave us the day off this Saturday. So now we won't have to rush to get ready for formal."

"I don't know why you need so much time," Malik muttered. "I'm gonna get ready like twenty minutes before we have to leave."

"Of course you are." Scarlett rolled her eyes before turning to Sam. "Are you sure you don't want to come with us?"

Sam shook her head. "Not this time."

Scarlett frowned at her. "Okay, but you're coming to the after party at my house, right?"

Sam smiled. "Yeah, I'll definitely be there."

"Okay, good. And you can spend the night if you want. We have an extra bed now in the guest room, so you won't be stuck on the couch."

"Oh sweet, thanks."

Jess checked the time on her phone. "Hey," she said to Sam, "I'm going to shower super quick and then I'll meet you in the parking lot."

"Alright," Sam replied with a nod.

Jess gave Luke a quick hug before jogging off to the locker rooms.

She hastily rinsed her hair and body before the water could get cold, then dried off and threw on a loose hoodie and sweats.

Sitting on the bench to tie her shoes, she could feel the adrenaline from the game disappearing, exhaustion quickly taking its place. She closed her eyes and drew in a deep breath. Every muscle in her body ached, even more than usual, and she felt a headache beginning to form between her eyes. She tried to recall the lesson in biology that said how many hours of sleep the human body could survive on before it shut down. Three? Maybe four? She made a mental note to google it later that night.

She cracked her eyes open and pulled her bag from the locker.

Outside, dark clouds blotted the sky, threatening another night of rain. She tucked her hands into the front pocket of her hoodie, rubbing them together for warmth. As she rounded the corner of the last building, she scanned the parking lot.

The bike was there. But no Sam.

She pulled out her phone.

No missed texts or calls. Maybe she'd stayed back to talk to Scarlett or the boys.

Jess turned back towards the field. Her tired legs trudged along the path between the school buildings, leading her back toward where she'd come.

Once she reached the far side of the field, she squinted to see who was still lingering there. She saw a few of her teammates talking to family members, and then her eyes landed on Sam, standing at the bottom of the bleachers talking to someone in a lacrosse uniform.

Jacie.

"Hey," she said to Sam as she approached them. "I thought we were meeting in the parking lot?"

"Oh, sorry," Sam frowned, looking at the time on her phone. "I didn't think you'd be done that fast."

Jacie flashed her a friendly smile. "It's my fault," she said, bumping her shoulder against Sam. "I was trying to convince her to come to the dance."

"Yeah, I probably won't budge on that," Sam said with a smile. "But I'll see you afterwards at Scarlett's party if you're going to be there."

Jess noticed the way Jacie's eyes lit up.

"Okay, yeah. I'll definitely be there," she said.

The tone of her voice reminded Jess of a giddy child. It usually wouldn't have bothered her, but given her extreme state of exhaustion, she sorely lacked patience.

Jess watched Sam nod, smiling at the girl and letting her eyes linger for an extra unnecessary second.

"Are you ready to go?" Jess cut in abruptly, crossing her arms over her chest.

Both girls broke their eye contact, looking over at her.

"Oh—uh, yeah," Sam answered.

"Well," Jacie said, placing her hand on Sam's arm. "Text me about that English project. I promise I'll be a good partner and won't make you do all the work." She finished with a smile that, for some reason, left Jess' stomach feeling uneasy.

"Yeah, I will," Sam replied with a smile as she turned to walk with Jess.

They walked in silence to the parking lot.

Jess slid her helmet down over her head and sat on the bike behind Sam, leaving some space between them on the seat. She placed her hands on the other girl's hips, instinctively moving to wrap them around her torso, like she'd done every day since the diner. But this time, something in her head told her to stop.

There was a tight feeling in her throat accompanied by a heaviness in her stomach.

It must have just been the fatigue taking its toll.

"Ready?" Sam asked over the roar of the engine.

Jess nodded, forcing the feelings away.

***

Laura stood at the front desk, looking over her clipboard.

"Hey ladies." She greeted them with a smile.

"Hey. Sorry we're late," Jess said, setting her things down behind the desk.

Laura gave her a slightly confused look. "Oh, are you? I didn't even realize."

"She's more punctual than most people," Sam said to Laura, giving Jess a teasing smirk. Jess kept her head down, ignoring the comment as she pulled out her things.

Laura smiled, tucking the clipboard underneath her elbow. "I'm heading in. Let me know if you need anything."

Sam nodded and Jess pulled a paper out of her bag with the list of tasks left over from the previous day. She scanned the list, aware of Sam's lingering eyes.

She glanced up at her. "What?"

"What's wrong?" Sam asked, giving her a curious look.

"Nothing."

Sam frowned, pursing her lips. "Seriously, what is it?"

She rolled her eyes, suddenly feeling self-conscious. The truth was that she'd felt off ever since they left the school and honestly didn't really have a good reason why. But she didn't want to admit that. So she chose the next best alternative.

"That's the second time you flirting with someone has made me late for something. It just annoyed me, okay?"

Sam looked at her in disbelief. "You're joking, right?"

116

Jess stared hard at her, folding her arms.

"First," Sam continued, "I wasn't flirting. And second, we were literally here, like," she looked down at the time on her phone, "barely even two minutes later than usual."

Jess rolled her eyes. "You weren't flirting? Really? Try telling that to Jacie."

Sam cocked her head slightly, her eyes probing every inch of Jess' face. "Is it the flirting you have a problem with? Or the fact that I'm flirting with a girl?" she asked in a low, serious voice.

"What?" Jess blurted out, shaking her head in disbelief. "Don't even try to pull that. You know that's not what this is."

Sam folded her arms across her chest, still glaring at her. "I'm not sure I do. You are trying to get into Trinity, after all."

Jess matched her glare. "So what?" she asked in a low voice, spitting the words out like venom.

"So, they would probably reject you just for *knowing* a lesbian. I know how they work and the students that get in are the ones who have the same beliefs they do."

Jess clenched her jaw. "I'm not arguing with you about this again."

"Yeah, whatever." Sam spat, turning back to the desk.

Jess' blood boiled. She wanted to yell. She wanted to scream and tell her that *she* was the one who should be mad, not the other way around.

Her jaw physically hurt from being clenched as she sat there, glaring into Sam's side. Sam was clearly in the wrong. Yet again, she hadn't valued Jess' time. And to top it all off, she chose to flirt with her teammate, when she could've chosen anyone else at their school. They were friends now, and friends wouldn't do that to each other. It was disrespectful.

She pushed up from the chair and walked down the hallway to the bathrooms.

She shoved the door open, letting it slam against the wall with a crack. She paced to the sink, putting her hands on the edge and resting her bodyweight against the counter. Taking a deep breath, she looked up at her reflection in the mirror.

Dark circles peered back.

She swallowed hard, rubbing her eyes until spots appeared behind her lids.

A frustrated exhale puffed from her lips. She felt stupid for letting it all bother her so much. For letting herself get so exhausted. For letting the interaction with Sam get so blown out of proportion.

She looked at the mirror again. Rubbing her eyes had made them red and slightly swollen.

Great, now Sam would probably think she was crying or something.

She bent over the porcelain sink and turned the knob for cold water. It sputtered out, and she cupped some in her hand. She splashed in over her eyes, then looked up at her reflection. It didn't seem to help the puffiness, but at least it woke her up a little.

She took one last look in the mirror before exiting back into the hallway.

As she approached the desk, she saw Sam sitting with her headphones on, studying her computer.

Sitting in front of Jess' chair was a small cup of coffee and a donut carefully placed atop a napkin.

She sat down and cocked her eyebrow curiously at the items.

Sam jumped when she saw her. She removed her headphones and shifted awkwardly in her seat to partially faced her. "Uh—I know you like the ones with the pink frosting. I grabbed you one from the meeting before they ran out."

Jess stared down at the donut. The area behind her eyes started to prickle.

Sam cleared her throat in a way that Jess hadn't heard from her before. It sounded cautious. Careful even. "I'm sorry," she said in a low voice. "I didn't mean to assume anything, and I shouldn't have accused you like that."

A lump formed in Jess' throat, and it took everything in her to hold back the tears that threatened to flow from her eyes. She swallowed hard, afraid that if she said anything, the tears would pour out along with the words.

Sam shifted again in her chair. Jess felt her eyes on her, and she wished desperately that Sam would keep talking so that she wouldn't have to.

"I'm sorry if that wasn't the right thing to do. I just thought you might be hungry and tired after the game," Sam mumbled, her hands fidgeting in her lap.

The soft, apologetic tone of her voice made Jess' heart pounded furiously in her chest, and she felt a tear threatening to fall from her eye.

She panicked and, before she could process what she was doing, she turned, throwing her arms around Sam's neck and shoulders.

Sam froze. But only for a second.

Then she gently wrapped her arms around Jess' torso.

Sam slowly stood, pulling them both up until they were standing. She kept her arms wrapped securely around her.

Jess took a deep, shaky breath, inhaling the soft scent of mint and eucalyptus in Sam's hair. Somewhere in her subconscious, she thought it was faintly familiar. A distant memory she couldn't quite place. She closed her eyes, resting her chin on Sam's shoulder and let her body relax.

Sam's hand began rubbing slow, soothing circles on her back, and Jess' body melted into her touch. She silently prayed that Sam wouldn't be able to feel her rapid heartbeat.

"Better?" Sam whispered. Jess felt tingles run down her neck and back, settling as a warmth in her lower abdomen.

She nodded, wiping her eyes with the back of her hand as she slowly released her arms from the other girl's neck. When she pulled back, she could see concern and curiosity written across Sam's face. She hoped that her own facial expressions weren't giving away as much.

"Sorry," she murmured, casting her eyes down toward the ground. "I think I'm just tired from the game and everything."

Sam pursed her lips, still watching her closely. She didn't believe her. Jess knew that. Still, she hoped she'd let the matter drop, anyway.

Eventually, Sam nodded. "Do you want me to take you home?"

Jess shook her head. "No, that's okay. I need to get this stuff done."

Sam frowned. "Okay, well, let me know if you change your mind."

Jess looked at the donut and coffee on the desk, another small wave of affection washing over her.

"Thank you for everything," Jess said softly. "You're a really good friend."

Sam smiled at her, but Jess could see the hint of concern still lingering in her eyes.

"Just glad you don't hate me anymore," Sam replied, nudging her arm gently.

Jess exhaled with a small smile, feeling the tension between them finally break.

Chapter 9

T he rides with Sam were over.

That morning, Jess had woken to a message from the repair shop letting her know the car was fixed and ready to be picked up. She sent a quick text to Sam, letting her know, then went with her dad to pick up the car.

It was bittersweet. A couple of weeks before, she would've done anything to get her car back, but things had changed.

It felt foreign pulling up to the clinic that day in her car. It even felt odd walking through the doors and seeing Sam already sitting at the desk, talking to Ricky. She'd gotten used to being with her most days after school. Now it felt like something was missing.

"Hey," she greeted them as she walked up to the front desk.

"Happy finally having your car back?" Sam asked with a smile.

She shrugged, rounding the corner of the desk and setting her things down. "Yeah, I guess."

"Be glad you won't stick out like a sore thumb on that bike anymore," Ricky said with a chuckle.

Sam rolled her eyes and threw a wadded up paper ball at him. He laughed, ducking out of the way. Jess noticed he looked a little different from the last time she'd seen him. Dark circles enveloped his eyes, and his face seemed a little thinner than before. Exhaustion clung to his cheeks, his smile only reaching halfway to his eyes.

"I don't know," Jess said. "The green kind of grew on me."

A brilliant smile spread across Sam's face. "See! Girls love it."

Ricky groaned. "Please don't encourage her."

Jess laughed, shaking her head at the two of them.

The front door opened as she shuffled through her backpack, pulling out her things. Out of the corner of her eye, she could see a man in a military uniform walking toward them.

"Chris?" Sam asked, standing up from her chair. She walked around the desk, meeting him a few feet away. "What're you doing here? Is everything okay?"

"Why haven't you answered my texts?" he demanded.

"Oh, uh, sorry. My phone's still in my backpack from the ride over here. I haven't checked it in a little while."

He stared at her hard, unblinking. "You owe me rent. Today."

"What?" Sam asked, lowering her voice a bit and pulling him to the side of the hallway. Jess tried to focus on her work and give them their privacy. She glanced up and saw Ricky watching them intently.

"You said that rent was due on the first of every month," Sam continued.

"Not for you. I need half of your portion every two weeks."

Sam frowned. "I didn't know that."

He stared at her with a blank face. Jess could only detect a hint of annoyance in the way his eyes crinkled slightly, and he seemed to puff his chest out while deeply exhaling. He must have been Sam's uncle, given the military uniform and the fact that they clearly lived together on some level. But Jess could see no family resemblance between the two of them. Sam was like the sun; warm and bright. He seemed cold. Harsh.

"I stopped getting checks for you when you turned eighteen, so it's your responsibility to make up the difference."

"Hey," Ricky suddenly snapped, moving toward them. "How about you stop being such a prick and give her a break? She's your fuckin family, for god's sake."

Jess' head snapped up in surprise.

Sam's uncle watched with a mildly annoyed but unfazed expression as Ricky approached them. His eyes scanned him from top to bottom, like a machine assessing a potential threat before deciding it was harmless.

"Hey," Sam said softly, looking at Ricky with obvious concern and confusion in her eyes. She seemed just as surprised by his sudden outburst. "It's okay. I got this."

The two men continued staring each other down until Chris finally broke eye contact, turning back to Sam with a small exhale. His shoulders loosened a fraction from their tight position.

"Look, I'm not trying to be the bad guy." Jess thought she could detect the faintest bit of regret in his eyes. "You know the deal, though. If you can't cover the other half, then I have to get a roommate instead. It's just the reality of things."

Ricky scoffed, and Sam threw him another curious glance.

"I know," she said, looking back at Chris. "I only have like half right now, though. Can you give me another week to get the rest? I'm finishing a project next week and it should pay out by next Friday."

He pursed his lips slightly, but otherwise remained completely stoic. "Fine."

"Thank you."

He nodded, but said nothing as he turned to leave. He walked briskly through the hallway and out the front door.

After a second, Sam turned to Ricky. "Why'd you do that?" she asked, confusion laced in her voice.

"He was being a dick," Ricky huffed, his hands still clenched tight at his sides.

Sam stared at him intently, scanning over every inch of his face. Jess wondered what Sam saw there that she didn't.

"What?" he demanded, looking at her and crossing his arms over his chest.

"What's going on?" she asked, lowering her voice.

His jaw clenched, and Jess thought another angry outburst might be on its way. But this time, he stopped, closing his mouth before it could release any words. He looked down at the ground and dropped one arm from his chest, rubbing his hand roughly against his face.

"I lost my job," he breathed.

Sam glanced over at Jess, who was still watching them. She didn't need to see the look on her face to know they needed some privacy.

She stood up from the desk and walked into the auditorium to help Laura set up for the next meeting. They were far enough away from the doorway that Jess couldn't hear what they were saying, but she glanced in their direction every few seconds to see when Sam would return to the desk.

Finally, after a few minutes had passed, she saw Sam walk to the desk and crouch down next to her backpack on the floor. She opened one of the side pockets and pull out a wallet.

Jess leaned to the side, trying to get a better view.

Sam shuffled through it for a few seconds before pulling out what looked like a small fold of bills. Then she stood back up and walked toward where she'd been talking to Ricky.

A few seconds later, Ricky stomped through the doorway, shaking his head. Two more people followed, and Jess glanced up at the clock on the wall. The meeting was about to begin.

She quickly finished setting the rest of the items on the table and walked back out into the hallway. As she approached the desk, she could see Sam kneeling back over her backpack, returning the cash to her wallet. Jess sat down in her chair and watched a few small groups of people enter the hallway, then file into the main room.

After a minute, the last of them made their way in, and Laura closed the door behind them, leaving Jess and Sam alone in the hallway.

Sam pulled her headphones out of their case, and Jess knew that her window to talk was closing.

"So, your uncle seems like a nice guy."

Sam snorted, frowning down at the headphones in her hands. "He has his moments."

Jess pursed her lips. "Seems like a tough situation to be in."

"It's not bad," Sam answered, shaking her head. "Just some misunderstandings here and there."

She pulled her phone out of her backpack, and Jess watched her scroll through for a moment before typing and sending a quick text.

Jess wanted the conversation to continue, but knew that if Sam was open to talk about something, she would do it on her own.

Sam pulled her headphones over her ears, and Jess got the hint. She began working on the list of tasks from Laura, letting the matter drop.

When the hour was nearly up, the front doors of the building opened and a young woman holding the hand of a little girl walked through. Sam's head snapped up, and she immediately stripped her headphones off before walking to meet them at the entrance.

"Sam!" the little girl said, reaching her arm out toward her.

"Hey," Sam replied in a low, excited whisper.

The woman gave her a small, apologetic smile before pulling her in for a hug. She held her like that for a few seconds, and Jess looked away, feeling like she was intruding on a private moment for the second time that day.

They spoke in hushed tones for a minute or so, and Jess had to make a conscious effort to avoid eavesdropping.

Eventually, Sam walked back to the desk and leaned over to retrieve something from her backpack. She walked back to the woman and Jess watched her pull the folded cash out of her wallet once more. The woman stared at it hesitantly. Then, after a few moments, she gently took it and pushed it into her front pants pocket. She said something to Sam before pulling her into another tight hug.

Jess' head snapped up when the door to the auditorium opened. People shuffled out of the meeting and into the hallway.

Ricky walked through the door, eyes cast down at the floor.

"Daddy!" the little girl yelled. His head jerked up, spotting her at the end of the hallway.

"Hey baby," he said, as he walked up and scooped her into his arms.

Sam gave the woman a small smile before leaving to walk back to the desk, avoiding Ricky's gaze.

He hugged the woman and the three of them walked out the door, with the little girl waving to Sam over his shoulder.

Sam dropped into her chair with a deep sigh, letting her body slump and her head rest against the back.

Jess kept her eyes on the papers in front of her, trying to pretend that her focus hadn't just been entirely on Sam and what she was doing.

After a few seconds, Sam shifted in her chair until she was facing her. Jess continued, trying to keep her concentration, until she could practically feel her eyes burning into her.

She glanced sideways, her hands still ruffling through the papers. "What?"

To her surprise, Sam looked at her with an amused smirk.

"Are you excited for the dance tonight?" she asked, her chin resting against her hand on the back of the chair.

Jess cracked a smile, tilting her head curiously. "Um—I guess," she answered.

Sam's smile widened. "What color is your dress?"

Jess wrinkled her nose, amused at the turn this had taken. "It's green—wait, no," she paused, thinking for a moment. "No, it's blue."

"You don't remember what dress you're wearing?" Sam asked with a chuckle.

Jess shrugged. "Scarlett helped me pick it out a few months ago. It's been in the bag in my closet ever since."

Sam laughed again, shaking her head. "Then how'd you make sure Luke's tie is gonna match?"

Jess frowned, looking down at the stack of papers in front of her. "I actually don't even know what he's wearing. We never talked about it."

"Really? Aren't all the couples supposed to match?"

"I guess," Jess shrugged. "We've never really done that stuff, though."

Sam nodded, but gave no response. Jess felt something soothing in the way Sam was watching her, like she was the only thing in the room. It made her want to continue.

"Besides, it's sort of hard to be a normal couple when you barely see each other," Jess muttered as she continued rifling through the stack of papers.

"Because of your new schedule?"

"Yeah," Jess replied, pausing for a beat. "But I think it was already starting before that. I guess that's what happens when you're about to go your separate ways to college."

Silence fell between them for a few seconds as Sam looked at her thoughtfully.

"So," Jess said, using the opportunity. "You wanna talk about what happened earlier?"

Sam frowned, but she didn't look away. "What about it?"

Jess pursed her lips. "Did you give Ricky money?"

"No," she said, glancing away and finally breaking eye contact.

"Did you give it to his wife?" Jess asked.

Sam looked at her, resting her chin lazily on the back of the chair again. Something about her demeanor and the conversation felt different. There was an air of trust and comfort, but also a hint of something else. The way Sam watched her reminded her of the way she looked at her computer when she was working; like it was the only thing that existed in her world at that moment. Jess wondered if this was her way of coping with stress; by placing her focus entirely on something or some*one* else.

"Don't you need it for rent?" Jess continued, when she realized Sam wasn't going to give her an answer.

Sam shrugged. "It'll be fine. I'm getting paid for a big job next week." She kept her eyes fixed on Jess, looking at her with an unreadable expression.

"Hey girls," Laura said as she walked up to them. The sound startled her, but it still took a second for her to rip her eyes away from Sam, who seemed entirely unfazed. "You can head out early if you want," she said, setting her clipboard on the desk next to Sam. "There's only one more meeting and then I can close up."

Jess cleared her throat, trying to focus on what Laura was saying. "Are you sure? I can stay longer and help—"

Laura waved her off. "No, no. I can handle it. You girls go enjoy your weekend."

Jess nodded appreciatively. "Okay, thanks."

They each packed up their things, and although they were no longer driving together, Sam still waited for her to finish.

"So, what time should I get to Scarlett's tonight?" she asked, as they made their way out to the parking lot.

Jess thought for a second, pulling her keys out of her bag. "Hm—maybe like ten? I think her and Malik are leaving the dance a little early to set up, so they should be there around then."

Sam nodded as they walked up to her bike. She unfastened the jacket that Jess had become accustomed to wearing.

"You know, it feels kinda weird riding alone now," Sam said with a chuckle.

A small smile passed over Jess' lips. "I know what you mean. I think I actually missed it this morning," she said, shaking her head.

"Glad it finally grew on you," Sam said with a smirk as she slid her helmet on.

"Yeah, I guess it did," Jess said as she turned to walk toward her car. "See you tonight," she called over her shoulder.

"Have fun at the dance!" Sam yelled back, her voice muffled through the helmet.

Jess opened the door to her car and slid into the driver's seat. She kissed the fingertips of her right hand and reached up to touch them against her mother's gold pin on the car's visor. But instead of cold metal, she felt smooth fabric.

Her stomach dropped as her eyes snapped up.

It was gone. Just an empty space on the visor where the pin usually sat, the fabric a slightly lighter color in that one circle.

She slammed the visor up, hitting the ceiling of the car. It had to be there somewhere. It must have fallen.

She shot her hand beneath the seat, running it across the bare carpet.

"No, no, no." Jess muttered as she jumped out of the car and frantically searched the cup holder in the door.

"Fuck!" she yelled, ripping items out of the center console and throwing them onto the ground of the front passenger seat.

"Hey," she heard Sam's concerned voice behind her. "What's wrong?"

"It's gone," she answered, her voice quivering as she dug through wadded up receipts in the drink holder.

"What's gone?"

"My mom's college pin," she cried, waving her hand at the visor above her seat. "It's always right here. I've never moved it."

"Okay," Sam said, her voice calm. "It's okay, we'll find it." She walked to the other side of the car and opened the door, looking on the floor and under the seat.

After a few seconds, she began rifling through the center console.

"I already checked there," Jess snapped. Sam frowned, avoiding her gaze, and Jess' chest immediately filled with guilt.

Her eyes burned and she couldn't tell if it was from her near constant state of exhaustion or from the tears that were now rushing into her eyes.

All at once, she felt the buried emotions of the last few weeks swell inside her, forcing their way to the surface.

They sliced through her, one after the other, like the sharp gusts of wind in a hurricane.

She felt anger—no, *rage*—that she'd worked so hard the last few years and still wasn't a top choice for the college she wanted.

And she felt rage at Sam. She hated her for being there. She hated her for making her miss riding on the motorcycle. She hated her for the way she made her feel that night at the diner. She hated the way her wet skin had shimmered in the streetlights, burning the image into her memory. She hated her for making her feel less alone; for making her feel like she wasn't crazy for how she felt about her mother's death.

What if the pin was gone forever?

Fear spread through her body like sheets of ice scraping against her veins.

What if this was the closest she'd ever get to knowing her mother?

What if, for the rest of her life, she was stuck with only these fading half memories of the woman who brought her into this world?

A cracked sob ripped through her chest.

Her hands went numb as she placed them over her face, covering the tears that flowed freely down her cheeks.

She felt the ground shaking around her and she was sure it was about to break open and swallow her whole.

Suddenly, two strong arms wrapped around her, and she felt the pressure of a body holding her tight.

"It's okay, breathe," the body said. "Deep breaths."

She did as she was told and inhaled as much air as her still sobbing lungs would allow. The soothing scent of eucalyptus flowed into her nostrils, settling deep inside her chest.

"Good. Keep going."

She felt a warm hand rubbing circles between her shoulder blades. Her hands, wet with tears, slid off of her face and grabbed onto the chest in front of her. Clinging to the only solid object in the middle of a stormy sea.

"It's okay. I got you."

Another deep breath and a smaller sob shuddered through her chest.

Another deep breath, this time the smell of mint.

"Good."

The voice seemed less worried this time, and Jess enjoyed the sound. She curled her head slightly, moving closer to it.

The hand continued rubbing circles, and she felt the pressure in her chest finally subsiding; the hurricane inside her dying out into a light rain.

"Keep breathing."

Another deep breath. More mint.

She felt the chest beneath her hands moving in a steady rhythm, slower than her own.

She tried to sync her breathing to it.

Up. Down.

Up. Down.

Her head felt light, and her hands tingled from her fingertips down into her wrists. The sudden realization hit her that she might faint.

Like an all-knowing god, the voice said, "You're okay. I got you," and for some reason, she believed it.

She felt the body pushing against her and she took a step backward, her thighs hitting against something soft.

Two strong hands slid onto her thighs, hooking behind them. They lifted her off the ground, setting her onto the soft seat of the car behind her.

She took another deep breath and slowly cracked open her eyes.

Through the blurry tears, she could see her fists tangled in the black hoodie on Sam's chest, just inches from her face. Sam stood between her bent knees, arms still wrapped tightly around her.

Jess closed her eyes again, resting her forehead against Sam's chest in front of her.

Any other time, she might have felt shame or anxiety over how she'd just fallen apart, but she was honestly too exhausted to care. It felt like this was the first time in months that she'd closed her eyes, and she wasn't ready to let that feeling go.

She took another deep breath, not bothering to hide it when she pressed her nose against the warm fabric and inhaled the soothing scent of Sam's hoodie.

Breathe in. Breathe out.

Sam's chest moved up and down beneath her head, like waves pulling up onto shore and receding in a never-ending cycle.

Inhale. Exhale.

She wished she could stay there forever.

Her head felt impossibly heavy and, for a moment, she thought she might actually drift off to sleep. Or maybe she was already asleep. She couldn't tell.

A few seconds later, Sam shifted slightly, and the movement drew her back to reality.

She lifted her head a few inches and opened her eyes, blinking away the wetness that still clouded her vision. She slowly released one of her hands and wiped her eyes.

There was a thick feeling in her mouth that she tried and failed to swallow down.

She cleared her throat, keeping her gaze down on her lap.

"Sorry," she mumbled, her voice like two pieces of sandpaper scraping against one another.

"Don't be," Sam whispered, pulling back slightly, letting her arms unwrap from Jess' body.

Jess wiped her eyes again, sniffling as another slight tremor rippled through her. She loosened the grip of her other hand, but kept it there, resting against Sam's chest.

"Why'd you give her the money?"

"What?" Sam asked, pulling back an inch to look at her.

Jess stared blankly ahead. "Ricky's wife."

Sam watched her for a moment, then shrugged, looking down at Jess' lap. "They needed it."

"*You* needed it."

Sam exhaled. "They have a little girl." Jess finally glanced up at her, but this time it was Sam who avoided eye contact. "She needs it more than I do."

Jess pursed her lips and nodded slightly, letting her eyes drop back down.

"You're a good person," she whispered.

Sam drifted her hand up to where Jess' hand was still resting on her chest. She placed it over hers and rubbed a small circle with her thumb. Jess watched it in a daze.

"Do you want to go to the repair place and see if they have your mom's pin?" Sam asked gently.

Jess let out a deep exhale, closing her eyes as she finally released her hold on Sam and let her hand drop into her lap. "Yeah."

Sam took a small step back. "Do you want me to go with you?"

Jess looked down at the ground, finally feeling a twinge of embarrassment setting in. "Can you?"

"Yeah, of course," Sam replied. "Are you okay to drive or do you want to ride with me?"

"I'm fine. I can drive."

"Okay," Sam said, looking her over closely. "Are you sure? You look tired."

Jess let out a dry laugh. "That's nothing new."

Sam frowned, but didn't argue. "Okay, I'm gonna follow you on my bike, but call me if you need to pull over or anything."

Jess nodded and picked her keys up from where they sat on the dashboard.

She drove in a daze, still disconnected from her body, watching the world go by from afar.

When she pulled up to the shop, she shook her head in a useless attempt to clear the fog. Sam met her at the door and did all the talking after Jess explained in detail what the pin looked like. Then she sat in an uncomfortable plastic chair near the entrance while they waited for one of the workers to check the lost and found.

When he returned, she knew right away by the look on his face that it was a lost cause. She stood to walk out.

Through her daze, she was vaguely aware of Sam writing a phone number for them to call in case they found anything.

They walked back outside, and Sam followed her to her car.

"Are you sure you're okay to drive?" she asked, holding the car door open for her.

"Yeah," Jess mumbled. "I'm just gonna go home and try to take a nap before I have to get ready."

Sam frowned. "Maybe you should sit this one out and just take it easy tonight."

Jess snorted. "Yeah, right. I'm pretty sure Scarlett would actually murder me."

Sam sighed, crossing her arms over her chest.

"I'm fine," Jess said, trying to lighten her tone.

Sam studied her face for a few seconds before giving in. "Okay. If you say so."

Jess tried to give her a convincing smile.

"I guess I'll see you tonight then," Sam said, stepping back from the car to leave.

"Yeah," Jess muttered. She watched her turn to walk toward her bike. "Sam?"

"Yeah?"

"I feel like I've said this a hundred times since I've known you," she said, pausing. "But, thank you. Again."

Sam smiled at her, fiddling with the keys in her hand. "You're welcome. Again."

Chapter 10

"I can't believe they played the same song like four times," Scarlett complained as she poured a drink for herself. She motioned the bottle to Jess, asking if she wanted one, too.

Jess shook her head, chuckling at her friend's incessant complaints. "I think I'm gonna pass tonight."

Scarlett raised her eyebrows as she set the bottle back down on the granite countertop. "You sure? It's like our last Winter Formal after party ever."

Jess laughed again. "You're going to say that after every single dance this year."

"Yeah, because it's true!"

Jess shook her head, rolling her eyes with an amused smile.

"So?" Scarlett asked, motioning the bottle toward her again.

"Not right now. I'm just not in the mood. Kinda had a weird day," she mumbled, looking off into Scarlett's living room where dozens of their classmates were drinking and enjoying one of their last nights of high school.

"You wanna talk about it?"

Jess shook her head. "Not really."

"Okay, well, let me know if you change your mind," Scarlett said, squeezing her arm gently.

Jess smiled at her appreciatively before looking back at the sea of people. She scanned them until she saw Luke standing near the back, talking to Gabby. She watched her lean in to whisper something in his ear.

"She's been like that around him since she started volunteering at the hospital," Scarlett said, rolling her eyes. "I can't tell if she has an actual crush on him or if she's just trying to annoy you."

Jess shrugged. "I don't really care either way," she muttered.

The dance had been fine. Nothing special, but she was glad she'd gone and spent that time with her friends. The problem was that was all Luke felt like; just a friend. They'd danced and kissed a few times, but it felt like they were just going through the motions.

Scarlett looked at her curiously. "You wouldn't care if your arch nemesis was flirting with your boyfriend?"

Jess shrugged again. She really didn't think it would.

"Hm," Scarlett replied, eyeing her closely, before finally looking away. "Hey, I think your girl's finally here."

Jess followed her gaze and smiled when she saw Sam walking through the entryway of the house.

"Sam!" Scarlett called to her, holding up the liquor bottle in her hand. Sam turned, smiling when she saw them.

"Hey," she said, as Scarlett pulled her into a tight hug.

"Will you do a shot with me?" Scarlett asked with a pout. "Since my best friend is down for the count tonight."

Sam laughed. "Yeah, sure, just give me a second." She turned to Jess, lowering her voice a bit. "Come here, I have something for you," she said, taking her hand and pulling her out of the kitchen.

"What—guys, what the hell?!" Scarlett yelled.

"I promise I'll be back in thirty seconds and then I'll be your drinking buddy all night!" Sam called back over her shoulder as she led them down the hallway, where the house was mostly empty.

Jess snorted. "That's a big promise to make. Scar's not easy to keep up with."

Sam chuckled. "I think I can manage." She stopped at the end of the hall, turning to face her.

Jess looked at her questioningly. "What is it? Are you okay?"

Sam smiled, reaching her hand into her pocket and pulling something out. Jess looked down and gasped.

The gold pin.

"What?!" she yelled, grabbing it from her palm. "Are you serious? Where did you find it?"

"I called and asked if they'd let me go back into the work area after they closed so I could look around for it," she answered with a beaming smile. "I found it on the ground under one of the workbenches. Must have popped off when they were working on your car."

Jess looked up at her in awe.

It suddenly struck her how lucky she felt to have Sam as a friend—to have her in her life.

She pulled her into a tight hug, feeling a gigantic weight lift from her shoulders.

"Thank you so much," she whispered, her voice cracking as she felt fresh tears well up in her eyes. "You have no idea how much that means to me." She held her for a moment, then pulled back to wipe the tears from her eyes.

Sam smiled warmly at her. "Yeah, that's why I wanted to give it to you somewhere a little more private."

Jess nodded appreciatively. "Thank you."

"You're welcome," Sam replied, smiling back at her. "Okay, I better go back and have that drink with Scarlett before she loses it."

Jess laughed, wiping the rest of the tears from her eyes. "Yeah, alright. Let's go."

"Damn, finally!" Scarlett yelled, as they made their way back into the kitchen. Then she looked at Jess. "Hey, are you okay?" she asked, the protective best friend in her immediately taking over.

"Yeah. Yeah, I'm fine," Jess answered, nodding. "Happy tears," she said with a light laugh.

Scarlett scanned her face curiously before turning to look at Sam.

Sam nodded at the bottle she was still holding. "Shot? I could use one after today."

"Man, what the hell goes on at this clinic?" Scarlett muttered, grabbing two plastic shot glasses for them. "You guys both look fucking rough today."

Jess scoffed. "Thanks Scar."

Scarlett shrugged, pouring the thick clear liquid into the glasses.

"Some days are better than others," Sam muttered. "Today wasn't one of them."

Jess felt a small pang of guilt for having added to Sam's already stressful day. She watched her take the glass from Scarlett and quickly cheers before downing it.

"Wanna talk about it?" Scarlett asked, her face screwed up in disgust as she took a sip of soda to wash down the alcohol.

"Definitely not."

Scarlett nodded in understanding, looking off into the living room. "Well, if you need a distraction for the night, I'm pretty sure Jacie would volunteer herself in like half a second."

Sam and Jess both followed her gaze to where Jacie stood near the far wall. She looked to be in the middle of a conversation with some guy from their school, but she was clearly staring over his shoulder at Sam. She didn't even bother to hide it when they looked over at her. Instead, she met Sam's eyes with a coy smile.

"Not all problems can be fixed with sex, Scar," Jess said, although her eyes went to Sam.

Scarlett shrugged. "No, but some of them can." She looked back at Sam. "So, is this one of 'em?"

Sam continued silently staring back at Jacie, and Jess felt a sudden heaviness settle in her stomach as she waited for the answer. Finally, after a few seconds that felt more like an eternity, Sam turned back to them.

She picked up the liquor bottle, gesturing to the two shot glasses in front of them. "Another?" she asked Scarlett.

"Hell yeah," Scarlett answered, a wide grin breaking out across her face. "Man, I love this girl," she said, looking at Jess and nodding her head towards Sam.

Jess tried to return a convincing smile. She glanced back at Jacie, whose hungry eyes still clung to Sam.

The party raged on as more people arrived. Both the backyard and inside the house were packed, making it hard to walk anywhere without being shoved back and forth.

Some people had set up a speaker in the living room, dancing clumsily around the beer pong table in the center. Luke had convinced her to dance with him for a few minutes before she told him she was exhausted and needed a break. He'd given her his signature hurt puppy look, but forgot about it quickly when one of the guys on his baseball team pulled him away for some drinking game.

Jess pushed through the mass of people, slowly making her way to the kitchen, where she finally spotted Scarlett and Malik.

"This is crazy!" Jess yelled over the noise.

"I know, isn't it awesome?!" Scarlett yelled back with a beaming smile, her arms wrapped tightly around her boyfriend's waist.

Jess laughed, shaking her head. "Yeah, it is."

"Man, I called it," Malik said, nodding toward the dance floor. "I knew Jacie was gonna make a move. She was all over her when we were outside."

Jess looked back at the living room, following his gaze. Sam stood leaning against the wall, with Jacie only a few inches away. She had her hand resting on Sam's forearm as she whispered something into her ear.

Scarlett laughed. "I knew Sam would go for it!"

Jess felt a tightness wrap around her chest as she watched Jacie drag her hand up and down Sam's arm. She looked away, staring down at the granite island in front of her. Swallowing hard, she tried to force the unfamiliar feeling down as it bubbled up inside of her.

"Hey," Scarlett said, concern evident in her voice. "You okay?"

Jess swallowed hard again, the image of Sam and Jacie together still burned in her mind. She shook her head, confused at why it bothered her so much.

"Yeah. Fine," she mumbled, working to plant a fake smile on her lips.

Scarlett stared at her, eyes squinted. Her gaze flitted to Sam and Jacie again before returning to Jess. She tilted her head, and Jess could practically see the wheels spinning behind her eyes.

"I just think it's weird," Jess blurted out, before Scarlett had a chance to say anything. "It's weird to have your friend hook up with one of your teammates."

Scarlett stared at her silently, head still cocked in curiosity, and Jess felt heat rising in her cheeks.

Scarlett looked back at Sam and Jacie. "Hm," she grunted. "Well, the only way to get over it is by forcing yourself to get used to it."

Jess pursed her lips, her jaw automatically clenching.

"Come on," Scarlett said with a smile as she grabbed her hand. "Let's go say hi."

"What? Scarlett, no," Jess pleaded, trying to pull her hand away as she dragged her into the sea of people.

"Scar, seriously stop," she growled, her voice dying in her throat as they approached Sam and Jacie.

"Hey guys," Scarlett said, practically skipping up to them with a wide smile planted on her lips. Jess did her best to clear the angry look on her face.

Sam turned to them and Jess' chest felt some relief when Jacie dropped her hand from Sam's arm.

145

"Hey," Sam said with a grin. Her eyes bounced lazily between them. A small giggle escaped her lips, and Jess wondered how much she'd had to drink since she arrived.

"You guys look like you're having fun," Scarlett said with a smirk.

Jacie smiled shyly and looked down at her feet, a slight blush rising into her face.

Sam's smile spread even wider. "Yeah, this is awesome. I can't believe how many people are here," she answered, oblivious to Scarlett's innuendo.

Scarlett smiled at her the way she'd smile at a cute, clueless puppy. "Hey, I have an idea," she said, glancing at Jess with a mischievous look. "Beer pong. Me and Jess versus you guys."

Jess frowned at her, ready to decline. Jacie squealed with excitement beside her. "Yes! I'm so down!" she yelled over the loud music, before turning to Sam. "Do you want to?"

Jess rolled her eyes internally, knowing that Jacie would only want to do it if Sam did.

"Uh—yeah, sure," Sam said, scratching the back of her neck. "Why not?"

Jacie's smile stretched so wide it reminded Jess of a cartoon character. "Okay, let's do a shot first, though. I think I need to catch up to you guys," she said with a laugh.

Jacie took Sam's hand and pulled her past them as they all made their way back to the kitchen.

Jess instantly regretted standing on the opposite side of them, where her view was now filled with Jacie glued to Sam's side. She averted her gaze, watching Scarlett pour a round of drinks for the three of them.

In her peripherals, she could see Jacie's index finger slip through the front loop of Sam's faded black jeans.

Jacie whispered something into Sam's ear, making her lift her head in laughter, and Jacie took the opportunity to lean further into her space, her lips coming dangerously close to Sam's neck.

Jess' heart beat furiously in her chest.

Sam laughed again, and suddenly she couldn't take it anymore.

She opened her mouth, looking up at Scarlett, prepared to make some excuse as to why she had to leave the party. But her voice caught in her throat when she saw Scarlett already watching at her. She scanned Jess' face with the same curious expression she wore earlier as she screwed the cap back onto the liquor bottle.

After a moment, Scarlett turned away from her and slid the shot glasses toward the other two girls.

Jess remained quiet, watching them clink glasses and throw back the drinks.

Then after another second, she cleared her throat. "I–"

"Jacie," Scarlett said, quickly cutting her off. "Come with me to see if the BP table is open."

"Oh," Jacie said, frowning slightly as she glanced at Sam, who looked even more oblivious than before. "Okay, sure."

Scarlett grinned at her, grabbing her hand and pulling her away. "We'll be back in a bit," she called over her shoulder, but her eyes lingered on Jess for an extra second.

Jess stood there frozen, unsure of where to look.

Sam moved toward her from the opposite side until she was right beside her, their shoulders brushing against one another.

"So," Sam said, leaning over to let her elbows rest on the island in front of her. "How was the dance?" she asked, a goofy grin filling her face.

"Fine, I guess," Jess shrugged. "Kinda boring."

"What color tie did Luke wear?"

"Blue," Jess answered with a tiny smirk. "Apparently Scarlett told him what color my dress was."

Sam laughed, and Jess felt the sound vibrate through her body.

"Well, I'm sure you guys looked great together."

Jess gave no response, still looking down at her hands.

"So," Sam said, pushing herself up off her elbows. "You ready to get your ass handed to you in beer pong?"

Jess rolled her eyes, but couldn't stop the small smile from forming on her lips. "Better hope your new teammate doesn't suck," she muttered, the words coming out with more bite than she intended.

Sam's grin spread further across her face as she turned her body toward her. Jess glanced up, trying to even out her expression.

Sam reached one arm out and grabbed the liquor bottle off the counter. She pulled a new plastic shot glass out of the bag and poured into it, ignoring the drops of liquid sloshing out onto the counter. Jess thought for a moment that maybe she should stop her from having any more, but before she could say anything, Sam downed the shot.

She set the glass back down on the countertop and wiped her mouth with the back of her hand.

Jess frowned, seeing the slightly glazed over look in her eyes.

A large group of girls walked into the kitchen, and as they squeezed by, one of them knocked into Sam's back, pushing her forward into Jess.

Jess grabbed onto her, snaking her arms around her waist and pulling her out of the way. Sam glanced back over her shoulder, but Jess could feel her body still fully relaxed.

"Hey," Jess said, frowning as she wiped some strands of hair out of her face. "Are you okay?"

Sam opened her eyes to look at her, their faces now only a few inches apart. She smiled, an amused look slowly spreading through her face. She took a small step closer, and a shudder spread through Jess in every place where their bodies met.

Sam leaned her head toward her, and Jess froze in place, her breath catching in her throat. She inched closer until her lips reached the sensitive spot just before Jess' earlobe.

"If you wanted to be on my team instead, all you had to do was ask."

A chilling sensation bolted down her neck and through her back, transforming into a throbbing pulse between her thighs. Jess' eyelids fluttered, and she felt her hands subconsciously tighten their grip on Sam's back until the fabric of her shirt balled up inside her fists.

No, no, no.

"Sam," she warned, the word coming out broken, ringing more like a plea.

Then, before she could register anything else, she felt Sam's body pulling back out of her arms. The warmth rushed away, leaving a bitter, empty memory in its place.

Sam looked at her with that infectious, amused smile. "But you didn't ask," she said, grinning from ear to ear, the goofy drunk look reappearing. "So now you're gonna get your ass kicked."

Jess stared at her, lips slightly parted, finally feeling some oxygen seep back into her lungs. She could still feel the terrifyingly steady pulse between her legs.

"Okay!"

Jess jumped, hearing Scarlett's voice behind her.

"We got the next game. They should be done in a few minutes," Scarlett said, trotting up beside her. Jacie followed behind her and immediately nestled herself beside Sam.

This time, Jess' eyes refused to leave them, no matter how hard she tried to rip them away. She could feel Scarlett watching her, but she couldn't bring herself to care as her eyes shamelessly traced the near perfect contours of Sam's face before drifting to her neck and further down her body.

Jacie's hand lifted and settled on Sam's hip, as she turned to whisper something to her. A murderous heat boiled in Jess' stomach as her eyes landed on Jacie's fingertips, just barely hooked on the hem of Sam's jeans, pulling her closer.

Her chest burned. She felt both like she was breathing too fast and also not getting enough air.

She knew she needed to look away, but for some reason she couldn't bring herself to do it.

"Alright, if we're gonna play, I definitely need to pee first," Sam said.

"Okay," Jacie said, her fingers still lingering on Sam. "Well, when you come back, let's go outside for a minute before the game starts. I need some air."

Jess knew that line. Everyone knew that line. That was the classic excuse to go out in the dark backyard and make a move. And it only

150

just then occurred to her that she'd said the exact same thing to Sam weeks before at the last party.

"Kay," Sam mumbled, turning to head toward the bathroom.

Jess saw the hungry look in Jacie's eyes and felt her heart rate increase. She shot a glance back at Sam, watching her weave through hoards of people as she made her way to the bathroom at the back of the hall.

A terrible, sinking feeling filled her chest as she watched her walking away.

She looked back at Jacie again, seeing the coy smirk still present on her lips, and something inside her snapped.

"Uh—yeah," she mumbled. "I have to go too."

She ignored the look that Scarlett immediately shot her, and before she could say anything, she darted past them out of the kitchen.

She urgently pushed through people, mumbling quick apologies as she made her way to the hall. Once she reached it, she could see Sam at the end, walking into the bathroom and shutting the door behind her.

She wasn't sure what she was thinking, or if she was even thinking at all. Her body seemed to be running on its own, with no sign of slowing down.

She jogged the rest of the way to the door and turned the knob, shoving it open.

"Wha—" Sam spun around with a confused look.

Jess quickly shut the door behind her and turned the lock.

"What's wrong?" Sam asked, her concerned voice suddenly much sharper than before. "Are you okay?"

Jess' heart pounded like a hammer in her chest.

151

"Don't sleep with her."

Sam stared at her, dumbfounded. "What?"

"Don't sleep with Jacie."

"Are you serious?" Sam rolled her eyes. "I'm not arguing with you about this again. Just drop it."

Jess swallowed, her throat suddenly overwhelmingly dry. "Do you even like her?"

Sam exhaled. "Why does it matter? She's nice and we're both just having fun."

Jess looked away.

Sam watched her, waiting for some response that she couldn't give. Or that she wasn't willing to give.

After a few seconds, Sam shook her head. "Whatever," she muttered, walking toward the door.

"Wait—" Jess stepped in front of her at the last second, placing herself between Sam and the door. She held a hand up to stop her. It pressed against Sam's lower abdomen.

Their faces were mere inches apart, and Sam stared down into her eyes, waiting.

Jess could feel every beat of her heart rushing through her veins.

She slowly inched her hand down Sam's stomach, letting her nails drag against her until they reached the hem of her jeans.

Sam's body stilled. Her eyes flicked down.

Jess swallowed, raising her other hand to rest gently on Sam's hip.

Sam's eyes snapped back up, meeting hers. The look in them was entirely unreadable.

She stared back at her for a moment, then slowly tilted her head forward, past Sam's flushed cheek. She kept going until her lips brushed lightly against her ear.

"Please don't do it."

She felt a slight shudder run through Sam's body.

Her heart pounded so hard she was scared to say anything else, afraid that her voice would shake.

Sam's body completely stilled beneath her fingertips. Jess waited a second, feeling like an eternity had passed. Then finally, she pulled her head back a few inches, searching for Sam's eyes.

When she found them, her heart sank.

Maybe this had been a terrible mistake. She slid her hand off Sam's stomach to pull it away, but as she did, her nails brushed over the exposed skin between her shirt and the hem of her pants.

Sam's abdomen tightened beneath her fingertips and the look in her eyes changed from clouded to something else; something that made the pulsing between Jess' legs instantly return.

Sam remained still, but the feeling that ran through Jess spurred her forward. She leaned in an inch, and then paused, gauging the look in Sam's eyes again. Looking for anything that would tell her to stop. There was nothing besides the hungry new stare that burned in her eyes.

She leaned another inch forward until her lips were mere centimeters away from Sam's. Her eyes fluttered as she moved to close the remaining distance.

Her lips barely brushed Sam's.

Warmth bloomed through her entire body.

And that was it.

Whatever was holding Sam back completely crumbled in that instant.

Sam's lips kissed her back, and Jess felt life itself being breathed into her.

Every thought disappeared, replaced with pure and overwhelming instinct. Both of her hands shot up, desperately grabbing onto the back of Sam's neck.

Sam's arms wrapped around her securely, and Jess felt herself being turned, and then pushed back against the countertop of the sink. It barely registered when she hit the edge with a thud.

Somehow, her tongue ended up in Sam's mouth, and the second it touched Sam's, her body erupted in tingles. The sensation traveled downward and within seconds, the feeling between her legs was overwhelming.

She'd never experienced anything like it. It was like something inside her had taken over and there was no force that could stop it. A moan escaped her lips, more out of frustration than of pleasure, and she instantly felt Sam shift, somehow knowing exactly what she needed.

Sam's hands hooked onto the back of her knees, and Jess felt herself being lifted in the air until she sat on the bathroom countertop.

Then, before she knew it, Sam's body returned. Her lips came with a new urgency, and her body pressed tightly against her. Sam shifted her hips against the pulsating area between her legs, and Jess felt the entire universe shift in one instant.

The feeling turned into something else entirely; something deep and yearning.

She desperately clutched onto Sam, one hand digging into her back while the other tangled deep in her hair.

Sam's hands found her hips, her thumb stretching around, pressing into the delicate spot between her hip and thigh. She pulled Jess' hips toward her.

"Hey!"

A loud knock pounded on the door, and Jess was suddenly catapulted back to reality.

Sam jumped back, her hands immediately leaving Jess' body like they'd been burned.

"Hurry up! There's a line!"

Jess was too stunned to find words as her chest heaved, gulping in air. She stared wide-eyed at Sam.

"Uh—yeah," Sam said, calling through the door. "One second."

Sam avoided her gaze, and Jess felt a cold sensation sweeping through her. Fear and anxiety were rapidly replacing any other feelings. She was torn between wanting to touch Sam again to calm the storm that was building inside her, but also feeling terrified by the fact those thoughts entered her mind at all.

Jess slowly slid off the countertop.

"Wait a minute after I leave," Sam said, her words sounding oddly crisp and much sharper than before. Something in her tone added to the already present anxiety in Jess' chest.

Sam turned to the door, and Jess felt the wave of disappointment swelling inside her. She looked down at the ground, hugging her arms around her now ice cold chest.

The door opened, and the sounds of the party outside suddenly rushed in for a brief moment before the door shut again. She thought she heard Sam mumble something about another person in the bathroom, but she couldn't be sure. Her head felt like it was underwater, all of the noises and thoughts dull whispers of what they once were.

When Sam had finally kissed her back, it was like the volume of life had been turned all the way up and she could finally hear everything crisp and clear. Now that she'd walked away, the volume returned to a hushed static, and the quiet felt uncomfortably loud.

She closed her eyes and mentally counted to ten, both to calm herself and also to give enough time before she walked out after Sam.

When she finished, she walked out the door, back into the party, ignoring the mumbled discontent from the small line of people waiting outside. The music blared, and everything felt both too loud and too quiet at the same time.

She slowly made her way through the crowds of people that had somehow grown even larger in the few minutes since she'd been gone.

Scarlett and Jacie were talking as she approached them in the kitchen.

"All good?" Scarlett asked. Although her eyes seemed like they were asking an entirely different question.

Jess cleared her throat, her eyes searching for Sam among the bodies in the kitchen. "Uh—yeah. All good."

"Where's Sam?" Jacie asked, her tone hopeful.

Jess swallowed hard, avoiding her eyes. "I don't know. I thought she'd be out here with you guys."

Jacie frowned, and Jess could feel Scarlett's eyes watching her.

"I'm gonna check to see if she's outside," Jacie muttered, turning to walk away.

Jess was in a daze, barely registering what was happening around her, but she could still feel Scarlett's eyes piercing the side of her face.

"What?" she asked, trying and failing to sound confident.

Scarlett pursed her lips. She opened her mouth and then paused before closing it again and shaking her head. "Nothing," she muttered, finally looking away.

Jess gritted her teeth, turning back to face the countertop. She spotted the liquor bottle and leaned over to grab it before pulling out a fresh shot glass. Scarlett's eyes followed her every move.

Jacie returned a few minutes later wearing a dejected look on her face, letting them know Sam was nowhere to be found.

An hour passed and when they still hadn't seen her anywhere, Jess decided to sneak out to the street to check if her motorcycle was still there. She worried that she might have tried to drive home. When she spotted the bike parked along the street, she assumed she'd called an Uber to pick her up.

With Sam gone, Jess floated through the rest of the party, barely able to register anything else.

Eventually, the night turned to early morning and the party slowly died down. She checked her phone once, and when she saw no texts from Sam, the disappointment that flooded through her was overwhelming. When most of the people left, she made up the guest bed to go to sleep.

The next morning, she woke up and went outside to see if Sam's bike was still there. Her heart sank when she saw that it was gone.

Chapter 11

J ess trudged back into Scarlett's house to get her things, stepping
over an assortment of debris left over from the night before.

She cracked the door of Scarlett's room open and tiptoed to get her
bag and her phone where she'd left it on the charger the night before.
The screen lit up and her disappointment deepened when she saw the
only text was from her dad reminding her about church that morning.

She left the room quietly, careful not to wake Scarlett. The last thing
she needed was to deal with the questions she knew her best friend was
dying to ask.

She threw her clothes into her backpack and quickly left the house,
texting Scarlett an apology for not staying to help clean up.

When she got home, she jogged up the stairs to take a quick shower
before leaving with her dad for church. She rushed through as quick
as she could, then threw on some of her nicer clothes before heading
back downstairs.

When they walked into the church, she breathed a sigh of relief
at seeing Luke's parents there without him. They'd barely talked all
night after the dance, and the last thing she needed was awkward
conversations or explanations while she'd still barely processed the
events of the night herself.

Her dad led them to their usual spot in the back, and within minutes, the sermon began.

Finally, she had a minute to think.

Her mind instantly catapulted to the night before.

The feeling, the taste, the want, all flashing through her mind. No matter how hard she tried to think of something else—anything else—her thoughts always led back to Sam.

She pulled her phone out of her pocket, checking it once more for any missed texts or calls.

Again, there were none.

The heavy feeling from the night before returned to her stomach, and she realized that it was tinged with both regret and guilt. She'd been so consumed with where Sam was and what she was thinking that she hadn't really thought about how she felt about it herself.

Why did she snap when she saw the way Jacie looked at Sam?

Why did she follow her to the bathroom?

Why did she *kiss her*?

With each new thought, the pit in her stomach deepened.

I kissed her.

Why did I kiss her?

I kissed a girl.

The thought sent a wave of overwhelming nausea shooting through her, and she jumped up from her seat.

Her dad shot her a look as she squeezed by him into the aisle.

She'd never been so thankful before that they always sat in the back row near the main hallway. She shuffled through the doorway and jogged to the bathroom, throwing the door open when she got there.

Her stomach heaved right as she ran into the first stall.

She bent over the toilet, vomit burning through her throat. Tears streamed down her face, and she couldn't tell if she was actually crying or if it was her eyes reacting to the violent puking.

She stayed over the toilet for a minute, waiting to see if it was over.

Finally, when her stomach felt like it had no more to give, she straightened up, ripping a piece of toilet paper to wipe her mouth. She flushed the toilet and stepped out to the sink.

The mirror reflected red, puffy, swollen eyes back to her.

She rarely cried. Actually, before the last few weeks, she couldn't even remember the last time she'd cried. Maybe when she broke her arm as a child? No, not even then. She thought it must have been when she was much younger. Maybe years before, when she still cried for her mother.

Her *mother*.

What would she have thought of this?

What would she have thought of her kissing another *girl*?

This new thought sent paralyzing fear coursing through her and, for a second, she thought she might be sick again.

She swallowed down the thick feeling that filled her mouth and stung her raw throat.

What would her mother have thought of her kissing another girl?

The thought raced through her mind. She wrapped her arms around her torso, holding herself as a tremor ran through her body. She shut her eyes, waiting for it to pass.

Once she was sure she wouldn't be sick again, she pulled her phone out to text her dad. She told him she wasn't feeling well and would wait in the car. That would buy her some time to get herself together.

She tucked the phone into her pocket and walked back into the hallway. When she tiptoed into the main room, he shot her a concerned look as he handed over the keys. She shook it off, giving her best attempt at a reassuring smile.

In the car, her mind spiraled with thoughts of her mother.

She wished harder than ever that she could remember details of what she was like—anything that would give her a clue to how she would react to Jess feeling *something* for another girl.

All she could think of was how involved she was in the church. And that she went to Trinity.

Trinity. That was the next problem.

Sam wasn't wrong about what she'd said about them. Not that they'd ever said anything publicly, but they weren't exactly known for their acceptance.

She closed her eyes, leaning her head back against the seat of the truck.

Her chest and throat felt like they were being squeezed. She took a few breaths to calm herself and blinked away the approaching tears in her eyes.

Whatever it was that she was feeling had to go away. She couldn't do it. She couldn't want to kiss Sam.

She couldn't want Sam.

It was just one kiss, nothing more. It was one emotional day. Sam was there for her, and it made her confused about how she felt. That's all it was.

That's all it can be, a voice echoed in her head.

She swallowed hard, forcing out any thoughts of Sam. She just needed to focus. The stress of everything had gotten to her and made her weak. It had almost ruined everything, and now she needed to get back on track.

All she needed to do was go to the clinic and apologize. She'd tell Sam that she'd made a mistake and it wouldn't happen again. Because it wouldn't, right?

She stared blankly out the window.

How could she be around Sam and feel normal after what had happened? How could she not be constantly reminded of that night and how it felt?

That was the thing. She couldn't.

She couldn't sit next to her every night at the clinic without being reminded of her lips and the way it felt to have her body pressed against her.

The front doors of the church opened and people began flowing outside. She carefully wiped the wetness out of her eyes and flipped down the visor mirror. Little red veins shot through the whites of her eyes, and her face was red, but other than that, she just looked exhausted.

She flipped the visor back up and spotted her dad walking toward the car.

Taking a deep breath, she wiped her eyes one last time.

The car door opened, and he slid into the front seat beside her.

"What's wrong?" he asked, scanning her disheveled face.

She cleared her throat. "Nothing. Just felt nauseous."

"Did you drink at that party last night?"

"No," she answered, rolling her tired eyes. "I just—I don't know. My stomach was upset."

He glared at her suspiciously, and Jess avoided eye contact, staring straight ahead through the window.

"Hmph," he finally grunted, before turning away and putting the keys in the ignition.

Her shoulders relaxed a fraction.

The car ride was quiet, only filled with the light sounds of football on the radio. On the one hand, that meant she didn't have to answer any more of his questions. But on the other, it meant she had nothing to distract her from thinking. And thinking was the last thing she wanted to do.

When they eventually pulled back into the driveway, Jess muttered, "I'm going to the clinic."

He frowned at her. "Maybe you should take the day off. You look," he started, pausing as his eyes scanned over her, "tired or something."

She knew it was probably weird for him to see her like this. It was weird for her, too. She couldn't remember the last time she'd felt so mentally or emotionally exhausted. Actually, she couldn't really remember a time when she felt so many emotions, ever. And now, in the last two days, it was like everything she'd neglected and forced down for years had come back with a vengeance to punish her.

"I'm fine," she responded, trying to make her voice sound stronger than it felt.

He looked at her for a few seconds before giving a slight nod. It wasn't like them to check up on each other like this and, in that moment, she was grateful that he didn't feel comfortable enough to change that.

She opened the car door to get out, pausing as she remembered what she needed to do. "Um—dad?"

"Yeah?" he mumbled absentmindedly, probably already having mentally moved on to thinking about the rest of the football games being played that day.

"Do you still think your friend at the hospital could get me into the volunteer program there?"

He looked up at her curiously, his attention returning. "Uh—I don't know. I'd have to ask."

Jess nodded, her eyes drifting back to the ground as she stepped out of the car.

"Do you want me to?" he asked, eyeing her again with that suspicious look that reminded her he was a cop.

She pursed her lips, feeling the different emotions battling within her. "Maybe. Can I let you know later today?"

He looked like he wanted to push the conversation further and, for a second, Jess thought he might actually do it. But after a moment, he just grunted and shut his car door before trudging up the driveway and into the house.

She followed him inside and quickly changed her clothes into something more comfortable before leaving again for the clinic.

Everything played in her mind again on the drive there. Every thought and feeling she'd had the night before.

By the time she arrived and parked, her palms were sweating and the tightness in her chest had returned. She scanned the parking lot as she walked toward the entrance, surprised when she couldn't find Sam's bike.

She pushed through the front doors and saw Laura standing alone at the front desk, flipping through a small stack of blue papers.

"Hey!" Laura greeted her with a distracted smile, her eyes instantly dropping back to the pile in front of her. "Coming in on your day off?"

"Yeah," Jess said, equally distracted as she glanced around the hall for signs of Sam. She walked around the side of the desk and scanned the ground where Sam's backpack usually sat.

"Is Sam here today?" she asked, working to sound as nonchalant as possible.

"Hm?" Laura looked up at her from behind her thick rimmed black reading glasses. "Oh, um, no. I haven't seen her."

Jess frowned, sitting down at the desk. Her immediate nerves disappeared, but the heaviness in her stomach deepened.

She pulled her phone out of her pocket and opened the messaging app, staring at the conversation with Sam.

Maybe she could just text her?

No, she definitely wanted to talk in person. It felt weird to discuss what happened over something as impersonal as a text.

She pursed her lips and locked her phone, returning it to her pocket.

She sat there, looking around the empty hall. The next meeting wouldn't start for another thirty minutes, and if she was being honest, this was the last thing she wanted to be doing that day. Throwing up that morning plus the lack of sleep the night before had left her utterly drained. All she really wanted was to get this conversation over with and then curl up in bed with Netflix.

Her foot tapped on the ground impatiently.

She didn't think she could stand waiting another twenty-four hours before seeing Sam, and who knew if she would even show up? Maybe she was trying to avoid her.

She cleared her throat. "Um—actually, Laura, I had to give something to Sam today," she said as the woman finally looked up at her. "Something from school," she continued, clearing her throat awkwardly. Hopefully, it sounded more convincing than it felt coming out of her mouth. "Is there any chance you have her address? So I could drop it off real quick."

Laura looked away, thinking for a moment. "Hm, you know I probably do somewhere on my phone," she answered, reaching for her purse on the desk. "She left one of her little techy computer things here one time and I brought it to her after closing up."

She pulled the phone out of her purse and pushed her reading glasses up on her nose, holding the phone out until it was a full arm's length from her face. She tapped and scrolled through with her index finger, squinting at the screen.

"Ah! There it is," she said with a proud smile. "Here." Laura handed the phone to Jess.

"Oh perfect, thank you so much!" Jess said, taking a picture of the phone screen before handing it back to her. "Do you think it'd be okay if I went to go drop it off to her? That was really why I came in today."

"Oh honey, of course," Laura said, waving her off. "It's your day off. Besides, it's dead in here, anyway."

Jess smiled at her appreciatively as she stood up from the desk. "Thanks. I'll see you tomorrow."

She walked out to her car, switching between the picture of the address and the maps app on her phone, remembering bits and pieces each time to type into the search bar.

It was only about a ten-minute drive from where she was. That meant she had ten minutes to mentally prepare for what she needed to say. It'd probably be best to keep it short.

Short and to the point, she thought as she turned onto the highway, the app's robotic voice relaying the next instruction to her.

After a few minutes, it told her to take an exit. She glanced at the ETA on the screen, and her palms began to sweat.

A few turns later, she entered a neighborhood, and the voice told her the next directions in a matter of feet instead of miles.

She wiped her hands on the front of her hoodie as she examined the street. Chain-link fences lined overgrown front yards, some with rusted old cars, and others with children's toys littered over every inch of the grass. A few middle-aged men stood talking on the sidewalk, and she felt their eyes stalk her as she drove by.

After another hundred feet, the GPS declared her arrival.

She pulled the car over against the curb on her right side, but left it running with the windows locked. The dropped pin on the map showed that the house was on her left, and she glanced out the window to check the address.

This house appeared slightly less run down than the rest. The lawn was neatly trimmed, lacking the assortment of random items that the rest of them had. The peeling beige paint could definitely use a fresh coat, but otherwise, it looked to be holding up pretty well.

She glanced around the street for Sam's bike. Nothing.

Her eyes landed back on the house. In all of her thinking and planning what to say, she realized she hadn't imagined what she would do once she actually arrived.

Should she knock on the front door?

No, absolutely not. She didn't want to risk the possibility of an awkward run in with Sam's uncle if he answered the door. He wasn't exactly a friendly face she looked forward to seeing again.

She shifted uncomfortably in her seat, bouncing her leg as she weighed her options.

Calling would probably be the best. She would call and let her know she was there, then Sam could meet her at the door.

She reached into her pocket and pulled her phone out. Sam's contact filled the screen. She stared at the call button, her thumb hovering to the side. Anxiety crawled through her skin. She was starting to feel hot beneath her hoodie.

Taking a deep breath, she tapped her thumb down on the phone icon. It immediately switched to the black call screen. She tapped the speaker button and turned up the volume as the sounds of ringing filled the car.

Ring... Ring...

Ring... Ring...

By the time it got to the sixth ring, Jess knew she wasn't going to answer. She tapped the red button to end the call.

Groaning, she closed her eyes and threw her head back against the seat. She leaned her head to the side, opening her eyes to look at the house again.

The front door looked daunting.

Calling again wouldn't hurt. She could at least call a few more times before resorting to the uncomfortable door knock.

She tapped the phone icon, followed by the speaker button, and looked out the window to the house as it rang.

Ring... Ring...

"Hello?"

Jess jumped, snapping her head back. Seconds ticked off on the screen.

"Uh—" Jess stuttered as every ounce of preparation flew out the window. "Hi."

Silence.

Her heart pounded so hard she could hear it in her ears.

"What's up?" Sam asked, and although her voice sounded even enough, Jess could still detect a hint of irritation. She hated the way it caused a pang in her chest.

"Um—can we talk?"

"Yeah, I'm listening," Sam's tone seemed to soften slightly.

Jess squeezed her eyes shut, pressing her hand against her forehead as the sudden realization hit her that driving to her house completely unannounced was probably one of the most embarrassing things she's done.

"Actually," she sighed, peeking out the side of her hand to look at Sam's house again. "Are you home?"

A long, painful pause.

"Uh—yeah," Sam answered slowly. "Why?"

Jess closed her eyes again, feeling physical pain at having to say the next words. "I'm—uh," she sighed. "I'm outside your house."

A longer, even more painful pause.

She glanced down at the phone screen. "Hello?" she asked, wondering if the call had ended.

"You mean like—" The tone of Sam's voice was now amused, and Jess cringed when she could hear her holding back laughter. "You're physically here right now?"

Jess rolled her eyes, leaning her head against the palm of her hand. "Yes, Sam. I am physically here right now, sitting in my car, outside your house."

Another long pause, and this time Jess knew she was definitely holding back laughter.

"Sam," she warned, her voice a mixture of anger and exhaustion.

"Yeah—uh sorry," she answered, her voice returning to its even state. "Do you wanna come in?"

"That'd be great," she replied, tapping the red button to end the call.

She grabbed her keys and threw the car door open, every bit of patience leaving her body.

She walked up the driveway to an empty front walkway. If she didn't already know who lived there, she might think the house was vacant.

The door opened when she was still a few feet away and she saw Sam standing in the doorway. She wore a black t-shirt with gray sweatpants, her hands in her pockets as she leaned casually against the door frame. She said nothing, just tilting to the side to make room for Jess to walk into the house.

Jess took the cue, stepping past her through the threshold.

The inside looked about as untouched as the outside. There was a couch in the living room she walked into, but no coffee table or TV on the wall. The kitchen to her right had no table, and there was nothing on the walls. Without the couch and the one pair of shoes sitting inside the door, the house would've been completely empty.

"So," Sam started, and Jess turned around to look at her. "You want to talk about how you kissed me?"

Jess' eyes shot wide open, her mouth dropping open in surprise.

"Uh—" she stuttered, feeling heat rising in her cheeks. "Can we—can we talk about this somewhere private?" she said through a clenched jaw.

Sam shrugged, her expression completely unbothered, as if they were talking about something as mundane as the weather. "Sure, but Chris isn't here, anyway." She walked toward the hallway leading further into the house.

"Well, still," Jess muttered, following her.

They walked into a room at the end of the hall, and Jess was instantly struck by the smell. It smelled like Sam. That semi-sweet mint and eucalyptus that wafted off of her every time Jess got close.

This room was different. It was minimal, but still had an air of comfort about it. The bed was perfectly made with a dark gray comforter and matching pillow case. It was pushed into the corner, touching two walls. Beside it, sharing one wall, there was a desk with multiple computer monitors lined up and all turned on. Taped to the bottom of one monitor was a small, faded picture of a woman with a young girl.

Sam sat down in the chair in front of the desk and looked at her with a mildly bored but questioning expression.

Okay, this was it. She couldn't put it off any longer.

Jess cleared her throat and motioned to the bed. "Can I—?"

Sam nodded.

She sat down on the perfectly crisp comforter.

"I—I'm sorry for last night. It was a mistake. It was an emotional day, and I wasn't thinking straight."

She glanced up at Sam to gauge her reaction. Sam just watched her with that same bored look.

Jess shifted uncomfortably on the bed. "So, yeah. Um—that's it."

"Okay."

"Okay?" Jess repeated. "That's all? You have nothing you want to say?"

Sam shrugged. "Not really."

Jess scoffed, looking off to the side. "Great, okay. Glad this was all so easy for you," she snapped, standing up from the bed. She took a few steps toward the door before whipping her head back around. "If you're so unbothered by this entire thing, then why'd you disappear last night? Why didn't you stay and at least—I don't know—hook up with Jacie or something?" she asked, throwing her hand in the air.

Sam stood up and strode toward her. "Because I knew that *this* was going to happen," she said, gritting her teeth. "You were going to freak out even though *you're* the one who kissed *me*," she said, pointing between them as she took a step closer, leaving only a foot of space between them. "So why'd you do it?"

"I—"

"What? Were you bored with your boyfriend? Wanted to mix things up?"

Jess shook her head. "No—I just," she paused, a million thoughts racing through her head.

"You just what?"

"I—" she tried again, the overwhelming mass of feelings bubbling up inside her once more, begging to be released. "I don't know. I just couldn't stand the thought of Jacie kissing you," she said, shaking her head. She crossed her arms defensively, but it felt more like she was holding her body together to keep it from falling apart.

Sam stared at her for a moment.

The angry look slowly faded into something resembling curiosity. She opened her mouth, but closed it again before any words came out. Her eyes drifted across Jess' face.

"Okay," she began slowly, her tone much softer than before. "Do you know *why* you couldn't stand the thought of Jacie kissing me?"

Jess pursed her lips, clenching her teeth together as she felt tears prickling up into her eyes for what must have been the tenth time that day. She shrugged, looking down at the beige carpet.

Sam sighed, but this time it didn't sound like it was out of irritation. "Come here," she said softly, nodding to the bed that Jess had just vacated, the comforter now wrinkled where she'd been sitting.

Jess followed, sitting beside her on the bed. She tried to ignore how close their legs were to each other.

"Jess," Sam said, her voice soft and caring, but also cautious. It reminded her of the way teachers used to speak to her after her mother died. Like she would break if they used a normal tone. "Do you want to talk about what you were feeling last night?"

Her throat felt incredibly tight. The thought of speaking aloud, let alone trying to explain her feelings to someone, made her feel physically ill.

She shook her head, keeping her eyes trained on the hands in her lap.

"Okay. That's okay. You don't have to if you don't want to."

Something about the way Sam said it made the tightness in her throat subside.

"How are you feeling? Like physically?"

Jess shrugged. "Tired, I guess."

"Okay. Anything else?"

She shook her head and then paused. "I was sick to my stomach this morning, but it's better now," she muttered.

"You mean you threw up?"

Jess nodded, still staring down at her hands.

"How much water have you had today?"

She shrugged. Usually she was extremely good about making sure she stayed hydrated, but she'd obviously had bigger things on her mind that morning.

Sam stood and walked out of the room, disappearing into the hallway. Jess swallowed, still unable to look anywhere else other than her lap.

A minute later, Sam returned with a glass of ice water. She held it out to her and sat back down.

"Drink," Sam commanded.

Jess slowly lifted the glass to her lips, letting the ice cold water seep into her mouth. She hadn't realized how thirsty she'd been until the wetness touched her tongue. She took a few sips, letting it soothe her raw, burning throat.

When she finished, Sam took the glass from her and leaned off the bed to place it on the desk.

"Do you want to lie down for a bit and try to sleep?"

Jess looked up at her in surprise.

174

"I'll be right here on my computer," Sam said, probably feeling the need to clarify that she wasn't offering to join her in the bed. "And Chris won't be home at all today, or probably tonight either."

Jess looked back down at the comforter beside her, picking at a loose thread with her thumb.

Sam slowly lifted her hand, but paused in midair. She looked torn for a moment, as if making a decision. Then, she brought her hand the rest of the way, letting it rest over Jess'.

"I promise everything is going to be okay."

Her heart swelled both at the words and at the feeling of Sam's hand over hers. A pleasant and intense warmth spread from her chest through the rest of her body. It was crazy how easily her heart and body reacted to something so small.

Tears pricked up behind her eyes again. "Sam," she whispered, her voice cracking. "I don't think I can volunteer at the clinic anymore."

Jess couldn't see her face, but she saw Sam's head bob in an understanding nod.

"It's okay." She brushed her hand up and down Jess' forearm. "Why don't you just try to get some sleep now and we can talk about it more when you wake up?"

Jess swallowed, wiping away the tears that had pooled in her eyes. "Okay."

Sam gave her a small smile and stood up from the bed. She walked up to the bifold door in the wall and slid it open, revealing a neatly organized closet. Reaching up to the top shelf, she pulled down a perfectly folded auburn blanket.

"Here," she said, handing it to her. "I get hot when I sleep, so I usually just sleep on top of the comforter with this over me. But obviously, do whatever you're comfortable with."

Jess nodded, suddenly feeling self-conscious.

Was it a bad idea to sleep in Sam's bed while she was having these—feelings? Yes, she was exhausted, but she didn't really need to rest *there*. It would only be a twenty-minute drive back to her house, and then she could sleep in her own bed. Besides, it's not like Sam had invited her over. She'd just showed up unannounced on her doorstep. Sam was probably just trying to be nice by letting her stay there.

She glanced around the room, contemplating what to do. Sam sat down in the chair and turned to the computer, immediately getting sucked back into whatever was on the three screens in front of her.

Knowing that Sam wasn't paying attention to what she was doing eased her anxiety a bit. Maybe she could just nap for a few minutes. Then she'd leave.

The thought of being alone in her own bed, trying to sleep while everything raced through her mind, seemed like actual torture. At least being here, she was with someone who she didn't have to pretend to be okay in front of.

She slid her shoes off and pushed herself further back onto the bed, before laying down. She threw the blanket out over her, letting it drape across her body.

She turned onto her side, facing Sam, and pulled the blanket up to her chin. The smell that was so uniquely Sam instantly filled her nose, and she knew she wasn't lying when she said she slept with it every night.

Her drooping eyes slowly closed, and she shifted her body, trying to relax as much as possible.

The firmness of the bed felt foreign, and the neckline of her sweatshirt squeezed against her windpipe. She shifted again, pulling the blanket up higher around her face.

Relax, she told herself, and let out a deep breath. She tried to shut everything out, loosening the different muscle groups in her body.

Another deep breath.

Her sweatshirt tugged against her throat, and she swallowed against the uncomfortable pressure. Maybe it was the clothes or the unfamiliar surroundings. Or maybe it was the fact that Sam was just a few feet away from her. Maybe it was everything. Although, as much as she hated to admit, it was probably the latter more than the rest.

She let out a heavy sigh. "I don't think I'll be able to fall asleep," she muttered, pushing up onto her elbows. "I should probably just go home."

Sam looked over at her with a frown. "Have you been sleeping at home?"

Jess looked down at the floor and shook her head.

Sam nodded slowly. "You need it. I can see it in your eyes. Whatever's going on in your head is going to be worse if you're sleep deprived on top of it."

Jess grimaced. She didn't like feeling weak or vulnerable. And the last thing she wanted was someone else seeing her in those states.

Sam stood up from the chair and walked back to the closet. She reached for the top shelf, farther to the right this time, and pulled out three more pillows, identical to the one Jess had beneath her head.

Sam tucked them under her arms and walked back to the bed.

"Here, stand up real quick."

Jess watched her curiously, and slowly pushed herself up, swinging her legs off the side of the bed to stand. Sam pulled back the comforter and pushed one pillow in so that it was standing on its long side, wedged between the bed and the comforter.

Then Sam turned to her. She opened her mouth to say something, then paused. She tilted her head and looked her up and down.

"Do you usually sleep in a hoodie?"

Jess shook her head. "No."

"Do you want to take it off?" Sam asked, like it was the most obvious thing in the world, but was trying her hardest to be patient.

"I—have nothing on underneath it," Jess muttered.

Sam, unfazed, walked back to the closet. She pulled a white t-shirt off of its hanger and came back, handing it to Jess. She cleared her throat awkwardly. "Um—I'll go get you more water while you change."

Jess watched her take the cup off the desk and walk out of the room, closing the door behind her. She sighed, turning her back to the door, and pulled off the hoodie she had on. She looked at the white t-shirt in her hands and, for a second, thought about the night in the rain at the diner. The way she felt listening to Sam speak. Things had changed since then, but she wondered if what she felt now had already been there that night.

She brought the shirt up and slid it over her head before sitting back down on the bed. Her body already felt more relaxed without the constricting sleeves and heavy material around her torso.

A small knock echoed off the door.

"I'm done," Jess said.

Sam walked in with a full cup of water and set it down on the desk again.

"Alright, lay down."

Jess rolled her eyes. "I might be a little out of it, but I do know how to lay in a bed."

Sam smirked, and Jess' heart fluttered.

"Yeah, but clearly you need some help with the actual sleep part." She picked one pillow up off the bed. "I had a tough time sleeping when I was a kid. My mom used to put pillows around me in a certain way and it always helped me fall asleep."

Jess watched her flip the pillow in her hands. Knowing that Sam was using something from her childhood to help her suddenly made it feel much more intimate. A warmth filled her chest, while her brain told her she should leave.

She dismissed it.

A nap was a nap, no matter how many pillows there were or where the idea originated from. It changed nothing. She just needed to get her feelings under control.

She sat back down on the bed and shimmied under the comforter.

Sam reached down toward Jess' knee and then stopped her hand in midair. "Uh—lift your top leg up, so you can put this pillow between them," she muttered.

The corner of Jess' lip twisted up in a small smirk. She'd never seen Sam look nervous before.

Jess took the next pillow from her and wedged it between her legs.

"Okay, now you hug this one," she said, handing her the last pillow. Then she pulled the comforter and blanket back over her before walking to the fan that was standing in the corner. Sam turned the dial, and it whirred to life, blowing cold air directly over the bed.

A chill ran through her body, and she pulled the blanket back up over her chin, tilting her head down into it.

"I'll wake you up if anyone calls your phone or anything," Sam said, returning to her seat in front of the computer.

Jess nodded slightly, watching Sam for a few more seconds before shutting her eyes.

She wasn't sure if it was the pillows, the cold air, or the new t-shirt, but she actually did feel more settled and comfortable than before.

Her mind began running through different thoughts and memories, one after the other. They started with Sam and the night before, then moved onto that morning and eventually her mother. She let her mind wander until the thoughts became too dark, and she forced them onto something else. Winter break would come soon, and she looked forward to the time off from school and lacrosse. She thought about what she might do over the break and wondered if she would see Sam. She wondered what their friendship would become once the volunteer program was over.

That thought drifted into another, and then another after that, until the thoughts morphed into dreams.

Dreams of Sam.

Dreams of her mother.

Dreams of her future.

Then, eventually, the dreams turned back into thoughts, and she slowly felt herself being pulled back into reality.

She tucked her chin further into the blanket surrounding her, relishing the warmth and comfort, not yet ready to let go of the sleepy, foggy feeling still lingering in her head.

The smell surrounding her felt good in her lungs and she inhaled deeply, letting the heaviness of sleep suck her in once more.

Finally, after what felt like a years-long sleep, she felt coherence fully re-entering her mind. She stirred beneath the heavy comforter, swallowing away the thickness in her mouth. Then she became faintly aware of clicking and tapping sounds coming from somewhere nearby.

She cracked one eye open, expecting to see her familiar bedroom. Instead, her vision filled with Sam in a dark room, the light of computer monitors illuminating her face in a whitish blue tint as her fingers jabbed at the keyboard in front of her.

All the memories of the day and the previous night flooded back to her at once, explaining where she was and why. She couldn't remember the last time she'd slept so deeply. Or so contently.

She shifted, and her muscles protested like she hadn't moved in years. Reaching up next to the pillow under her head, she tapped the screen of her phone.

It lit up, showing the time, one text from her dad, and one text from Scarlett.

5:27pm.

Her eyebrows raised. She'd slept for almost six hours. That was probably longer than any full night's sleep she'd gotten in months.

She cleared her throat, shifting again and pulling the comforter down to her waist.

Sam's head snapped up from the computer, a startled look on her face. "Hey," she said, blinking as her face softened. "How are you feeling?"

Jess cleared her throat. "Um—good actually." Her voice scraped out like gravel. She cleared her throat again. "I don't think I've slept that good in a while. Totally forgot where I was for a sec."

A pleased grin spread across Sam's face. "I told you. It's the pillow thing. Works every time."

Jess smiled sleepily, shaking her head. "I guess so." She pushed up off the bed, shifting into a sitting position with her back leaned against the wall, facing Sam. "Thanks for letting me ruin your perfectly made bed."

Sam laughed, and it sounded like music. "Anytime."

She tried not to read too much into that response.

Sam stood up from her chair and grabbed the cup of water from the desk, reaching out to hand it to her.

She stood above her, waiting as Jess took a few big gulps. When she was done, Sam placed the cup back down and, to Jess' surprise, climbed onto the bed, settling in next to her with her back against the wall.

They sat in silence for a few moments before Sam finally turned to her.

"Do you want to talk about it now?"

Jess pursed her lips, staring straight ahead.

Sam watched her for a few moments. "Whatever it is you felt last night is okay. But it's also okay to feel scared."

Jess shook her head. "I'm not scared."

"Then what are you?"

She shrugged. She didn't know what she was. Maybe she was scared, but she didn't feel like thinking about it.

She turned back to Sam. The glow from the computer was the only light in the room, and it cast perfect highlights over her face. She wasn't sure if it was the sleep or something else, but this was the first time she'd felt perfectly calm in a while. Like the permanently crushing weight of everything in her life had been temporarily lifted, and she could finally take a full breath.

She let her eyes wander shamelessly over Sam's face and neck, appreciating the sharp curves. Her mouth felt dry, and she swallowed hard when Sam's eyes met hers with an intense, curious stare.

"Why'd you leave last night?" Jess asked, her voice barely above a whisper.

Sam's face fell slightly, but she kept eye contact. "I won't be the person you cheat with."

Jess pulled her head back, stunned by the words. Technically, it was true, but it had never actually crossed her mind. She hated to admit it, but she hadn't even really thought about or considered Luke in it at all.

Guilt seeped into her chest. Sam was right to have left.

She closed her eyes, leaning her head back against the wall. "Why didn't you go to the clinic today?"

"I figured things would be awkward." Sam muttered. "I just wanted to put it off as long as possible."

Jess frowned, but kept her eyes shut, desperately trying to hold on to the calm feeling she'd had a few moments before.

She opened her eyes, tilting her head to look at Sam again. "Do you wish it was Jacie that kissed you instead?" she asked, her voice barely louder than a whisper.

Sam stared back for a few moments, then she dropped her eyes and exhaled. "I don't know."

Jess clenched her jaw to keep the hurt from showing on her face. The last thing she wanted was for Sam to think she was some pathetic girl with a crush.

She shifted her body slightly, turning toward Sam. "It felt like you wanted to kiss me back."

"It's not that I didn't *want* to kiss you," Sam replied, shaking her head. "It's just that—with Jacie, it would've been easy. Like scratching an itch. Stress relief with no strings attached. But with you, obviously it's different."

"Why? Why can't it just be that? Stress relief with no strings attached."

Sam frowned at her. "Look at how upset you were today."

Jess pursed her lips, her eyes flicking down to her lap.

"Correct me if I'm wrong, but it seems like the whole kissing a girl thing kind of freaked you out, so I'm assuming it's not something you'd ever thought about or wanted before."

Jess stayed silent.

"I don't know what's going through your head now, but I know from experience that if you think it is more than just a random spur-of-the-moment thing, then it can be a lot to process and work through."

Jess sighed. Thinking about it was the absolute last thing she wanted to do. For once in her life, she just wanted to act without thinking.

"Why can't it just be this?" she asked, embarrassed by how much it sounded like a plea. "No emotions. No strings attached."

Sam sighed. "You know it won't just be that."

If she let herself really think about it—about the implications of kissing Sam—it felt like the whole world was crumbling. But if she only thought about her lips on hers, her hands grasping her hips, then it felt like she'd discovered a whole new world. And she wasn't ready to let that go just yet.

"What if it really is just that?" she asked. "Why does it have to mean anything?"

Sam scoffed. "It's not like I'm just some random girl anymore. We're *frie*nds. We see each other every day. You want to screw that up for some random feeling you had at a party?"

Jess pursed her lips and looked away. She hated that Sam was right. They'd gotten closer over the last few weeks, and she didn't want to lose that.

"Why don't you just go for one of the girls at school? Like Jacie or something?"

Jess rolled her eyes, shooting Sam a pointed look. "Yeah, I'm pretty sure she only has eyes for you. Besides," she muttered, "it's not the same."

"What do you mean?"

Jess sighed. "I don't know. It's just different."

Sam gave her a slight nod. "Well, if you need someone to talk to about any of it, I'm here."

"Thanks," Jess said with a small, appreciative smile. Things hadn't gone exactly how she'd hoped, but she did feel better than before.

"Are you hungry? You want to grab dinner or something?" Sam asked.

"I wish, but I should probably go home. I have a lot of homework I need to finish before tomorrow."

Sam nodded and moved to get up from the bed. Jess slowly followed, stretching her sore muscles.

Sam walked her out to her car, and Jess was thankful for the company when she saw different groups of men standing near the street, laughing and drinking together. Their eyes followed them as they approached the car, and she felt uneasy knowing that Sam would be alone in the house after she left.

"Text me when you get back inside. And make sure you lock the door right away," she said, lowering her voice a few octaves.

Sam chuckled, following her gaze down the street toward the closest group of obnoxious men. "I'll be fine."

Jess grunted, watching them for a second longer, before looking back at Sam. "Thank you. For everything today."

"Anytime. I'm glad you decided to randomly show up," Sam replied with a teasing smirk.

Jess rolled her eyes, but couldn't help the grin that spread across her face. She felt the now familiar warmth reappearing in her chest, but this time there was no panic with it, like there had been the night before or that morning. That seemed like progress.

Jess stepped up into her car. She turned the key in the ignition but waited to leave until she watched Sam walk through the front door.

On the drive home, she rolled down the windows, letting the ice cold air rush over her and numb her mind. She focused on the slight sting against her skin, keeping her from being sucked into the thoughts in her head.

When she walked into her house, she saw her dad sitting on the couch, reading his iPad.

"Hey," he said, glancing up at her. "You're home late."

"Yeah, sorry," she mumbled.

"They keep you late at the clinic?"

"Uh—no. I went to a friend's house afterwards," she answered.

He grunted, looking back down at the iPad. "I texted you about dinner. There's some leftover food in the fridge if you're hungry."

"Thanks," she said, walking toward the stairs.

"Hey, wait," he called. "Do you still want me to ask that nurse about getting you into their program?"

Jess paused with one foot on the first step. She'd completely forgotten about that. Nothing had changed since that morning, so technically, she should still try to transfer out of the program. But for some reason, it just felt different. She didn't want to leave. Besides, there were only a few more weeks until winter break, and then the program would be over.

"No. No, that's okay," she answered, as she walked up the stairs. "Thanks though."

When she reached her bedroom, she glanced in the mirror and remembered that she was still wearing Sam's t-shirt. She gently pulled the neckline up to her nose, closing her eyes and inhaling the familiar scent.

If she was being honest, she hadn't actually forgotten to give it back. She'd thought about it before she left, but decided not to say anything. It was definitely up there on the list of the most pathetic things she'd done in her life, but she just wanted something that made her feel calm. And as much as she hated to admit it, Sam did that. Even just a small reminder of her was enough to make her relax.

She sighed, opening her eyes again and sitting down on her bed. She pulled her phone out of her pocket and felt a rush when she saw a new text.

SAM HAYES: Made it into the house alive :)

A smile spread over her face as she read it, the warmth in her chest instantly returning.

She tapped the screen, hovering her fingers over the keys to respond as Sam's words from earlier played in her mind.

I won't be the person you cheat with.

Guilt seeped back into her stomach. She knew what she needed to do.

She clicked out of the conversation and pulled up Luke's contact instead, sending him a quick text to meet in the morning before school started.

Chapter 12

"So then, why'd you break up with him?" Scarlett asked, her breath labored as they ran their third lap of the practice.

"We barely ever saw each other," Jess answered with a shrug. "I'm busy all the time and it wasn't fair to him."

Breaking up with Luke that morning had actually been a lot harder than she'd expected. She sort of assumed that he'd also become detached recently, given that they barely ever saw each other.

She was wrong. He argued the whole time, trying to convince her to give it a chance until winter break, when both their schedules would lighten up. And she hated to admit it, but he actually had a good point. If that was the *only* reason for the breakup, then it might have changed her mind.

But it wasn't. And she wasn't even ready to admit that to herself, much less to anyone else.

Sam's words the day before had stung, and the guilt clung to her all night. She felt horrible for never having considered Luke's feelings at all. And even worse for betraying his trust. Even though Sam had made it clear nothing else would happen between them, it still wouldn't be fair to stay with Luke after what happened.

"Are you gonna tell me what went down on Saturday?" Scarlett asked, although her tone said she already knew something.

Jess frowned, quickly glancing behind them to see if any of their teammates were within earshot.

She lowered her voice a bit. "I—" Anxiety crept up along the back of her neck. "I kissed Sam."

Scarlett gave no reaction.

Besides the huffing of their breaths, silence filled the air between them, and Jess felt the anxiety spreading further through her body as she waited for Scarlett to say something.

Finally, she glanced over at Jess. "Is that it?" she asked, almost sounding disappointed.

"Uh—yeah?" Jess answered, her eyebrows pulling together.

"Hmph," Scarlett grunted, looking straight ahead again.

"What?"

"Nothing, I guess I just expected more. Figured you guys fucked in the bathroom or something."

"Scar!" Jess yelled under her breath, turning to make sure no one was near them.

"Wait—*you* kissed *her*?" Scarlett asked, suddenly intrigued again.

"Yeah," Jess muttered.

"And then what? Did she kiss you back? Wait—is that why she left that night?"

"Yes, and yes."

They turned the last corner of the track and slowed to a walk as Coach Lowe blew his whistle, signaling the end of practice. Scarlett hung back, waiting until the rest of the team had crossed the field ahead of them.

"So, what now? Are you gonna do it again?"

"Do what again?"

"Kiss her, obviously. Or—I don't know—more than kissing?" Scarlett asked, her lips tilting up into a smirk.

Jess rolled her eyes. "No. It won't happen again. The kissing or anything else."

"What? Why not?"

The last thing she wanted to do was recount how Sam had technically rejected her the night before.

"She doesn't want to. Besides, I'm not throwing away everything I've worked for just because of some stupid onetime crush."

Scarlett frowned. "Do you think that's all it is?"

"Yes. Definitely. I spend like four hours a day with her almost every day of the week. I spend more time with her than I do with anyone else right now. So of course I developed some type of attraction." she paused, looking around again before lowering her voice. "I'm not a lesbian or bi or anything like that."

Scarlett stopped their slow walk and turned to look at her. "You know it'd be okay if you were, though, right?"

Jess pursed her lips, peering down at the ground. "It doesn't matter, because I'm not," she crossed her arms over her chest. "It was an emotional day, and I wasn't thinking."

Scarlett looked like she wanted to say more. Jess was glad she didn't. "Okay, if you say so."

Jess gave a quick nod before walking to where the coach and team had huddled together to go over the practice schedule for the next few days.

After they finished, the team dispersed, and Jess changed in the locker room before heading to the clinic.

By the time she arrived, Sam was already there, laser focused on her laptop. When Jess walked in, she pulled her headphones off, resting them around her neck.

"Hey," she said with a wide smile. "How was practice?"

"It was okay," she replied, settling into her usual spot at the desk. "Lots of conditioning, though."

Sam made a disgusted face. "I'm surprised they're having you do conditioning this close to the finals."

"Yeah," Jess answered, immediately followed by a yawn.

The front door opened and Sam's eyes darted up, watching a few people walk into the hallway. She frowned as she looked over at them, then tapped the screen on her phone.

"Waiting for someone?" Jess asked.

"Uh—no," Sam muttered, craning her neck to look through the open door to the main auditorium. Right on cue, Laura walked through the door, writing something on her clipboard.

"Hey, Laura," Sam said as she approached them at the desk. "Is Ricky in there?"

"No," she replied absentmindedly. "I haven't seen him."

Sam leaned back in her chair as she watched the front door again. "Was he here yesterday?"

"Um, no. I don't think so. Why?"

Sam frowned. "Just wondering."

Laura watched her for a moment before dropping the clipboard on the desk and returning to the auditorium.

"Everything okay?" Jess asked.

"Yeah. Yeah, I'm sure it's fine," Sam shook her head before standing up and stretching her arms. "You want any coffee? Before they close the doors."

"Yeah, sure. Thanks."

Sam disappeared into the room as Jess organized her work for the night. When she walked back out holding two coffees, she shut the door behind her, leaving them alone in the hallway.

"Thanks," Jess said as Sam handed her one of the cups. They took a few sips in comfortable silence.

"So," Jess started, clearing her throat. "I told Scarlett about the other night."

"Yeah?" Sam asked, her eyebrows raising.

Jess nodded. "Yeah. I just wanted you to know that she knows now."

"Oh, okay. Thanks for the heads up."

Jess took another careful sip of the hot coffee. "Um—also, I broke up with Luke this morning."

This time, Sam's head jerked back. "Really? Why?"

Jess shrugged. "It wasn't working," she said, not wanting to go into too many details. "And I wasn't being fair to him."

Sam nodded, giving her an apologetic look. "I'm sorry it didn't work out."

"Yeah," Jess mumbled as she took another sip from her cup. She wasn't sure what else to say. Now that it was done, she just wanted to move past it.

Jess finished her coffee and then they both settled into their tasks for the night, only talking occasionally when Sam offered to get more coffee or during the rare times she removed her headphones.

Finally, when the last of the patrons had left, Laura said goodbye and the two of them gathered their things to lock up.

Jess pulled her phone out as she waited for Sam to lock the front doors. There was a new text from her dad letting her know he'd be home late and wouldn't make it for dinner. She actually felt a little disappointed since this was the first night in a long time that she wasn't buried in homework and projects that had to get done by the next day. Sitting at home alone didn't sound like the worst, but it also didn't sound super appealing.

"Hey, are you doing anything after this?" Jess asked.

"Uh, no," Sam said, zipping the keys back into her backpack. "Why?"

"Do you want to hang out?" Jess asked, suddenly feeling a pang of nerves rise in her stomach.

A wide grin spread across Sam's face. "Yeah, sure. What do you wanna do?"

Jess shrugged, feeling Sam's smile infect her as a smirk pulled itself onto her own lips. "Is Chris at your house?"

Sam snorted. "No, he's almost never there. I basically live alone."

Jess felt a small surge of anger course through her at the thought of Sam being left alone in that neighborhood.

"Could we watch a movie or something at your house?" she asked. "My dad's working late and I just don't really feel like being alone."

"Yeah, of course" Sam gave her a warm, understanding smile as they walked together to the parking lot.

Chapter 13

"That was the dumbest ending they could've ever chosen," Sam said, grunting as she sat up to grab the remote from the foot of the bed.

"It was not!" Jess argued, taking a handful of chips from the bag between them. "You just hate it because it wasn't a *happy* ending. But really, if you think about it, him dying at the end was the most realistic."

Sam scoffed, laying back down beside her, one arm tucked behind her head on top of the pillow they were sharing.

This had quickly become their new routine after that first night earlier in the week. They'd leave the clinic and she would follow Sam to her house, where they would eat dinner together and either work on homework or watch movies, or both.

And they quickly learned they had extreme opposite tastes in movies. Sam loved romantic comedies and anything with guns or fight scenes in it. And, much to her dismay, Jess had a preference for thrillers and horror movies.

If she were being fully honest though, horror movies hadn't been her favorite until after they'd watched the first one. Sam had basically kept her face tucked into Jess' shoulder for two hours straight, only peaking out when she promised her there was nothing scary about to happen.

Maybe it was wrong, but those two hours with her tucked into her shoulder had made her smile more than every other night combined. And it was hard to let go of that.

"What was the point of it, then? No one got the gold and literally every single person died. Why did we just watch that whole thing if it ended with things being exactly the same as they were at the beginning of the movie?" Sam replied as she scrolled through her Hulu account.

"*That* is exactly the point. It was *realistic.*"

"Hmph," Sam grunted. "More like depressing."

Jess smiled, shaking her head. Arguing with Sam about the movie endings was an experience all on its own.

She picked up her phone, frowning when she saw the time. "I should probably go home," she said, trying not to sound as reluctant as she felt.

"What? Why?" Sam asked, turning her head on the pillow. It left their faces only inches apart.

"It's late," she answered as a wide yawn pulled through her mouth, right on cue. "And if I lay here any longer, I'm definitely gonna fall asleep."

Sam shrugged, turning back to the TV. "You can stay the night if you want."

Her heart rate ticked up a few notches.

"I mean," Sam continued absentmindedly, still scrolling through movies. "It's Friday, so it's not like we have to be at school in the morning."

She thought about it for a moment. Laying in bed next to Sam watching a movie was hard enough. Spending the entire night sleeping next to her was probably not a good idea.

But, on the other hand, Sam had made it very clear that she didn't want anything to happen between them. They were just friends, and Sam would make sure it stayed that way. So, maybe she was overthinking the whole thing.

"Uh—okay. Yeah, sure."

"Sweet, another movie?" Sam asked with a wide smile. Her heart fluttered again.

"Yeah," she replied, pulling her phone out to text her dad. "But this one better be scary."

Sam rolled her eyes. "I don't understand how you actually enjoy those. Why would anyone want to make themselves feel scared on purpose? It's like voluntary torture."

Jess shrugged, a hidden smirk on her lips as she texted her dad that she'd be staying the night.

She paused, looking over the message. The way he'd reacted when Sam came to pick her up that one day popped into her mind. It wasn't that she wanted to lie to him, but she also didn't want to deal with him acting weird for no reason. She tapped the screen and changed the message to say that she was staying the night at Scarlett's house.

"Alright, what about this one?" Sam asked, motioning toward the TV.

There was a young woman on the screen with blood covering her face, and a man with an ax standing behind her. She cringed. It looked terrible. Maybe this was a good time to end the scary movie watching.

Then a warmth touched her shoulder. She felt Sam leaning into her, subconsciously moving farther from the TV. That fiery feeling bloomed in her chest at the contact.

"Sure, looks great."

The first thirty minutes of the movie were so awful that she almost gave in, ready to tell Sam to put on one of the romantic comedies she wanted instead. But for what it lacked in plot, and just about anything story related, it made up for in jump scares. Almost every couple of minutes, there was something popping up on the screen that made Sam jump and curl up into Jess' side. At one point, she even tucked her head so close to her that Jess could swear she felt her breath against her neck.

So, no, she was definitely not going to give in and change the movie, even if it meant sitting through another hour of crappy plot points.

"Tell me when it's over," Sam groaned, for what was probably the tenth time that night.

Jess smiled. She'd never seen her so out of her element. "It's over. You can look now."

Sam pulled her hand down from her face and, as if on cue, the ax murderer popped out behind the main character.

"Ah!" she yelled, covering her eyes again and shoving Jess' arm. "You asshole!"

Jess laughed, pushing her back.

"Ugh," Sam groaned, pausing the movie. "I need more snacks if I'm gonna sit through another hour of this."

She climbed over Jess and walked to the door. "You want anything?" she called over her shoulder, disappearing into the hallway.

"I'm good," Jess called back, picking up her phone to scroll TikTok as she waited.

A minute later, Sam re-appeared with a Kitkat and another bag of chips, plopping down on her usual spot of the bed before pressing play on the remote. She tore the Kitkat open, chomping down on a big bite.

"I can't believe you actually enjoy this," she mumbled through a mouthful of chocolate.

"You would too if you weren't such a baby," Jess answered, swiping the Kitkat from her hand. She peeled the wrapper back another inch and took a bite.

"If this doesn't terrify you, I'm pretty sure you're a psychopath."

Sam reached to take the Kitkat back, but Jess pulled it out of her reach. "You're scared of this, but you're not scared of riding on your motorcycle?" She took another bit. "Pretty sure *you're* the psychopath."

Sam rolled her eyes, stretching again to snatch the Kitkat back. Jess pulled it back just before she could get it.

"At least the motorcycle wouldn't jump out and scare me before killing me."

"Yeah, but your chances of dying on that are much higher than dying from a serial killer."

Sam shot her hand out once more, but Jess yanked it back just in time. Sam threw her a determined look and Jess let a teasing smirk spread across her mouth.

Then Sam lunged toward the Kitkat, twisting her body over her.

Jess erupted in laughter, pulling the Kitkat up by her head to keep it out of Sam's reach. She felt Sam laughing above her as she tried and failed again to reach it.

Sam let her body drop down, settling on top of her. "This is why I asked if you wanted anything! I knew you'd steal whatever I got," she laughed.

Jess could hardly focus on formulating a response while Sam's body pressed on top of hers.

Sam pulled her head up to look at her with that mischievous smirk, and Jess broke out into laughter, knowing she was about to try again.

Suddenly, Sam jolted upward, her hand outstretched once more.

Jess' breath instantly caught in her throat. Sam's hips pressed tightly against her as she stretched, making the contact much more intimate than before.

Her whole body froze, not bothering to pull the Kitkat back this time.

"Ha!" Sam yelled, still laughing as Jess felt it being pulled from her hand.

Her heart beat furiously in her chest as she felt other parts of her body reacting to the contact.

"Sam," she croaked, her voice a warning.

The girl stopped laughing, looking down at her in concern, their faces only inches apart.

Jess swallowed hard, completely frozen.

Sam scanned her face for a moment before her expression changed from confusion to understanding.

Jess turned her head to the side, too embarrassed to meet her gaze. "I'm sorry," she whispered.

Sam shook her head softly. "Don't be. You didn't do anything wrong."

She felt a sting prickle behind her eyes and looked up at the ceiling, taking a slow, steadying breath.

Then she looked back at Sam. There was something in her eyes that she hadn't expected to see. She couldn't exactly pinpoint what it was, but it reminded her of the night they kissed.

Sam remained perfectly still and, for a moment, Jess wondered if maybe Sam wanted to be there just as much as she wanted her there.

The thought sent a fresh jolt of electricity through her body.

Sam's mouth seemed to inch closer to hers, their eye contact never breaking.

Jess' mouth went dry.

Finally, she was so close that Jess could feel the heat radiating off her lips. She subconsciously held her breath.

Sam's lips brushed against hers, so lightly she almost wondered if she'd imagined it.

Then, fire erupted across her skin in one gigantic wave.

Every thought disappeared. Every other feeling in her body disappeared.

And all at once, she forgot why she'd ever thought it was a bad idea.

The feeling of Sam's lips against hers was the only thing that mattered in the entire world at that moment.

She lifted one hand, grabbing the back of Sam's neck, and she instantly felt her deepen the kiss. Within a second, every feeling coursing through her took over, telling her body what to do. It felt almost primal. So natural, it was like taking that first breath after being submerged under water for too long.

Sam kissed her faster, their tongues quickly finding each other, shooting electricity through Jess' mouth and down her neck.

This was it.

If she lived her entire life never feeling another human being again, that would be okay. The thought ran through her head that nothing in the world could be better than Sam's mouth pressed against hers.

But she was wrong.

A second later, Sam shifted, and her hips ground down between Jess' now wide open legs. The effect was instant.

It ignited the urgent pulsating once again.

Her body tightened, and she grabbed a fistful of Sam's shirt on her lower back, her nails scraping against the exposed flesh.

She felt Sam's body contract as she pulled her hips back a fraction before grinding down against her once again.

Jess' eyelids fluttered, waves of pleasure crashing through her body. She wrapped her left leg around Sam, desperately working to keep the girl's body right where she needed it most. Sam's teeth nipped at her lower lip. A tremor ran through her, the feeling between her legs building to a new high.

That's when she realized.

It was building too much.

Too fast.

No, no, no.

This couldn't be happening already.

Sam said they couldn't do this, and she had no idea how far gone Jess already was. It wasn't right for her to let it happen.

Another burst of feeling shot through her body and she knew that she only had seconds to stop what was about to happen.

"S–Sam," she managed to get out, her voice a shaky warning.

Sam pulled her face back an inch, resting her forehead against Jess' as she looked into her eyes with that deep hunger she'd seen a minute earlier.

"I know," she whispered. "It's okay."

Every fiber in her body erupted at the sound of those words.

Everything that had built up suddenly released and crashed through her in one massive tidal wave of sensation.

She wrapped both her legs around Sam's waist, bucking her hips against her in short, wild bursts as the feelings pumped relentlessly through her.

Her back arched up off the bed. She frantically grabbed onto Sam, digging her nails into the skin on her back.

Every inch of Sam's body pressed against her, satisfying her desperate cravings.

Then finally, when she almost thought she couldn't take it anymore, the last wave subsided, and all at once her body relaxed in a way it never had before.

Her back dropped down onto the bed.

She gently loosened her grip on Sam's back. One leg dropped back down to the bed, but she kept the other wrapped loosely around Sam's waist.

Her breath came out in ragged bursts as Sam shifted above her, carefully moving her hips to the side so they no longer pushed against Jess' now extremely sensitive area.

She laid there with her eyes closed, one hand still clinging to Sam's shirt, enjoying the feeling of bliss that engulfed her.

Perfectly calm relaxation.

That feeling lasted about three and a half seconds.

Then the rush of thoughts pounded their way back in, each one delivering its own special blend of fear and anxiety.

What does this mean?

What if Trinity somehow found out?

What would mom think if she were still alive?

Her eyes shot open. That last thought looped in her mind, practically screaming at her.

Sam was still halfway on top of her, watching like she knew what was about to happen.

"Are yo—"

"I need to go to the bathroom," Jess said, cutting her off as she pushed up onto her elbows.

Sam immediately moved to the side, making room for her to get up off the bed. Jess pushed herself up and rushed out of the room into the hallway. Her eyes darted around, finding the bathroom door. She shoved it open, bursting inside with a heaving breath.

What would mom think if she were still alive?

She shut the door behind her and dropped onto the closed lid on top of the toilet.

What would mom think?

What about Trinity?

Mom.

Trinity.

The thoughts attacked, each one like a fresh punch in her already beat up gut. Her breathing became fast and shallow, and she couldn't tell if it was still from the orgasm or from the anxiety that now wreaked havoc on her body.

She squeezed her eyes shut, pressing her palms against her brow with so much force it made pain radiate through her forehead.

Trinity.

Mom.

Mom.

What would she think?

A familiar buzz formed in her hands, and she knew she needed to force herself to take full breaths.

She dropped her hands into her lap as she opened her eyes. Spots swam through her vision, and the edges of her eyes darkened in a rhythm that she assumed was her pulse.

"Hey, are you okay?" Sam's muffled voice came through the door.

The words snapped her back to reality for the moment. She tried to say something, but the it caught in her throat, dried out by the quick puffs of air going in and out of her lungs.

What would she think?

What would she think?

The buzzing spread from her hands up into her biceps.

Blood rushed in her ears.

What would she think?

"Jess?"

What would she think?

She opened her mouth, but again no sound came out.

The air caught in her throat. A strangled cough escaping her lips.

What would she think?

Suddenly, the door swung open. Within an instant, Sam was crouched on her knees in front of her.

"Hey," she said, her tone commanding and urgent, yet still gentle. "Look at me."

Jess' eyes frantically shot up.

Sam lifted her hands to rest them on Jess' thighs, but paused at the last second, dropping them by her sides.

"Jess, what color are my eyes?"

Jess stared at her, trying to calm her breathing enough to speak. She knew what she was doing. She had a vague memory of her therapist doing this when she was little. Trying to distract her when she had panic attacks after her mother died.

The buzzing in her arms rose to her neck. Maybe this was actually a heart attack.

A breath released from her chest, but for some reason, a new one refused to come in.

Her vision darkened a shade.

Too dark.

Her arms tensed, and she reached forward, grabbing onto Sam's arm.

"Jess, do you have a Costco membership?"

What?

This yanked her back for a second.

She stared at her, blinking, unsure of what she'd heard.

"Or does your dad have one?" Sam continued.

"I–" Jess choked on the word, but some sound came out.

"Jess," Sam repeated, with so much intensity it sounded like her life depended on it. "Do you or your dad have a Costco membership?"

Jess stared at her, wondering if she'd gone completely insane since she'd entered the bathroom and was actually imagining this whole thing.

"I—don't—" the words stung against her throat. "Well—yeah," she shook her head slightly. "He has one."

"Do you have cable TV?"

Jess blinked at her.

Yeah, she was definitely going insane.

"Uh—" she swallowed, the sting in her throat subsiding a fraction. "No. No, we—don't. Just—Netflix," she swallowed again, shaking her head slightly. "And Hulu."

Sam nodded seriously, like she was contemplating a life or death situation. "More people in the US now have Costco memberships than cable TV in their house."

Jess blinked again, her mouth parting slightly. "What?"

"There are more households in the US that have Costco memberships than cable TV."

Jess stared at her, her eyebrows slowly pulling together.

"I—" she shook her head slightly, still wondering if she had somehow misunderstood every word Sam had just said. "Are you—okay?" she asked, her voice an even mixture of concern and suspicion.

The corners of Sam's mouth tugged upward just enough for Jess to notice. "Yeah. Are you?"

That's when she realized she was breathing again. Full, deep breaths.

The buzzing in her limbs had subsided, and her vision appeared to be back to normal as she stared at Sam's face.

"Um—yeah actually," she said, still feeling like she was in a mild daze.

Sam gave her a small, warm smile. "What do you need now?"

Jess watched the way her perfectly curved lips moved when she spoke, unable to form a response.

"Do you want me to take you home?"

Jess shook her head once to clear the fog that had formed. "No. No, that's okay." She stood up, her legs trembling like she'd just run a marathon.

Sam lifted her arm to hold on to her, but froze midway in the air. "Is this okay?" she asked, glancing at her hand.

Jess nodded and felt instant relief as Sam's arm snaked around her waist, keeping her stable as they walked back to the bedroom.

They sat down on the bed, and Jess noticed Sam shift a few extra inches away from her.

"I'm sorry," she whispered, her voice raw and foreign to her own ears.

Sam frowned. "Why are you sorry?"

Jess shook her head, trying to push down the guilt in her chest. "I just—don't want you to think it's because of you."

Sam's eyes flicked down to her lap for a split second before shooting back up. Something about it made Jess' heart ache.

"I wanted that so much," Jess whispered. "I wanted *you* so much. I still do."

The look in Sam's eyes shifted the smallest amount.

"Is that why you're upset?" Sam asked. "You hoped that would get it out of your system, but it didn't?"

"No, I—" she paused, looking down. For the first time, she wished desperately that she could explain everything she was feeling to another person. If Sam could hear the torturous thoughts that ripped her to pieces just moments ago, maybe she would understand.

Sam waited, watching her intently.

"I just—" she tried again, the words sticking in the back of her throat. She opened her mouth a fraction, hoping something would come up, but nothing did. Finally, she shook her head, the trapped words in her mouth sliding back down to their lifelong prison in her chest. "Can we just lay down?" she asked, hating how small her voice sounded.

Sam frowned. "Are you sure you don't want me to take you home?"

Jess shook her head once. "I want to stay here," she paused, looking up at her. "If that's still okay?"

"Of course it is," Sam answered with a sympathetic smile. "I just want to make sure you're okay."

"I am. I promise."

Sam watched her for another second before nodding and getting up off the bed. "Do you want some of my clothes to sleep in?"

Jess looked down at the jeans and hoodie she was wearing. "Yeah, sure. Thanks."

Sam retrieved a plain black t-shirt and a pair of soccer shorts from the closet, handing them to her. "Uh—" she shifted on her feet, scratching the back of her neck. She seemed to do that every time she felt uncomfortable. Probably a nervous habit. "I'll go grab us some water while you change."

Sam walked out into the hallway, closing the door behind her. Jess stood up from the bed, her muscles aching in protest. Her lower abdomen felt tight, which didn't come as a surprise. The soreness in her chest, however, was a surprise. The muscles had probably cramped up from the fast, short breathing in the bathroom. Hopefully, a few hours of sleep would loosen them again.

A light knock came through the door.

She quickly slid on the pair of shorts and pulled the shirt over her head. "Yeah, come in."

Sam walked past her, setting two cups of ice water on the desk. She cleared her throat awkwardly as she turned around. "Um—I can sleep out on the couch and you can sleep in here."

"Oh," Jess mumbled, hating the disappointment that bloomed in her chest. "Okay, yeah. If that's what you want."

"Well, what do you want?"

Jess looked back up at her. She was tired. Too tired to continue hiding her feelings.

"I want you to sleep in here."

Sam's throat bobbed as she swallowed. "Okay."

"But," Jess continued, "only if you're comfortable with that."

A hint of a smile skittered across Sam's face and Jess' heart swelled. "Yeah. I am."

Sam went to the closet again, and Jess slid under the comforter, shifting closer to the wall to make room. She watched as Sam dropped another pillow on the edge of the bed and then returned to the closet. She pulled out a new pair of gray sweats with a white t-shirt and walked out into the hallway.

A minute later, the sound of running water floated down the hall. Jess closed her eyes, taking a deep breath. No matter what, she needed to keep those thoughts from re-entering her mind. She pulled the comforter up to her chin, inhaling another deep breath.

A few minutes later, Sam reappeared in the doorway wearing the new outfit, the old items clutched in her hands. She tossed them into a hamper in the closet as she made her way toward the desk.

"Do you want me to plug your phone in to charge overnight?" she asked, taking a big gulp from one of the cups of water.

"Yeah, thanks."

Jess checked the phone one last time before handing it to her.

She plugged it in and then shut off the lights before getting into the bed. She shifted onto her back, leaving a wide space between them.

Jess shifted onto her right side, facing her.

After a moment, Sam tilted her head, meeting her gaze with a soft smile. The TV was still on, and the light perfectly illuminated the curves of her face in the dark.

"Are you tired?" Sam asked.

Jess nodded. "My body is."

"You probably shouldn't play in the football game tomorrow."

"Oh," Jess replied, her voice thick with exhaustion. "I forgot to tell you. I won't be there tomorrow. We have an extra long practice in the morning to go over things for the first semi-final game next week."

"Man, now I won't have any competition at all," Sam answered with a smirk.

Jess smiled, shifting her body an inch closer to Sam. She held her hand up to her mouth as she yawned, then dropped it back onto the bed, just an inch from Sam's shoulder.

"At least you'll have Ricky there to play against."

She watched the crinkles around Sam's smiling eyes release.

211

"Yeah, maybe. If he shows up." A hint of worry came through her voice.

"You don't think he will?"

Sam shrugged, her shoulder moving just enough to brush against Jess' fingers for a fraction of a second.

"As far as I know, he hasn't been to the clinic since that last day we talked."

Jess' heart ached as she watched the worry fill Sam's face. She wished she could say something to make her more at ease, but soothing words weren't exactly her strong suit.

Instead, she lifted her hand and gently laid it on Sam's bicep. She waited a beat to see if Sam would reject the touch, but when she remained still, Jess began rubbing slow circles with her thumb against the soft skin beneath her sleeve.

It wasn't much, but it did the trick.

Sam's eyes changed as she looked at her, like she was being pulled back into the present moment. Just like when she'd rubbed her hand that night in the diner.

"That feels good," Sam whispered, her voice low and coarse.

A tiny jolt of electricity ran through Jess' body. Those words mixed with the tone of her voice inspired something inside of her.

Jess carefully leaned her head forward, never breaking eye contact. She watched Sam's eyes for any sign that told her she shouldn't continue the advance.

There was none.

Sam's lips were mere millimeters away. Her heart raced, adrenaline coursing through her veins, despite the exhaustion.

She scanned her face one last time.

Then she closed her eyes and gently pressed her lips against Sam's.

The kiss was painstakingly slow.

She felt each tiny movement and texture against her lips.

It was completely different from any other kiss they'd. Any other kiss she'd *ever* had.

When she finally pulled her mouth back, her lips tingled. The now familiar pulse between her thighs had returned, but it felt different this time. Deeper, but less urgent.

She watched Sam's throat move as she swallowed.

Jess let her head rest on the pillow next to Sam's, their eyes still locked together.

"I'm glad I stayed tonight," Jess whispered, her eyes drooping as the adrenaline slowly dissipated.

"Me too."

Chapter 14

J ess' legs burned as she sprinted down the field toward the ball.

Again, she beat everyone else to it, easily scooping it off the turf. She eyed the defense and quickly spotted an opening to the goal.

Cradling the ball close to her chest, she juked around one defender then sprinted past another. The opportunity presented itself and she took it, swinging her arms down hard as she launched the ball toward the upper corner of the net.

The goalie's stick shot up just a second too late, and Jess watched the ball ripple across the back of the net.

Coach Lowe whistled, signaling the score as he jogged toward the net. "Good hustle, Miller."

"Fuck yeah! Scrimmage MVP!" Scarlett yelled as she ran up, tapping her stick against hers.

"Hey!" Coach Lowe shot her a scolding look. "Language, Scarlett."

"Yeah, yeah. Sorry," she muttered.

"Alright ladies, that's it for today," he called across the field to the rest of the team. "Let's wrap it up. You know the drill."

The team dispersed, dropping their gear on the sidelines before working together to remove each bright orange goal post from the field. Jess, along with a few other girls, dropped one of the goal posts near the shed where they stored them. She turned, scanning the field, and spotted a group of left over cones on the far side. As she walked toward them, Scarlett jogged up behind her.

"So, how was your date last night?"

Jess glanced at her, unamused. "I told you, they're not dates. We just—" she paused, her mind replaying the events of the previous night, "hangout."

Scarlett raised her eyebrow. "Um, what was that hesitation? I was just teasing, but did something happen?"

Jess swallowed, glancing around them on the field to ensure no one was listening. "We kissed again last night."

Scarlett beamed like a giddy child. "Ah finally! Fuck!"

Jess couldn't help the smirk that drew up on her lips.

"Just a kiss?" Scarlett asked, her tone the slightest bit skeptical.

Jess looked at the ground, watching her feet trudge through the turf. She cleared the awkward feeling out of her throat. "We kinda made out."

Scarlett's grin grew impossibly wide. "Oh, my god!" she squealed.

Jess shushed her, quickly glancing around. A few of the girls on their team had wandered toward them, huddled in a group talking. Luckily, they were still far enough away that she didn't think they'd heard Scarlett's outburst.

Jess crossed her arms over her chest, glaring at her. "Can you please try not to announce it to our entire team?"

"Yeah, yeah. So, how was it?" she asked with a beaming smile.

The memories of the night flashed through her mind. She looked away.

215

"I don't know. I kinda freaked out afterwards."

Scarlett frowned, a sympathetic smile replacing the one already adorning her face. "Why?"

Jess shrugged. She wasn't willing to let those thoughts fill her head again, even if it was just to get them off her chest.

"I don't know," she muttered.

Scarlett stared at her, and Jess could tell there were things she wanted to say.

A whistle blew behind them, and the coach called for everyone to gather. They jogged the rest of the way to the stray cones, quickly collecting them before running back to the team. He then ran through the practice schedule for the following week leading up to their next semi-final game.

Between the extended practice schedule and volunteering, on top of her normal school work and college prep courses, her week would be packed. But surprisingly, one of the first worries she had was about whether she'd be able to fit in her nightly hangouts with Sam. She forced it away, convincing herself that Sam was only on her mind because of the conversation with Scarlett.

After the team finished meeting, they all scattered to collect their things. Jess went to her bag and pulled out her phone. Her heart rate increased when she saw an unread text from Sam. She tapped on it, and a picture of the football field appeared.

> SAM HAYES: *The games are definitely more fun with you here*

Jess couldn't help the smile that fought its way onto her lips.

She typed out a quick reply.

I think I would've had more fun there. Coach kicked our asses today.

She sent the message and then paused, another thought running through her head.

Was Ricky there?

She sent the second text and turned up the volume on her phone before sliding it into the front pocket of her lacrosse backpack.

She swung the bag over her shoulders and walked to where Scarlett was sitting on the turf, packing up her things.

"Wanna get Chipotle?" Scarlett asked as she carelessly stuffed her equipment into her overflowing bag. It was a wonder she never lost anything in there.

"Sure," Jess answered, chuckling as she watched her struggle to zip up the bag.

The ding of her phone alert went off, and she reached around her back, pulling it out of the pocket.

SAM HAYES: Nope, never showed.

She frowned, reading the message.

try not to worry too much. I'm sure everything is fine

She sent the message and slid the phone back in the pocket as Scarlett stood up, finally ready to go.

***

Church the next day was a disaster.

"When did that happen?" her dad asked as they walked out of the building to the parking lot.

Jess shrugged. "A few days ago."

Apparently Luke had also forgotten to tell his parents about their breakup. Which made things pretty awkward when Luke's mom came over to invite them out to lunch, and Jess had to explain that they were no longer dating. Mrs. Adams looked as if she was the one that had been broken up with. That was the first time Jess realized where Luke got his puppy dog pout from.

"Hmph," her dad grunted as he got into the truck. Then he turned the radio on and an excited football announcers voice filled the car.

She knew then that the conversation was over, and she couldn't have been more grateful. The last thing she wanted to do was talk to her dad about a breakup.

"I'm going to the clinic after this," she said.

"Kay," he muttered, with a look that said everything besides the announcers voice was going in one ear and out the other.

It was raining by the time she pulled into the parking lot at the clinic, and she saw Sam outside wheeling her bike up near the entrance beneath the cover. The sight reminded her of the night at the diner, and she felt her stomach flutter the slightest bit at the memory.

She gathered her things and jumped out of the car, jogging to the entrance as the rain pounded against her shoulders.

"Hey," she called to Sam as she jogged the last few steps to the front door.

Sam turned around, and a smile instantly spread across her face. Maybe Sam was just as excited to see her.

Small droplets of water ran down Sam's face and neck, disappearing into her black hoodie. She ran one hand through her wet hair, shaking the water out of it.

Suddenly, Jess wished they were alone in Sam's room again.

No. She shook that thought from her head.

This couldn't be a regular thing. She needed to focus on getting into Trinity. She couldn't afford to be distracted by something, or someone, that could ruin her chances of accomplishing the one thing she'd wanted for most of her life.

"Have fun at church?" Sam asked as she wiped water off the bike seat.

Jess cringed, remembering the awkward run-in she'd had. "Definitely wish I'd skipped today."

Sam chuckled, looking up at her with questioning eyes. "Why didn't you?"

"We've never skipped," Jess shrugged, walking toward the front doors. "Not since my mom died."

She froze, realizing the words that had left her mouth.

The words that had so *easily* left her mouth.

She hadn't even thought about it. She just replied honestly, her brain not filtering the way it usually did.

"Why not?" Sam asked, her expression curious but also gentle. Jess wondered if the sudden honesty had surprised her, too.

She stood there for a second, still dumbfounded. "Uh, we—" she started, before feeling the familiar stickiness in her mouth. She waited for the words to come, but they were already long gone. A ghost of a conversation left unfinished.

"I don't know," she finished. It was an obvious lie, but she knew Sam wouldn't push her on it.

Sam watched her for a beat, then she nodded and took a step forward, pushing through the front doors.

The hallway was empty, but Jess could see a meeting in session through the small window of the closed door to the auditorium. She dropped her bag on the ground behind the desk as she sat in her usual chair and pulled out her camera.

"How's the video going?" Sam asked, opening her laptop.

Jess shrugged. "It's okay. Better now that I've been able to get a few people to do interviews. But I still don't think it's enough."

"I'll do one if you need it," Sam replied. "I mean, I'm not an addict, but it might be cool to have a different perspective on the video."

"Really?" Jess asked, raising her eyebrows. "Yeah, that would be amazing, but only if you're completely comfortable with it."

Sam smiled, draping her arm over the back of the chair, and resting her chin on her hand. "Totally cool with it. I'm an open book."

Jess' eyes flickered down, tracing the curves of her arm and hand.

No. Stop.

"Thank you. Seriously, this helps a ton." Jess smiled, pulling her eyes away and popping the lens cap off the camera.

"Do you want to do it now?" Jess asked.

"Sure. If you want to."

"Well, I'd be thrilled to do anything that's not filing. So, yes."

Sam chuckled beside her.

She turned the camera on and held it up, crossing her legs and resting her elbow on her thigh.

"Um—so." She suddenly felt subconscious. The past interviewees had all sort of talked on their own about whatever they felt was relevant. Jess hadn't really done much besides hold the camera and nod politely as they spoke.

Sam smirked, like she knew what she was thinking. Of course she did.

"What is—" Jess cleared her throat, unsure of how to phrase the question. "Or *was* the hardest part of being the child of an addict?"

Sam looked to the side for a moment. "I think probably the instability. Like always swinging back and forth between good months or weeks and bad ones." She cleared her throat before looking back at the camera. "When you're a kid, you don't really get it. You don't understand why they can't just stop if they say they want to stop, you know?"

"Do you think that causes resentment?" Jess asked.

"Oh, one hundred percent," Sam answered. "You have no real understanding of what they're going through. So, in your mind, they're just *choosing* to let you down most days. They're *choosing* to break their promises to you. And then you have all these adults in your life telling you it's not their fault or they can't help it. Which, I think, actually makes you resent them more because it feels like everyone is taking their side over yours."

Jess watched her carefully, gauging every tiny change in her expression.

"Do you remember a lot about her? About your mom." she asked, just above a whisper, and she wasn't sure if she was asking for the video or for herself.

Sam's face fell just a fraction. "I remember *everything*." She swallowed thickly, her eyes flitting off to the wall behind Jess, like she was watching the memories play out in front of her. The glazed over look in her eyes reminded Jess of their conversation at the diner.

"During the rough patches, she would always tell me how strong I was; how *resilient* I was. She would say it like she was so proud of me. It was almost like sometimes she thought she was doing me a favor. Like she was giving me this gift of strength or something," Sam finished, her voice trailing off as her eyes fell from the wall to her lap.

"Every time she said it, I just wanted to scream at her. It made me so angry," she whispered, and Jess could imagine a younger Sam with so much completely justified, pent up rage. "But then every time you get mad or scream or yell—or cry" she swallowed, pausing. "Eventually they relapse."

Her eyes glossed over and Jess could see her reliving some hellish pain from her childhood.

"And then you know it's all your fault for pushing them to the edge again." She shook her head, catching herself. "I mean, you *think* it's your fault. Even though it's not."

Jess' heart ached, wondering how long it took for her to truly learn and believe that distinction.

"Sometimes I wish I could forget her," Sam whispered.

The words broke her heart.

Jess thought of every time she'd cried as a child, wishing she could remember more of her mother. Wishing she could remember good, warm, loving memories. The existence of bad memories hadn't even crossed her mind. It wasn't even in the realm of possibility. Her mother passed away when she was too young, but even so, she did have a happy childhood. That much she knew.

And she'd never been more aware of that than now.

The door of the auditorium swung open and a few attendees flowed out into the hallway.

Jess cleared her throat, suddenly remembering that the camera was still recording. She pressed the button to stop.

"Sorry." Sam cleared her throat, blinking her way back to reality. "Um—what other questions do you want me to answer?"

Filming Sam wasn't like filming the others. It felt different. More intimate. Those were conversations she wanted to keep for herself, not share with the world.

"That's okay. That was long enough."

Sam nodded with a small, forced smile.

"Hey girls," she looked up and saw Laura standing in the doorway. "Would you mind grabbing a few more chairs for the next meeting?"

"Oh yeah, of course," Jess answered, setting her camera down. She stood up at the same time as Sam.

They walked down the hallway together, the noise of the people at the front of the building slowly fading until they were far enough for the silence to surround them again.

When they reached the familiar door, Sam turned the knob, and Jess followed her into the dark, musky room. She stopped just behind her. Stacks of chairs filled every inch of the room, leaving hardly any space for both of them to stand in there.

Sam turned halfway, looking to the right, her shoulder only an inch from Jess' chest.

"I guess these are probably the easiest to carry without having to break up the stacks," Sam muttered, nodding to a few stacks of chairs in front of her.

Jess couldn't care less.

The only thing she was aware of was the short distance between their hands and bodies.

Sam turned her head toward Jess, about to say something, but stopped before the words could make it out. Maybe she could guess what she was thinking.

Jess swallowed, squeezing her hand into a fist to keep herself from reaching out to touch her. She couldn't do it again, no matter how badly her body craved it. It would just make things more complicated.

The familiar warmth radiated in her chest, and the terrifying thought ran through her head that maybe it was more than just her *body* that wanted Sam. Maybe it was deeper than just physical attraction and need. She pushed that thought away, refusing to let it linger.

Sam's breathing seemed to become shallow, while Jess' almost stopped entirely.

In that moment, every fiber of her body screamed to touch Sam. She wanted to hug her, to hold her, to kiss her. Even just to touch her hand. Something.

But she couldn't.

It wasn't fair to Sam.

She couldn't yank her back and forth, one minute wanting her more than anything in the world, and the next minute feeling like the world was ending because of it.

She couldn't do that to her.

She wouldn't.

Her hand squeezed so hard against her palm that pain radiated up through her wrist.

She would *not* give in.

"Jess," Sam whispered, her voice dripping with want and need.

Sam's hand gently snaked around her waist.

Her heartbeat skyrocketed.

Their faces inched closer together, and she couldn't tell if it was her or Sam leaning in.

Sam's eyes held a familiar look, and it took her a split second to realize that it was the same heated look they'd had when they spent the night together. The realization sent a shock of warmth from her chest down into her stomach, landing between her legs.

The resolve she'd been so determined to keep was diminishing by the second.

Her fist loosened.

Sam's face inched closer, their lips almost touching.

Jess swallowed, trying to find her voice before it was too late.

"I—I don't want to hurt you," she whispered.

Sam's eyes flicked up, meeting hers once again. She saw the hunger in them, but now she also saw a softness—an understanding.

"You won't."

Then Sam's lips met hers.

A jolt of electricity shot through her body.

Everything she'd been holding back suddenly came rushing forward.

She grabbed the front of Sam's hoodie with one hand, pulling their bodies flush against one another. The other hand reached up, grasping the back of her neck, desperately holding it in place.

Sam's arm tightened around her waist, pulling their bodies flush against each other.

Jess ran her tongue over Sam's bottom lip, and a soft moan escaped.

A fire ignited within her. She couldn't get enough. She needed more. She needed to feel Sam's entire body.

Jess reluctantly pulled back, breaking the kiss. She rested her forehead against Sam's.

"Can we—" she paused, catching her breath. "Do you want to—"

"Go to my place after this?" Sam asked, cutting her off with a small smirk that made her stomach tingle.

Jess nodded.

"Yes," Sam breathed, the smirk growing into a wide grin. "Definitely."

Jess smiled, closing her eyes. She let her forehead fall to rest on Sam's shoulder. "And there's no way we could just leave now, right?"

Sam laughed, unwrapping her arm from Jess' waist. "Technically, I can leave whenever I want. I'm here by choice. You, on the other hand," she said, tapping her finger against her hip, "are here by force."

Jess grumbled, lifting her head. "Right. Guess we should bring these chairs then. Can't keep my boss waiting."

Sam laughed again, turning to the stack next to them. She pulled two stacks out into the hallway, and they each carried one back to the auditorium.

"Thanks girls." Laura greeted them with a warm smile as they broke the stacks apart, setting them out one-by-one. "I need them to replace these," she said, pointing to a group of chairs in the back row. "Someone spilled coffee on them."

Sam grunted. "Not as bad as some of the other things people have gotten on these chairs."

"That is very true," Laura answered with a grimace.

Jess raised her brow at Sam.

"Trust me, you don't wanna know," Sam muttered, shaking her head.

"You girls don't have to stick around if you don't want to," Laura said as she moved the old chairs out of the way. "The rest of the meetings will probably be pretty empty. No one likes to go out in the rain."

A smile broke out on Jess' face as she glanced at Sam. "Actually, yeah, that would be great. I have a lot of—stuff—to do."

Sam instantly shot her back an amused look.

"Well," Laura said absentmindedly. "Remember, you don't actually have to come in on Sundays. It's not required in the program."

"Right, yeah," Jess muttered. She noticed Sam smirking at her again.

"I'm gonna head out too," Sam added. "I also have *lots* to do."

Laura frowned, looking up at Sam. "*Please* be careful riding home. Make sure your lights are on so the cars see you. You know they all become idiots the second the rain rolls in."

"Yeah, yeah, I got it," Sam replied, giving Laura a half hug as she walked past her to the door. Jess followed her out to the desk and began packing up the camera, popping the lens cap on first.

"So," Sam said, "you just can't stay away from me on Sundays, huh?"

Jess' mouth dropped slightly open. "What—no—I" she stuttered, and Sam burst out laughing. Warmth spread through her cheeks. Sam seemed to be able to fluster her in ways no one else could. She wasn't used to caring so much about what someone thought of her.

Sam's laugh died out and a new smile filled her face as she took a step toward Jess, leaving only a foot of space between them.

"I'd do the same thing to see you," she said, her voice low.

Tingles erupted in Jess' stomach. She looked down, feeling warmth in her cheeks again. She didn't want Sam to see how much the words affected her.

"Whatever," she muttered, rolling her eyes. But she couldn't hide the small smile on her face.

Sam's head cocked to one side with an amused smile, like she was trying to piece together the most interesting puzzle in the world.

Jess cleared her throat, her own smile refusing to leave her face, no matter how hard she tried. "You ready to go?"

Sam's smile widened, like this somehow amused her even more. She nodded. "Ready when you are."

They grabbed their bags and walked down the hallway. The rain outside drizzled from the dark sky, leaving a reflective sheen on the dark pavement.

Jess frowned as Sam walked to her bike beneath the overhang.

"Are you sure you should be riding right now?"

"It's fine," Sam replied, untying the thick jacket from the bike. "It's not coming down too hard yet."

Jess glanced up at the sky again. "It doesn't matter," she muttered. "The road could still be slick, and it'll be hard for other cars to see you."

Sam gave her a small, reassuring smile. "I'll be safe. I promise."

She opened her mouth to argue, but stopped herself. Sam probably wouldn't budge, anyway.

"Fine. I'll meet you there," she replied, walking out into the rain toward her car. She hunched her shoulders and ducked her head, trying to avoid the droplets that sprinkled into her eyes. "Be careful!" she called once more over her shoulder.

She knew the drive by heart, but still somehow managed to miss the exit for Sam's house. Truth be told, she'd only really been half paying attention to where she was going as her eyes incessantly scanned the road for Sam's bike. She'd seen her in the rearview mirror for the first few minutes, then she'd disappeared by the time she looked up again.

Jess cursed as she took the next exit and pulled her phone out to map the rest of the way.

She eventually turned into Sam's neighborhood and slowed as she approached her usual spot on the opposite side of the street. Throwing the car in park, her head swiveled back and forth. She'd expected to see Sam in the garage waiting for her to arrive since she'd taken a few extra minutes with the missed turn, but the house and garage looked dark and empty.

Rain splattered down harder now, beating against the roof of the car in a steady rhythm.

She frowned, checking the time. It shouldn't be taking her so long.

The fingers of her left hand tapped against the steering wheel as the other hand pulled Sam's contact up on her phone.

Right as she was about to click the call icon, she heard the low rumble of an engine approaching from the neighborhood entrance. She whipped her head around, her shoulders instantly relaxing at the sight of Sam coming down the street towards her.

Sam accelerated to the top of the driveway, then hopped off her bike once she got to the garage door. Jess waited for the garage to open before she jumped out of the car and ran toward it, trying to avoid getting soaked in the rain.

"You're late," Jess called, as she jogged the last few steps into the dimly lit garage. She'd only been in there a few times in the last week since they'd started hanging out each day, but the smell of the garage already felt a little familiar. It was a mix of sawdust and gasoline and something else she couldn't quite place, but somehow reminded her of Sam.

"I was *being careful*, as per your instructions," Sam answered with a teasing smirk as she stripped off the top layered jacket. It hadn't seemed to help her much. Jess could clearly see the water line on the black hoodie beneath. Water dripped off the soaked cuffs onto the cement floor.

"If you were being careful, you would've pulled over when it started raining harder."

Sam chuckled, running her hands through her wet hair. "Then I would've never shown up, and you'd be even more worried than you already were."

"I wasn't worried," Jess muttered. "I was just wondering where you were."

A wide smile spread across Sam's face, and she stepped toward Jess until they were only a few inches apart.

Her stomach fluttered, and she instantly forgot about everything except Sam's lips in front of her.

Sam leaned towards her, and Jess felt her hand rest against her hip.

"It's okay if you were," she said in a low voice, leaving their faces only an inch apart.

She reached up, snaking her hand around the back of Sam's neck and pulling her in. Their lips met, and warmth bloomed in her chest, but it somehow felt a little different from the times before. Her body craved the contact, but something else inside her craved it too—something deeper.

She pulled her lips back, breaking the kiss and opening her eyes.

Water dripped down Sam's face onto her neck. A slight tremble rippled beneath the hand that was still on Sam's neck. She pulled it away and gently wiped a water droplet off of her forehead.

"You should change into dry clothes," Jess whispered, reluctantly dropping her hand from Sam's cold skin.

Sam swallowed as a small shiver ran through her body. She looked dazed, and Jess wondered if it was from the kiss or cold. Probably the latter.

"Come on," Jess whispered, taking her hand and leading her toward the door that led into the house. Sam paused at the threshold, untying and removing her wet boots.

It was just as dark and cold inside the house as it was outside, and Jess' heart ached at the thought of Sam spending most nights there alone.

She took Sam's hand and led them to the back room.

Jess sat down on the bed, removing her shoes. Then she leaned her back against the wall and watched as Sam pulled out a new set of dry clothes.

She peeled the soaking wet hoodie up her body and tossed it into the hamper. Jess' eyes lingered on her toned, glistening body as she walked out into the hallway.

When she returned, she was wearing a cozy looking pair of gray sweats with a new white t-shirt. Outfits like this were a common occurrence during their movie nights, but something about the casual look still made her heart flutter.

Sam swiped the TV remote off the desk before sitting next to her on the bed. "Wanna watch something?" she asked.

Jess felt the heat of their thighs pressing together, making it difficult to think about much else. All she really wanted was to feel Sam as much as possible.

"Um—yeah. Pick whatever horror movie."

The corners of Sam's mouth pulled up slightly, like she was trying to hold back laughter.

"What?" Jess asked, her brows knitting together.

Sam turned, smiling like she was about to tease her for something. Then she let the smile drop, closing her mouth. She leaned her body a little closer.

"If you want to touch me, there are much easier ways of making it happen."

Jess felt heat rush into her cheeks. "I—" she stuttered, hating that she'd been so transparent.

Before she could argue, Sam leaned the rest of the way and kissed her.

She tensed for a moment, still wanting to rebut what she'd said. Then, the warmth of Sam's tongue ran against her bottom lip, and she instantly melted into the kiss. Nothing else mattered.

Both of her hands wrapped around the back of Sam's neck, pulling her closer, like it was the most natural thing in the world.

Need and want pumped through her veins.

Sam's hand slid further up her leg, stopping to grip the base of her hip.

Tingles erupted across her body. Her fingers clenched Sam's neck, nails scraping against her skin.

Sam moaned into her mouth, and the sound awakened something deep within her. Her body reacted instinctively. She pushed herself up and swung her leg over Sam's thighs, straddling her. Sam wrapped her toned arms securely around her waist, pulling her down and grinding them together.

Electricity shot through her, and she pressed her mouth hard against Sam's in order to stop the desperate sounds in her throat from fighting their way out.

Sam pulled her down again, and she felt a familiar pressure building.

But it wasn't enough.

She wanted more.

She needed more.

She needed to *feel* more of *her*.

Jess broke the kiss and swung her leg back over until she was sitting beside her. She quickly unzipped her jeans, pulling them down past her hips and knees until they were completely off, leaving her in just a black satin thong.

Her body seemed to move on its own, quickly swinging back into its previous position.

Sam's eyes raked down her like she was a meal ready to be devoured.

The feeling of Sam's hands grasping her bare thighs sent a rush of feeling between her legs.

Sam pulled her down again, grinding them both together, and this time Jess couldn't stop the deep moan before it escaped her lips.

Sam's fingertips grazed dangerously close to her underwear line, and the area between her thighs beat furiously with need.

She wanted Sam to touch her everywhere.

Everywhere.

Jess rolled her hips towards Sam's hand, desperately trying to move it a few more inches toward her center.

Sam's fingertips shifted slightly, hooking beneath the edge of the fabric that covered her throbbing clit.

Jess inhaled sharply.

The feeling of her fingers so close to where she needed them most sent an almost overwhelming wave of adrenaline rushing through her body.

She rolled her hips once more, Sam's fingertips moving another few centimeters past the edge of her thong.

So close.

They were so close now that if she moved her hips just slightly to the left, they would be right on top of where she needed them most.

But before she could move, Sam pulled her head back and looked into her eyes.

Want and need filled her eyes, but there was also something else—a question.

Jess gave a small nod before crashing their lips back together.

Sam's hand slipped beneath the edge of her thong, and Jess' eyelids fluttered shut. Fingers lightly traced over her throbbing clit, sending a bolt of lightning crackling through her.

The fingers continued their path toward her center until they traced light, teasing circles at her dripping wet entrance.

So much sensation flowed through her, it almost forced the air out of her lungs. She pulled her lips back from Sam's and wrapped her arms securely around her neck and shoulders, keeping herself upright.

Sam's fingers circled her again.

They were so close.

So close.

Jess' hips jerked forward, begging for more contact, but Sam pulled her hand back with them, carefully keeping her fingers where they gave Jess just enough pleasure to keep her on the edge without teetering over.

She couldn't take it anymore.

She needed to feel her.

Jess slid her head forward a few inches until her lips grazed Sam's ear. She bit her earlobe softly and almost came completely undone by the noise it brought from Sam's throat.

"*Please,*" she begged.

Every inch of Sam tightened beneath her, and she barely had time to register the movements before Sam's fingers pushed past her opening, plunging deep inside.

Waves of pleasure rippled through her body.

Her arms immediately tightened again around Sam's shoulders as a deep moan erupted from her throat. Stars swam in her vision as Sam's hand pumped furiously in and out of her again and again. The palm of her hand brushed against her clit with every movement, and the sensation made her body feel as though it were building and crumbling all at once.

She rocked her hips in a rhythm with Sam's hand and with each thrust, her core tightened.

Her hands grasped wildly for flesh, never getting enough of her body or her skin.

She grabbed the hem of Sam's shirt in her fist and lifted it an inch before pulling her head back to look her in the eyes.

"I—" Her voice shook with the ragged breaths that forced their way out. "Can I?"

Sam nodded quickly before pulling her own shirt over her head. She had no bra on underneath, and for a second, Jess paused, mesmerized by the beautiful sight before her. Then Sam swiftly turned them over, reversing their positions, and pinning Jess on her back against the bed.

She watched through hazy eyes as Sam sat back and pulled her sweatpants down, dropping them on the floor. Then she pulled down her underwear, dropping them to the ground, and this time Jess' mouth parted in awe. Just the mere sight of Sam like this inspired so much feeling between her legs that she thought that alone might push her over the edge.

Jess reached for her, desperately grabbing for the newly exposed skin, trying to pull her body against hers.

Sam's fingers instantly moved down to her thong, pulling it down over her hips. Jess lifted herself an inch off the bed, letting Sam pull them the rest of the way down her legs.

Cold air hit against her slit, sending a shiver through her body.

Jess grabbed onto her side and pulled her body toward her, desperate to feel every inch of her skin against her own. Their eyes met as Sam slowly lowered her body on top of her.

The feeling of her warm, bare skin was like heaven on earth. Like their bodies were two halves of a mold that fit perfectly together.

She gasped when Sam's thigh slide between her legs, instantly reigniting the urgency she'd felt just seconds before.

Nothing in the world could be better.

Nothing.

Then Sam's wet center lowered onto her inner thigh, just inches from her own, and Sam moaned as she slid herself against her thigh.

In that instant, the entire world shifted.

She would do anything—*everything*—to give Sam that feeling again.

Jess pulled their mouths together and kissed her hard as she rolled her hips against Sam. She moaned again, and they fell into a fast rhythm, sliding against each other. Jess' entire body buzzed. She could feel her wetness gushing out onto Sam's thigh, making her clit slide easily against her with barely any friction.

Her arms wrapped around Sam's back, grabbing onto every inch of her like her life depended on it.

Then Sam's hand dropped behind her knee and she pulled her leg up, spreading her legs further, completely exposing her most sensitive area.

Sam shifted her hips lower and lifted one leg slightly.

Before Jess could wonder what she was doing, she settled back down on top of her.

Sam's clit rubbed against hers.

A gush of wetness spilled out of her, and a noise that was more animal than human came from her mouth.

She couldn't even move. She couldn't do anything but lie there, relishing the sensation. The world felt like it was spinning.

Sam thrusted faster, and Jess felt the orgasm quickly building inside her. She wanted to stop it, to make the moment last forever.

Then Sam's raspy, ragged voice whimpered in her ear. "I—I'm gonna—"

Jess felt the girl's body trembling above her as her rhythmic thrusts turned to quick, sporadic bursts. She knew what was about to happen, and that was all it took to send her own body crashing over the edge.

Her arms tightened around Sam's shoulders, her back arching off the bed.

Sam groaned and her arm snaked around Jess' waist, crashing their hips together. Sounds of pleasure echoed through the air, and Jess felt wave after wave of the orgasm pump through her body.

Every inch tingled with sensation. It was stronger than anything she'd ever felt before.

It was so incredible.

So right.

The feelings coursing within her began to subside, and she relaxed her back, letting it fall onto the bed. Sam was still gripping her tightly, panting hard in her ear. That alone was almost enough to make her body ready for more.

She slowly unwrapped her arms from Sam's waist, pulling her hands up towards the back of her neck. She let her nails drag along her spine and felt Sam inhale sharply, jerking her hips forward into Jess' sensitive area. Seeing Sam's body react to her touch sent a wave of new feeling through her.

Her hands reached the base of Sam's neck and she let her fingers massage the tight muscles there.

She turned her face toward Sam, her lips perfectly meeting her neck, and kissed the soft spot right below her ear. Her lips lightly dragged over Sam's earlobe, and she felt a shiver run through her.

"You feel so good," she purred in her ear.

Another shiver.

Then Sam's body slowed, and she felt the girl relax into her once again, the orgasm having finally run its course.

They stayed like that, bodies completely intertwined, while Jess caressed the tight muscles in Sam's neck and shoulders, leaving occasional kisses on her jaw or temple.

She'd never been so intimate with another person before, but laying there with Sam, feeling her breathing slow and her head relax against her, just somehow felt right. It felt natural. All she had to do was allow her hands and body to do what they wanted—what they craved.

After a few minutes, Sam's breathing deepened, and Jess knew she'd fallen asleep.

She slowly shifted their bodies to move out from beneath her.

Sam groaned softly and cracked her eyes open, blinking a few times.

"Oh," she mumbled, her eyes flitting over Jess and then herself. "Sorry."

The corners of Jess' lips curled upward at the sight of Sam, laying naked in front of her, with satisfied exhaustion written across her face. It was beautiful. One of the most beautiful things she'd ever seen.

Jess sat up and reached for the blanket at the end of the bed. She grabbed one side and threw it out, letting it settle over them. Then she laid on her side, facing Sam, and pulled the blanket up to their waists.

"How long was I asleep?" Sam asked softly, her eyes still drooping.

"Just a few minutes."

Jess lifted her hand and let her fingers trace down Sam's jaw, working to savor every last detail of the moment.

Sam's eyes fluttered, and she shifted closer to Jess, letting her arm drape over her bare hip.

"Are you okay?" Sam asked, scanning her face and eyes.

Jess gave a small nod. This moment was something she refused to let any thought in her head ruin. If they wanted to rush in and try to destroy her afterward, then so be it, but they would have to wait.

"Are you sure?" Sam asked, eyeing her carefully.

"Yes," she said, leaning forward and pressing her lips against Sam's. "I'm not letting anything ruin this. At least not right now."

Sam frowned, opening her eyes a little more. "I hope nothing ruins it later, either."

Jess let her hand wander up to Sam's face, tracing her bottom lip with her thumb.

"You know you can call me if it does," Sam continued, a serious expression filling her face. "I mean—if you want to talk about it or anything."

She continued mindlessly tracing her lip. "Can I ask you something?"

"Of course," Sam answered, her eyes burning into Jess' face.

"What are you?" Jess asked, watching her finger carefully glide from her lip down to her jaw. "I mean—are you a lesbian? Or bi? Or?"

"Oh," Sam blinked like she wasn't expecting that to be the question. "I'm a lesbian. One hundred percent."

"How did you know?" Jess' eyes stayed glued to her trailing hand.

Sam shrugged. "I just always did. I don't remember ever *not* knowing."

Jess frowned, her lips forming a hard line as she watched her fingers drag down onto Sam's neck, finally stopping at her collarbone.

"But it's different for everyone. Just because that's how it was for me, that doesn't mean it has to be like that for—" Sam paused, thinking for a moment, "other people," she finished carefully.

Jess shifted her body forward until her head rested against Sam's bare chest.

"I've never thought about it before," she whispered, her lips brushing against Sam's skin. "I never had a reason to."

"And now?"

Jess frowned, closing her eyes as she buried her head deeper into Sam's chest. "I don't know."

Chapter 15

"Watch your left!" Jess screamed to her teammate from the sideline, her arms waving wildly in the direction of the goal.

She tensed, watching the other team's player sprint past one of their defenders and take a hard shot at the goal. The ball whipped through the air, smashing into the orange metal edge of the goal post and ricocheting out of bounds.

Jess released the breath she'd been holding and turned to Coach Lowe. "Put me back in."

His side glance made it clear he was about to protest. Probably something about how she needed more time to rest.

"I'm good. I had enough time," she continued, before he had the chance to disagree.

He examined her for a second. "Fine," he finally answered, crossing his arms. "Sub for Jacie."

She turned and snatched her stick off the bench before running up the sideline.

Watching the play, she waited until the ball moved to the other side of the field. Then she waved Jacie over.

"Jacie! Sub!" she yelled. The girl whipped her head around and immediately sprinted towards her.

Right when her foot touched the sideline, Jess darted out onto the field.

Her eyes tracked the ball as she watched Gabby bend down and seamlessly scoop it up. But just as she did, a girl on the opposing team charged at her, slamming into her side. Gabby's body hurled to the right and went crashing down onto the turf.

The referee immediately blew his whistle, and Jess ran across the field toward her.

Gabby clutched her knee, pulling it to her chest as she writhed in pain on the ground.

"What the fuck was that?!" Scarlett yelled from beside them. Jess watched her charge toward the opposing player, the referee immediately stepping between them.

"Can you stand?" Jess asked, kneeling beside her.

Although she was the last person she'd ever choose to tend to, a teammate was a teammate at the end of the day. And teammates take care of each other, whether they want to or not. Also, as much as it pained her to admit, Gabby was an okay player. Better than okay, even. So if she went out with an injury, it would make it that much harder for them to win.

Gabby stretched her leg a few inches, instantly groaning in pain. Jess frowned, watching her attempt and fail one more time before waving the coach and trainer over from the sidelines.

They examined her on the field as the rest of the team stood by, waiting.

Jess glanced up at the bleachers. Her dad sat by himself on the far left, watching the huddle of people gathered around Gabby.

Her eyes continued scanning the crowd until they landed on two more familiar faces.

Malik and Sam were sitting together near the center of the bleachers. Malik seemed to be in the middle of telling some animated story, his arms waving wildly in the air, while Sam laughed beside him.

After a moment, Sam turned her head toward the field, and their eyes instantly met. Sam's lips curled up into a small smile, and something about the look in her eyes made Jess' stomach fill with butterflies.

A smile formed on her lips, and she quickly wiped the sweat off her face with the back of her hand, hiding it as best as she could.

"They're playing rough," Scarlett said from beside her. "Watch out for that one especially," she jerked her head toward the player who ran into Gabby.

Jess grunted, her eyes flitting back up to the bleachers.

"Distracted?" Scarlett asked, a light smirk on her face.

"Never." Jess shook her head, turning back to the field to check on the progress with Gabby.

The referee blew his whistle, and they jogged toward the center, where their team huddled together. They were up by one goal, with only six minutes left. If they could keep the other team from scoring, or widen the scoring gap, then they would make it to the championships.

"Number three is good when she shoots from the right side," Jess said in a low voice, eyes bouncing between her teammates. "But she barely even gets close to the net when she's on the left. Keep her there and block her any time she tries to get on the right."

The three defenders in front of her nodded.

"If the ref would call any of the million fucking times they've fouled me, then I could get the free shot I deserve and put us two goals ahead," Scarlett said, throwing a glare at the referee.

"Wouldn't count on that," Jess said, walking away from the huddle toward center field.

The game had been rough from the start, and now that it was nearing the end, the other team was growing more agitated by the minute.

They all took their positions on the field, and the referee blew the whistle to resume the game. A girl on the other team had the ball, and Jess watched as she quickly passed it off to number three. As she'd expected, the girl immediately tried to move to the right side of the goal. Jess watched with pride as her teammate moved with her, blocking her path and keeping her at the top-center of the arc.

The girl moved back, her head swiveling from side to side, weighing her options before finally passing it off to her teammate.

Jess watched the seconds ticking down on the clock, her eyes bouncing between the field and the scoreboard.

Finally, the clock hit four minutes, and number three had the ball once again. Jess watched the way her hips turned, and she knew right away that she was going to make her move.

The girl jerked her body hard to the left before attempting to pivot around Jess' teammate. She managed to slip just inches past her, opening up a small lane for a shot.

Jess held her breath as she watched the girl whip her stick forward, the ball hurling out toward the goal.

The yellow ball sliced through the air, but even from where she was, Jess could see right away that it was angled too high. It shot over the goal post by almost a full foot.

Jess let out a breath of relief.

One of her teammates on that side of the field grabbed the ball and threw it back in bounds to another teammate once the referee blew his whistle to resume.

Jess sprinted toward the ball, easily losing the defender that was supposed to be guarding her.

"Here!" she yelled, crossing the field. She'd created the perfect opening, and the girl found her easily, lobbing the ball through the air.

Jess looked up, squinting past the sun to find the ball falling a few more feet ahead of her. She kicked her legs as hard as she could, reaching her net out at just the right time. The ball landed perfectly in the net, barely disrupting her stride.

Further up the field, she could see Scarlett struggling to break free from her defender.

Jess sprinted, her legs burning with every step.

Three defenders stood between her and the goal. If she was going to get a good shot, she'd need to weave between them.

Scarlett must have known what she was thinking, because once Jess reached the top of the arc, she sprinted to the side, drawing one of the defenders out with her.

That left only two people between her and the goal.

The first one descended on her instantly, and she dodged to the left, easily making it past them. When the second defender charged at her, she knew she already had them beat. They were too far away to get there in time.

The opening was there. It was time to take it.

She pulled back the head of her stick, and in one fluid motion, whipped it forward, hurling the ball at the lower corner of the net.

The goalie kicked her leg out in an attempt to block it, but it was just a fraction of a second too late.

A ripple cascaded through the net as the ball struck its target.

Cheers erupted all around her before it had even registered in her mind that she scored.

She turned to find Scarlett, but her eyes magnetically pulled to the bleachers instead. They instantly met with Sam, who stood with Malik, cheering and clapping.

She felt a surge of something flow through her body. Happiness? Pride? Maybe both? It was like she was floating, but at the same time, she'd never felt more calm and anchored before in her life.

Out of the corner of her eye, she could see Scarlett running toward her. She smiled, bracing herself as Scarlett crashed into her, wrapping her arms around her in a tight hug.

"Yes!" she shouted, and all Jess could do was laugh. She couldn't remember the last time she'd felt so content. So happy.

After a quick on field celebration, both teams lined up at center field to faceoff. But now, with only two minutes left of the game, Jess knew it was basically over. And she could see the other team knew it too. She could see their frustration in the way they played. They were sloppy, committing two hard fouls in less than thirty seconds.

When the game resumed again, Scarlett had the ball and Jess instantly saw a player on the opposing team charging towards her.

Jess sprinted to the side closest to Scarlett, easily losing her defender. She yelled for the ball, and Scarlett spun around to throw it to her.

Right as the ball left her net, the defender running at her slammed her stick down, causing the ball to shoot off course. It looked to be sailing about ten feet past where she was, and she quickly sped up her stride to make it there. Her eyes stayed glued to the ball, watching as it fell. She kicked her legs as hard as she could and reached her stick out to catch it.

Then, right as the ball was within inches of landing in her net, suddenly, what felt like a train crashed into her side.

Her whole body spun and twisted in the air before landing hard on the grass.

Excruciating pain radiated out all over her torso.

She squeezed her eyes shut, biting her lip to keep from crying out. Her ears rang, but she could still hear the faint sound of Scarlett yelling, followed by the sharp crack of a whistle.

She groaned, rolling from her side onto her back. Pain shot out over her ribcage and chest.

Her eyes cracked open, and she stared at the sky, blinking away the spots that glided through her vision.

Coach Lowe appeared first, followed shortly by the trainer. They both knelt above her with expressions that said the collision probably looked as bad as it felt.

"What hurts?" the trainer asked, her eyes scanning over Jess' body.

"Ribs," she hissed, clutching her side as another wave of pain rolled through her.

They each went through their usual checklist of injury questions, and by the time they'd finished, she felt well enough to sit up.

"Take it slow," the trainer said, holding onto her arm to keep her steady.

She paused, a wave of dizziness passing through her.

"I'm okay," she replied, swallowing down the lump in the back of her throat.

She kept her eyes shut until she was sure she wouldn't vomit. Once the bile in her mouth subsided, she opened her eyes. She could see all the fans in the bleachers, and wasn't surprised that the first thing she saw was her dad standing near the fence right next to the field, his eyes glued to her.

She turned slightly and what she saw next did surprise her.

Sam stood with her hands clutched around the metal bar of the chain-link fence that separated the bleachers from the field. Her body looked tense and for a split second, it almost looked like she might be about to jump over the fence onto the field. It made Jess wonder how bad the hit must have looked. Maybe as bad as it felt.

"How's it feeling?" the trainer asked, watching her intently.

"A little better," she answered, lightly running the tips of her fingers over her ribcage.

"Can you stand up?"

Jess nodded, planting one hand in the grass beside her to push herself up.

The trainer and coach both grabbed hold of each of her arms. Once she was standing, she heard clapping from the fans in the bleachers, and the players on the opposing team.

"Let's get you to the bench. Then I'll grab you an ice pack," the trainer said, slowly guiding her to the sideline.

Each step she took sent fresh surges of pain through her torso. Nausea crept up in her stomach again, and she squeezed her eyes shut, drawing in slow breaths to calm her body. That worried her. The only time in her life she'd been in enough pain to make her sick was when she'd broken her arm in sixth grade. As she sat down, feeling the cold metal of the bench press against her thighs, she silently prayed that nothing was broken. They were minutes away from making it into the championship, and she wasn't about to let anything stop her from playing.

"I'm gonna get you an ice pack," the trainer said, stepping away.

She squeezed her eyes shut as another wave of pain radiated through her. When she opened them again, Scarlett was standing in front of her, a worried expression painted on her face.

A whistle blew on the field, and Sam could see girls sprinting about in her peripherals.

She glanced up at the scoreboard before looking back at Scarlett. "Why aren't you in?"

"Got a yellow."

"What? Why?"

"Yelled at the ref," she grumbled, taking a seat beside her.

Jess smirked, easily picturing it in her head: her best friend yelling some profanity before being ejected.

Seconds later, the trainer returned, handing her a packed bag of ice. "Keep icing it tonight and if the pain hasn't improved or gets worse by tomorrow, then you need to go see a doctor."

Jess nodded, gently pressing the bag against her ribs.

They watched the remaining minute of the game quickly wind down. Luckily for everyone, it was uneventful and ended without any more injuries.

When the final whistle blew to signal the end, their whole team cheered and celebrated, Jess and Scarlett watching from the sideline with their own smiles.

They'd done it. They'd be playing in the championship game the following week.

The rest of the team gathered around Jess and Gabby on the bench while Coach Lowe congratulated them and spoke about the schedule for the next seven days. As she listened to him drone on, her thoughts wandered. The following week, win or lose, they'd play their last game of the season. Then the semester would end with winter break. Lacrosse season would be over. The volunteer program would be over.

Her eyes skipped to the bleachers. Sam was now sitting next to Malik, but she was watching the team. Watching Jess. They locked eyes for a moment before Jess looked back at the coach.

A few minutes later, he dismissed them, and Scarlett began packing up both of their things while Jess rested on the bench. Her eyes skipped across the field, and she saw her dad walking around the fence. Once he reached the opening, he walked onto the field, making his way toward them. He'd never been one to fuss over her sports injuries, but he did always at least check on her.

"You okay?" he asked once he was only a few feet away.

Jess grunted in response, wincing when her chest muscles constricted. "A little better now."

He pursed his lips, watching her. She wondered if, in these moments, he ever tried to think of what her mother might have done.

How she would've handled things. Would she have insisted that she see a doctor? Or would she have known that Jess was okay just by seeing her?

"Think you're fine to drive?"

"Yea–"

"You did it!" Malik's voice rang out, and she glanced over to see him and Sam approaching Scarlett at the other end of the bench. Scarlett laughed as he picked her up and swung her around in the air.

"Yeah," she giggled. "And I made it through the whole season with only one yellow card. Who knew that was possible?"

"Well," Sam said, "I don't think a single person would blame you for being carded today." She looked up and met eyes with Jess. "I know I sure as hell would've been ejected if I was on the field when that happened."

Jess looked away, back at her father, who glanced suspiciously between her and her friends.

"I'm fine to drive," she continued.

He grunted, his attention returning to her. "You gonna be okay by yourself tonight?" he asked. "I have a shift scheduled."

"Yeah, I'll be fine," she lied. In truth, the thought of being home alone and in pain sounded like the worst night possible. But she'd never tell him that.

"You sure?" he asked. "I can see if someone could cover it for me."

She gave him a small smile, appreciating the effort even though they both knew what her answer would be.

"No, that's okay."

"Alright, well, I won't be home too late," he replied, turning away from her. She thought she caught a glimpse of him looking over at Sam as he turned. He cleared his throat awkwardly. "And good job on the win."

She smiled. He may not have been the type for big emotional displays, but she always knew when he was proud. This was one of those moments.

"Thanks dad," she murmured, sliding her body down a few inches until her head leaned against the back of the bench. She let out a slow exhale, careful not to move her chest too much.

After he'd walked a few dozen feet, she saw Sam approaching. She both loved and hated the way her heart rate ticked up with anticipation.

When Sam reached her, she sat down on the bench, sliding close enough that their thighs just barely touched. The warmth of Sam's skin behind her black jeans pressed against Jess' cold, bare knee. Sam looked straight ahead at the field, and Jess tilted her head sideways to look at her. The cold metal of the bench pressed against her cheek. Her eyes shamelessly traced the curves of her face.

It wasn't just that she was attractive. It was everything else. Her mannerisms. Her confidence. The smile that formed on her lips when she was about to tease someone. The way she rubbed the back of her neck when she was nervous.

It was all of it.

It was *everything*.

"You won the game for them," Sam said beside her, still looking out over the field. Jess watched the way her throat bobbed as she said the words. She watched the way she licked her lips when she paused. "How does it feel?"

"Terrifying," Jess whispered.

Sam turned to her with a questioning expression. "You mean it was terrifying to get hit that hard?"

Jess let her eyes silently wander over the lines of Sam's face. She wasn't sure what she meant.

Sam frowned. "How does it feel now?"

"Hurts."

"Do you think you shou—"

"Can you come over tonight?" Jess asked, cutting her off.

That familiar teasing smile formed on Sam's face. The sight of it made Jess feel like she'd just reached the summit of the highest mountain on earth.

"Like, to your house?" Sam asked. "Are you sure your dad would be—"

"He won't be there. He's working tonight."

"Oh, okay," Sam replied. "Then yeah."

"Yeah?" Jess mimicked, a teasing smile forming on her own face. She wondered when Sam's playfulness had seeped so far into her own personality.

Sam smiled at her, and Jess wondered if she was thinking the same thing. "Yes."

"Now?" Jess asked.

"What, like leave straight from here and go to your house?"

Jess nodded, and Sam chuckled, shaking her head. "Sure, why not?"

Jess' smile grew wide across her face. Something about the moment felt so perfect, and for a second, she forgot every reason why she could ever think that this—being with Sam—wasn't a good idea.

"You ready to go now?" Sam asked, glancing around at the few people still lingering near the bench.

"Yeah," Jess said, pushing against the bench until she was sitting up straight. She closed her eyes, taking slow steadying breaths as a dull ache throbbed in her side.

"Which bag is yours? I'll get your stuff ready to go," Sam said, standing up from the bench.

Jess cracked one eye open and saw her bag on the ground by Scarlett and Malik. "The black one with the neon green tape on the top," she answered, jerking her head towards it.

Sam let out a snort of laughter. "How could you have ever hated on my bike seat? You basically have the exact same thing."

Jess smirked as she closed her eyes again, feeling relief when the pain finally dulled once more.

"Ya know," she heard Malik's voice approaching, "Luke wanted to come to the game today."

Jess' eyes snapped open again. She saw Scarlett behind him, their gazes instantly locking. Sam was still close enough to hear, but gave no visible reaction.

"Why?" Jess asked, her brows pulling together.

Malik shrugged. "Don't tell him I said this, but I think he misses you. He still talks about you all the time."

Jess frowned and looked away. Luke was the last thing she wanted to talk about, especially with Sam just a few feet away. But she knew Scarlett hadn't told Malik about her and Sam, so she couldn't exactly blame him for bringing it up.

"Well," Scarlett cut in, "tell him he needs to move on. He flirts with Gabby all the time anyway, so he's halfway there already."

Malik shrugged again. "Pretty sure he just does that to try to make you jealous."

255

Jess rolled her eyes, and Scarlett let out an exasperated groan.

"You really wouldn't give it another shot with him?" Malik asked with genuine curiosity. "I mean, I don't really get why you guys broke up in the first place. You seemed fine together."

Sam walked back towards them and dropped the backpack on the ground in front of her. Jess searched her face, but Sam avoided her gaze.

"I wanted more than just *fine*," Jess answered. Sam's eyes flickered up to hers for a split second before looking away again, her expression unreadable.

"Hmph," Malik grunted. Within seconds, he turned to Scarlett to ask about dinner options, the entire conversation already long forgotten.

Sam stood in front of her, hands tucked in the front pockets of her black jeans. She cleared her throat awkwardly, and Jess wondered if the conversation had bothered her, or if it bothered her that Malik didn't know about them.

"Ready?" Sam asked.

Jess nodded and slowly pushed herself up off the bench. Sam reached out, placing a secure hold on her arm to help her stand.

"Take it slow," Sam said softly as she scooped up Jess' backpack and threw it over her own shoulder. "We're not in a hurry."

Although that was true, Jess was dying to be home. All she could think about was laying in her bed with Sam after a hot shower. Her dad wouldn't be gone all night, and Jess wanted to take advantage of those few hours while she could.

"You guys wanna get dinner with us?" Malik asked.

Sam looked at Jess, who instantly shook her head.

"The only thing I'm doing tonight is a shower and movies," she answered, wincing as she took her first steps.

Malik nodded in understanding before turning his gaze to Sam. "You down for dinner?"

Sam glanced at Jess again before answering. "Um—I think I'm gonna take it easy tonight, too. Joining in the shower and movies."

Scarlett's head whipped up to look at her with a stunned and amused expression.

"I mean—" Sam stuttered, her face turning red as she realized what she'd just said. "The movies! Joining in on watching the movies only! Not uh—the shower part." She looked down at the ground and raised her hand, scratching the back of her neck.

Jess had never seen her so flustered before. She almost broke out in laughter, but was too busy looking back at Malik to gauge his reaction. He seemed to have missed the slip up entirely, just nodding along distractedly as he pulled out his phone.

"Right," Scarlett muttered under her breath, looking down to hide her smirk as she finished packing her bag.

Jess chuckled, taking another couple of steps. "Have fun at dinner," she called over her shoulder.

"Yeah, you guys have fun tonight too!" Scarlett called back, and Jess could hear the teasing lull thickly laid over her voice.

Sam groaned beside her, and Jess couldn't help the smile that broke out across her face. "Well, that was smooth."

Sam glared at her sideways. "Not exactly my best moment," she grumbled.

They slowly made their way to the parking lot, with Sam helping her into her car once they arrived. After a minute of getting settled in the driver's seat, with the ice pack tucked between her ribs and the center console, they each departed separately.

Luckily, traffic was light, and they both made it to the house quickly, arriving at almost the exact same time.

Jess pulled her car into her usual spot in the driveway, then checked her rearview mirror to see Sam parking along the street. She unbuckled her seatbelt slowly, taking her time before sliding out of the car.

She heard the rumbling of Sam's bike abruptly cut off, and then the sound of footsteps treading toward her.

The few small steps up to the front door were a bigger bother than she'd anticipated, and Sam placed a steadying hand on her back to help guide her. When she finally reached the front door, she took a deep breath, already feeling the exhaustion settling in her bones. The full flight of stairs inside definitely wouldn't be pleasant.

She fiddled with the keys in her hand until she found the one she was searching for. The door clicked open easily, and before she knew it, the smell of home filled her nostrils.

The house was dark, and she reached one hand to the wall inside, immediately finding and flipping up the light switch.

Light sprang out over the front hallway, and Jess reached up to hang her keys on the hook by the door.

She glanced back and forth between the kitchen and the stairs, wondering whether she would have the energy to come back downstairs for food and drinks after her shower.

"If you tell me where things are," Sam said, "I can get whatever you want."

Jess turned, smiling at her with appreciation. "There's some chips and random snacks in the pantry. Can you get whatever you think sounds good?"

"Of course," Sam answered, sliding past her toward the kitchen.

Jess took a couple of steps to the stairs, then called out to her. "Oh, and water too, please!"

"Got it!" Sam called back.

Jess heard the ruffling of chip bags as she took her first steps up the stairs. By the time she made it to the top, her side throbbed in pain, and she desperately wanted to lie down. For a second, she considered just changing and getting straight into bed, but the thought of going to sleep covered in sweat made her too uncomfortable.

She waded into the bathroom and turned the shower on before sitting down on top of the closed toilet, waiting for the water to heat. Sam's footsteps echoed on the wooden floor as she came up the stairs.

"It's the room on your right," Jess called out when she heard her get to the top of the stairs.

Sam stopped in the bathroom doorway. There were at least six different snack bags cradled in her arms, with a tall glass of ice water balanced in one hand.

"That one," Jess nodded her head past where Sam stood.

She grunted as she turned and walked into the room behind her. Jess heard the bags drop onto what she assumed was her bed before Sam walked back out, returning to the bathroom doorway.

"You need anything?" she asked, crossing her arms and leaning against the doorframe.

"Shouldn't I be the one asking you that?" Jess asked, pushing herself up from the toilet seat lid. "Ya know, with you being the guest and all that."

"Maybe," Sam answered with a smirk. "But only one of us got tackled by a brick wall today."

Jess snorted and shook her head. It felt more like being tackled by ten brick walls.

"I'm fine. I'll be out in a minute," she said, sliding her shoes off one foot at a time.

"Alright, well, yell if you need anything."

Jess smirked as she reached up to let her hair down. "Trying to shower with me?"

Sam matched her smirk in a way that made Jess' stomach burn. "Maybe someday," she said, letting her eyes linger for an unnecessary moment before walking back to the bedroom.

Jess' smile widened as she closed the door and began carefully stripping off her clothes. The cold air hit her skin, sending a painful shiver through her chest. She dropped the last item of clothing to the ground and stepped into the shower.

The hot water felt so good cascading against her back that she groaned softly without realizing it. Her eyes fluttered closed as she leaned her head back, relishing the moment of peace as the water ran through her hair.

She stayed like that for a minute, just breathing the steam in and out through her nostrils, letting the calm wash over her. Once her body finally felt warm enough, she gently washed herself and shampooed her hair, gritting through the pain that flared up when she raised her right arm above her head.

Usually she would wash her face and slather copious amounts of conditioner all over her hair, but the mixture of pain and exhaustion kept her from doing any more than the bare minimum.

She rinsed off and sat under the stream of scalding hot water for another few seconds before finally shutting it off. She reached out and grabbed the towel hanging on the back of the door. Still standing in the shower, she ran it through her hair a few times and then wrapped it around her body. When she opened the door and stepped out into the hallway, she could hear videos playing from her bedroom.

Sam glanced up from her phone as Jess walked in. She caught Sam's eyes lingering on her bare thighs for a moment before snapping back to her phone.

She was sitting in the chair at the desk in the corner of her room. It'd been a gift from her father when she got into middle school. He insisted she'd need a dedicated spot in the house to do her homework every day. In reality, it just turned into the spot in her room where she threw the clothes she'd worn but didn't really consider dirty yet.

"Pretty sure that's like the third time ever that anyone has actually sat in that chair," Jess muttered as she rifled through her dresser drawer, looking for clothes.

Sam grunted, her attention still glued to whatever she was watching on her phone. "I could tell. Had to move like ten pounds of clothes before I sat down."

Jess finally found the pair of old sweats she was searching for. She took the clothes and changed in the bathroom before returning. When she entered the room again, she made a beeline for the bed.

Pulling the comforter back, she slowly tucked herself beneath its warm weight.

Sam looked up from her phone, watching her.

Once she was in, she pulled the comforter securely up to her chin and exhaled, finally feeling her body fully relax. After a moment, she looked at Sam expectantly, and the girl looked back at her, raising her eyebrows in question.

"You probably don't want me laying in your bed with these clothes on after I sat on those dirty bleachers at the game."

Jess smirked at her. "Are you trying to come up with an excuse to take your clothes off?"

Sam laughed, shaking her head. She looked off to the side. "I'm just trying to be respectful."

Jess' smile widened. She wanted to tease her again, but more than that, she wanted her in bed beside her. She glanced down at the empty space next to her, the teasing smile dropping from her face.

"Please?" she whispered.

Sam swallowed, her eyes meeting Jess' stare with equal intensity. They held the look for a moment before Sam stood from the chair and walked to the edge of the bed. She removed her boots and pushed the snacks out of the way, then lifted the comforter and slid inside the cocoon of warmth.

Jess reached out to the nightstand and grabbed the remote, handing it to Sam.

"What do you wanna watch?" Sam asked as she reached for the closest bag of chips with her free hand.

Jess hummed, letting her tired eyes close. "You pick."

"Horror?" Sam asked, and Jess could hear the teasing lilt in her voice.

The corners of Jess' lips curled up, and she shook her head lightly.

"Or do you no longer need the excuse to touch me?" Sam asked with a chuckle.

Jess opened her eyes again and glared at her. Then she shifted her body forward, ignoring the pain in her torso as she pushed herself across the bed. She kept going until her body was flush against Sam's, then dropped her head down on her chest, letting her arm drape lazily across the girl's stomach.

"No, I don't," she said, closing her eyes once more.

Sam froze for a few seconds. Then she finally felt the girl's arm wrap gently around her waist, holding her in place.

She heard the click of the remote again as Sam continued searching for something to watch.

"You know," Sam said after a moment, "somehow this is exactly how I would've imagined your house."

Jess hummed, the rise and fall of Sam's chest already lulling her to sleep. "What did you imagine?"

"I don't know," Sam answered. "I figured it'd be comforting and homey, but not like the way that you see in movies or magazines. Just in the way you know, people actually live their lives here, I guess. If that makes sense."

Jess hummed again, breathing in the scent of Sam's shirt.

"Have you always lived here?" Sam asked.

"Mhm. My parents bought it before they had me," Jess replied with a yawn.

Sam was silent for a few seconds before she continued. "I can't even imagine that—living in one place your whole life."

Jess' eyes cracked open, and she pulled her head back a few inches to look up at her. "How many places have you lived?"

Sam shrugged lightly. "Honestly, I don't even know. Sometimes I think I've remembered them all and then randomly a memory will pop into my head of somewhere that I'd completely forgotten."

Jess nodded slowly, letting her head drop back down to the girl's rhythmic chest.

They laid in silence for a few moments, and Jess thought the conversation might have ended. Then Sam cleared her throat.

"Was it hard—to live here after your mom passed away?"

Jess blinked a few times, processing the words.

Was it? She hadn't really thought about that before. No one had ever asked her that. Not even the therapists.

"No," she answered, her voice sounding a little distant from her own ears. "I—" She knew what she wanted to say, but it was like her brain and her mouth had disconnected. She closed her eyes and took a deep breath, trying to reconnect them.

"I—think it was actually better." Jess cleared her throat, now feeling more awake than she had in the last few hours. "It helped me remember things—about her."

"That didn't make it harder for you? To remember things all the time?" Sam asked softly, and Jess could hear the genuine curiosity in her voice.

"I needed that. I—" she cleared her throat again. "There isn't much that I really remember, so the reminders are—good—I think."

She felt Sam's head nod above her.

An unfamiliar feeling swept through her. She *wanted* to keep talking about her. She *wanted* someone else to hear the thoughts that constantly swirled in her head. She wanted *Sam* to hear them.

"My dad never wanted to talk about her," she whispered.

Silence fell between them again for a few seconds before Sam spoke. "Did that make it harder for you?"

Did it?

No one had ever asked her that before. However, to be fair, she'd never told that to anyone in the first place.

"I don't know," she whispered. "Maybe." Thinking about it for a few more seconds, she swallowed. "Yeah. Yeah, I think it did."

"Is that her in the picture by your mirror?"

Jess' eyes flickered to the picture taped on the edge of the mirror beside the dresser. She nodded.

"You guys have the same eyes."

"Really?" Jess asked, surprised. No one had ever mentioned any resemblance to her mother. Although, she wouldn't expect it since her father never spoke of her and she barely ever saw her relatives.

"Yeah," Sam said. "I saw it right away when I looked at the picture."

Jess hummed, shifting her body closer to Sam's and draping her leg over the other girl's thigh. No matter how close she got, it somehow never seemed like enough.

"It's always been kind of—" Jess paused, thinking of the words she wanted to say. "Hard, I guess. To talk about her." She cleared her throat. "With anyone."

Sam's hand ran up and down her back in a soothing motion. "Everyone handles grief at their own pace and in their own way," she whispered.

Jess nodded, her eyes drooping again, begging to close. But she knew she had one more thing she needed to say.

"I think it's been good for me—to talk to you. Or even just listen to you. When you talk about your mom, it makes me feel—" she paused, exhaling a breath she hadn't realized she was holding. "It makes me feel understood. Like I'm not crazy for feeling the way I do."

Sam was quiet for a moment, then Jess felt lips press down against her forehead. A warm, soothing feeling bloomed in her chest, and she wondered how she'd gone her whole life without feeing the way she did now. It was like her life had permanently split in two. The life before she knew Sam. And now.

Because it wasn't really minutes, or hours, or days that marked the passage of time. It was this. Life before knowing someone or something that changed your whole world. And life after.

She couldn't think of the exact moment that it happened—when the split happened. But she knew now with complete and utter certainty that this was the after.

Her eyelids fluttered closed, listening to the steady thrum of Sam's heart.

This time, when the familiar worries of Trinity and what her mother would have thought entered her mind, they didn't spark the usual anxiety. She heard them and accepted them. She allowed them all to fill her mind—to consume it.

They played alongside memories. Both memories of her mother, and more recent memories with Sam. A pleasant calm filled her bones, and before long, she could no longer tell if she was awake or if she was dreaming.

When she saw her mother standing before her in their kitchen, she realized that she was, in fact, dreaming. She watched her—studied the woman in front of her.

Sam was right. They did have the same eyes.

The image of her mother floated away, and she continued drifting in and out of sleep, feeling perfectly at ease.

Then, in one of the dreams, she heard the sound of a door open somewhere far away. Then she heard it close, a little louder this time.

"Jess?" she heard her dad's voice calling out, this time much louder. The body beneath her head jerked, and Jess' eyes snapped open. She instantly sat up, vaguely aware of Sam doing the same. Her vision swam, coming into focus.

Sam stared at her with caution and concern painted on her face.

"Jess? Is someone here?" her dad called out again. Footsteps echoed from the stairs.

"Uh—" she stuttered, pushing herself up until she was sitting as far on the other side of the bed as she could, her left leg slightly hanging off. "Yeah!" she called back as his footsteps grew closer.

The bedroom door opened, and her dad stepped in. His eyes met hers for the briefest moment before snapping to Sam.

"Um—dad, you remember Sam, right?" She cleared her throat, looking back at him. His gaze was still held firmly on Sam, his lips pursed in a tight line. "From the clinic," she continued. Her heart sank at reducing their *relationsh*—well, whatever they were, down to something so insignificant.

"We um—" she glanced at the TV. "We wanted to have a movie night." She waved her arm toward the TV in a way that she hoped seemed nonchalant. She knew she'd failed by the suspicious look her dad finally gave her.

"Getting late, don't you think?" The look he gave her said that it wasn't actually a question as much as an unspoken command.

Before she could respond, Sam spoke up.

"Yeah," she said, her voice sounding much calmer than Jess' had. "I should head home."

Jess felt the bed shift as she stood up, but she kept her eyes on her lap. She couldn't bring herself to look up and see whatever emotion was on Sam's face.

She could hear Sam sliding on her boots and then heard the scrape of her keys as she grabbed them off the desk.

"Hope your ribs feel better tomorrow."

Jess nodded, still refusing to look up at her.

"Good to see you again, Officer Miller. Glad that it was under better circumstances this time."

Her dad only grunted in response as she walked through the doorway, and Jess finally looked up to gauge the look on his face.

They were both silent for a minute as they listened to Sam's footsteps going down the stairs. Then the door opened and shut, and then eventually the motorcycle outside rumbled to life.

Finally, her dad spoke.

"I told you I didn't want you spending time with her."

Jess suddenly felt both hot and cold, and she matched his angry stare.

"Well, I'm eighteen so you can't really tell me who I can and can't hangout with." She said it with a bite that made his eyes widen slightly.

He gave her a new look now. One that made her stomach instantly knot up and feel sick. It was like he was searching her face, looking for something hidden that she hoped wouldn't show. It reminded her of the way Scarlett had looked at her the night of Winter Formal.

After a handful of seconds, he finally crossed his arms, leaning against the doorway.

"I don't care how old you are, I still choose who comes under my roof. And I don't want a criminal here."

Jess stared at him for a moment, utterly dumbfounded.

"What?"

He looked back at her with pursed lips and slightly squinted eyes, like he was daring her to argue with him.

"You heard me, Jess. I don't want a thief in my house. And maybe I can't control who you see when you're not here, but I'd hope you'd make better choices in friends. I raised you better than that."

Her eyebrows pinched in confusion. "What do you mean, a *criminal*?"

The look on his face said that he didn't believe that she didn't know what he was talking about. He was silent for a moment, his jaw set.

"She has a record. I saw it when I logged the incident report that day at the clinic." He shook his head. "Wasn't even fifteen the first time she got caught for trespassing and burglary."

Jess was stunned. It's not like she expected Sam to share every detail of her life with her, but if she didn't know about this, what else could she not know about?

"I—I didn't know that," she muttered.

He unfolded his arms and stuck his hands in his front pockets instead. "Okay, well now you do, and I expect you to make the right decisions from here on out."

Then he turned and walked back into the hallway.

Jess sat there, stunned by everything. She played it all back in her mind. Falling asleep, waking up to her dad calling her name. Sam leaving.

A vibrating noise buzzed from the nightstand.

Sam's name filled the screen.

Jess grabbed the phone and immediately tapped to open the new message.

SAM HAYES: Well that was awkward.. Everything ok?

She stared at the phone, fingers hovering above the keyboard. It wasn't that she didn't want to talk to her. Something just somehow felt different. How could she feel so strongly about someone when she didn't even know about huge pieces of their life? And if she didn't know that about her, what else could she not know?

It left her with a pit in her stomach.

She pushed the comforter back and stood up from the bed, quickly crossing the room to shut the door and turn the light off. When she got back in bed, she picked up the phone and stared at the message once more.

One half of her brain silently pleaded with the other to respond. But the reluctant half wouldn't budge. The reluctant half told her she was insane for feeling the way she did about someone she'd only known for a few short weeks. And in that moment, the reluctant half was making a lot more sense.

She stared for a few more seconds, contemplating. Then she plugged the phone into the charging cord on her nightstand and set it down beside the alarm clock.

She closed her eyes, but this time the calm feeling from before never came.

Chapter 16

J ess stared through the windshield at the run-down building of the clinic.

It'd been two days.

Two full days of avoiding Sam.

To be fair, though, some of it was actually justified. The day after the game, she'd genuinely felt so sore and tired that she knew she'd be doing more harm than good if she pushed herself and went to the clinic to volunteer. But she'd also be lying if she denied that a small part of her wasn't also using it as an excuse to avoid seeing Sam.

Ever since the argument with her dad, she felt the need to take a step back. It made her realize not only how quickly they'd gotten so close but also how much she *felt* for her. And both of those things were equally terrifying.

She never responded to Sam's text that night. Every time she tried, she got stuck on what to say or how to say it.

Should she bring up what her dad had said? It felt like something they should speak about in person. And when Sam texted her again, the next night to check in on her after Laura had presumably told her she'd called out sick, she still wasn't sure what to say. But she decided she had to say something or else it would look like she was avoiding her.

She settled for something short and generic, then decided she would speak to her the next day in person about everything.

Unfortunately, the extra twenty-four hours had done little to clear her head.

She stared at the building for another few seconds before reaching to grab her things from the passenger seat. When she picked up her phone, she saw a new email notification pop up on the screen. She slid it open and recognized Miss Williams' email.

Hi Jess,

I had the pleasure of speaking with a member of the admissions staff at Trinity University yesterday. She said their women's lacrosse program hasn't had many eligible students admitted this year. Due to this, their coach has decided to scout the eligible student athletes in the area who have applied. If they're impressed with what they see, they'll most likely push through the admission to make you a top candidate. This, along with your volunteer project, could possibly guarantee your acceptance as long as everything goes smoothly.

However, I wanted to run it by you first. Their assistant coach would come watch both you and the other top candidate, Gabby Earnheart, in the championship game.

*So, if this is still the college you'd like to pursue, let me
know, and I will set it up!*

Jess stared at the screen. Lacrosse was easy. She wasn't worried about
that part, but still something felt off. Her thumb hovered over the
reply button, frozen. For some reason, the obvious answer didn't come
as quick as it always had. She thought about what her dad had said
about Sam, and the pit in her stomach returned.

She stared at the screen for another few seconds. Then she tapped
the reply button.

*Sounds great! Yes, Trinity is still the goal, and I'll do
anything necessary to get in.*

Before she could dwell on it any further, she grabbed her things and
slid out of the car.

When she opened the front door of the building, she immediately
saw Sam sitting behind the desk with her usual headphones on, eyes
glued to the screen in front of her.

Sam finally noticed her once she was a few feet from the desk. "Oh,
hey," she said, pulling her headphones down and resting them around
her neck.

"Hey," Jess replied with the best smile she could muster.

"How are you feeling?" Sam asked as her eyes scanned over her.

Jess set her things down on the desk. "Good. Much better." She felt
awkward, like she was avoiding eye contact too much.

"Oh good," Sam replied. Her eyes lingered for a few extra seconds before she turned back to her computer.

Jess pulled her camera out of the bag with an unnecessarily high level of focus. She couldn't help cringing at herself as she needlessly adjusted settings she'd never seen before, just so she had something to do.

After a few more seconds, Sam stopped typing again and looked at her.

"Is everything okay?" she asked, her voice slightly lower.

Jess swallowed, still looking at the camera screen that now displayed an unfamiliar error message. "Yeah, just tired."

Sam studied her for a few moments. Then she finally asked, "Was everything okay with your dad the other night?"

Truthfully, this was about as perfect an opening as she could've gotten to bring up what he'd said, but she really didn't want to talk about it just yet.

"Yeah," she lied. "Fine."

Sam kept watching her, but remained silent.

Luckily, Laura walked out and interrupted them before the conversation could continue.

"Hey," she greeted her, smiling warmly, like always. "It's been kind of empty so far today. If you want me to do another interview for your video and answer more questions, today would probably be best."

"Oh, yeah, that'd be great," Jess answered. She tried to match the woman's smile, but truthfully, doing anything more than sitting at the desk sounded exhausting.

"Wonderful!" Laura said with another bright smile. "Just grab me in between meetings whenever you're ready."

"Okay, I will," Jess responded with a nod.

Then Laura walked back into the auditorium, leaving them alone in the hall once more.

"So," Sam began again, "really, how was it with your dad that night?"

Jess pursed her lips, eyes lingering on the camera bag in front of her.

"He mentioned something," she said. "About you."

Sam's expression remained even as Jess finally turned to look at her. She cleared her throat, unsure of which words to choose.

"He said that you—" she glanced around and lowered her voice before continuing. "He said you had a record."

Sam's eyes widened just a fraction. Barely enough for Jess to notice. She watched her face go from surprised to hurt to angry in less than a second.

"Is that why you've been so weird?" Sam spat. "You think less of me because of that?"

"What? No, of course not—well yes, that is probably why I've been a little weird. I just didn't know how to bring it up and I—"

"You didn't know how to bring it up?" Sam scoffed, and Jess hated hearing the anger in her voice. "If you wanted to know something, you could've just asked instead of—" she paused suddenly, like she'd just remembered something. She opened her mouth to continue, but instead just shook her head. She closed her mouth, lips pursed and jaw clenched. "You know what," she started again, "you don't really have a right to ask me about stuff like that, anyway. We're not dating. You're not my girlfriend. We're just friends, right?"

Jess was trying her hardest to listen, but her brain was stuck on the way Sam's voice sounded when she said "my girlfriend".

"Maybe," Sam continued, "at most, some days we're fuck buddies. But definitely nothing more than that."

This got Jess' attention. Shame washed over her when she instinctively scanned the surrounding area to see if anyone was within earshot. Sam must've noticed, because the hurt look reappeared on her face.

"You can't blame this all on me," Jess said, finally feeling her defenses rise. "The second time, you—" she glanced around again, lowering her voice. "You kissed me, okay? So don't act like this is all my fault, because you knew exactly what you were getting into, and you chose to do it, anyway."

"Yeah, but what I didn't choose was for you to treat me like your girlfriend one minute, and a stranger the next. Just some girl you volunteer with at the clinic, right?" Sam spat back. "If that's the case, then why would you expect me to share every intimate detail of my life with you? How could you possibly be upset that I hadn't told you about that?"

Jess shook her head in frustration. "I wasn't upset that you hadn't told me. I was upset that I—" she paused, trying to think of how to explain what she'd felt when she found out. "It just—it made me feel like I didn't really know you." She looked down at her lap. "Which didn't feel good or right, given how I *feel* about you."

Sam was quiet for a second, watching her, but Jess could still feel the anger coming through the stare.

"When this all started, you wanted to figure things out. Figure out what you were feeling. I think you've had enough time to do that."

Jess closed her eyes, hoping that didn't mean what she thought it did.

276

Sam shut her laptop and picked her backpack up off the floor, placing it in her lap. She paused then, contemplating for a second.

"I was in a—" she paused again, and Jess looked up at her. Sam shook her head slightly, looking off to the side. "I was in a bad home. I was young and stupid, and I thought it'd be easy to just run away. Live on my own or something." Jess saw the muscle in her jaw tighten. "I snuck out and didn't know where to go."

She cleared her throat and picked up her laptop, stuffing it messily into her backpack. "I was walking in a neighborhood and there was a Jeep parked against the sidewalk. It had one of those soft tops that you could just open through the zipper on the back to get into the trunk."

She pursed her lips, staring hard at the backpack in her lap. "I was tired and cold, and I didn't know where else to go, so I unzipped the back and climbed into the trunk to sleep for the night. The owner found me in the morning and called the cops."

Sam was quiet for a moment. "They had some random snacks in the car. Chips and stuff. Probably groceries that they'd forgotten to bring inside." She rolled her eyes. "I was hungry. The cops called it burglary."

She shook her head one more time, then zipped her backpack closed and stood up. "I knew exactly what I signed up for the day I kissed you. I know what this is supposed to be," Sam said, motioning her hand between them. "I think you're the one who's forgetting."

Jess sat there, stunned, staring at the girl who had come to mean so much to her.

She wished more than anything that she could tell her she was what she wanted. But as she thought that, she also thought of the email from Miss Williams'. The email about Trinity. Then she thought about her dad the night before. She thought about the way he'd looked at her, studying her reaction. Then, like clockwork, she thought of what her mother would've thought. She wished she could honestly tell herself that her mother would've been fine with it—would've loved her and supported her. But she didn't know if it was a lie.

Sam took a few steps towards the door.

"Sam," Jess said, her voice cracking. "I—I'm sorry."

Sam paused her steps for a moment, but didn't turn around.

"Yeah, me too," she muttered. Then she walked out the door.

***

Jess pushed the front door of her house open and stepped inside. The sounds of food popping and sizzling made their way to her. It smelled good, and on any other day she would've been excited to eat whatever it was. But this time, she had no appetite.

Sam never came back after she walked out, and although Jess desperately wanted to text or call her. She had no clue what to say. And the longer she'd sat there alone thinking about it, the more angry she got. Anger at her dad for causing her doubt. Anger at herself for not being able to choose.

She hung her keys on the hook before slowly trudging to the kitchen.

Her dad glanced up from his phone as she walked in.

"Hey," he said, his voice rough. She wondered if he also hadn't slept great the night before. "Didn't see you this morning. You skipped your run?"

Jess stopped when she reached the other side of the countertop, and by the time she was there, her blood was boiling.

"Did you even read the actual report?" She practically spit the words at him.

His eyebrows pulled together slightly, and he looked utterly lost. The fact that he didn't even know what she was talking about just added fuel to the fire.

"Sam's arrest," she gritted out through a clenched jaw.

Finally, understanding dawned on his face. He leaned back with a sigh.

"Did you read the full report?" she repeated with a venom she hadn't ever heard in her own voice.

"No," he answered nonchalantly. "I didn't."

The anger boiled over into rage.

"What is wrong with you?" she shouted, her fists squeezing together. "How could you possibly think it was okay to judge someone off of two words that you saw on the summary of their record?"

"Jess, I think you're overreacting—"

"No! You don't know the whole story. You don't know what happened—"

"Well, I don't think there's any excuse for doing something that gets you arrested for trespassing or burglary," he said, crossing his arms over his chest.

She opened her mouth, ready to argue—ready to tell him the full story. But then she stopped.

She shook her head and scoffed. "You're so worried about me being around such a terrible influence. But in reality, she's probably a better person than I'll ever be." She felt a burning sensation in the back of her eyes. "She's strong, and she's—" Jess paused, her voice having lost some of the anger it previously held. "She's just—*good*." The word somehow felt both completely inadequate and also perfect.

He looked at her again with that penetrating stare, and she wondered if her face revealed anything new to him this time.

After a few moments of silence, he finally spoke. "I didn't realize you were so *close* to this girl."

A prickling sensation ran down the back of her neck.

"Jess," he continued, and it instantly reminded her of the way he spoke when he was taking someone's statement. "How much time have you two been spending together? Have you been hanging out with her and keeping it from me?"

She immediately thought of the first night they'd spent together, when she texted him and said that she was spending the night at Scarlett's instead. That had actually been the only time she'd flat out lied to him about it. Every other time, she left it vague and hadn't specified who she was with. She figured he would just assume she was with Scarlett, and she wouldn't go out of her way to correct that. Technically, that wasn't really lying. After all, it wasn't her fault if he made assumptions on his own.

"No," she started, but quickly changed her mind. She didn't want to lie to him again. "Well, yeah, I guess we've been hanging out," she muttered.

The muscle in his jaw twitched, and she knew he was trying hard to keep his cool.

"So you've been lying to me?"

"Technically, just once," she muttered. "The other times you never asked who I was with."

"But you knew I didn't want you spending time with her, and you did it anyway behind my back?" The anger had now broken through his cool facade.

"Well, you clearly only had a problem with it for the wrong reason anyway," she said, letting every drop of annoyance seep into her voice.

"You've never been one to lie, but now you've lied to me so you could," he paused, slowly articulating the next words, "spend time with this girl?"

The tone of suspicion in his voice made her stomach feel sick.

She didn't answer.

They sat in silence for what felt like an eternity. Then finally, he spoke again.

"If you're doing something that you feel the need to hide from other people, then you probably shouldn't be doing it in the first place."

She looked away, the last few words looping in her head.

"You only have one week left before winter break. Then lacrosse will be over and colleges will finish their early decision choices."

She gritted her teeth and met his stare again.

"Jess," he continued, his voice cutting through the air. "Do not screw it up."

She wanted to argue with him—to tell him she'd worked her ass off her whole life, and she didn't need anyone reminding her of the stakes. But she kept her mouth shut. Maybe it was the fear that he would see through her even more than he already had. Or maybe she was afraid of the conversation continuing and somehow accidentally revealing even more of the truth about her feelings for Sam.

So she stayed quiet.

After he'd stared her down for a sufficient amount of time, he finally relaxed a bit, uncrossing his arms and leaning back against the countertop. He cleared his throat, changing his tone to something nonchalant and much less intimidating. Somehow, that was even worse.

"Luke's dad invited us over to their house Monday night for a holiday dinner."

Jess' eyes snapped up, her mouth already opening to protest.

He put up a hand, stopping her. "Originally, I said no. But I think it would actually be good for you."

Jess scoffed. "That's ridiculous! Luke and I broke up. That would literally be the most awkward dinner ever. How could that possibly be good for me?"

The look in his eyes told her she'd said exactly what he'd wanted. "Did you two break up before or after all of these hangouts with Sam started?"

It felt like ice water had trickled down the back of her neck, and the sick feeling instantly returned to her stomach. He was getting closer. Too close.

She opened her mouth to respond, but nothing came out. She felt like a deer in headlights.

"Jess," he said slowly, "is there anything else you need to tell me?"

She looked down at her hands to avoid his piercing stare, then shook her head.

"Are you sure?" he asked again.

She paused for a beat before giving one final nod of defeat.

He watched her for a few seconds, then finally sighed. "I think it'll be good for you to be around people who've always been good influences on you. You need normalcy and support right now. Not—" he paused, clearing his throat and looking away, "distractions."

This time, she didn't argue. She couldn't risk saying something else that would eventually lead to the truth about her and Sam. The mere thought of it was enough to make her feel sick.

So instead, she nodded once again.

"Good," he said, picking his phone up off the counter. "I'll let them know we can make it."

Chapter 17

I t's possible Sam was avoiding her.

Okay, no. Sam was most definitely avoiding her.

Jess' eyelids sagged as she pulled into the clinic parking lot that Saturday morning. She'd texted Sam an apology but hadn't gotten any response. Then, the next day when she'd arrived at the clinic, Sam never showed up. Laura said she hadn't heard from her and that she must've been busy, but Jess knew better.

Sam was putting some distance between them. And now Jess had to figure out how to fix things.

Showing up at her house again unannounced had initially been an option, but she quickly scratched it off the list. It was probably best not to look too overbearing. If Sam needed space, that's what she'd get.

She put the car in park and leaned her head back on the seat, closing her eyes. Between the extended practices leading up to the championship game, studying for school finals, and volunteering, she could feel herself wearing thin. And when she could finally lie down to sleep, it didn't come easy.

She swung the car door open and picked up her bag, stifling a yawn as she let her feet drop to the pavement. Her eyes glazed over, staring blankly at the floor as she trudged to the front door of the building.

Another big yawn, and she shook her head, blinking the wetness out of her eyes. This was going to be a long day. She mentally berated herself for not having picked up coffee on the way.

She pulled the handle and walked through the entrance, her eyes automatically flitting to the front desk in search of the one face she wanted to see.

Instead, she just saw Laura standing there, her back turned to her.

She tried her best not to frown in disappointment.

"Hey Laura," she said, walking around the side of the desk.

"Oh," Laura turned to her, startled, and Jess could instantly see her red, swollen eyes. "Sorry honey, I didn't hear you come in."

"What's wrong?" Jess asked, instantly forgetting her own worries. "Are you okay?"

She threw her bag onto the chair and rounded the desk to the woman.

Laura opened her mouth to speak, but closed it again as a sob wracked through her body. Jess grabbed a tissue from the counter, glancing down the hallway, searching for any sign of Sam.

"Here." She handed her the tissue, rubbing gentle circles on the older woman's upper arm.

Laura dabbed her watery eyes. "Thanks honey," she said through a sniffle. "You haven't talked to Sam?"

Jess stiffened.

"No, why?" she asked, concern creeping around the edges of her voice.

Laura sniffled again, wiping her eyes and nose.

"Laura, what's wrong?" she urged with a little more force than she meant to use. "Where is she? Where's Sam?"

Laura shook her head lightly. "She called this morning." The woman opened her mouth to continue, and Jess watched fresh tears well up in her eyes. "R—Ricky, he—" her bottom lip trembled as tears streamed down her face. "He passed last night."

Jess' breath caught in her throat.

"I—I guess his wife called Sam to come help when she—" A fresh sob shook through her. "When she found him."

"Oh Laura, I'm so, so sorry," Jess said, wrapping her arms around her.

"I didn't r—realize he was stru—struggling so much." She felt the woman shaking beneath her, tears falling freely once more.

They stayed like that for a minute before Jess gently released her grip. The woman needed consoling, but Jess couldn't stand one more minute without seeing Sam. Not when she *knew* she was hurting.

"When did you talk to her last?"

Laura blew her nose into the crumpled tissue. "A few hours ago, maybe. She called when she left their house."

Jess' heart ached thinking of Sam being there all night, putting her own feelings aside to help his family.

"Will you be okay here?" Jess asked, handing her a fresh tissue from the box on the desk.

The woman nodded with a small, sad smile. "You're not staying?"

Jess frowned, looking away to avoid Laura's questioning eyes. "I—I want to go check on Sam," she said. "I mean, if that's okay with you."

Laura waved her off. "Yes. Yes, of course it is, honey. I'm so glad you girls have become such good friends."

Jess nodded slightly, her lips pressed into a hard line. "Do you need me to help with anything before I go?" she asked, her hand itching to pull the phone out of her pocket and call Sam.

"No, that's okay. You go ahead," she answered, blowing her nose. "Give her a big hug for me."

"I will," Jess said, grabbing her bag off the desk. "And call me if you need anything."

She spun and practically jogged out of the building toward her car, pulling her phone out as she got to the driver-side door. Scrolling through her recent text conversations, she quickly found the thread with Sam and clicked the call icon.

The phone rang a handful of times before going to voicemail, but even before then, Jess had already begun the familiar drive to her house.

She called two more times on the way, knowing every call would end the same, but she still had to try.

Ignoring every yellow light, she sped down the road, fingers tapping hard against the steering wheel.

Her phone buzzed in her lap, and she jumped, her hand dropping down to grab it.

A text from Scarlett.

She groaned, dropping it back into her lap.

A few lights later, she finally turned into the familiar neighborhood. Her eyes instantly flicked to Sam's house at the end of the street. She pulled up and parked in her usual spot, then jumped out of the car without a second thought.

The porch light was on, which was new, but at least told her that Sam was probably still there.

She knocked twice, then stood on the top step, waiting, her right hand tapping against her upper left bicep.

A few seconds passed, and she raised her hand to knock again.

Suddenly, the door swung open.

"Oh." Jess' eyes widened in surprise.

Chris stood in front of her, staring back with a mildly intrigued expression.

"Hi," she said, working to regain her composure. In all honesty, she'd almost forgotten that he even technically lived there at all. She'd spent a lot of time at the house over the previous few weeks and hadn't run into him even once.

"I'm uh—"

"I'm sorry for your loss," he cut her off.

She blinked, confused for a second at what he'd said.

"I remember seeing you at the clinic that day with them," he continued. "I assume you knew him, too."

"Oh," she mumbled, shaking her head slightly. "Yeah. I did, but not as well as Sam did."

He nodded, pressing his lips together in a tight line.

"Um—" her eyes flicked past him into the house. "Is she here?"

He squinted slightly, watching her. She could tell he was reading something on her face, and she tried to keep from shrinking beneath his gaze.

"She was out all night. I'm not sure she's up for visitors."

Something rose inside her. Almost like anger, but also something else. Maybe protectiveness?

She crossed her arms over her chest, feeling her eyes tighten into a slight glare. "Well, I'd like to check with her myself, if that's okay."

His face changed into something that resembled amusement, and suddenly Jess could see Sam in his expression. The way his eyes crinkled just slightly. The way one corner of his mouth curled up the smallest amount. It was the first time she could see the resemblance between them, and any other day, it might have actually been sort of heartwarming. But not now. Not when Sam was hurting on the other side of the door.

She straightened her back, standing a little taller.

He watched her for a few more seconds, his eyes scanning over her. Then, finally, he moved to the side and nodded his head inside.

Her shoulders relaxed slightly as she exhaled and brushed past him. "Thanks," she muttered.

She made it a few feet down the hall before Chris called after her.

"Wrong way."

Jess turned around, giving him a quizzical look.

He jerked his head toward the door leading to the garage.

"Oh," she mumbled, awkwardly walking back to the front of the house. When she got to the door, she held up her hand to knock, but decided she'd rather not endure Chris' penetrating stare any longer than necessary.

Pushing open the door, her eyes instantly landed on Sam sitting in a chair in front of the workbench, faced partially away from her.

She cleared her throat, taking a slow step toward her and pulling the door closed behind her.

When Sam remained still, with no reaction whatsoever, Jess took another step in her direction. Now she could see the open laptop resting on her thighs, with a black screen. Sam stared at it, her jaw set, a vacant look in her eyes.

"Sam," she said softly, taking another careful step toward her.

The girl flinched then, whipping her head around. Dark, angry circles hugged her eyes, and even from a few feet away, Jess could easily see the red rims around them.

Sam's face softened just a fraction. "Oh, hey," she muttered. "What are you—"

"I talked to Laura," Jess answered, coming up slowly beside her. She knelt in front of her, carefully resting both hands on her knees. "I tried calling, but you didn't answer."

Sam's eyes hardened again, a complete emotional barrier put up between them. And for the second time that day, Jess saw a resemblance between her and her uncle. This time, it wasn't heart-warming.

"Oh," she mumbled, looking down at the computer. "Sorry. Phone's on the charger."

Jess watched her closely, scanning her face and body language. Sam tapped a key on the laptop and the screen came back to life. She started typing, hitting the keys a little harder than usual.

Jess waited a few seconds until she realized Sam wasn't going to say anything more.

Memories flickered into her mind of how it was after her mother died and the things people had said and asked her. The most common one was if she was okay. It was also her least favorite. Of course, she wasn't *okay*, but if she ever actually told them that, they'd get uncomfortable, as if she'd said something inappropriate. As she got older, she realized they weren't really asking because they wanted to know the answer. They were just asking because, what else do you say to a grieving six-year-old?

It killed her to realize it, but the only thing she wanted to ask Sam at that moment was if she was okay.

Pain clearly radiated from behind her clouded, red eyes, although it also seemed to be coated in anger. And still, that was the only question Jess wanted to ask. Maybe she'd been a little too hard on all those people who'd asked her that after her mother died.

She watched the way Sam's eyelids drooped as she scrolled and clicked.

"Have you slept at all?"

Sam shook her head slightly, her eyes never leaving the screen in front of her.

Jess frowned. "Do you think you should try?"

Sam gritted her teeth and closed the laptop before abruptly standing up from the chair.

"I'm not tired," she growled, callously shoving the computer onto the workbench. Jess flinched, hearing the metal scrape against the wooden top.

"But maybe you should try—"

"Why are you here?" Sam demanded, spinning to face her.

Jess stared at her, dumbfounded. "What do you mean?"

Sam crossed her arms over her chest and leaned back against the workbench. "*Why* are you here?" she asked again, her voice low and dangerous.

"I—I don't know," Jess stammered, beginning to feel flustered. "I knew you'd be upset and—I—I don't know. You're my friend. I wanted to be here for you."

The muscle in Sam's jaw twitched. "So today we're *friends*? Not *fuck* buddies?"

Jess flinched. She hated herself for instantly worrying if Chris could hear them through the door. Her arms folded defensively over her chest and she looked off to the side.

After a few seconds of silence, Sam dropped her arms to her sides and rested her palms behind her on the edge of the wood. Her head tilted down, sagging between her shoulders, and Jess could see the exhaustion riddled throughout her body.

"You know, eventually you're gonna have to choose."

Jess pressed her lips together, ignoring the dread that bubbled up in her chest. "Well, *eventually* isn't today."

Sam looked up, and they locked eyes for a few seconds before her gaze fell back to the floor. She didn't look angry or defensive anymore. She just looked sad. Defeated.

It was enough to make Jess' chest ache, and she wondered when she'd let her own feelings become so intertwined with another person. Become so dependent on another person. Maybe it was the day they'd slept together, or the day they kissed for the first time.

Or maybe it happened long before that.

She took a small step toward her and paused, gauging her reaction. Sam didn't even seem to notice, so she took another. Then another. And another, until she was finally standing right in front of her. She moved another few inches until they were closer than any *friends* would be.

Finally, Sam raised her eyes and looked at her. There was still anger in them, and Jess wondered if it was directed at her or something

292

else. Underneath the anger, she could see pain and uncertainty. Maybe fear?

She raised both hands, never breaking eye contact, and rested them against Sam's chest near her collarbone. Then, inch-by-inch, she slowly slid them up and around her shoulders onto the back of her neck. She worked her hands back and forth against the tight muscles there before dragging her fingernails up into her hair at the base of her neck.

Sam's eyes fluttered for a second, then opened again. They held a determined stare, and it reminded Jess of the way a child looks when they're utterly exhausted but refuse to let themselves fall asleep. Jess might not have known the perfect thing to say or ask, but she did know this. She knew how to make Sam's body relax.

"I'm not tired," Sam repeated, her voice scraping like gravel.

"Then what are you?" she asked, her fingers tangling up into the girl's hair, nails dragging in the place she knew would make her yawn, eventually.

Sam opened her mouth to say something and then paused, shaking her head lightly, her jaw clenching again. "Angry," she growled.

Jess nodded, expecting something along those lines. "Okay, and what are you angry at?"

Sam's eyes darkened, and Jess swore she could see the actual emotion flooding them. A darkness enveloping the deep green. She clenched her teeth harder, the muscle in her jaw twitching back and forth. Jess waited a few seconds, but Sam remained silently seething, avoiding her gaze.

"What are you angry at?" she repeated the question, sliding her palms back down onto the girl's shoulders.

A storm of pain and fury raged in her expression, each one fighting to come out, and Jess wished she could take some of the burden for her.

"Him."

"Why are you angry at him?" Jess asked, her voice calm and gentle.

"I just—I can't believe he did that to her," Sam forced out through gritted teeth.

Sam's body tensed even more, her shoulders raising and her back straightening.

"He just left!" She swung her hand through the air. "After everything he said and everything he promised them, he just fucking left!"

The tone in her voice was furious, but it held an edge of despair that reminded Jess of the soft cracking sound glass makes when it has too much pressure on it. Right before it shatters. She kept quiet, hoping Sam would fill the silence with everything she was holding in. With everything she was feeling.

But she didn't.

Jess waited and watched her for what felt like an eternity, but Sam just stood there silently, anger rippling off of her. She knew why Sam was really so angry, but she needed to be the one to say it. She needed to admit it to herself. Jess couldn't do it for her.

"What else does it make you feel?"

Sam shook her head slightly, and Jess could see the moment slipping away. It was like she was watching a wall in Sam's head being built right before her eyes and she was powerless to stop it.

"Nothing." Sam's eyes went vacant. There wasn't a single trace of the warmth they usually had when they looked at her.

Jess waited for her to say something else, anything that would help her let out the pent up rage and sadness. But nothing came.

Finally, Sam sighed and pushed herself forward off of the workbench, taking a step past Jess.

"I'm sorry you came all the way here," Sam started, and the way she said it made Jess' stomach hurt. "But I have a lot to do. A lot to help with."

This wasn't how it was supposed to go. Sam wasn't supposed to shut her out. Or at least, that wasn't how Jess had imagined it going.

"I was angry at my mom for a long time after she died," Jess whispered.

Sam froze a few feet away.

"When she was sick, people would say things like 'she's a fighter' and 'she'll beat this'." Jess paused as the memories crept into her mind. Memories she hadn't recalled in years. Memories she wasn't even sure she still had. "I think—I didn't really understand cancer or sickness. I was too young. Everyone saying things that like put the idea in my head that it was up to her to—" she shook her head, eyes dropping to the floor. "I don't know, win or something."

It was odd, saying these things aloud. Sometimes she'd let herself think about them, but even then it'd been years since she had.

"So when she didn't—*win*—" Jess continued, feeling the familiar tightness finally squeezing into her mouth and throat. She closed her eyes, forcing herself to finish. "I blamed her."

She took a deep breath and felt her chest tremble slightly on the exhale.

"Do you still blame her?" Sam whispered, and her eyes looked like they were begging for a certain answer.

Jess pursed her lips, knowing what she wanted to hear. But that wouldn't be the truth.

"Yeah," she whispered. "I know it's not fair. I know it wasn't her choice, and that it was an awful thing that happened. But I think sometimes, when you're grieving, you just need something to hate. *Someone* to hate."

She sighed, suddenly feeling completely drained.

"I know it's not the same," she continued, her eyes meeting Sam's. "I'm not trying to say that cancer and addiction are equal or anything. I just—I hope you remember that whatever you're feeling is okay."

Sam's eyes flitted to the ground, and she gave a small nod.

Jess waited a few seconds for her to say something before finally breaking the silence.

"I'm sorry for just showing up. I—I just wanted to make sure you were okay." She pulled her car keys out of her pocket and fiddled with them in her hand. "Call me—if you need anything, okay?"

"I'm sorry I snapped at you," Sam said, regret evident in her eyes and voice.

Jess nodded, letting silence fill the space between them for a moment. "Is it starting to bother you? Us doing—whatever it is we're doing."

Sam looked thoughtful for a moment before she spoke. "Honestly, I don't know. I didn't think so before today."

"What changed?" Jess asked, selfishly hoping it would be something she could change back.

Sam shrugged, staying quiet for a few moments.

Jess waited, hoping she would eventually answer. Finally, she sighed, turning towards the door.

"I wanted to see you," Sam said in a low, defeated voice.

Jess stopped where she was, her back facing Sam.

"Last night," Sam continued, "in the middle of everything, I just wanted to see you."

Jess' throat suddenly felt tight.

"It wasn't to kiss you or to hook up or anything else. I just wanted to *be with you*."

Jess swallowed the lump in her throat and felt a sting in her eyes.

Sam sighed, shaking her head. "That's not how I should feel about someone who's just a *friend*. Or even someone I'm just sleeping with."

Jess shook her head, finally turning to face her. "I'm sorry. I tried—"

"No," Sam said, cutting her off. "I know. I'm not blaming you. If anything, it's my fault." A sad smile skipped across her lips. "Like you said, I knew what I was getting into."

Jess bit her lip to distract from the pain she felt in her chest as Sam spoke those words. She knew where this was going, and she wasn't ready to let it happen. She wasn't ready to let her end things.

"Please," Jess whispered. "Please don't do this now. We can talk about everything tomorrow if you still want to, but today just please let me take care of you."

Sam exhaled, and she reached one hand up to rub her eyes.

Jess stepped towards her, reaching to take the hand that still hung limply by her side. "Lay down with me."

"I—"

"You don't need to sleep." Jess cut her off. "Not if you don't want to." She ran her hand up and down Sam's forearm in a soothing rhythm.

Sam frowned, and Jess could tell that she wasn't ready to give in. Not yet.

"Just for a few minutes," Jess continued. "Let your eyes rest, then you can get back to doing what you need to do."

Sam looked at her wearily for a moment before nodding in submission. "Fine."

Jess gave her a soft smile before turning to walk toward the door. She waited for a moment before Sam followed her, shoes dragging along the concrete floor.

She opened the door and felt relief when she saw the kitchen was no longer occupied. They walked down the hall, with Jess leading the way. She pushed the bedroom door open and went straight to the closet, pulling out the two pillows that Sam had given her to sleep with weeks before.

Funny that it had only been a couple of weeks. It felt like a lifetime had passed.

Sam stood at the foot of the bed, watching her curiously.

"Lay down," Jess said, her voice gentle but commanding.

Sam did as she was told, pulling the comforter back.

"Wait." Jess stopped her and turned back to the closet. She opened a drawer, scanning the contents before quickly pulling out a large gray t-shirt and sweat shorts.

"Here," she said, handing them to Sam.

Jess paused for a beat, awkwardly debating in her mind before turning around and facing her back to Sam.

She heard a chuckle behind her. "Are you turning around so I can change?"

A hint of amusement laced Sam's voice, and Jess couldn't believe how much she'd missed the sound. It was like taking a gulp of ice water after a long summer run.

"Just hurry up," she muttered, the corners of her mouth turning up slightly.

She heard another chuckle and then the light ruffling of clothing falling to the floor. Then the bedsprings creaked.

"You can turn around now," Sam said from behind her.

Jess turned around and saw Sam sliding under the comforter into the bed. She was about to kick off her own shoes out of habit when she suddenly stopped.

"Do you—" she cleared her throat awkwardly. "I can go if you want to be alone—"

"No," Sam cut her off, shaking her head.

Jess nodded, ignoring the relief she felt. She kicked off her shoes and then stepped toward Sam, holding the two pillows.

She held one out towards the girl's knees. "Here."

Sam smirked, taking the pillow and placing it between her legs. Then she handed her the next one.

"You forgot the third one," Sam said, a teasing lilt in her voice as she tucked the pillow between her arms.

Jess shook her head. "You don't need that one."

She knelt on the bed, crawling her way over Sam before laying down behind her. Then she pulled the comforter up over them and wrapped her arm tightly around her.

Sam stiffened for what felt like a millisecond before Jess felt her whole body relax, like she was melting into her.

She knew she probably shouldn't, but she couldn't help nestling her face into the crook of Sam's neck. Her lips grazed the girl's ear and, almost out of habit, she left a kiss on the soft skin.

Sam sighed, and Jess felt her relax even further into the embrace.

"If you keep doing things like that, it'll make it harder," Sam lulled, her voice already sounding lazy and half-asleep.

"Make what harder?" Jess whispered as her hand found Sam's and intertwined their fingers.

"Choosing."

Jess swallowed, closing her eyes. "Harder for me? Or harder for you"

"Both of us," she mumbled, and by the way her voice swayed, Jess knew she'd be asleep in minutes, if not seconds.

She leaned forward and kissed her shoulder, inhaling the scent of her hair, trying to savor the moment as much as possible.

Within a minute, she could feel the rise and fall of Sam's chest deepen with sleep. She closed her eyes, focusing on the rhythm, hoping that sleep would come for her too. But after a few minutes, the thoughts began seeping into her head, and she couldn't stop them. She thought of her and Sam, and then, like always, the thoughts turned to her mother.

What would she think?

Chapter 18

Jess walked out of her last class on Monday afternoon and immediately paced down the hallway toward the parking lot.

Sam had spent all day Sunday with Ricky's wife and daughter, doing as much as she could to help. And as much as Jess admired her selflessness, she also didn't want her sacrificing her own well-being in the process. So when she'd texted her that morning that she'd be at school at the end of the day to pick something up, Jess jumped at the opportunity to make sure she was alright and wasn't pushing herself too hard.

As she reached the end of the building and turned the corner, she squinted against the sun, scanning the front row of parking spots for her motorcycle.

There it was.

She paced across the grass, making her way to the bike. She stopped next to it and glanced back at the building. Sam was nowhere in sight. Jess pulled out her phone, checking the time. In all the days that Sam had given her rides to the clinic, Jess had never once beaten her to the parking lot at the end of the day.

That's okay, she had to turn up eventually if her bike was there. It didn't matter how long it took. She'd wait there all night if she had to.

She unlocked her phone and began scrolling through her TikTok feed while she waited. As the minutes passed, the parking lot slowly cleared, leaving only a handful of cars and Jess waiting alone beside the bike.

She checked the time again.

Just when she began contemplating whether or not she should call her, a door at the front of the counselor's building swung open. Her eyes shot up.

There she was.

Sam hadn't seemed to notice her yet. She was too busy staring down at a big red folder in her hands. By the time she was ten feet away from the bike, she still hadn't looked up.

Jess cleared her throat softly.

Sam's head snapped up, finally broken from her daze.

"Oh," Sam said with a small smile. "Hey."

She looked exhausted, with dark circles hugging her eyes. But there was something else there, too.

"I think this is the first time I made it out here before you."

"Oh, yeah. I guess so," Sam said, her eyes dropping back down to the folder in her hands.

"How are you doing?" Jess asked, hating that it seemed like such a stupid question.

Sam shrugged.

"Will you be at the clinic at all tonight?" Jess asked.

Sam shook her head. "Chris has some stuff he wants to talk to me about when I get home, and I don't know how long it'll take."

"Oh, okay."

They stood in silence for a moment. Jess had to keep her hand gripped tightly around her phone to keep from reaching for Sam's hand.

"You're here later than usual," Jess continued, trying to keep the conversation going as long as possible. Trying to keep Sam from leaving and spending another night wearing herself thin.

A small smile formed and spread across Sam's lips. "Yeah," she pulled the red folder out from under her arm. "I—um," she chuckled and shook her head slightly. "I got in." She turned the folder around, and Jess saw the words '*Welcome To MIT*' printed on the front.

"Are you serious!?" Jess yelled, a smile breaking across her face. "That's amazing!" She stepped forward and threw her arms around Sam's neck, hugging her as tight as possible.

Sam laughed lightly beneath her. "Thanks," she said softly, wrapping one arm around Jess' waist.

After a second, Jess knew that she should pull back and end the hug. She knew that would be the appropriate thing to do. That's what a friend would do. But no matter what her brain said, her arms wouldn't budge. Even when she felt Sam's arm loosen its grip around her, she still couldn't bring herself to let go. If anything, she held on even tighter.

Sam seemed to understand then, and she wrapped both arms securely around her waist, pulling her close.

Jess closed her eyes, absorbing every feeling of having Sam this close. She focused on every detail, burning the memory in her mind.

"You're incredible," Jess whispered. "I'm so proud of you."

Sam's arms squeeze just a bit tighter around her.

After a few seconds, Jess exhaled softly and finally let her arms loosen, letting them unwrap and hang at her sides. But she didn't step back. And when Sam removed her arms from Jess' waist, she didn't step back, either.

Jess looked at her and, for a second, she couldn't believe that she'd been lucky enough to meet the girl standing in front of her.

Sam looked back at her, and Jess could see the careful look in her eyes. She knew then that Sam was following her lead, putting the ball in her court. Letting her choose what they were to each other. Friends—or something more.

Jess swallowed, her eyes flitting to Sam's lips for a fraction of a second before meeting her eyes once more.

Sam became perfectly still, watching and waiting. Jess could see a curious anticipation forming in her gaze.

She felt herself subconsciously leaning in.

Sam's throat bobbed as she swallowed, her eyes looking at Jess' lips.

Then suddenly the door to the building swung open, the sounds of a group of students erupting into the air outside.

Jess jumped back instinctively, her head jerking up toward the sound.

She watched them walk toward the other end of the parking lot, completely oblivious to anyone else. Oblivious to the way they'd caused her heart to leap into her throat.

When she turned back, Sam hadn't moved an inch.

Jess expected to see disappointment in her eyes. Maybe frustration. Or maybe even a little anger.

Instead, they were full of understanding.

They held no judgment, only compassion.

"I'm sorry," Jess croaked, wrapping her arms around her own torso as she looked down at the ground.

Sam shook her head. "You didn't do anything wrong." She took a careful step forward. "It's okay to not be ready. And it's okay to not know what you want." A sad smile formed on her face. "I just can't do this hidden thing anymore when I have no idea how it's going to end."

Jess' heart leapt into her throat.

No. Don't do this. Not yet.

"Can you please just give me a little more time?" Jess pleaded, hating how weak she sounded. "Or at least just this last week before winter break. Then lacrosse and school will be over and I can really focus on figuring things out."

Sam frowned. "You really think that'll make a difference?"

"Yes," Jess said, her voice finally regaining its strength and confidence. She just needed Sam to wait a little longer—to give her a little more time.

Sam pursed her lips, thinking for a moment. "Okay."

"Okay," Jess repeated, a wide smile spreading across her face.

Sam chuckled, shaking her head. "Do you want to hangout later tonight? After I talk to Chris. Celebrate the whole MIT thing."

"Absolutely," Jess answered, with a smile so wide it hurt her cheeks. Then it instantly fell as she remembered the dinner she'd agreed to go to that night. She frowned. "Actually, sorry, I forgot I'm having dinner with—" she paused, her brain reluctant to give all the details, "my dad."

She knew she should tell Sam that it was with Luke's family, but it just didn't seem like the right time. Those details could wait at least a few more days. Besides, the dinner was just that: a dinner. Nothing more. Maybe there wouldn't be any reason to mention it to Sam at all.

"Oh, okay. Yeah, no worries," Sam said, and the understanding smile she gave created a small speck of guilt in Jess' chest. "Are you going to be at the clinic the rest of the nights this week?"

"Yeah, I need to finish a few things for the video essay. I have to submit it before Friday." Jess internally groaned, thinking about her workload for the next few days. She had finals, volunteering, editing the video, and on top of everything, their championship game on Friday.

"Are you still coming to the game?" Jess asked.

"Of course. As long as you still want me there?"

"Yes," Jess answered, a little too quick. "I mean," she continued, catching herself, "as long as you still want to come?"

She hated that it was ever a question to begin with. Sam had come to almost every game since that first week when she started giving her rides after school.

"Yes," Sam answered with a soft smile. "I do."

Jess smiled back at her.

Sam turned to her bike and began preparing to leave. Jess watched her swing the jacket over her shoulders, followed by her backpack, and she missed the days that she had done it with her. She missed knowing that she'd see Sam at the end of each day. By the time she realized how much it had meant to her, it was over. She wondered if Sam missed those days as much as she did.

The rumble of the engine broke through the air as Sam started the bike.

"See you tomorrow?" Sam called over the roar.

"Yeah," Jess answered with a smile. Sam nodded beneath the helmet, and Jess watched her pull out of the space and drive away.

***

They pulled up to Luke's parent's house, and Jess immediately exhaled a breath of relief. A handful of cars were parked along the street, which meant that her dad hadn't been lying when he'd said that other families would also be at the dinner.

She watched her dad put the car in park as his eyes drifted across the house in front of them. His lips were tight, and he wore the same mildly annoyed expression he always did when they attended social gatherings. At least that gave her one piece of satisfaction. She knew he would hate doing this just as much as she did.

They both slid out of the car and plodded up the driveway to the front door.

Jess stopped a couple of feet away, letting her dad be the one to knock. He cleared his throat, shoving his hands in his pockets as they waited.

After a few seconds, the door swung open, revealing Luke's mom, who smiled so wide, it almost looked unnatural.

"Oh my gosh, I'm so glad you guys could make it!" she screeched, clapping her hands together.

"Yeah." Jess' dad cleared his throat again, shifting his weight between his feet. "Yeah, we're uh—glad to be here."

If she wasn't so distracted thinking of an excuse to leave, Jess might've laughed at his response. Formal gatherings were definitely not his thing. And in the almost year she'd dated Luke, he'd never once shown any interest in getting to know Luke's parents. She'd actually always really liked them. They were sweet and welcoming, but they could also definitely push the line of being a little overbearing at times. And she had a feeling this dinner would be one of those times.

"Oh, sweetie, we've missed having you over!" Mrs. Adams cooed as she stepped out onto the porch and wrapped her in a tight hug. Jess hugged her back, feeling a little more at ease. At least she wasn't treating her differently now that she was no longer dating her son.

"I missed you guys too," Jess replied as she slowly released her grip on the woman.

Mrs. Adams stepped back, looking at her with another, more mischievous smile. "Well, maybe after tonight you'll start coming around again."

Jess stared at her blankly as she whipped around and waved them inside. Any ease the initial greeting had given her was instantly washed away by that comment.

Her father stepped past the threshold, and Jess reluctantly stepped in after him.

The inside of the house wasn't as crowded as she'd hoped. Luke found her within seconds, his eyes instantly lighting up as he jumped off the barstool he was perched on.

"Hey," he greeted her with a wide grin.

"Hey," she smiled back. This was really the first time they'd actually spoken since the breakup, and so far, he didn't seem awkward. That was a win she desperately needed.

He pulled her into a big hug that maybe lasted a few seconds too long.

"I'm so glad you came," he said, finally letting her go. He stepped back, but remained closer than any platonic friend would.

"Yeah," she muttered, her eyes scanning the once familiar living room.

"Hi Mr. Miller," he said, giving her dad a smile that was just a little too big.

The older man nodded at him, then continued walking toward the kitchen where beers sat the countertop.

"Come on," Luke said, taking her by the hand. "We can help my mom bring out the food."

Jess wondered if it was a friendly or flirtatious gesture. His hand wrapped around hers felt so wrong. Had it always felt that way? Maybe it had, and she just never had anything *right* to compare it to.

Once they reached the kitchen, he dropped her hand and Jess felt herself relax slightly.

"What can we help with, mom?" he asked.

There it was again. *We.* Like they still came in a pair. Even when they were technically a couple, Jess never really felt like they were a *we*.

"Oh, thanks honey," Mrs. Adams replied, looking over two full baking dishes resting on top of the stove. "You guys can bring these out now."

Jess picked up a dish, grateful to have something to do, and followed Luke out into the dining room, carefully setting it between a few others. They went back and repeated the process until every item had made its way to the table. And within a few minutes, people began sitting to eat.

"Here," Luke said with a smile, pulling out the chair next to his and motioning for her to sit down.

Mrs. Adams watched from a few seats down, a hopeful smile tugging at her lips. She wanted to make some excuse to sit somewhere else, but the intense looks from both of them dampened the words in her mouth. After a pause, she reluctantly gave in and sat down in the chair beside him.

Once everyone was seated, Mr. Adams led the table in a prayer that lasted an eternity. When it was finally over, he asked that everyone go around and say what they were most grateful for that year.

Wonderful. Her least favorite dinner activity. There was no way to make it not feel awkward.

She tuned out the first couple of answers, picking at the food on her late, until it got to Luke.

"I'm grateful for the special people in my life," he answered, glancing at her. This time, the smile he gave her seemed natural. It seemed sweet.

Then it was her turn.

"Um—" she paused, glancing down at her plate. She hadn't been paying attention and didn't bother coming up with something while the other people answered.

She took a second to think before finally answering, looking over at her dad. "I'm grateful for the new people I've gotten to know this year."

A flash of annoyance crossed his face. He looked away, and the person next to her began speaking.

After that, the dinner went on and Jess actually found herself enjoying it. It helped that Luke seemed to relax once they started eating. He stopped trying so hard and went back to being his usual self, which Jess remembered she actually liked when they were just friends. Even her dad seemed like he was having a good time, cracking the occasional laugh. Granted, he'd quickly downed two beers on arrival, so that was probably helping. Too bad she couldn't have done the same.

By the time dinner was done, Jess actually felt herself wanting to stay longer. She hadn't realized it, but she did miss Luke's family. And she now realized that she even missed him a little bit.

As the other families began saying their goodbyes and drifting out, Jess offered to help Mrs. Adams cleanup. The older woman accepted with a warm smile, and she and Luke worked together to bring the dirty dishes into the kitchen. Once everything was cleared, they began washing and drying at the kitchen sink, with Mrs. Adams packaging up the leftovers behind them.

Jess laughed hard, her cheeks hurting after Luke recounted another embarrassing story about Malik from their younger high school days.

Luke smiled, shaking his head as he dried his hands and leaned against the sink. "Man, I've missed this so much."

Jess looked down, her smile closing a bit as she finished drying the last dish in her hands. She reached over, setting it with the others.

He leaned a little closer to her, but Jess remained where she was, looking down at her hands as she fiddled with the dishrag.

"I've missed *you* so much," he said in a low voice. He leaned closer until his mouth was only inches from her face.

Her brain froze. She couldn't think of anything to say. Had she missed him, too? Maybe if she thought about it, there were probably some things that she did miss. But she really *hadn't* thought about it. She couldn't even remember the last time she'd thought about him since they broke up.

She swallowed hard, knowing she had to be honest.

311

"I—" She turned, ready to let him down gently. But right when she did, he surged forward, pressing his lips to hers.

Her entire body froze.

His lips moved against hers.

It felt wrong. *He* felt wrong.

But also—it felt *familiar*.

Her heart didn't race or jump in the way she'd become accustomed to every time she kissed Sam.

She didn't feel like every inch of her body was on fire. She didn't feel the excitement shooting through her bones. Instead, she was too aware of the way his lips felt. Too aware of the way they moved against hers. It felt like they were each dancing, but to an entirely different song.

But again, it felt familiar.

It didn't scare or excite her. She could probably do it forever and never even feel a fraction of the good—or *bad*—she'd felt every time Sam's lips touched hers.

She might never feel like life was blooming inside her when she kissed Luke, but she also knew with certainty that she would never feel the doubt and terror she did in the darkest moments after being with Sam.

And maybe that was worth it. Maybe that could be enough for her. Maybe she could learn to accept a life of *maybe* and *almost*. A life where her heart wouldn't threaten to explode every time she looked in *her* eyes.

Luke finally pulled back, breaking the kiss, and Jess' body thawed from its frozen position.

He gave her a small smile, but it didn't seem to reach his eyes this time, and Jess wondered if he sensed that something had changed in her. If he knew she was searching for someone else in his lips.

She looked away and saw Mrs. Adams peeking up at them from the other side of the kitchen, a half-hidden smile on her face.

Jess glanced down, something turning in her stomach. "I should probably go," she mumbled, setting the dish rag on the counter top. "Thank you, Mrs. Adams, for dinner. Everything was great."

"You're so welcome," she replied with a smile that was again too big.

She took a few steps toward the end of the kitchen before turning back to Luke. "See you at school?" she asked.

"Yeah," he said with a smile that didn't seem as bright as before.

She nodded, looking down at the ground as she exited the room to find her dad.

"Seemed like you were having a good time," he said gruffly, as they got into the car.

She didn't respond.

She felt like she was on autopilot.

For the first time in a long time, no thoughts, good or bad, swirled in her head.

Chapter 19

It wasn't cheating. So why did she feel so guilty?

It was Wednesday, two days later, and Jess weaved between students to get to the parking lot.

All day on Tuesday, she'd dreaded both running into Luke at school and also seeing Sam at the clinic that night. She knew she had to talk to her, but still had no idea what to say. So on Tuesday, she'd lost her nerve and texted Laura that she was sick and couldn't make it to the clinic that night. It made her feel like a coward, but it was better than seeing Sam before she really knew what she was going to say to her. Or if she was going to say anything at all.

Laura must have mentioned that she was sick, because Sam had called her later that night. Jess didn't answer. She'd called twice more, but Jess couldn't muster up the courage to answer.

She kept reminding herself that she didn't really have a reason to feel guilty. It's not like they were in a relationship. They hadn't made any agreements about not seeing other people. Far from it.

But still, it felt wrong. It felt like she'd cheated. Which was ironic considering that the only time she'd ever actually cheated on someone was on Luke when she'd kissed Sam the night of Winter Formal.

And somehow, this felt more like cheating than that did.

Now, as she made her way to the parking lot, she still didn't know what she was going to say. Worse, she still didn't know what she actually wanted.

She gritted her teeth in frustration as she rounded the side of the student building. She pushed through a few people until she'd made it past the hoard of students, and right when she broke out of the group, giving her the first clear shot to the parking lot, she saw her.

Sam was standing next to her motorcycle, smiling at Jacie beside her. Jacie was laughing, and to her credit, it looked more friendly than it did flirtatious this time.

Still, the sight stirred something within her.

The fact that she'd been tortured by guilt over the last two days while Sam just went about her life, probably still being hit on by multiple girls, lit a fire in her stomach.

It wasn't fair.

Jess was still far enough away that they hadn't seen her yet. She could easily go around the side of the parking lot and avoid them altogether.

That would be the smart thing to do.

And for a second, she really was about to do that.

But then Sam laughed, shaking her head in a way that made her hair fall perfectly around the base of her neck. And blood boiled under Jess' skin.

She turned, making a beeline toward them.

Sam was still oblivious by the time she got within ten feet of them, but Jacie saw her.

"Jess," she said with her usual sweet smile. "Hey."

She tried her best to smile back before immediately directing her attention to Sam.

"Surprised you're here," she said, her tone coming out more clipped than she expected.

"Yeah," Sam replied, her smile quickly fading into a confused look. "I had to talk to Miss Williams. And actually, I was hoping to talk to you, too."

Jacie glanced back and forth between them, probably picking up on the tense vibe. "I'm gonna head home. Sam, text me if you need help finishing the project for English."

"Yeah, I will. Thanks," Sam replied, smiling at her.

Jess watched her walk away, letting silence fall between them.

Finally, Sam cleared her throat. "I wanted to talk to you—"

"I didn't realize you and Jacie actually talked," Jess interrupted.

Sam looked at her, tilting her head to one side as her eyes squinted the smallest amount. "We have the same English teacher, just in different periods. She offered to help me get some of the work done before winter break."

Jess scoffed, and even she cringed at how jealous it sounded. "We both know you're smarter than everyone in that class. You're the last person that would need help with schoolwork."

"Well, I'm in a time crunch," Sam replied coolly.

Jess pursed her lips, looking away. "Right," she mumbled under her breath.

Sam stared at her for a moment, the confusion on her face finally replaced with something else. She crossed her arms, matching Jess' defensive stance. Then she took a step toward her, leaving only a foot between them.

"You can't ignore me one day, then show up the next acting like a jealous girlfriend," she growled in a low voice.

Jess' eyes snapped up, rage suddenly filling her chest. "I'm not jealous. If you want Jacie, I'm sure as hell not going to stop you."

For a split second, she thought she could see something resembling hurt flash across Sam's face.

Then, before she could stop them, more words came spilling out. "Honestly, it probably should've been her all along, anyway. She should've kissed you that night, not me."

The words scraped and cut against her lips like glass as they left her mouth.

She hated saying it. It felt like she was punching herself in the gut. But the thought had swirled in her head ever since the kiss with Luke.

She wasn't good for Sam.

Maybe she could be one day, but not now. No matter how painful it was to admit. The truth was that someone like Jacie would be better for her. Someone who knew what they wanted. Someone who wasn't *afraid* of what they wanted.

And that's when she realized it.

This wasn't just an argument. It wasn't just a fight.

It was *the* fight.

"Do you regret kissing me that night?" Sam asked in a low voice. It sounded angry, but Jess could hear the hint of pain behind it, and it broke her heart.

But it also made her even more sure of what she had to do.

Sam deserved better.

She deserved so much more than what Jess could give her.

"I wish I hadn't kissed you that night." Her voice cracked, but at that moment, she was sure it was the sound of her heart beginning to break.

Sam's head pulled back, her lips parting slightly. She looked like she'd been slapped across the face, and Jess knew right away that her blow had landed.

She instantly wanted to take it back, to tell her she was lying. That she would've absolutely lost her mind if anyone else had kissed her that night.

But she couldn't.

She couldn't keep Sam from living her life and being truly happy with someone else. It wasn't fair.

Her eyes burned as tears threatened to well up inside them. She blinked, forcing them away so she could land the final blow.

"We both knew this wouldn't turn into anything real, anyway."

The look in Sam's eyes as she processed the words was almost too much for Jess to watch. Pain and betrayal filled them, but the worst part was that she didn't look all that surprised. She almost looked like she'd half expected to hear those words. Like she'd known they were coming, and it was just a matter of time.

Sam looked down, swallowing. She stared at the ground and Jess waited for the anger. She waited for the harsh words to be hurled at her. The words she deserved.

"Okay," Sam said, uncrossing her arms and turning to pick her helmet up off the seat of her bike.

Jess blinked once, watching as she picked up her hoodie and slid it over her head. Then she paused, like she was wrestling with something in her head. Finally, she looked up at Jess again.

Her eyes and face were softer than before, but something about them already felt cold and distant. Nothing like the Sam she knew.

"I really hope you find everything you want in life," she said with a sad smile. "You deserve it."

And with that, the small fracture that had formed in Jess' heart turned into an irreparable break. The tears she'd worked so hard to keep at bay surged forward. She blinked furiously, looking down at her shoes to keep Sam from seeing the wetness in her eyes. Then she felt the familiar tightness forming in her chest, and she knew she had to get away.

She spun around without another word, walking in the direction of her car without really seeing where she was going.

She just knew she needed to get far away from Sam before she fell apart. But what hurt even worse was knowing that Sam was the only person she really wanted when she felt like this. Like the world was crumbling around her.

The familiar roar of the motorcycle filled the air behind her as she finally spotted her car.

She practically ran the last few feet before ripping the door open and pulling herself inside.

Right as the door shut behind her, the tears she'd worked so hard to hold back poured down her face. A gushing stream of despair leaking from her shattered heart.

Chapter 20

Sam's frozen face stared at her.

Jess watched the recording finish for what was probably the hundredth time in the last two days, the last frame ending on Sam's face. She clicked the button on her laptop to play the video again.

She'd spent the last two days compiling all the footage she'd taken to create the final video essay to submit to Trinity.

Every interview and every clip fit and blended perfectly together, and the interview with Sam would be the perfect final piece.

But now, she couldn't bring herself to do it.

She watched the way Sam's eyes changed. How they lit up and then dulled as she spoke about her childhood and her mother. It felt different from all the other videos. Even the one of Ricky. It was raw. The emotion poured through the screen.

And the more she watched it, the more she wanted to keep this memory for herself.

She didn't want a college admissions board to see it. She didn't want *anyone* else to see it. That moment was for her, and her alone.

"Jess!" her father called up the stairs. "You almost ready? Are you gonna drive with me?"

She blinked, watching the video roll to an end. "Yeah, one minute," she called back.

Staring at the screen, frozen once again on Sam's face, she finally removed the clip from the end of the video. Then she saved the file and attached it to the email she'd already prepared.

Taking a deep breath, she hit the send button and shut her laptop. She glanced at the time on her phone and jumped off the bed, grabbing her lacrosse bag.

***

"Fuck, there's like actually a lot of people here to watch us," Scarlett said, stretching her arm across her chest as she scanned the bleachers.

Jess' eyes followed hers, instinctively searching for Sam's face among them. Her eyes dropped back down when she saw the empty spot beside Malik. It's not like she'd expected Sam to show up, but it still hurt to see.

"Jess! Gabby!"

She turned, looking toward Coach Lowe, who was standing with a middle-aged woman and waving them both over. Her eyes flickered to the stands once more before jogging away from the stretching circle.

"Ladies," he said, as they both stopped in front of him. "This is Coach K." He nodded to the woman beside him. "She's the assistant coach for the lacrosse team at Trinity, and she'll be watching you play today."

"It's a pleasure to meet you," Gabby said beside her, holding out her hand. "I've heard such great things about you and your team."

Jess internally rolled her eyes, but she was also a little impressed by the girl's quick composure.

"Great to meet you," Jess said, reaching her hand out after Gabby's.

"Likewise. Good luck out there today," the woman replied with a tight smile before turning back to their coach. "I think I'm going to go find a seat before it gets too crowded."

He nodded at her, then waited until she was a few feet away. "I know having a college coach watching today could add some extra pressure, but try to push that aside and play like she's not here." His eyes skipped between them. "You're both incredible players. Play like you always do and she'll see that."

"Thank you," they both mumbled together as he walked back toward the bench.

Jess tilted her head back and rolled her shoulders. She wasn't one to get nervous, and this game was no exception. In fact, added pressure usually brought out the best in her.

Gabby, on the other hand, looked like she could use some help. One hand tapped against her thigh in an uneven rhythm as her eyes jumped back and forth, looking between the field and the stands.

"You need to block it out," Jess said in the most gentle tone she could muster.

Gabby scoffed, crossing her arms defensively. "I'm fine. Worry about yourself."

Apparently, nerves made her even more unlikeable.

Jess bit her cheek to keep from snapping back. "Look, this isn't a competition. We're literally on the same team."

"Right." Gabby rolled her eyes.

It took everything she had to keep her patience. She turned to fully face her. "Gabby, I'm serious," she said, taking a deep breath. "I'm sick of doing whatever this *thing* is with you. There's no point. We're both good, and we both deserve to get into any colleges we want."

Gabby squinted at her like she was trying to figure out if it was some kind of trick.

Jess exhaled her frustration. "Look, at least for now we're still on the same team, which means I care a lot more about beating them," she nodded toward the opposing team's bench, "than I care about beating you."

The referee whistled, signaling the two-minute mark before the start of the game.

Gabby looked at him for a moment before returning her gaze to Jess. "Fine," she said, her face softening a bit. "Truce."

Jess' lips tilted up into a small, satisfied half smile as she nodded. "Truce."

***

Apparently, the pressure *had* done something to Jess, because she was playing absolutely terrible.

She cussed under her breath as she watched the pass she'd just thrown sail wildly over Scarlett's head, landing out of bounds. None of her passes were going where they were supposed to, and the one shot she'd taken had gone straight into the center of the goalie. Luckily, the other team wasn't playing great either and hadn't managed to capitalize on any of her mistakes.

As Scarlett jogged to get the stray ball, the buzzer went off, signaling the end of the first quarter.

She walked to the benches and saw Scarlett jogging toward her.

"I know," Jess growled through her clenched teeth. "I don't need to hear it."

Scarlett's face softened. "Dude, it's okay. It's still early in the first half. Just clear your head." She squeezed Jess' shoulder as she sat down on the bench. "You got this."

Jess exhaled, snatching a bottle off the ground. She squeezed it, spraying water into her mouth. Her eyes naturally drifted over the crowd in the bleachers on the opposite side of the field. She spotted Coach K sitting near the center, talking on her phone. Jess' eyes skipped past her. If having her there was in fact throwing her off, she didn't want to dwell on it any more than necessary.

Her eyes drifted farther down to the end of the bleachers and abruptly stopped.

There, standing off to the side, leaning against the metal rail, was a girl she would recognize from a thousand miles away.

She couldn't clearly see Sam's face from that distance, but she knew without a doubt that it was her.

Her eyes froze in place. She couldn't have ripped them away if her life depended on it. Nerves shot through her chest, yet somehow this was the calmest she'd felt all day.

"Jess!"

Her eyes finally broke away, but the image of her remained burned behind her eyelids. She stood and walked into the huddle, only half-listening to what Coach Lowe was saying.

Why would she have come?

Maybe for one last goodbye?

Or maybe, just maybe, she missed Jess as much as Jess missed her.

"Jess?"

Her eyes snapped up to see Gabby glaring at her. "Did you get that?" she asked, her tone much more aggressive than it needed to be.

"Yeah," she lied, shaking her head slightly to clear any lingering thoughts.

The whistle blew, and the team dispersed to retake their positions on the field.

Jess turned to follow, but Gabby stepped in her way.

"Whatevers distracting you, you need to let it go. Now."

Jess rolled her eyes and stepped around her, but Gabby moved into her path again. Over her shoulder, she could see Scarlett in the middle of the field, watching them with the murderous look that any protective best friend would have.

"Look I'm not trying to be a dick," Gabby said, although her tone said differently. Then she exhaled and softened her face, like she really was trying to come off nicer. "You need to take the advice you gave me at the beginning. Push it aside for now and just focus on one play at a time."

To her credit, Gabby really did sound genuine once she tried. It almost felt like talking to a friend. Almost.

Jess pulled her shoulders back, nodding once. "Yeah. I got it."

***

And she did.

Maybe it was the pep talk from Gabby, or maybe it was seeing Sam. Or a combination of both. Either way, her energy and focus came back with a vengeance in the second quarter. And that seemed to re-energize the whole team. Everyone played better, and by the time the second quarter was almost over, they were up by two goals.

Jess sprinted down the sideline, cradling the ball and scanning her options for a pass. She saw Scarlett open off to the left side, and she quickly threw the ball to her.

Each player took a position around the crease, and Jess watched a few passes go around the circle while they tested different cuts.

She felt something wet hit her shoulder. Then she felt it again on her face, and then on her hand.

She glanced up for a second and saw rain droplets falling from the sky.

When she looked back down, she noticed her defender looking up as well. She saw the opportunity and cut straight toward the goal, waving her stick in the air and yelling for the ball.

Her teammate spotted her immediately and shot the pass straight to her. The ball smacked into her net with perfect precision, and she immediately shot it into the upper left corner of the goal, before the goalie had any time to react.

It was perfect.

The net rippled behind the goalie, and her teammates erupted in cheers, along with half the people in the stands.

Every teammate around her ran up, hugging and high-fiving her. Even Gabby gave her a wide smile and a nod as she tapped her stick against hers.

By the time their celebration was over, the rain was pouring down on them. She glanced at the bleachers and saw umbrellas going up everywhere. Her eyes drifted farther along to where she really wanted to look.

Sam stood farther away now, watching the last of the on-field celebration. She stood in the rain, wearing just her white t-shirt, with no umbrella to protect her from the downpour.

Their eyes met for a second, and she felt the familiar buzz of electricity run through her veins.

She thought she could see the ghost of a smile pass over Sam's lips.

Then, like it was the easiest thing in the world, the girl turned and walked away.

***

The second half was a very different game.

Jess played well, but both teams generally seemed to struggle to get much of anything done. The rain was gushing down, making it both difficult to see and get traction on the field. She'd already slipped and fallen twice, even with her cleats.

Nearing the end of the fourth quarter, neither team had scored any more goals, and every player was soaked from head to toe. They could barely make it twenty feet down the field without slipping, and with only a few minutes left in the game, the frustration was obvious.

Both teams were making sloppy fouls and letting avoidable mistakes slip by.

Jess watched Scarlett drop an easy pass, allowing the defender closest to her to scoop it up.

Her eyes flitted to the scoreboard. They were still up by three goals, and now there were only two minutes left in the game. Even if the other team did score, the likelihood of them scoring two more goals to tie the game was slim.

Jess jogged down the field, trailing after her teammates, who'd successfully stopped the player.

The girl was distracted looking for an open pass, and Jess saw the opportunity for a steal. She ran up from the side she was looking away from and checked her stick, knocking the ball out of her net.

Jess scooped it up from the puddled turf, spraying water into the air.

She heard ragged cheers from the now thinned out crowd in the stands as she ran back down the field. Glancing up at the scoreboard, she could see the clock ticking down now with less than a minute. The safe thing to do would be to hold the ball and let the clock run down, securing their championship win.

But something in her didn't want to be safe.

Something within her begged to make the unobvious choice. To do what she really wanted for once.

She glanced up at the scoreboard again.

Twenty-eight seconds.

There were three defenders around her, leaving no clear openings to the goal. She pulled back a few feet and jogged to the right, pretending to look for an open teammate to pass to.

It gave her a little more space, but not enough for a clear shot. If she wanted to go for it, she'd just have to take the risk.

She moved a few more feet to the right, giving her a full view of the bleachers on the other side of the goal. Before she could stop it, her eyes skipped up to the now empty space where Sam had been standing. The rain poured down, making it hard to see. If she squinted a little more, she could almost pretend that Sam's outline was still there, watching her.

Sixteen seconds.

The words of their last conversation played in her mind.

Eleven seconds.

She'd made the right choice. She knew that. Sam deserved better. And at least this way, maybe the torment of wondering what her mother would've thought would finally disappear. That was the silver lining. Although, if she were being honest, Sam was worth any amount of mental anguish she had to endure.

Seven seconds.

She scanned the defenders once more before finally making her move.

Jess faked a pass to the left, drawing one defender out of her lane. She stepped hard to the right, keeping her head down as she blew past the opponent in front of her. The girl tried to block her, but was just a second too late. This left just one more player between her and the goal. She tried to step around her, but the girl easily blocked her path.

"Jess!"

She heard the yell and looked up to see Gabby cutting through the middle, with a wide open lane to the goal.

There was a split second of hesitation as she realized that passing would mean giving up the last goal of her high school career. And also giving up her last chance to impress Trinity's coach in the stands.

Then, she passed the ball.

It cut through the air like a bullet, hitting Gabby's net with perfect precision.

In one fluid motion, Gabby caught and shot the ball.

Before Jess could blink, she saw the ripple as it crashed into the net behind the goalie.

The crowd cheered, although they could barely be heard over the pounding of the rain.

It was perfect. Probably the best shot she'd seen all season.

Then, right on time, the buzzer rang out, signaling the end of the championship game. The end of the season. The end of her high school lacrosse career.

"We fucking did it!" Before Jess could turn around, she felt Scarlett crash into her, jumping onto her back.

"We did." The words broke through her laughter as she watched her teammates run and slide through the wet turf in celebration.

They'd done it. The hard work they'd all put in—the hard work Jess had put in—finally paid off. This was the moment they'd been waiting for.

They continued celebrating on the field for another minute before the coach called them to the bench.

He gave them the speech they all expected to hear. Words that made them proud of their last season playing high school lacrosse. And by the time he had finished, the rain had finally slowed to a light drizzle. Jess looked behind him and saw Coach K approaching the team.

"You girls played very well. Congratulations," she said, glancing between her and Gabby.

"Thank you," they replied in unison, sharing a small smile.

"Our team at Trinity would be lucky to have you both," she said, shifting her umbrella above them. "I'll definitely be putting in a good word with the admissions board."

"Thank you so much," Gabby said with a wide smile.

Jess nodded, smiling politely.

Then the woman excused herself to congratulate their coach.

Gabby cleared her throat, turning to her. "Thank you," she said, with an uncharacteristically friendly smile. "I know you probably could've taken that last shot on your own and made it. You didn't really have to let me take it."

Jess shook her head. "No, you made the right cut. It was yours."

Gabby nodded slowly, looking at the ground. "Trinity isn't the only school I applied to." She looked back up, and Jess thought she could detect a hint of guilt in her eyes. "Don't get me wrong, I have wanted to get in there this whole time, but—" She looked down again, her voice lowering. "I think I've been doing it for the wrong reasons." She paused for a moment before clearing her throat again. "You deserve to get in, if that's still really what you want."

Jess stared at her, blinking raindrops out of her eyes. She'd never seen a genuine side of Gabby, and it left her stunned. In addition to that, her last few words were still ringing in her head.

Was it still what she really wanted?

She thought the answer would be an easy 'yes', but something made her hesitate.

"Anyway," Gabby continued after a few seconds of silence, "good game today."

"Yeah, thanks," Jess mumbled, her brain slowly catching up. "You too."

Gabby walked away, leaving her standing alone on the sideline. She watched some of her teammates still celebrating, smiling from ear to ear and hugging their parents as they congratulated them.

"Hey," she heard her dad's voice behind her and turned around. He held an umbrella that wasn't nearly big enough for him, leaving the shoulders of his jacket completely soaked through. "Congratulations."

"Thanks," she said, pulling the corners of her lips into a small smile. It felt more forced than she expected.

Everything she'd wanted—everything she'd worked for—was now basically hers. She should be happy.

He frowned at her. "You okay?"

"Yeah," she answered quickly, shaking her head. "Just cold and tired. Ready to go home."

He nodded, probably more than ready to get out of the rain himself. "Grab your stuff."

She quickly gathered her things and said goodbye to her teammates before walking to the car with her dad. By the time they left the parking lot, she felt completely mentally and physically exhausted. Like everything from the past few months had finally fully caught up with her. And now that it was done, she just wanted to block it all out and rest.

She leaned her head against the window, watching the blur of cars and street signs flash by against the dark sky. When they got onto the highway, she saw a sea of red brake lights ahead and felt the car slowing down.

"Wanna grab some food?" her dad asked as he looked over his shoulder to switch into a faster lane. This was one of the times she would've actually preferred to be in his squad car. People usually moved out of their way.

"I'm fine," she muttered, still staring mindlessly out the window. "Not hungry."

He switched lanes again, muttering something under his breath about how no one knew how to drive in the rain.

They rolled along for another minute before flashing lights appeared on the road ahead. From where they were, Jess could make out two fire trucks, one ambulance, and at least six or seven cop cars lining the side of the highway, completely blocking the two farthest lanes.

Her dad grunted. "Surprised I didn't get called in for this one."

It took another couple of minutes, and lots of merging lanes, before they were close enough to see parts of the crash.

There was one SUV turned sideways, with the front end smashed into the center divider. The ambulance was pulled up next to it, and Jess could see a middle-aged man lying in the back, surrounded by paramedics.

"Hope everyone's okay," her dad muttered, scanning the wreckage.

There was another fire truck further ahead, surrounded by most of the cop cars, and when they finally reached that part of the crash, Jess understood why.

A large truck had been completely smashed and flipped over, tilting at an unnatural angle, like it was halfway on top of something. A trail of debris led up to it for at least fifty feet, and Jess wondered if the car had rolled the entire way. The thought gave her chills.

Their car inched forward as they merged with the next lane over, and now Jess could see with the glow of the red flares and the flashing lights that the truck had in fact landed on top of something. Another car maybe? No, it was too small.

Then she saw the front wheel of a motorcycle.

From the angle they were at, the truck's mangled passenger door blocked the rest of the bike from view. Still, something felt wrong. Something about it felt too familiar.

A prickling sensation rose in her chest.

They rolled a few more feet forward, and now she could see more of the bike. It's bent black frame.

Too familiar.

The shattered side mirrors.

A few more inches, then they came to a full stop, and she saw it.

The seat.

The unmistakable neon green seat.

Her brain stopped working.

The entire world froze.

This couldn't be happening. She'd just seen her at the game.

She'd *just* seen her standing there.

Bile filled her mouth.

She'd watched her *leave* after the rain started.

Her hands and arms went numb.

She watched her *leave.*

Everything in her exploded.

She ripped her seatbelt off and threw her door open, her feet crashing out onto the wet pavement.

"Wha—Jess!" She heard her dad cry out from the car, but it sounded like it came from a thousand miles away—like she was underwater.

This couldn't be happening.

She sprinted through the next lane, barely registering the array of horns that blared at her.

Her leg hit the side of one car that was rolling forward.

It didn't matter.

None of it mattered.

It was as if there was nothing left in the world but the mangled bike in front of her.

Suddenly, strong arms grabbed her from behind.

"Hey, hey!"

Everything rushed back. It felt like time had frozen, and then in an instant switched to fast forward. The blaring sirens rushed into her ears and the lights blinded her as she struggled desperately to break free of the tight grip.

"Stop! You can't go up there!" an older man's voice yelled in her ear as she struggled against him. She turned, shoving him as hard as she could. His grip wasn't tight enough, and she broke free from his grasp, falling backward.

She spun around, sprinting the last few feet until she reached where the motorcycle stuck out from beneath the overturned truck. She dropped to her knees grabbing at the wreckage.

"Stop! You can't—"

"Where is she?!" Jess screamed, whipping her head frantically from side to side.

"Jess!" She heard her father's voice, like it was some foreign movie playing in the background. His car was pulled up next to the wreckage with both doors wide open.

"Where the fuck is she?!" Jess shrieked, spinning around to face the officer that had tried to stop her.

"Wha—" His head cocked to the side, now looking more concerned.

"Jess what are you—"

She took a step toward the officer.

"Sam Hayes," she said, and something in her broke as she spoke her name aloud. "The girl on the motorcycle—where is she?"

It took a second for the officer to understand, and another second for his face to change from understanding to pity.

The look made her feel sick.

Literally, sick. She choked down the vomit that rushed into her mouth.

The officer glanced at her father, and it was only then that she realized she recognized him. She'd seen him at the station a few times when she'd visited her dad, but couldn't recall his name.

"We had a young female motorcyclist on the scene when we arrived," he said, looking at Jess. Then he looked back at her dad. "She was the first to go to the hospital."

Hospital. That was good. That meant she was alive when they took her.

She pushed through the two men and ran back to her dad's car.

"Jess!" She heard him call from behind her, but she was already approaching the driver-side door.

"Wait!"

A firm hand grabbed her shoulder, stopping her from getting into the car.

"No!" She spun around, coming face to face with her father. "I have to—" She choked on the words, suddenly not knowing how to finish that sentence. What did she have to do? Sam wasn't her girlfriend. In

336

fact, she wasn't even really sure if they were even friends anymore. But none of that mattered. Every word they'd said, or hadn't said, didn't change the feeling that consumed her now.

"I have to—" she tried, again unable to find the words.

Her dad's face softened as much as she'd ever seen it. "Okay. But I'll drive. Get in the car," he said, his voice taking on the commanding tone she usually only heard while he was working.

She walked to the passenger side. When she slid into the seat and shut the door, she realized her face and neck were wet with tears. She wondered when she'd started crying.

"Put your seatbelt on."

She did as she was told and felt the car move forward, slowly merging back into the traffic.

"It should clear up now that we'll be past the accident."

He was right. Once they moved back out onto the highway, the traffic cleared. But Jess was only vaguely aware of the outside world.

She tried to focus on the car in front of them. She tried to keep her mind anchored on something. But it was no use.

The terror that had gripped her wasn't letting go, and she could feel her chest growing tighter by the minute.

The edges of her vision pulsated, and the familiar buzz filled her hands.

She closed her eyes, squeezing her fists as she forced herself to take deep breaths. The air scraped against her dry throat and for a second, she thought she might be suffocating.

She squeezed her eyes shut and forced one more deep breath.

Breathe, she told herself.

It reminded her of the day Sam held her in the parking lot after she'd realized that her mom's pin was gone.

The memory flowed so easily into her mind. She could almost pretend Sam was there with her again, arms wrapped around her like a shield from the world.

Breathe.

Sam's voice whispered in her ear like a lullaby, and she felt her forehead resting against her chest. She could imagine the way it would move up and down with her breath.

The memory consumed her. Every sight, smell, and touch recreating itself in her mind.

Breathe.

***

She stepped through the automatic doors.

The lobby was large. Too large for the few scattered people sitting inside. The sea of empty seats made it feel quiet and calm, like it was just any other boring Friday night.

It felt wrong.

Her father stepped in beside her and immediately walked to the front desk.

Jess followed closely behind, relieved that he'd taken the lead.

He cleared his throat as he approached. "Excuse me," he started, and Jess again recognized his cop voice. "A female motorcyclist was brought in—"

"Hey."

Jess jumped, hearing a man's voice behind her.

"You're Sam's friend, right?"

She turned to her right and saw Chris standing there in his military uniform.

"Uh—" She was dumbfounded. Somehow it hadn't occurred to her that he would be there. "Yeah," she shook her head, collecting herself. "Yes. Is she—" She swallowed and her throat grated like sandpaper. "Where is she?"

Even with his stoic facade, she saw a hint of worry flash over her face. He glanced down at the half-filled styrofoam coffee cup in his hand. "They took her in for surgery. There haven't been any more updates since I got here."

She forced herself to nod as the sick feeling returned to her stomach.

"How did you.." his voice trailed off with the question.

"We saw the accident," she answered, but her voice didn't sound like her own. "I saw—" The image of the bike crushed beneath the truck flashed in her mind. This time the sick feeling rose into her throat. She was about to either throw up or cry. Maybe both.

"I believe my daughter recognized the motorcycle," her dad cut in beside her.

She'd almost entirely forgotten he was there. A pang of relief ran through her when Chris' eyes left hers to look at him instead.

Chris nodded as he gently swirled the coffee in his cup. Then he looked back at her. "I'm sorry you had to see it."

The back of her throat burned, and she felt a fresh tear spill over and rush down her face. She quickly wiped it away with the back of her hand.

"I'm not sure how long it'll be," he continued, "but I can text you an update when I get one."

There was no way she could bring herself to walk out of the building while Sam was still in there.

"Do you mind if we wait with you?" her dad cut in. Jess' eyes snapped up at him in surprise.

"Oh, sure," Chris answered with a nod. "Of course."

He turned and walked a few steps around a row of chairs before sitting down. Jess wondered if she was supposed to follow. Before she could think too hard, her dad stepped in front of her and walked to one of the seats beside him. Jess took the cue and did the same.

An uncomfortable silence filled the air for a few moments, and Jess was grateful when her dad broke it with something about thanking Chris for his military service. The conversation continued after that, but Jess couldn't process any of what they were saying.

A clock hung on the wall above the double doors that she assumed led further into the hospital to where Sam was. She watched the longest hand tick by, counting every second. It gave her something to focus on. Something to keep her grounded.

The men alternated between silence and light conversation, and after about an hour, her dad got up to get coffee. Actually, it was about fifty-three minutes, to be exact. She'd been counting.

Right when he rose from his seat, the double doors pushed open.

Jess' eyes snapped down from the clock and saw a woman in scrubs holding a clipboard. Her heart leapt into her chest as she watched her scan the paper.

Finally, the woman looked up. "Family of Sam Hayes?"

Jess practically jumped out of her seat.

"Yes," Chris cleared his throat beside her, raising his hand as he stood up. "Here."

340

The woman walked toward them, stopping a couple of feet in front.

"Hi," she said with a smile that somehow wasn't a smile at all. "I'm Dr. Walker. I helped perform part of Sam's surgery tonight, so I can give you an update and an overview of where we're at now. Is there anyone else that should be here or that we need to wait for?"

"No," Chris answered, shaking his head.

"Okay," she replied, glancing down at the clipboard briefly. "Sam is now fully out of surgery and in a recovery room."

Jess felt a tiny fraction of the tension in her shoulders release.

"She was brought in unconscious, with multiple lacerations on her face, neck, and arms. There is also one large abrasion covering most of her right leg. One of the lacerations on her neck was fairly deep and contributed to a significant amount of blood loss. We took her in for surgery immediately to stop the bleeding. While she was in surgery, we conducted a thorough check over the rest of her wounds." She glanced down at the clipboard again. "We found three broken ribs, as well as a broken clavicle on the left side. The clavicle was broken in multiple places, so surgery was needed in order to ensure that it healed properly." She paused, taking a small breath. Her lips pursed for just a split second as she glanced at the clipboard once more. "Roughly forty seconds after we began work on the clavicle, Sam's oxygen levels sharply decreased. We found that one of the broken ribs had shifted and punctured her right lung. We quickly inserted a chest tube, and so far she's been showing positive signs with that."

The woman glanced across the three of them. "Do you have any questions so far?"

A million questions circled in Jess' mind, but only one came out. "Is she—so she's going to be okay?"

The doctor nodded. "She'll need time to heal, but yes, she should make a full recovery." She paused for a moment. "Sam was very lucky."

Jess' lip trembled, and she bit down a sob of relief.

"When can she have visitors?" Chris asked.

"I'll check on her again after this and make sure she's still doing well and if she's awake yet. If so, then we can allow a maximum of two people to see her tonight, one at a time. But it's important that she gets enough rest tonight and over the next couple of days. Her body has been through a lot. It needs time to heal."

He nodded.

The doctor glanced at Jess for a moment before tucking the clipboard under her arm. "Let me go check on her and if she's awake, I'll let her know she has some family here to see her."

Chris leaned back in the chair, his body visibly more relaxed than before. She met eyes with her father, and he gave her a small nod before looking away.

A few minutes later, a nurse came out of the double doors and informed them Sam was awake enough to see visitors. Chris stood first, and Jess watched him follow her and disappear through the doors.

It felt like only a minute had passed before the doors slid back open and he walked out to the waiting room, looking just as stoic as he had the day she first met him. She glanced at the round clock above the doors. Six minutes had passed. It made sense. She couldn't really imagine him saying much more than a simple 'glad you didn't die'.

The nurse followed him out.

"Do either of you want to see her next?" she asked, looking between Jess and her father.

"Yes, me." Her voice scratched, and she wondered how obvious it was that she'd been crying. She wondered if Sam would notice.

She followed the nurse through the double doors and into a wide hallway lined with empty hospital beds. Nurses and doctors ambled past them. She overheard two discussing their lunch break plans. It felt surreal that while this would be a night she'd never forget, to them this was just another day at work. Mundane enough that it didn't even interfere with their lunch break.

They took a turn down a different hallway and her heart rate ticked up a few more beats. They'd walked a good bit, which meant they had to be getting close.

In the six minutes that Chris had been gone, she'd tried to think of what she wanted to say. To explain that while she knew nothing had changed between them, she still had to see her. She had to see with her own eyes that she was okay.

Potential words flowed through her head as the nurse slowed beside a room with an open door.

Her heart rate rose even higher.

A few feet inside the room, a blue curtain fanned out, blocking the view.

The nurse turned to her. "She didn't want the stronger pain medication, so she might be a little uncomfortable, but she'll be moderately alert."

Jess nodded, her heart now full on pounding in her chest.

The woman gave her a small smile before taking a step back down the hall. "Press the call button if you need anything," she said over her shoulder.

Jess turned back and looked at the closed curtain. It reminded her of visiting her mother in the hospital. As morbid as it was, it had always sort of felt like one of those mystery toys you open and discover what's inside. On the front of the box, they show the potential toys it could be, and there's always one that's ten times better than the others. That's the one you cross your fingers for. That's the reason why you bought the stupid mystery box in the first place. But everyone knows, that's never what you get.

As a child, the mystery of what waited behind that blue curtain terrified her. The fear of what version of her mother would be there. Each time, the blue mystery curtain revealed something worse.

Staring at this one, she had a similar fear.

She swallowed and took a slow step into the room. The first thing she heard was the beeping. A steady rhythm of machines assuring her that whatever version of Sam lay on the other side of that curtain, at least she was alive.

She reached out, slowly pushing the curtain to the side, the metal hooks screeching in protest.

Her eyes immediately skipped to the top of the bed.

Green eyes stared back at her.

They were bloodshot and tired, but they were there. They were open. And that's all that mattered.

One side of Sam's face was littered with cuts, and a large bandage covered that side of her neck.

Sam's mouth twitched up slightly. "Hey," she said. Her voice sounded like two sheets of sandpaper grinding against one another.

Fresh tears welled in Jess' eyes at the sound.

"Did you guys win?" Sam asked, barely louder than a whisper.

The tears spilled over, rolling down her cheeks. Jess raised a hand to cover her mouth as a sob ripped through her. Never in her life had she been so overcome by fear.

"I—I thought you were gone," she choked out between sobs.

Sam tried to speak, but coughing overcame the words. Jess rushed to the other side of the bed, searching for the call button.

Sam shook her head. "No. It's okay," she said, but her voice sounded much weaker than before. "I'm okay." She gave her a small smile, her cheeks lifting the oxygen tube that ran across her face into her nostrils. Then she opened the hand that sat in front of Jess on the bed. Her palm faced up, waiting.

Jess stared at it for a second before gently placing her hand on Sam's and sitting in the chair beside her.

It felt different. Colder than usual.

Jess wiped the wetness from her cheeks and traced her thumb across Sam's hand. "What happened?"

"I'm not really sure," Sam whispered, and Jess could hear a wheezing sound from her lungs. Like wind whistling through the cracks of a door. "It started raining a lot harder when I was on the highway. I heard a crash and then something slammed into me from behind." She paused, her breathing labored. "I think I remember being on the ground and hearing people yelling. I felt wet everywhere but," she stopped again, catching her breath, "I don't know if it was the rain or if it was blood."

Jess looked down at their hands again, the thought of Sam covered in blood making her feel sick. She laced their fingers together, squeezing a little tighter.

"Did Chris call you?" Sam asked, her voice even raspier than before.

Images of the crash flashed behind Jess' eyes. She closed them and shook her head. "I saw it when we were driving home," she whispered, trying to keep her voice from shaking. "I saw your bike."

Another tear rolled down her face, and she quickly wiped it away, turning her head away from Sam.

"I'm sorry," Sam said, lightly squeezing her hand.

"No." Jess shook her head. "I'm sorry."

Tears rose in her eyes once again. She bit the inside of her cheek to keep her jaw from trembling. There were so many things she wanted to say, but none of them seemed like enough.

She leaned her head down and closed her eyes, pressing her lips gently against Sam's bare wrist.

Footsteps echoed through the door, and Jess pulled her head back, but kept her hand firmly holding onto Sam's. Then the curtain opened, and Mrs. Adams stood there in her nurse's uniform.

Jess froze for a split second. In the midst of everything, she'd entirely forgotten that Mrs. Adams usually worked the evening shifts at the hospital.

"Jess?" the older woman asked, her eyebrows arching as she stepped into the room.

She slowly pulled her hand away from Sam, using it to brush the remaining wetness off of her face. "Oh, hi Mrs. Adams."

The woman frowned at her, before glancing at Sam. "I'm so sorry. If I'd known you girls were friends, I would've called you to let you know when she arrived here."

"Oh, that's okay," Jess mumbled, suddenly feeling the need to avoid eye contact.

The woman looked back at Sam with a warm smile. "How are you feeling, sweetie?" She walked to the top of the bed on the opposite side of Jess, immediately checking the monitors.

Sam tried to clear her throat, but it turned into a cough instead.

"Here," Mrs. Adams said, handing her a cup of water from the table beside her bed. "Small sips."

"Thanks," Sam hissed, taking the cup from her and placing the straw between her lips.

"Your throat will be a little raw and irritated like that for a few days. Warm liquids will be your best friend. Try tea or bone broth. No coffee, though, for at least a week."

Sam groaned from behind the cup.

The woman grabbed the clipboard that hung on the end of the bed, scanning over it. "We haven't given you much for the pain." She glanced up at Sam. "How are you feeling?"

Sam tried her best to shrug, but Jess could see the slight wince on her face when she moved. She wondered how much pain she was really in.

"I'm fine for now," she whispered.

Mrs. Adams watched her for a second before nodding and flipping the paper back down on the clipboard. "Okay. Tell me if that changes and we can give you something to help," she replied, hanging the clipboard back up on the end of the bed. "Do you need anything else while I'm here?"

Sam shook her head lightly.

The woman nodded, giving her a small smile before turning to walk out. She was almost to the curtain again before she stopped, turning to look at Jess.

"You let me know if you need anything while you're here, okay?" she said with a warm smile.

Jess nodded, pressing her lips together. "Okay, thanks," she mumbled.

For a second, it looked like she was about to leave, but then she paused again. "I just have to say, I'm so happy that you and Luke were able to work things out."

Jess' entire body froze.

"Seeing you two together the other night just warmed my heart. I haven't seen him that happy since you were dating."

Jess swallowed, her mind completely blank. "We're—"

"I know, I know," she waved her hand, shaking her head. "He probably wouldn't have wanted me to say anything, but I couldn't help it. You both just looked so cute together."

Jess looked down at her lap, avoiding the woman's gaze. Avoiding Sam's gaze.

"Hopefully, I'll see you at the house again soon?" Mrs. Adams asked, and Jess hated the hopeful lilt in her voice.

She just nodded, keeping her eyes down. After a second, she could hear the woman finally leave.

Silence filled the room, the only sound the beep of the heart rate monitor.

Then, finally, Sam's raspy voice broke through. "So you and Luke, huh?"

Jess looked up at her, surprised by the even tone in her voice. She had a small smile on her face, but it looked more polite than genuine.

"No it's—"

"It's okay," Sam cut in. This time her smile seemed slightly less forced, but it still didn't reach anywhere near her eyes. "You don't have to explain—"

"No," Jess said quickly, "It's not like that. We just had dinner on Monday and we—"

"Wait," Sam looked at her, any hint of a smile dropping from her face. "You were with Luke that night? You told me you couldn't hang out because you were having dinner with your dad?"

Jess' mouth stopped.

"You lied to me?" Sam asked, and the tone of her wheezing voice made something in Jess' chest constrict.

"I just didn't want you to think—" Jess paused. She really didn't know how to finish that sentence. Why hadn't she told Sam the full truth about the dinner? Maybe she was scared that Sam would then fully close off the possibility of anything romantic between them.

Sam shook her head. "After everything between us, you don't even care enough to be honest with me?"

"No, Sam—"

"I asked you that night as a fucking *friend*—" Sam spat, holding one hand up to her mouth as a string of coughs came out.

Jess waited for them to subside. But really, she didn't know what she could say to make it better, anyway. She knew she shouldn't have held back the full truth. She knew it right when the words left her mouth.

349

The coughing finally stopped, but Sam laid there for a moment, taking deep, wheezing breaths.

Jess waited for them to slow before speaking again. "I know I messed up," she whispered, feeling tears sting her eyes for what was probably the hundredth time that night. "I'm so sorry for—"

"Just leave."

Jess' eyes snapped up to look at her. Her expression was ice cold.

"Sam, please," Jess whispered, her voice shaking now as she held back the fresh tears that welled in her eyes.

"No." Sam shook her head. "This is done. We're done."

Jess stared at her, mouth hung open, as her brain desperately searched for something to say.

Anything that could fix it.

But there was nothing.

What could she possibly say that would make any difference now?

Her legs tingled as she slowly stood from the chair. She took one slow step toward the door. It was like she was in a trance. Like her body and her mind were entirely separate from each other. She focused on each step, one after the other. When she reached the curtain, she paused. Something in her screamed to turn around. Screamed that leaving would be a mistake. A mistake she'd never be able to fix.

But it didn't matter. It was already past the point of being fixed, whether she left or not.

She took another step, pushing the curtain to the side.

Her legs kept moving until she was finally past the door, the beeping of the machines fading behind her. Then she was moving down the hall. When she eventually reached the waiting room, she didn't bother finding her dad. Instead, her legs kept moving on their own, taking her out into the parking lot, like they knew that if she stopped moving, she would fall apart.

Chapter 21

Eleven days.

Eleven days had passed since Sam's accident.

Eleven days had passed since Jess had last seen her. Actually, it'd probably been eleven days since she'd last seen anyone other than her dad. Since the night of the accident, she just hadn't felt like spending time with anyone. Just the thought of having to hold an actual conversation with an actual person sounded like *actual* torture. She'd even rejected each of Scarlett's attempts to hangout, giving half-assed excuses that Scarlett luckily knew better than to question.

So there she was. Laying in her bed on an extra frigid Tuesday morning, scrolling mindlessly on her phone, switching back and forth between Instagram and TikTok, like she'd done every morning for the last eleven days.

Jess closed her eyes, dropping the phone on the bed beside her head and pulling the comforter tight around her chin. The thought of spending another day in bed watching Netflix seemed a good bit less appealing that morning than it had the last ten mornings.

Coffee, she thought. *At least start this day with coffee.*

She opened her eyes again and reluctantly pulled off the comforter. Cold air hit her bare arms. For a second, she considered abandoning the idea altogether to continue her morning scrolling.

But no, she had to do something semi-productive. At least just that one thing. Then she would let herself continue wallowing in her empty Netflix and social media filled day.

She hurried over to her dresser and pulled a heavy sweatshirt and a pair of sweatpants out of the drawer. She quickly threw them both on, then grabbed her phone off the bed before heading out of the room. A few more minutes of scrolling while she drank her coffee couldn't hurt.

The cold floorboards stung her bare feet. She should've grabbed socks for the short journey downstairs.

As she descended the last of the steps, already hating every second of being out of bed, her phone buzzed in her hand.

She glanced down at the lit up screen.

An email from Miss Williams. Weren't guidance counselors also supposed to be off for winter break?

She stared at the unopened email, coming to a stop at the bottom of the stairs. If it was bad news, she probably would've waited to email her until after school had resumed. So an email now probably either meant that she had good news, or she needed something urgent that couldn't wait until the end of break. At least, that's what Jess hoped as she tapped to open the email.

Hello Jess!

I just received an exciting email from the assistant coach at Trinity University. She was very impressed with your performance in the championship game (congrats on the win, by the way!), and she emailed me to ask about your volunteer project. I sent her the video, and she loved it. She's going to personally speak with the admissions board after break to push for your acceptance. Given all of your hard work and impressive qualifications, she's confident you'll receive early admission.

Congratulations and great job on all the hard work you put in to achieve this! If anyone deserves this, it's you!

Sincerely,

Miss Williams

Jess blinked, re-reading the email a second time.

This was it. Everything she'd worked for, for as long as she could remember.

She finally had it.

Jess read over the email one more time, then locked the phone, dropping her hand by her side.

She stared blankly at the front door. This was everything she wanted. She should be happy. Over the moon with excitement.

Coffee. She needed coffee.

Turning to continue her trip to the kitchen, her eyes caught on the family picture hanging on the wall. It still had smudges on the glass from where she pressed her fingers each time she left the house.

The image of her mother stared back at her.

Usually, it felt lively. Happy, even. But this time, her mother's stare felt hollow. It didn't feel like her mother looking back at her. It just felt like any old picture of a family of three people who didn't know they would eventually be just two.

She looked at it with an indifference she'd never felt before.

No matter how many times she looked at that photo, no matter how many times she pressed her fingers to it, it would always just be a picture on a wall. And the woman in the picture would never again truly smile back at her.

She looked at it for another second before finally pulling her eyes away.

They landed on her keys hanging on the wall, and a new idea for the morning entered her mind.

***

It'd only been a couple of weeks since she'd last pulled up to the clinic, but still, something about it felt different. Maybe it was that this time she wasn't there for a school project. Or maybe it was knowing that Sam wouldn't be waiting for her inside.

She slid out of the car, grabbing her cup of coffee with the unfamiliar logo from the drink holder. She'd decided to go out of her way to try a new coffee stand that morning, rather than going to her usual one. The excuse, she told herself, was that it would be good for her to try something new. But in reality, she was just trying to avoid the extra reminder of Sam. Going to the clinic was hard enough already.

When she walked in, her eyes instantly spotted Laura behind the front desk, holding a stack of papers. She was so focused on what she was doing, she didn't even notice Jess until she was a few feet away.

"Hey," Jess said, trying her best to smile. It felt weird on her face after going so long without one. It felt weird speaking aloud at all.

The woman's eyes shot up in surprise, clearly unaware of her presence. "Oh! Jess, hi, honey!" She dropped the stack of papers on the desk and rounded the corner, pulling her into a tight hug. "What're you doing here? Is everything okay?" she asked, pulling back a bit to look at her.

"Oh yeah. Yeah, everything is fine. I was just in the area and wanted to stop by to say hi," she lied, glancing down the hall. She figured Sam would still be healing and wouldn't be there, but she still had to double check. It was a habit.

"Oh, that's so sweet of you," Laura replied with her signature warm smile. "It's been a little crazy here this week," she said, looking back at the messy desk.

Jess felt a pang of guilt. She should've thought about Laura and the clinic sooner. She should've realized they would need more help after losing both her and Sam.

"Anyway, how are you doing, honey?" Laura continued. "Are you having a good winter break?"

"Oh, yeah," she lied. "It's been great."

The woman gave her a small smile, and something about it told Jess she knew it was a lie. For some reason, that made her feel the need to continue.

"I got some good news this morning," Jess said, trying once more to resurrect a smile. "So that was—good."

Laura just gave her that same smile, like she was waiting for Jess to say something else. After two more seconds of silence, Jess shifted uncomfortably.

"So, do you need any help?" she asked, looking at the stack of papers. "I'm free right now. I can help with whatever you need."

The woman's smile grew, showing her white teeth. She opened her mouth to speak, but then stopped. "You know," she started, glancing at the open door of the auditorium. "It might actually be helpful to have you sit in on the next meeting if you're open to it. Sometimes it works out better if two people are in there to organize and help keep things on track. It runs a little smoother."

"Oh," she answered, surprised that Laura had never asked for her help with it before. "Yeah, of course. Whatever you need."

"Great," Laura grinned. She turned to the auditorium, and Jess followed behind her.

She set her coffee down on the fold-out table and dove into the familiar rhythm of setting things up while the attendees trickled in. It wasn't the most engaging work, but it felt nice to have something to do. It felt nice to be needed. To be helpful.

Some people came in quietly, sitting by themselves toward the back rows, and others were louder, coming in pairs and laughing or joking with one another. The latter reminded her of Sam and Ricky. It was a reminder she could've done without.

"Okay," Laura said, coming up behind her. "I'm going to get started. Feel free to sit down in the back and just listen in. I'll let you know when I need something."

"Okay. Sounds good." Jess grabbed her coffee from the table and sat down in the back row, with only one other person sitting a few chairs away.

Laura went through her usual introduction. Then the meeting began with people choosing to stand up and speak to the group about their experience and what they were struggling with.

Jess had overheard bits and pieces of the attendees speaking throughout her time volunteering, but she'd never actually sat through a meeting to hear it all. Again, their sheer honesty about how they were feeling, what they struggled with, and all of their worries left her in awe. It reminded her of the interview she filmed with Ricky. The ease at which he spoke about things that made Jess uncomfortable just hearing.

She tucked her coffee between her legs and clapped with the rest of the group as the young woman at the podium finished and walked back to her seat.

The next person stood up, a friendly-looking man, maybe in his late early thirties.

He cleared his throat before smiling. "Hi. I'm Elijah and I'm an addict."

A murmur of greetings echoed through the room.

"Um—I'm not super good at this whole sharing thing," he said, glancing down. Jess could sense his nerves, and she couldn't blame him. It wasn't something she'd ever want to do. "Well I guess I used to not be good at it. But I've really been trying and I think I'm getting better at it. At least, I hope I am."

He threw Laura a sheepish grin, and Jess wondered how long he'd been coming to the meetings. She didn't recognize him.

"I um—I made a couple of big mistakes recently, and I'm trying really hard to fix them." His face became more serious, and Jess watched a new intensity fill his eyes. A new determination. "I think it's really helped to be able to come here and talk about it with all of you," he said, nodding his head out to the small audience. "Even just saying it out loud to another person—" His throat bobbed up and down as he swallowed. "It makes it feel—I don't know, it just makes it—better somehow."

Jess saw a few people nod, and she wondered how many of them felt the way he did.

He continued speaking, but she was so focused on what he'd just said that the rest turned into background noise.

What would Sam have said if she knew every thought and feeling that went through Jess the night of the crash? Or even earlier that week? Would she have forgiven her?

Would things be different?

Maybe.

Did she *want* things to be different?

Maybe.

She thought about the email she'd gotten that morning. Everything she'd worked for had paid off. Yet somehow, she felt no different from before. She hadn't even cared enough to tell anyone.

What did she want?

Trinity. The answer popped into her head like a habitual response.

What did she *really* want?

This time, it wasn't a word that entered her mind, but an image. An image of one person in particular.

And that response *wasn't* out of habit.

The sounds of slow, uneven clapping broke her from her thoughts. She looked up and saw the man walking back to his seat, with Laura stepping up in his place.

"Thank you for sharing, Elijah," she said with a smile. "Okay, we're going to take a quick break. I'll see you all back here in ten minutes."

Jess' fingers drummed anxiously against her coffee cup. Wheels spun in her head. What did she really want? Would things be different if Sam knew how she felt?

Her foot bounced on the ground.

What did she want?

Sam.

The voice in her head finally spoke the truth.

She wanted Sam.

No, she thought. It was more than that. So much more than that.

She *loved* Sam. She was *in love* with Sam.

The realization hit her so hard that it felt like the entire world had come to a stop. Then, when it started again, everything looked different—*felt* different.

She was in love with Sam. Unequivocally, heart-wrenchingly *in love* with her.

And no matter what, nothing could change that. Not her college plans. Not her dad. Not even the fear of what her mother would have thought if she were still there.

It was a fact. As simple as knowing that she needed air in order to breathe.

And somehow, it also made her feel like she was suffocating. Like if she went just one more minute without telling Sam how she felt, she would choke and die on that unspoken truth.

She stood up from the chair, her mind racing as she scanned the room, quickly finding Laura near the podium. She crossed the room, tossing her coffee into the trash as she weaved between the chairs.

"Hey Laura," she said, the adrenaline in her veins making her voice almost shake. "Would it be okay if I left now? I need to go do something and it can't wait."

Laura gave her a look that said she'd expected this from the start. "Of course, honey," she replied with a warm, knowing smile.

Chapter 22

J ess put the car in park and stared out the driver-side window.

Although it was still early in the day, the sky was already dark with rain clouds.

She looked at the familiar house, and it reminded her of the first time she'd been there. The circumstances had been different, but the nerves were the same.

Before she could talk herself out of it, she threw the door open and slid out onto the pavement.

She jogged across the street, forcing any sense of doubt from her mind.

By the time she reached the front door, she was ready. All she wanted was to see Sam and tell her how she really felt.

She raised her hand and knocked twice.

Her heart pounded in her chest with every second that passed.

Then the seconds ticked on. When it felt like too much time had passed, she knocked again.

And again, the seconds ticked by.

A sinking feeling seeped into her stomach.

Please be here, she thought.

She raised her hand to knock one more time, when suddenly the door opened.

Sam.

She stood there with a tired expression, slightly out of breath. A large white bandage covered one side of her neck, and her left arm hung close to her chest, held up in a light blue sling. Her face had a pale, ghost-like glow that enhanced the purple circles beneath her eyes.

She should've gone to see her sooner.

Sam watched her for a moment before finally speaking.

"Hi," she said, and Jess noticed the slight wheeze that encompassed the word.

"Hey," Jess replied. "Can we talk?"

Sam's face remained unreadable. "Actually, I'm pretty busy."

Disappointment surged in her chest, but if she was being honest, she'd halfway expected a response like that. Still, rejection stings no matter how much you expect it.

"It won't take long, I promise."

Sam let out a small sigh, and she couldn't tell if it was out of annoyance or exasperation. Probably a bit of both.

"Fine," Sam said, stepping to the side of the doorway.

Jess walked in, her confidence coming back with the small win. She knew Sam would understand if she could just explain everything to her. Then she would forgive her and maybe they could move on as—whatever they were. Something more than friends, she hoped.

She paused, waiting for Sam to lead the way to her bedroom. Sam stepped down the hall, moving much slower than usual and with a slight limp. She wondered how much pain she was in.

When they reached the end of the hall, she could hear Sam's labored breathing as she pushed the bedroom door open.

Jess followed her in and immediately stopped.

Boxes.

There were moving boxes all over the room, and her desk was gone, along with every other major item besides her bed.

"Uh—what is.." Jess trailed off, her eyes bouncing around the mostly empty room.

Sam limped to the bed and dropped onto it, resting on the edge. She closed her eyes, taking a few deep breaths.

"I tried to tell you." She paused. "I called you a few times a few days before the accident to tell you, but you never picked up."

"Tell me what?" Jess whispered, a sick feeling creeping into her stomach.

"Chris is getting deployed again in a few weeks."

"Okay," Jess nodded, absorbing the new information. So Sam would just move in with someone else for the rest of the school year. That wasn't so bad. She just hoped it wouldn't be too far.

"Who are you going to live with until the school year ends?" she asked.

Sam looked up at her, and this time Jess thought she could see something slightly more than indifference in her eyes. Maybe a hint of regret.

Sam took another deep breath, dropping her gaze to the boxes on the floor in front of her. "I'm not finishing the school year. At least, not here." She paused, clearing her throat before looking up at Jess again. "I'm moving to Cambridge. I talked to the admissions office at MIT and explained what happened. They said that if I finished all of my high school credits before the end of winter break, then I could get my diploma and start living in student housing a semester early. I just have to do the work-study program there until my classes start."

Jess stared at her, the information slowly filtering into her brain.

Sam took another deep breath. "I was already ahead in all the classes, anyway. Miss Williams helped me get everything organized and submitted, though."

Silence filled the air around them. The only sound was Sam's slow, steady breathing.

"I don't—" Jess shook her head. "I don't understand. You're leaving?"

Sam nodded, her eyes on the ground.

"When?" Jess whispered.

Sam's eyes flicked up, meeting hers. Now Jess was sure she could see regret in them.

"Tomorrow."

Jess' throat tightened. "Tomorrow," she repeated.

Sam sighed, shaking her head. "I tried to tell you," she said with a hint of frustration in her voice.

Jess remembered the missed calls. She remembered watching her phone buzz and letting them go to voicemail. It was the day after the kiss with Luke. Would answering them have made a difference?

"Right," Jess whispered. She swallowed, trying not to think about how horribly wrong everything had gone. Trying not to think about how, just an hour before, she'd thought they'd be ending the day together.

Sam sighed, shifting on the bed. "I'm sorry—"

"No," Jess shook her head. "You have nothing to be sorry for. You didn't do anything wrong."

Sam pursed her lips, nodding slightly.

"Um—" Jess started, trying desperately to distract herself so that she wouldn't cry. "Do you—do you need help packing or anything? I could—" Her eyes darted around the room, looking for anything to avoid Sam's eyes. "I could help you—with whatever you—"

"No," Sam cut her off, and although Jess refused to look at her, she could hear the pity in her voice. "That's okay. Chris is going to help finish up tomorrow morning."

"Oh, okay," Jess replied, dropping her eyes to the ground. "Well—I guess I should head out then and let you finish." She swallowed hard, blinking away the emerging wetness in her eyes. "Sorry for just showing up."

"Jess," Sam said, her voice sounding softer, like the Sam she'd always known. The Sam she'd *fallen in love* with. "I really am sorry. I wish things could've gone differently."

"It's fine," she replied with a smile as the last of her heart shattered.

She turned away when the first tear fell down her still smiling face. She took a step toward the door, walking away from Sam Hayes one last time. The Sam Hayes she'd fallen in love with. The Sam Hayes she was *still* in love with.

She paused in the doorway, lifting her hand to brush the lone tear away. "You know, you have no idea how lucky you are," she said, her voice trembling. "You get to hate me because I'm the one who fucked us up." She swallowed the lump in her throat as more tears streamed down her face. "I know it's dumb, but I wish you'd done something horrible to me. Because then at least I'd get to hate you instead of hating myself."

Speaking those words aloud felt like lifting one of one hundred weights from her chest.

"I don't hate you," Sam whispered. "I'm just ready to move on."

Jess tilted her head back, a light laugh escaping her lips. "For some reason, that's even worse."

She took her next step into the hallway and kept going as the tears fell freely down her face.

***

By the time she walked through the front door of her house, the tears had finally stopped, but the ache in her chest had turned into a throbbing pit of despair.

She stepped through the door, barely aware of her dad sitting at the kitchen table.

"Hey," he grunted, briefly glancing up, then back down at his iPad. "Where've you been?"

Jess opened her mouth, ready to give some generic response, before heading to her room. But this time, she stopped herself.

She was tired.

Tired of hiding. Tired of lying.

Too tired to do anything but tell the truth.

She walked through the living room into the kitchen and pulled out the chair across from him to sit. When he looked up at her, she saw his expression immediately change to one of worry.

"What's wrong?" he asked, dropping his iPad on the table.

"I—" her lip trembled. "I messed something up and now it's too late to fix it."

He frowned at her, looking even more concerned than before. "What is it? Did you mess up on your college application or something?"

"No," she answered with a sigh, shaking her head. "Nevermind. I'm just tired," she said, pushing the chair back to stand up. "I'm gonna—"

"Is this about that girl?"

Jess froze. "What?"

He crossed his arms over his chest. "The girl that was in the motorcycle accident. Sam."

Her eyes dropped to her lap as her brain ricocheted between all the possible lies she could tell. All the excuses. But none of them made it past her lips.

"Jess," he said in an uncharacteristically soft tone. Like he was actively working to sound gentle. "Is there anything you want to tell me?"

She swallowed the last of the lies away. "Yeah," she whispered. "It's about her."

He nodded slowly. "Okay. What happened? Is she okay?"

"Yeah, she's okay." Jess took a deep breath. "She's um—" she felt tears stinging the back of her eyes. "She's moving away tomorrow."

He leaned back in his chair. "I'm sorry to hear that. But you'll still have your other friends here."

She nodded slowly, staring blankly at her lap.

"Unless," he continued, "is there something more going on?" He cleared his throat and this time Jess recognized his usual awkwardness. "You know, between you two."

She waited a few beats.

What else could she lose? She nodded again and tears flowed freely down her face once more.

Silence fell between them.

Finally, he released a long breath. "Okay." He cleared his throat again and rubbed the back of his neck. She hated that it reminded her of Sam. "Is it like a onetime—I don't know—teenage thing or something?"

Jess felt her heart pounding in her chest. She slowly shook her head.

He pursed his lips, nodding and placing his hands on the table in front of him. He was quiet for a few moments. Then finally he spoke.

"Why didn't you tell me?"

Jess bit her lip to keep it from shaking. She gave a small shrug.

He sighed. "I kind of figured something was going on," he said, pausing and looking to the side. "A person only reacts the way you did on the highway when they're in love."

Her eyes shot up.

He cleared his throat again and swallowed. "That's basically how I reacted when I found out your mom was sick."

Jess was almost too shocked to register his words. She'd never heard him talk about it before. She'd never even really heard him talk about *her* before.

He sighed again, looking down at his hands on the table. The look on his face was reminiscent, but also broken. The look of a broken man thinking of the woman he'd lost.

One question entered her mind. The question she'd asked herself relentlessly, day after day, since the night she kissed Sam. It forced its way into her mouth, refusing to stay choked down for another second longer.

"D—dad," she said, her voice shaking through her quivering jaw like it never had before. "Do you think m—mom would've still l—loved me if she knew?"

His face contorted in pain, mirroring the way Jess had felt every time the thought entered her mind. "Jess, your mom loved you more than anything in this world. There is *nothing* that would've *ever* changed that."

A sob ripped through her chest, and with it, the weight of everything she'd held in for so long.

She covered her face with her hands, tears pouring into her palms. The scrape of a chair on the floor echoed across the room, and then suddenly she felt her dad's solid arms wrap around her. She sobbed, letting every bottled up emotion finally find freedom and peace. There were tears of sorrow, but also tears of immense relief.

It could've been seconds, minutes, or hours that they stayed like that. She wasn't sure. All she knew was that with every passing moment, the void in her chest felt just a little bit smaller.

***

Rain pounded against the windshield. She could barely make out the sidewalk as she made the last turn onto Sam's street for the second time that day. Even with the windshield wipers turned all the way up, they couldn't keep up with the torrent of rain dumping from the sky.

She slowed the car to a roll as she entered the neighborhood. Her usual spot on the street was open, and she pulled up against the curb. Light from across the street at Sam's house instantly caught her eye.

The garage was completely open, and she squinted, trying to see through the rain. It looked like a person pushing something up the driveway.

She squinted harder.

What the fu—

Jess turned the keys and jumped out of the car, running across the street.

"What the hell are you doing?" she yelled over the hammering rain.

Sam turned to her, startled. Water poured down her face. A face that was somehow even more pale than before. The rain had soaked through the sling, turning it dark blue. She had her one good arm holding onto the handlebars of a motorcycle that Jess was sure hadn't run in at least ten years.

"What are—" Sam started, right as her hand slipped against the wet metal. She fell towards the bike, and Jess jumped forward, grabbing the seat of the bike with one hand and wrapping the other around Sam's waist.

Sam released a hiss of pain, and her hand instantly went to cradle her ribs.

Jess released her hold on her and placed both hands on the bike, straining to push it the rest of the way to the garage. It was heavier than she imagined, and she wondered how Sam had managed to move it even a few inches in her condition.

Water dripped onto the floor of the garage as she rolled it in. She kicked the stand down, rusted metal screeching in protest.

"Thanks," Sam's wheezing, breathless whisper came from behind her.

Jess whipped around, water droplets flinging off her face. "What the hell were you thinking? You shouldn't even be outside in the rain, let alone trying to move something like that on your own!"

Sam looked down, her jaw clenched tight. Jess couldn't tell if it was from anger or to keep herself from shivering in the cold. "I didn't want it getting rained on," she mumbled.

Jess looked at the motorcycle again, and honestly, she thought the rain might have done it a favor. It looked like it could use a rinse. Or more than a rinse.

Sam took a couple of slow steps further into the garage, stopping beside Jess and the bike. "This is the other old motorcycle Chris had. He said I could take this one with me to fix up since mine got totalled."

Jess stared at her with a blank look. "Are you joking?"

"Wha—"

She stepped into Sam's space, a raging fury consuming her. "You could've fucking *died* that night, Sam. You almost *did* die—"

"I—"

"No!" she yelled, a dam breaking inside her. "I was *there*! I *saw* the accident with my own eyes!" Her voice broke, and it felt like every emotion from that night was returning in one giant wave. "You almost died." Anguish dripped from her voice.

Sam's eyes softened. She took a step forward, taking Jess' hand in her own. "Hey, it's okay."

"No." Jess shook her head furiously. "It's not okay. Do you even understand how scared I was?" She paused when her voice cracked. "When I saw you at the game, I—" Her voice suddenly felt foreign

372

and fragile. "I thought everything was going to be okay." Tears made their way to the surface for the third time that day. For once, she didn't bother blinking them away. "I thought you and I would be okay. I thought—" The tears spilled over the edge and ran down her cheeks. "I thought I had more time."

Sam frowned, shaking her head the smallest bit. "More time wouldn't have changed anything. I'm still leaving, and you made your choice. You chose Luke."

Jess couldn't help the laugh that escaped her lips. It was ridiculous to think that there really was ever any choice between them.

"I never chose him," she said. "There was one night when I let my fear get the best of me. One night where I thought maybe I could try to just be satisfied with easy. With someone who didn't make me feel everything you do." Jess leaned in a little closer and took Sam's other hand. "I am so beyond sorry for not being fully honest about that night. I should've told you everything from the start. I know that, and you have every right to be angry with me. But," her heart beat faster, "that's not the only thing I kept from you."

Sam's brow tightened the slightest bit, a guarded look filling her features.

"I should've told you weeks ago," Jess continued, "but I think I was also hiding it from myself."

She looked into Sam's eyes. The same eyes that kept her company every night in her dreams. The eyes that made her heart feel like it would explode one second, while also being all that could keep it calm the next.

The words filled her mouth, and she almost laughed at the simplicity of it. How could she have ever truly thought that it would've ended any other way? Falling in love with Sam wasn't a choice. It was like breathing. And denying it would be sentencing herself to drown.

"I'm in love with you," she said, a teary smile spreading across her face. "I think I have been for a while, but I didn't let myself realize it." She wrapped both her hands around Sam's one. "Falling in love with you was one of the easiest things I've ever done. The hard part was admitting to myself that it had happened. The hard part was the absolute terror I felt every time my heart burned when I looked at you. And knowing that every time I walked away from you, I was leaving a piece of me behind and taking a piece of you instead." She shook her head, a laugh dancing out of her lips as she felt the final weight lift from her shoulders. "Fuck, Sam, I'm *so* in love with you—"

She only noticed the change in Sam's eyes for a split second before her lips crash against hers.

And instantly, everything felt right again.

Her hands released Sam's and moved to the back of her neck instead. All she wanted was to keep her there forever, never letting her go.

Their lips moved against each other, first in a rushed hunger, then slowing into something else entirely; something Jess had never felt before. It was like Sam was using her lips to say that she loved her, too.

She relished the feeling against her mouth, burning the memory into her mind. One hand released from Sam's neck and gently moved to wrap around her back.

Instantly, her eyes opened. She pulled back from the kiss. Sam's body shook beneath her hand.

"Hey," she whispered, only a few inches of space between them. "Are you okay?"

"Yeah," Sam mumbled, leaning forward to kiss her again. Jess stopped her, putting a light hand on her chest. She could feel her heart racing, but she could also feel the tremors quaking through her body.

"No," Jess said, her brows knitting together in concern. "You're not."

She stepped back to get a better look at her. Sam's face was pale, her eyes drooping slightly as she looked back at her. Water dripped down her neck and off her hair. Her clothes were soaked through, and Jess wondered if it was the cold or the injuries that were affecting her body the most.

"I'm okay. I promise," Sam said, opening her eyes a little wider, as if trying to prove it to her. "I just—this is my last night here," she whispered, "and I want to spend every second of it with you."

Jess' heart ached, both from the sweet words, and also from the reminder of the limited time they had left.

"Okay," she replied, gently wrapping her arm around Sam's waist. She kissed her cheek and felt Sam's body relax into her slightly. "But let's go inside so you can change into something dry."

She felt Sam nod against the side of her face. Jess pulled one of her arms over her shoulder, holding some of her weight as they walked to the door that led into the house.

Pulling open the door, she weaved them around the boxes lying in the middle of the walkway. The house felt even more empty than usual.

They moved slowly, but eventually made it to Sam's bedroom at the end of the hall. She let go of Sam, letting her walk through the open doorway first, but kept her hand hovering over her back, just in case.

Sam limped a few feet in before dropping onto the bed. Jess immediately went to the closet and found a few things that hadn't been packed yet. She grabbed a t-shirt and stopped herself as she went to pick up a pair of sweats, choosing the pair of shorts next to them instead when she remembered the road rash on Sam's leg.

She went back to Sam with the dry items.

"Can you lift this arm up?" she asked, nodding to the arm that wasn't wrapped in the sling.

Sam nodded, and even with only that one small movement, Jess could see the pain radiate through her.

She slowly lifted the arm, and Jess helped pull it through the wet shirt.

"Can we take the sling off?" she asked, unsure of how much pain that would leave her in.

"Yeah," Sam croaked as she moved her good arm to pull the strap of the sling over her head. Jess stopped her, replacing Sam's hand with her own. She pulled it the rest of the way, being as careful as possible.

"Sorry," she mumbled when Sam flinched in pain.

She pulled the rest of the shirt off, too concerned for Sam's health to even notice the beautiful half-naked girl in front of her.

"Here," she said, helping direct Sam's arm through one sleeve of the new shirt. It took them a minute, but after a few tries, she was fully dressed and dry again.

"Thanks," Sam said, one arm held tight, cradling her ribs.

Jess looked at the wide gauze bandage still stuck firmly to her neck. "Do we need to change that?"

Sam lifted her hand to her neck and skimmed her fingertips against it. She let out a soft sigh and nodded.

"Where's the stuff to change it?" Jess asked, glancing around the room.

"Bathroom."

"Can I bring it in here so you don't have to get up again?"

Sam nodded, and Jess could see the appreciation in her eyes. She walked out and quickly found the bag of medical supplies on the counter in the bathroom. She grabbed everything and took it back to the room.

"We don't need to clean it right now," Sam said, sounding slightly out of breath. "I just need a dry gauze pad."

Jess pulled out a box filled with them and set it on the bed beside Sam. Then she pulled out a roll of medical tape.

She stepped between Sam's legs and leaned down to examine the bandage. When she lifted her hands to peel up the edge of the tape, Sam's hand stopped her. The look in her eyes was one of caution and reluctance.

"You don't have to do this," she said.

Jess frowned. "I want to help you."

Sam swallowed. "It looks pretty bad," she said, looking away. "You already had to see the accident. I don't want you to have to see this, too."

Jess lifted her hand to touch Sam's cheek. She pulled her head back until their eyes met again.

"Thank you." She pressed a gentle kiss against her lips. "But I want to help you."

Sam watched her for a moment before nodding.

"Tell me if it hurts or if you need me to stop," Jess said as she slowly peeled one side of the tape up. By the time she got one more side peeled off, she could see the beginning of the gash beneath. Even calling it a gash seemed like it wasn't enough.

When she peeled the third side of the tape off, the bandage pulled back entirely, and she could see the wound from start to finish.

Sam was right. It was bad.

The doctor had said that it was a deep wound that caused a lot of blood loss, but even that hadn't prepared her for what was hiding beneath the bandage. It looked like something that would only be found on a corpse. Not someone alive. Not someone she loved.

It made her feel sick.

She waited a moment or two for the bile in her throat to subside. When it didn't, she felt a gentle hand rest against her hip.

"Hey," Sam's soft voice said. "It's okay. I can do the rest."

"No." Jess shook her head. "No. It's okay. I can do it."

She peeled off the last side of the old tape and dropped the wet gauze onto the bed. Then, trying to keep her hands steady, she peeled off a strip of tape and stuck it to the new sheet of gauze. She gently pressed it against Sam's skin, using the tips of her fingers to smooth it out.

She repeated that three more times until the bandage was secure, then gathered the old strips of tape and gauze and dropped them into the small trash can where Sam's desk used to be.

When she looked back, she could see a light layer of sweat over Sam's forehead, and her body looked tense.

"Are you okay?" she asked, sitting beside her on the bed.

"Mhm," Sam replied, but her eyes squeezed shut gave a different answer.

"I think you should lie down and rest," Jess said, watching her every movement with concern. "You're pushing yourself too hard."

Sam turned to her, and the look in her eyes reminded her of a small child.

"Will you lay with me?" she asked, her voice raspy and worn.

"Of course."

She helped Sam maneuver until she was laying down comfortably. Then she crawled beside her, throwing a blanket over both their bodies.

They faced each other, both their heads resting on the same pillow. Sam seemed to be a little more relaxed laying down, and when Jess began running her fingers through her hair, she relaxed even further.

"Is this better?"

Sam hummed. "Way better. Don't let me fall asleep, though. I don't wanna waste my last day with you."

Jess knew that sound in her voice. The way it rumbled over her words in a steady rhythm. She knew it meant Sam would be fast asleep within minutes if she kept running her fingers through her hair.

"Okay," she whispered, stroking her hand in a soothing motion until Sam's eyes closed.

This was what she really needed. Comfort. *Love.*

After a minute or so, Sam stirred slightly, and Jess knew she'd caught herself right as she'd begun to fall asleep.

She cleared her throat a bit, her eyes flickering open and instantly finding Jess.

"Hey," she said, and the sound of her tired voice reminded Jess of all the late nights they'd spent together.

"Yeah?" Jess whispered back.

"I love you, too."

Jess' stomach fluttered, and she couldn't help the smile that broke through her lips. She leaned forward, pressing a gentle kiss into her forehead. For once, there was no anxiety or fear. Only pure happiness.

She leaned back and continued stroking her fingers through Sam's hair. After a few minutes, she knew she was asleep.

Jess wasn't sure how long she stayed there, watching over her. Watching her chest move up and down with every breath.

Eventually, when she knew that Sam wouldn't be waking back up anytime soon, she pressed a careful kiss to her temple and whispered "I love you" one last time.

Chapter 23

"Jess Miller!" The principal called out her name, and she walked across the stage, her long graduation gown brushing against her ankles with every step.

He shook her hand and gave her the same smile he'd given to hundreds of other students that day. She smiled back politely, trying to absorb the significance of the moment.

She took the paper he handed her and continued her walk to the other side of the stage. Glancing out into the crowd of seated students, she quickly spotted Scarlett among them, pumping her fist up in the air and cheering. Jess shot her a smile as she found her seat.

The warm summer sun beat down on her forehead, and she tilted her graduation cap to block it from her eyes. A few dozen more students made their way across the stage, each one with the same giddy smile as they accepted their diplomas. When the last of the students finally crossed and took their seats, the principal proceeded with a speech about their hard work and their futures.

He spoke about the difficult decisions they would one day face, and Jess thought about the ones she'd already made. She thought about that first long talk with her dad, and every other one since. They still contained an air of tension and discomfort, but they both powered through, nonetheless.

She looked down at the Bucknell University pin attached to her gown beside her mother's pin from Trinity. She smiled, remembering the day she'd finally made the decision to turn down the Trinity admission. The day she'd chosen a different path for herself.

She thought about winning the lacrosse championship and receiving the MVP award at their banquet the following month, surrounded by her friends and teammates.

Then she looked back, smiling at Scarlett when she thought about how they'd enjoyed their last few months of high school.

Finally, she thought about Sam and wondered what it would've been like if she had stayed. Would things be different? Maybe they would've spent every moment together as a real couple, making up for lost time, enjoying the last few months of their waning youth.

After Sam left, they'd decided together not to start a real relationship with thousands of miles between them. They decided to wait until if or when they lived in the same city again. But that didn't stop them from speaking every day. And it didn't stop Jess' heart from fluttering every time she heard a motorcycle drive by, or saw Sam's name appear on her phone screen.

"—and now, a final congratulations to our graduating class!" Jess glanced up at the stage. "You did it!"

The whole student body cheered and threw their caps in the air. Jess smiled and tossed hers only high enough that she knew she could catch it again. It was something she wanted to keep. Something to remember the events of her senior year.

She turned and made her way through the crowd of students, spotting Scarlett as she jumped into Malik's arms.

"We're officially no longer in high school!" she yelled when she spotted Jess. He dropped her, and she ran and smashed into Jess with a crushing hug.

Jess laughed, hugging her back as tight as she could. She knew this was something she'd miss once she no longer had it. And soon, in a couple of months, they'd both be off at new colleges, making new friends.

She talked to Scarlett and Malik for a few moments, Scarlett making her promise that she'd be at her graduation party that night. Then she left to find her dad among the sea of parents. As she'd expected, he was alone, hanging near the back with his hands in his pockets, sunglasses blocking his eyes.

"Hey," he said, pulling his hands out when he saw her.

She gave him a one-armed hug. "Hope you didn't get too bored."

He grunted. "Can't believe how many kids are graduating with you. Took him an hour just to get through the first half of the alphabet."

Jess smiled and shook her head. "At least you weren't stuck in a full-body graduation gown. I don't know why they thought it'd be a good idea for us to wear these and then spend two hours standing in the sun."

He hummed in agreement, lazily scanning the crowd.

Jess watched as his head turned and came to an abrupt stop, looking somewhere behind her. After a moment, he nodded his head in that direction. "Think someone's here to see you."

She shot him a puzzled look before turning around and squinting against the sun.

Her lips parted slightly in shock.

Sam smiled at her, and Jess felt the all too familiar warmth surge in her chest.

"Hey," Sam said, and Jess closed the space between them, throwing her arms around her neck.

"What are you doing here?" she asked, unwilling to let go. "You didn't tell me you were coming."

Sam laughed beneath her. "I wanted to surprise you," she said. "Scarlett gave me all the details."

She pulled back, her mouth hanging open. "You mean Scarlett knew you were coming, and she actually kept it a secret?"

Sam laughed again, and Jess swore it was the best sound she'd ever heard. "I made her promise," she said. Then she nudged her shoulder against Jess'. "I definitely wouldn't have missed this."

Jess smiled at her, finally feeling like everything had fallen into place.

A phone rang, and Sam looked down, fishing it out of her pocket. She glanced at the screen with a small smile. "Sorry," she shot Jess an apologetic look. "Just give me one second."

Jess nodded in understanding as Sam stepped away to answer the phone call. She watched the way she smiled and laughed as she spoke. There was one other thing they'd agreed on when Sam left. They agreed that if either of them were to date someone, they'd only tell each other once it became serious. *If* it became serious.

The last thing Jess wanted was to feel jealous about every little interaction Sam had with other girls while she was thousands of miles away. But as the months passed, she worried more and more. She worried that one of the phone calls would be to tell her that she'd met someone. That she'd fallen in love with someone else.

Sam put her phone back in her pocket and walked back to her. "Sorry," she said with a smile.

"It's okay," Jess replied with the best smile she could muster, trying to shake the previous thoughts from her mind. "Was that," she cringed at the words about to leave her mouth, but she couldn't help it, "someone special waiting for you to come home?"

Great. It sounded even more pathetic out loud.

Sam tilted her head at her curiously. Then realization dawned on her, and a smirk danced over her lips. She took a half-step closer to her.

"There is someone special," she said, her voice lower than before. "That's why I came to see her."

Jess couldn't help the wide smile that broke out across her face. Sam was something else entirely. She was like the sun, and Jess couldn't help but yearn for every ounce of her warmth.

She took a step forward, leaving only a few inches between them. Sam stilled, watching her carefully, with eyes that looked straight into her soul.

Jess lifted her hand, gently placing it on Sam's neck. Her fingers traced over the end of the scar that peaked out from the collar of her shirt. It reminded her of their last day together. It reminded her of how many times she'd walked away from her. And how many times she'd walked back.

Their eyes met, and Jess ran her thumb across her jaw, down to her chin. Sam stayed perfectly still, frozen in place.

Every ounce of love and longing she'd felt since Sam left poured out of her. She leaned forward, inch-by-inch, closing her eyes.

Then their lips finally met.

Sam melted into her, taking her other hand in her own.

When Jess pulled back, she left her forehead leaned against Sam's. "I love you so much," she exhaled, feeling lighter than she ever had before.

"Me too," Sam whispered, pulling back and kissing her cheek.

A loud whistle and hollering from beside them got their attention. Jess looked over to see Scarlett wiggling her eyebrows at them with perhaps the biggest smile she'd ever seen.

Jess laughed, leaning her head forward to rest on Sam's shoulder. "You know she's going to force you to go to her graduation party tonight, right?"

"Oh yeah," Sam answered. "We already talked about it."

Jess laughed again, shaking her head. She turned and saw her dad still standing a little ways behind them. Sam followed her gaze and gave him a short wave. He nodded back at her and gave them both a small smile before walking to them.

"Didn't know you were back in town," he said, looking at Sam.

"Yeah, just for a quick visit," she replied. "Good to see you again."

He nodded, returning his hands to his pockets. "Jess and I were gonna grab dinner after this." He cleared his throat. "You should join us."

"Really?" Sam asked in surprise. "I mean, yeah. Yes. That would be great. I'd love to."

He nodded again, then looked at Jess with a small smile. "You ready?"

She smiled at him and laced her fingers through Sam's. Her other hand reached up, and she traced her fingers over her mother's pin on her gown.

"Yeah, I'm ready."

(Maybe Not) THE END

Seeing you is the rising sun spilling onto the floor of a frostbitten valley

Kissing you is jumping into the deepest bend of the river in November

Loving you is the unfurling of fresh leaves in the first three days of spring

Keeping you is a child holding onto a lady bug, forgetting to leave cracks for air

Losing you is lightning shattering the roots of the strongest redwood with a single bolt

So I ask you now
If your wings don't flap
and you're not all red and black
Please do come back
Find me
But also
I warn you now don't take too long
don't take
too long

Printed in Great Britain
by Amazon

23248467R00223